Sonoma Rose

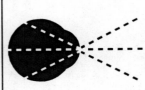

This Large Print Book carries the
Seal of Approval of N.A.V.H.

AN ELM CREEK QUILTS NOVEL

SONOMA ROSE

JENNIFER CHIAVERINI

LARGE PRINT PRESS
A part of Gale, Cengage Learning

GALE
CENGAGE Learning·

Detroit • New York • San Francisco • New Haven, Conn • Waterville, Maine • London

GALE
CENGAGE Learning

Copyright © 2012 by Jennifer Chiaverini.
Large Print Press, a part of Gale, Cengage Learning.

LIBRARY OF CONGRESS CATALOGING-IN-PUBLICATION DATA

Chiaverini, Jennifer.
    Sonoma rose : an Elm Creek novel / by Jennifer Chiaverini.
        pages ; cm. — (Thorndike Press large print core)
    ISBN-13: 978-1-4104-4512-4 (hardcover)
    ISBN-10: 1-4104-4512-7 (hardcover)
    1. Hispanic American women—California—Fiction. 2. Abused wives—Fiction. 3. Distilling, Illicit—Fiction. 4. Prohibition—Fiction. 5. Wineries—California—Fiction. 6. Quiltmakers—Fiction. 7. Domestic fiction. 8. Large type books. I. Title.
    PS3553.H473S66 2012b
    813'.54—dc23   2011047435

ISBN 13: 978-1-59413-597-2 (pbk. : alk. paper)
ISBN 10: 1-59413-597-5 (pbk. : alk. paper)

Published in 2013 by arrangement with Dutton, a member of Penguin Group (USA), Inc.

Printed in the United States of America
2 3 4 5 6   17 16 15 14 13

For Marty, Nicholas, and Michael,
with all my love.

CHAPTER ONE

Clad in the faded apron she had sewn from a cotton feed sack, Rosa sat at the foot of the kitchen table sipping a cup of coffee and planning her day while her husband bolted down his bacon and eggs. Sitting quietly side by side on her left, twelve-year-old Marta, and Lupita, almost five, ate their oatmeal in silence, sneaking furtive glances at each other or at Rosa but avoiding John. Rosa couldn't blame them. She didn't like to draw his attention either.

John wiped his mouth, pushed back his chair, and stood. "I'm going out."

"When will you be back?" She knew as soon as she spoke that the question was a mistake.

"Why?" he asked, immediately suspicious. "Are you planning to have company?"

"Not unless someone comes for their mail." John was the postmaster for the entire Arboles Valley and ran the post office out of their front room. Residents from the small town a few miles to the west and neighbors from nearby farms might stop by at any time throughout the day to post letters or pick up the bundles of envelopes and catalogues Rosa tied up with twine for them. "I only wanted to know when I should have your lunch ready."

"I won't be back for lunch."

The girls incautiously brightened, but John had already left the kitchen and didn't glimpse their sudden smiles. The front door squeaked open and banged shut, and a few moments later, Rosa heard John's roadster roar to life in the garage. She listened for the sound of gravel churning beneath the new tires as he pulled out, and for the sound of the engine fading as he sped away. Only then could she take a deep breath and feel the tension leave her face and neck and shoulders. Even the kitchen windows seemed to let in more of the warm California sunshine in her husband's absence, and the breeze that had felt clammy and oppressive as she served him his breakfast seemed newly refreshing as it carried ocean mists over the Santa Monica Mountains to the small adobe farmhouse on the mesa where Rosa had lived since her wedding day. Even after thirteen years of marriage and eight children, four of whom still lived, the adobe felt more like John's home than theirs together.

As soon as only birdsong and the wind drifted through the open windows, Marta and Lupita began planning their Saturday adventures in earnest. "Mamá, do you think Ana will feel good enough to play today?" asked Lupita.

Rosa glanced down the hallway toward the bedroom where her middle daughter slept fitfully in the bedroom with Miguel, who at two years old was still her baby. "I don't know, *mija*. I hope so."

She hoped so every morning, but far too often, Ana could do little more than sit on the front step and smile as she watched her sisters play beneath the orange trees. She had become so accustomed to her illness that she had long ago forgotten to be jealous.

Rosa's anger rose, sharp and sudden. John insisted he had no money to spare to search for a better doctor for Ana and Miguel, one wise and skilled enough to cure them of the terrible affliction that had already taken the lives of four of their brothers and sisters, and yet he had enough to waste on that ridiculous roadster, a lavish, impractical, and frivolous expense for a rye farmer in the rural Arboles Valley. When John first brought it home, beaming proudly through the open top, he demanded that Rosa go for a ride with him. "I will never set foot in that machine," Rosa declared, "unless it's to take Ana and Miguel to Oxnard or Los Angeles to see a new doctor."

"I've told you," said John, his dark blue eyes narrowing. "We can't afford it."

"We can't afford it now," she retorted, gesturing to the car angrily — and then she reeled as he struck her across the face.

In the weeks that followed, Rosa decided that the only good to come of John's extravagance was that the roadster took him away from home, and kept him away for hours at a time on errands he did not bother to explain. As the harvest approached, the rye fields lay forgotten beneath the September sun, except when Lars Jorgensen — her childhood sweetheart and dearest friend until she married John — tended them for Rosa and the children's sake. They would not starve, thanks to Lars's kindness, but if John had mortgaged the farm to pay for that roadster, what would become of them when the bill came due?

As much as Rosa despised the roadster, sometimes she was tempted to lift the keys from John's coat pocket while he slept, steal out into the night with the children, help them into the car, and speed away, far, far away where John would never find them. But there the dream came to an abrupt halt, because she knew that escape alone was not enough to ensure the children's safety. Where would they go? How would they live? What could she do to keep a roof over their heads, clothes on their backs, and food in their tummies? The litany of questions always led to the same bleak conclusion: She had nowhere to go, no money, no means to provide for her children. And she was certain John would pursue them no matter how great a distance separated them. He would not relent. If Rosa ran off with the children, she could never stop running. John would want her back, even though he no longer loved her. He would want the children back, even those he surely suspected were not his.

Ana and Miguel woke by mid-morning to a day that had turned overcast and breezy, with a metallic taste in the air that hinted at coming rain. While Marta and Lupita played outside, Rosa tried to entice Ana and Miguel to eat by drizzling honey on their biscuits and promising them a story if they each ate a little. Miguel turned his head

11

away every time she brought the fork close to his mouth, but Ana bravely took a few bites and glowed when Rosa praised her. Rosa had saved the best of the milk for them, but no sooner had they drained their cups than it all came back up again — milk, biscuits, honey, everything. After Rosa cleaned them up and helped Ana change into a fresh blouse, she asked Ana to mind her little brother while she cleaned the floor. Tearfully Ana apologized for the mess, wiping her eyes with her sleeve as she held a restless Miguel on her lap.

"It's all right, *mija*," Rosa assured her, on her hands and knees with the rag and bucket of soapy water. "It's not your fault."

Drawn by the sound of Ana's sobs, Marta darted into the adobe with Lupita close behind. "What's wrong?" asked Marta, eyeing the scene from the doorway before hurrying to take Miguel from Ana.

"Breakfast didn't agree with them," replied Rosa as calmly as she could manage, but Marta caught her eye, and she saw her own worry reflected in her eldest daughter's face. At twelve, Marta had seen two younger brothers and two sisters waste away, and she knew as well as Rosa did that not one of them had reached their sixth birthday. At eight years old, Ana had endured the affliction longer than any of her siblings. Sometimes Ana's refusal to succumb gave Rosa hope that Ana might yet survive to adulthood. More often, Rosa feared that each passing day brought Ana closer to the end. Miguel, who had fallen ill shortly after his second birthday, was much weaker than his sister and probably would not reach his third birthday.

Quickly Rosa turned her head away and closed her eyes to hold back her tears. If she gave in to her grief and anger, she might never stop weeping. She must not let the children know how close she had come to despair.

While Rosa finished cleaning the floor, Marta took charge of her younger siblings, carrying Miguel on her hip as she led her sisters outside. When Rosa went to empty the bucket, she spotted the children in the shade of the barn playing school — Ana's favorite game, one she could play while seated and without tiring herself. Although her sisters preferred to run and dance, they indulged her, knowing Ana longed to attend the Arboles School with them. She had for a single year, but when she began missing too many days, the teacher suggested that it would be best if Rosa kept her home.

"But Ana is so bright," Rosa had protested. "She loves to learn. Her heart would break if we didn't let her go to school."

"The long day exhausts her," the teacher had gently replied. "And some of the other parents are . . . concerned."

She didn't need to elaborate. Rosa had already lost three children by then, and the Barclay children's mysterious illnesses had become the source of much speculation and suspicion throughout the valley. Rosa was well aware of the rumors, the whispered conversations that fell silent when she approached neighbors and former friends in the grocery store. She knew some parents warned their children not to play with her girls, and entire families changed pews if the Barclays sat next to them in church. There had even been talk of moving the Arboles Valley Post Office from the Barclays' front room, but since John was postmaster and no one wanted to spend the money to build a new post office, the grumblings eventually faded. Rosa told herself that her neighbors did not mean to be unkind, that it would be difficult not to be suspicious, even fearful, when so much misfortune had beset their family. But understanding her neighbors' fears did not mean giving in to them, especially when her daughter's happiness was at stake.

"The other students are in no danger," Rosa had replied tightly. "Marta and Lupita are with Ana every day, and they haven't fallen ill."

"I'm not agreeing that their fears are reasonable, but either way, Ana would be far better off at home with you. And for your sake —" The teacher hesitated. "In the years to come, won't you regret every moment you didn't spend with the poor dear?"

Rosa's throat closed around a retort, and without another word, she gathered up her girls and took them home. She taught Ana herself after that, going over Marta's old lessons in reading, math, and spelling at the kitchen table. Some days Ana was too weary to study, but when she was strong enough, she absorbed every lesson with quiet, solemn purposefulness, as if she were determined to learn as much as possible in the brief time fate would grant her.

She rarely studied anymore, and when she was too tired to hold up a book, Marta read to her. "If I grow up, I want to be a librarian," she told Rosa dreamily one evening as Rosa tucked her in. "Think of all those books. Think of reading all day long, every day."

"I think there's more to being a librarian than reading all day," said Rosa, with a catch in her throat. She longed to assure Ana that of course she would grow up, that it was nonsense to think she might not, but Rosa wouldn't lie, and Ana wouldn't believe her if she did.

While the children played outside, Rosa made the beds, brought in the laundry from the line, and tended her garden. Gray clouds filled the sky from west to east, so she worked quickly, spurred on by the threat of rain. At noon she called the children in for lunch — corn tortillas and rice with fresh tomatoes and mild peppers, with water to drink, since they had no more milk. Miraculously, Ana and Miguel kept the food down, but the nourishment failed to invigorate them, so Rosa put them down for a nap while Marta and Lupita played with dolls in the front room.

She was tidying the kitchen when she heard an automobile approaching — not the smooth purr of John's roadster but the rattle and growl of an older and far more welcome vehicle.

Quickly she smoothed her hair back from her face and snatched off her soiled apron. When a knock sounded on the door, she hastened to answer it only to find Elizabeth Nelson standing on the doorstep, a tan cloche with a jaunty upturned brim upon her bobbed blonde curls. Behind her, Rosa glimpsed the Jorgensens' car parked near the garage, but Lars was nowhere to be seen.

Rosa quickly quashed her disappointment. Elizabeth, a newcomer to the Arboles Valley, had flouted local custom by befriending her, undeterred by her children's strange sickness and John's sarcastic malice. She and her husband, Henry, had moved to the Arboles Valley a few months before, carrying with them the photographs and maps of the thriving cattle ranch they believed they had purchased from a land agent back in Pennsylvania. When they came to the post office to pick up the deed of trust, they discovered that they had been swindled. Triumph Ranch did not exist — or rather, it had once, but Rosa's great-grandparents had sold it to the Jorgensen family long ago and the old Spanish name had all but faded into memory. Suddenly penniless, the Nelsons found work as hired hands on the Jorgensen ranch, and ever since, John had never missed an opportunity to mock Elizabeth when she came to the post office to collect letters addressed to Mrs. Henry Nelson of Triumph Ranch. Apparently Elizabeth would rather endure his jeers than admit to her family back in Pennsylvania

17

that she and Henry had been cheated out of their life savings.

Before Rosa could greet her, Elizabeth's pretty features drew together in concern. "What's wrong?"

"Nothing." When Elizabeth looked dubious, Rosa quickly amended, "Nothing new. Nothing that hasn't been wrong for a very long time." She opened the door wider and beckoned Elizabeth inside. "Please come in while I get your letters."

Marta and Lupita glanced up warily when Rosa led Elizabeth into the front room, but they quickly recognized the pretty young farmwife with the blonde bob, so after returning her bright smile with bashful grins, they returned to their play.

Rosa left them and went to retrieve the Nelsons' and Jorgensens' mail from the kitchen. Although John bore the title of postmaster and collected the paycheck, Rosa sorted the mail and was most often the one who met the valley's residents at the door when they came to collect their letters and parcels. Since purchasing the roadster, John had been too busy touring the countryside to pay any more attention to the daily mail than he did the ripening crops. The work had fallen entirely to Rosa, and as she sorted envelopes and boxes on the kitchen table in between tending children and folding laundry and preparing meals, she wished that she could claim John's wages for herself. She couldn't help tallying his income in her mind and calculating how many months he would have had to work, saving every dime, in order to purchase that loathsome automobile. How could he have amassed enough money unless he had mortgaged the farm?

Rosa had to know.

As soon as Elizabeth left, she would search John's desk for bank documents. She had already checked the strongbox where they kept the deed to the farm and other important papers safe from brush fires and earthquakes, but of course he had not put any mortgage papers there, where she could easily find them. He would have put them somewhere out of sight, someplace where she wouldn't accidentally discover them while dusting or putting away clothes.

Rosa brought the bundles of letters back to the front room and gave them to Elizabeth, who thanked her and added, "I found something in the cabin that belongs to you."

The ramshackle cabin on the Jorgensen ranch? Rosa had visited it many times, long before the Nelsons had made it their home, but she had always been careful to leave nothing behind. Bewildered, Rosa waited while Elizabeth took the mail out to Lars's car and returned with two folded quilts — but Rosa knew she had never left any quilts at the cabin.

While Rosa, Marta, and Lupita looked on, Elizabeth set one quilt on the sofa and began to unfold the other. Rosa glimpsed homespun plaids and wools in deep blues and dark barn reds and forest greens, sturdy and warm — and suddenly she recognized the pattern. With an eager gasp, she reached out to take the bottom corners of the quilt, lifting them so the quilt unfurled between her hands and Elizabeth's. The quilt was comprised not of square blocks but of hexagons, each composed of twelve triangular wedges with a smaller hexagon appliquéd in the center where the points met. The quilt had been well used and well loved, with tiny quilting stitches outlining each piece and many more arranged in concentric curves so the hexagons resembled wagon wheels in motion. The slight shrinkage of the wool and batting in the wash throughout the years had created a patina of wrinkles all over the quilt, and Rosa could almost imagine she knew each one by heart.

"Dios mío," she murmured.

"It is your great-grandmother's, isn't it?" prompted Elizabeth. "I recognized it from the photograph you showed me."

"Without a doubt, it is hers." As Rosa's gaze traveled over the quilt, long-forgotten memories came alive — her grandmother in a rocking chair, the quilt tucked around her lap. Rosa and her younger brother, Carlos, draping the quilt over a table and pretending it was a tent high in the Santa Monica Mountains. Climbing beneath it and snuggling up to her mother after fleeing to her parents' bedroom in the dark hours of the night, frightened awake by nightmares. Yes, she knew the quilt intimately. "It is just as I remember it."

"Almost but not exactly," said Elizabeth. "It needed some mending. I matched the fabric as best as I could when I replaced worn pieces."

Rosa smiled, touched by her friend's thoughtfulness, pained by the realization that it had been a long time since anyone had shown her such kindness. "Then it is even lovelier than I remember." She sat down in a rocking chair, draped the quilt across her lap, and ran her hands over it. The fabric had softened with age, the colors mellowed, but it was no less beautiful. "I remember my mother cuddling me in this

21

quilt when I was a little girl no bigger than Lupita. My great-grandmother made it when she was a young bride-to-be in Texas. Her parents had arranged for her to marry my great-grandfather through a cousin who lived in Los Angeles. The first time she saw him was the day he came to San Antonio to bring her back to El Rancho Triunfo."

"Triumph Ranch," said Elizabeth.

"Yes, and for many years the name rang true." Rosa could almost hear her grandmother's voice as she remembered her stories of days gone by, so full of happiness and sorrow, joy and disappointment. "They raised barley and rye. One hundred head of cattle grazed where the sheep pasture and the apricot orchard stand today. But my family lost everything in a terrible drought, the worst ever to strike the Arboles Valley. Every farm in the valley suffered. Some families sold their land after the first summer without rain, but by the time my great-grandparents decided to put El Rancho Triunfo up for sale the following year, there were no buyers. My great-grandparents sold all the cattle to slaughterhouses rather than let them starve. They were thankful and relieved when Mrs. Jorgensen's grandfather bought the ranch and permitted them to remain on the land in exchange for their labor. The rains fell two months later. My great-grandparents never forgave themselves for not holding out a little while longer, for giving up too soon and accepting less than the land was truly worth."

"They never forgave the Jorgensens either," said Elizabeth carefully, "or so I've heard."

"That is also true." The elder Rodriguezes had passed their anger on to their children, who had passed it on to Rosa's mother, Isabel. Isabel had mourned the loss of the land all her life, and she had resented the Jorgensens from the time she was a young woman until she took her last breath. Her enmity extended even to the Jorgensen descendants, who had nothing to do with the sale of El Rancho Triunfo.

Rosa stroked her great-grandmother's quilt in wonder while Elizabeth unfolded the second quilt and held it up high by the corners so that only the bottom edge touched the floor. "It's lovely," Rosa said, wondering why Elizabeth believed the wrinkled, faded quilt belonged to her. Instead of the dark homespun plaids and wools of the hexagon quilt, it had been pieced from a variety of cottons, satins, and other fabrics that looked to be decades more recent. Rosa admired it politely, but she soon felt her gaze drawn back to her great-grandmother's quilt. She could hardly believe she held it once more, and she could not imagine how it had come to be in the dilapidated old cabin on the Jorgensen ranch, especially knowing how her mother had felt about the Jorgensens. The last time Rosa had seen the quilt, it had been spread upon her parents' bed in her childhood home.

"I call this quilt the Arboles Valley Star." Elizabeth folded the second quilt in half with the pieced top showing and draped it over the sofa. "I found it with your great-grandmother's. Don't you recognize it?"

Although Rosa didn't, she examined it more carefully for Elizabeth's sake. The complex, intricate pattern resembled the traditional Blazing Star in that each segment of the eight-pointed stars was comprised of four congruent diamonds, but the smaller diamonds fanned out in a half star in the four corner squares of each block, giving the quilt the illusion of brilliance and fire. Great care must have gone into the making of each block for the divided stars to fit the corners exactly so. Few quilters had the patience for such painstaking work, and she knew only one personally — her late mother. But Rosa had never seen this

24

quilt among her mother's collection.

"I've never seen it before," she finally admitted, reluctant to disappoint Elizabeth. "I suppose I could look through the album and see if it appears in any of my family's photographs, but I've looked at them so many times. I think I would have recognized this quilt if it were in any of them. It seems too new for my great-grandmother's handi-work."

"I thought you had made it."

"Me?" Rosa shook her head. "Why would you think that?"

"Because of this."

Elizabeth turned over the quilt and showed Rosa a square of lace-trimmed satin appliquéd to the back. Upon the square, a wreath of needlepoint rosebuds surrounded a pair of intertwined initials embroidered in silk — R. D. and L. J.

For a moment, Rosa could only stare in stunned amazement at the letters, but then she tentatively touched her fingertips to the embroidered monograms. R. D. for Rosa Diaz, her maiden name. And L. J. could refer only to —

"What is it?" Elizabeth asked, concerned. "Do you remember the quilt now?"

"No," Rosa replied, bewildered. "I've never seen this quilt, but I — I do know this embroidery. This is my mother's work. She made these stitches. And this satin and lace. It came from Ana's baptismal cap."

Ana's baptism, an occasion that should have been full of joy, had been shrouded in grief, following soon after the death of Rosa's firstborn son. Though John had banished Isabel from the Barclay farm, he was unaware that she had come to the church to share in her granddaughter's holy day. But Rosa had known her mother would attend, just as she had attended her other grandchildren's christenings.

After the ceremony, Rosa had spotted her mother at the back of the church, standing in a darkened alcove and disguised by a heavy black veil, and she felt a pang of gratitude and shame. Her mother shouldn't have to lurk in the back of the church at her granddaughter's baptism; she should have sat proudly in the first pew, as John's mother had done, as was a grandmother's privilege. Trailing behind the others as they left the church, Rosa drew the quilt over Ana's head to protect her from the cold November rain, and as she did, she gently swept off Ana's soft satin cap, trimmed in lace to match her baptismal gown, and let it fall to the floor of the vestibule behind them. Rosa knew her mother would keep it, recognizing it not only as a memento of the blessed occasion but also an apology for all that Isabel had been denied that day — and had been in days past, and would be in years yet to come.

"But — why? And — when?" How had the pure white satin of Ana's christening cap come to appear in this unfamiliar quilt embroidered with Rosa's initials and Lars's — Lars, the man whose family Isabel had despised, the man Isabel had forbidden her to marry? Rosa swiftly turned the quilt over and studied the pieced stars, running her hands over the patches until her fingers came to rest on a piece of ivory sateen that was wondrously, painfully familiar. "This was from her wedding gown. I know it. And this —" She touched a triangle of pink floral calico. She could never forget the soft cotton print she herself had sewn so lovingly. "This was from the dress Marta wore on her first day of school. But how did my mother come to have it? I don't understand. Where did you find this quilt?"

"Both quilts were in an old steamer trunk in the cabin," said Elizabeth. "On the Jorgensen farm, where your family once lived. I assumed your grandmother had forgotten the older quilt there when they moved out, but as for the newer —"

"Oh, no, no. They left nothing behind. The homespun-and-wool quilt was in my mother's home all my life. It never left her bed. But this star quilt —" Rosa looked from one quilt to the other, thinking. "My mother must have taken the quilts to the cabin and left them there. But I don't understand —" Suddenly Rosa grew very still, and all at once, she knew. "She wanted me to have them. And she could not bring them to me here."

"Why not?"

"My husband would not allow my parents on his property, not even to visit their grandchildren. When I wanted to see my mother, we had to meet on the mesa. Once a week, when John went to pick up the mail from the train station, I would take the children to see her. You know the place." Everyone knew the story; everyone knew the place her mother had dearly loved, the place where she had slipped and fallen to her death. The authorities had declared it a suicide, but Rosa knew it must have been a terrible accident. Isabel never would have desecrated the place where they and the children had enjoyed brief moments of happiness.

"Rosa," said Elizabeth warily. "The day your mother died — were you supposed to

28

meet her on the mesa?"

"I was, but she didn't know that I could not come. A few days before, John had returned home with the mail and found me and the children gone. I — I had to tell him where we had been." Involuntarily, Rosa touched her left shoulder, the one he had dislocated when he forced the truth from her. "After that, he varied his schedule so I never knew when he would be gone or how soon he would return. I was never able to meet my mother again." Her hands tightened around the quilt, her mother's last gift to a penitent and sorrowful daughter. "I can't help but think of her waiting for me, waiting and waiting, every week without fail, hoping I would come. I can't help but imagine her despair when I never appeared. Perhaps she thought she would never see her grandchildren again. Perhaps — perhaps I've been fooling myself all these years, telling myself her death was an accident."

Elizabeth's eyes were wide and apprehensive. "Perhaps you were."

Rosa looked up sharply and read the fear written on Elizabeth's face. "No. No. I know what you're thinking. I can't believe it."

It was unimaginable — but was it any more likely that her mother had accidentally fallen from a place she knew so well or that

29

she had taken her own life? John had known that Isabel had waited faithfully for Rosa and the children on the mesa on the days he drove to the train station for the mail. He had known that she waited alone.

"Mamá?" said Lupita in a small, high voice full of fear.

With a start, Rosa remembered her daughters. "Marta, go and see if Miguel and Ana are still sleeping, would you, please?" she said. "Take Lupita with you."

Reluctantly, Marta did as she was told. The girls had been gone only a moment when Rosa heard the familiar, dreaded roar of John's roadster as it sped up the gravel road and braked hard in front of the adobe. Elizabeth looked out the window in alarm, but Rosa, strangely calm, folded her mother's quilt, set it aside, and stood. She was on her feet when the door burst open and John stormed in.

"Where is that son of a bitch?" John's sharp gaze scanned the room, alighting on Elizabeth for a moment before moving on. "I know he's here."

"No one else is here," said Rosa. "Only Elizabeth."

John shoved Rosa aside and strode into the kitchen. Rosa heard the table overturn and glass shatter, and then he appeared in

30

the doorway again, his eyes ablaze with fury. "I saw his car."

"I drove it," said Elizabeth. "I work for the Jorgensens."

"Did you come to help my dear wife plan the birthday party?" The glare John shot Rosa over his shoulder was full of anger, betrayal, and pain — a deep, deep hurt that must be avenged. "Lupita turns five next week, did you know that?"

Rosa could not breathe. Marta's birth only seven months after their marriage had raised John's suspicions, but he had drowned out Rosa's confession with his demands that they never speak of it again. He coveted Rosa, and silence was the price he paid for keeping her as his wife. In the years that followed, the other children Rosa had borne after Marta had fallen ill before their fifth birthdays — except for Lupita, whose continued good health was, in John's eyes, a mockery of his willingness to forgive Rosa's first betrayal.

"I just came for the mail," said Elizabeth steadily. She could not know the significance of Lupita's age, the reason for John's fury.

John threw her a look of utter contempt and strode off toward the children's room in the back of the adobe. At the sound of Lupita's cry of fear, Rosa drew in a shaky

31

breath and gripped the back of the rocking chair so hard her knuckles turned white. Elizabeth put her arm around Rosa's shoulders, but quickly released her when Rosa flinched from the pain of pressure on her recent injuries. Sometimes John remembered to be careful about hitting her only where her clothes would conceal the evidence.

Without warning John returned. Rosa drew back but not quickly enough to evade his grasp. He seized her by the shoulders and shook her. "Where is he?"

"I don't know," Rosa choked out, fighting for breath. "He's not here."

Elizabeth tried to put herself between them, but John knocked her to the floor. She grabbed for the rocking chair as she fell, but her hands slipped and her head struck the floor. Rosa turned to help her, but John seized her by the upper arm and punched her full-force in the face — once, twice, a third time. Her ears rang and her vision grayed over, and just when she felt herself slipping into darkness, John flung her down, kicked her in the side, and left her sprawled on the floor. Over the sound of blood pounding in her ears, she heard the door slam and the roadster roar to life. Somewhere nearby, Elizabeth groaned.

Rosa lay on the floor fighting for breath, gritting her teeth to hold back cries of anguish and pain, listening in vain for the children. They were so quiet. She hoped they had hidden themselves. Especially Marta and Lupita — they would be the next targets of John's rage. When he returned —

"Are you all right?" said Elizabeth shakily as she clutched the arm of the rocking chair and pulled herself to her feet, her blonde curls in her face.

Rosa felt blood and tears trickling down her face, and one of her molars was loose, but she managed a nod. "The children." Gasping from pain, she hurried to the children's room and found Marta standing defiantly in front of Miguel's crib, one arm around each of her sisters.

"I hate him," Marta said, fighting back tears. "I hate him. I hope he never comes home."

"Oh, *mija*." Rosa's composure shattered. Fighting back sobs, she placed her hands on Marta's face and kissed her on the forehead before hurrying back to the front room to assure Elizabeth that the children were safe, for now. "John's going after Lars. I'm sure of it."

"You shouldn't be here when he returns," said Elizabeth. "Gather the children and come with me. You can stay in the cabin with me and Henry."

Rosa shook her head. "It's not safe. We'll have to pass John on the way."

"Then take a room at the Grand Union Hotel. Carlos will look after you."

"No." Rosa knew not even her brother could protect her from John's vengeance. "I know a better place. A place my husband fears."

Elizabeth nodded; she knew the place Rosa meant. "Then take warm clothes and food. It looks like rain."

"I have to warn Lars. John keeps a pistol in the car."

"I'll warn Lars." Elizabeth went to the door. "Pack quickly. Take only what you need. John might double back at any time."

Rosa nodded and hurried back to the children. "Marta, *mija,* gather up clothes for you and your sisters and Miguel, enough for a few days. Put them in piles here on the floor. Lupita, help your sister."

"I can help too," said Ana.

"That's my good girl. If you get tired, stop and rest."

"Where are we going?" Lupita demanded tearfully.

Rosa paused in the doorway and forced calm into her voice. "To the mesa, to *Abue-*

la's favorite place. You like it there, don't you?" Without waiting for a reply, Rosa fled to her own room. Her heart in her throat, her ears straining for the sound of the roadster racing back to the adobe, she dug an old satchel from the back of her wardrobe and began filling it with her warmest, sturdiest clothes. When it was nearly full, she opened the top drawer of her bureau and retrieved the narrow wooden case that contained her few valuables — her mother's gold wedding ring, a pair of small diamond earrings John had given her for their first anniversary, and ten Indian Head Half Eagle gold coins her father had given her when she graduated from high school. "How are you doing, girls?" she called as she lay the case carefully on top of her clothing, closed the satchel, and fastened the clasps.

"Fine," Ana shouted from the children's room. "We're almost ready."

"Lupita wants to bring her doll," called Marta, "but I heard Mrs. Nelson say to take only what we need."

"I *need* Linda," Lupita argued.

Rosa lugged the satchel down the hall and dropped it in the front room. "You may each bring one toy," she called back. They would need something to occupy themselves while they waited for John's fury to abate. How long would it be, she wondered, before it would be safe for them to come home? Days? Weeks?

"What about a book?" asked Ana.

"One toy or one book." Rosa hurried into the kitchen and hastily packed food into a basket — tortillas, oranges, cheese, dried apricots — enough for a day, perhaps two. She lugged the basket into the front room and left it next to her satchel, and as she straightened, her gaze fell upon Elizabeth's tan cloche beneath the armchair. It must have fallen off when John knocked her to the ground.

"Hurry, children," she called as she tucked Elizabeth's cloche into her satchel for safekeeping. Her right eye was steadily swelling shut and blood trickled from her split lip. She wiped her mouth with the back of her hand and ran down the hall to the children's room. Marta had Miguel out of his crib and warmly dressed, and four neat piles of clothes sat on the floor. Lupita clutched her doll, gnawing on the inside of her lip as she fought back tears. Ana sat on her bed, her favorite book of fairy tales on her lap. Marta carried Miguel, and Miguel held his wooden train. By Marta's feet sat her backgammon set, the one covered in brown corduroy fabric that folded shut like a tiny suitcase.

Rosa murmured praise to her children, studying the piles and fighting to catch her breath, to calm the pounding of her heart. How would they carry it all? "If only we had another suitcase," she said, thinking aloud.

Lupita's lower lip trembled. "I know where there's suitcases."

Distracted, Rosa swept her long black hair out of her eyes, her fingers touching a gash in her scalp and the damp, matted hair around it. "*Mija,* we don't have any others."

"Papa does."

"No, he doesn't, honey." She needed bags — but she had feed sacks. She had washed and dried several empty cotton feed sacks and had put them in her sewing basket to make into undergarments for the girls. They would do.

"Yes, he does," Lupita insisted. "He put them in the barn. I saw him."

Her words sank in, and for a moment Rosa hesitated, studying her youngest daughter. "Marta and Ana, would you carry the clothing piles to the front room, please?" When they nodded, she turned back to Lupita. "Show me."

Lupita seized her hand and led her from

the adobe and across the yard to the barn. A few drops of rain pelted the dry earth around them as they ran. Inside the barn, Lupita dashed to the ladder and scrambled up to the hayloft. Rosa climbed gingerly after her, a sharp pain stabbing her in the side where John's boot had met her ribs. At the top she crawled through the square opening and out onto the hay-strewn floor, dizzy and gasping.

"There," Lupita said, tugging on Rosa's sleeve and pointing to a mound of hay in the corner. "He put them under there. He doesn't know I saw him."

Rosa forced herself to stand and made her way across the hayloft, picking up the discarded pitchfork on the way. Dubious that she would find anything useful, mindful of the swiftly passing minutes, she tossed the golden strands of hay aside until the tines struck something hard. Setting the pitchfork aside, she brushed the rest away with her hands and discovered several wooden crates, some large, some small, and three brown leather valises.

Rosa stared at the strange cache. What was John hiding?

"See?" said Lupita, slipping her hand into her mother's. "I told you."

"Yes, you did, sweetheart." Rosa squeezed

Lupita's hand, stooped to open one of the valises — and when it snapped open, she fell to her knees, stunned. The valise was stuffed with cash, hundreds of twenty- and fifty-dollar bills bound into neat, orderly stacks.

"That's a lot of money," said Lupita in a small, shocked voice. "Is that Papa's money?"

"I don't know." Rosa opened the second valise and found more of the same. "I suppose it must be."

"Where did he get it?"

"I don't know." Not by mortgaging the farm, that was certain. Rosa waded through the hay to the nearest large crate. It was nailed shut, but when she gave it a hard shove, she heard the tinkle of glass and a faint slosh of liquid. Surely it was alcohol. What other liquid would John need to hide? Somehow her husband had become entangled with bootleggers. That would explain everything — the cash, the roadster, and his mysterious errands.

The remaining large crates surely held more liquor, so Rosa turned to one of the four smaller crates. They were about half the height of the larger crates, long and shallow, but when Rosa nudged one, it made no sound, though it was heavy. She snatched up the pitchfork and tried to pry the nails loose, but her hands shook and the nails held fast. Turning the pitchfork around, she smashed the handle into the top of the crate, hitting it again and again, her teeth clenched against the pain in her side. Finally the plywood cracked and splintered. Dropping the pitchfork and falling to her knees beside the crate, she peered through the hole in the lid and glimpsed the gleaming, polished stock of a tommy gun.

She scrambled to her feet and backed away. "Lupita," she said as steadily as she could, "go back to the house and tell your sisters to put on their shoes." She took the handle of a brown leather valise in each hand and glanced up to find Lupita gaping at her. "Lupita, go!"

Lupita flew across the hayloft, down the ladder, and out of the barn. Rosa dropped the valises through the square opening one at a time, breathing a sigh of relief when they hit the stone floor of the barn and fell over without bursting open. Painfully she descended the ladder, seized the valises, and threw them into the back of the wagon. They had too much to carry to flee on foot.

She hitched up the horses and dashed back to the house through a thin drizzle, clutching her aching side. The girls waited in the front room. Marta carried Miguel, who rested his dark, curly head on her shoulder and whimpered.

"Mamá," said Ana, her little brow furrowed anxiously, "your face looks scary."

"Lupita, get my sewing basket, please." Rosa went to the kitchen sink, turned on the tap, and splashed water on her face. She could not bear to look in a mirror and see the ugliness of her marriage written in blood and bruises upon her features. A long time ago, she had been beautiful. She had been loved. Now — now she was frightened, and broken, and alone, and desperate to protect her children from the consequences of her mistakes. The children were all that mattered anymore.

She snatched up a towel from the counter and carefully patted her face dry, then hurried back to the children. "Better?" she asked Ana, who managed a small smile and nodded. Lupita had set the sewing basket next to the satchel; Rosa dug through it and found four cotton feed sacks, and she filled each with a pile of clothing. Distributing the bundles to the girls, she told them to get in the wagon as fast as they could and keep an eye on Miguel. As they darted away, Rosa glanced around for anything essential that they could not leave behind, listening for the roadster over the patter of rain. When John came home, he would be incensed, outraged — and once he climbed into the hayloft and discovered what Rosa had done, what she had found —

It would have been better, far better, if he had mortgaged the farm to pay for the roadster, but since he had not, she must make sure he couldn't. Clutching her side, she stepped around the baskets and hurried to John's desk, where she opened three drawers before she found John's strongbox containing their most important papers. It was locked, and John carried the key, but Rosa didn't need to open it. She only needed to keep them out of his hands so he could not sell or mortgage the farm in her absence.

As she loaded the strongbox into the food basket, Rosa's gaze fell upon the folded quilts, her mother's last gifts and a wordless promise of forgiveness. Rosa could not leave them behind. Her heart ached as she stacked up the two baskets and draped the quilts over them, and then, at the last moment, she remembered her precious family photo albums and tucked them within the folds of the quilts. For years she had believed her mother had died from a terrible accident, and she had censured all who whispered that it had been suicide. To discover, or even to suspect, that her husband had killed her — a day ago she wouldn't have believed it, but nothing seemed beyond him anymore, now that she knew what he had hidden in the hayloft.

She hefted the baskets and quilts, staggering back from the weight, and joined her children in the barn. She loaded her burdens into the back, fastened down a tarpaulin to keep the children and their belongings dry, shoved open the double doors, and climbed onto the wagon seat. A moment later they were on their way through a steady gray rain. From the corner of her eye Rosa saw the tarpaulin move, and she knew one of the children, probably Lupita, had come out from beneath the improvised tent to watch the small adobe as they drove away. Rosa did not turn around for one last glimpse of home, even though she had no idea when they might return.

She urged the horses into a trot, expecting at any minute to hear the roadster roaring after them. The main road wound south past the Barclay farm through rolling hills, and just beyond them, they came upon acres of land as flat as a tabletop, covered in brittle gold-brown grasses and dusty green scrub. The mesa plummeted abruptly at the canyon's edge, a descent so sharp it looked as if a blade had sliced into the earth. Rosa turned the horses off the road and drove them across the mesa. Even if John overlooked their tracks in the rainstorm, he could not fail to miss the wagon itself, standing out starkly against the light grasses of the mesa, visible from miles away. The wagon was no safe hiding place, but she had never intended to remain with it.

She pulled the horses to a halt a few yards away from the canyon's edge, in a spot with ample tender grass should they need to graze. "We need to be quick, but please, be careful on the rocks," she said, peering under the tarpaulin. The children blinked back at her, cold and miserable and scared. "The cave will be warm and dry. You'll see."

Marta was the first to move, crawling out from beneath the tarp and handing Miguel to Rosa. While the girls gathered their belongings and climbed from the wagon, Rosa carried her son on her hip and swiftly unfastened the tarpaulin with one hand, folded it twice, and draped it over the food basket, urging her daughters to hurry. When John came after them, and he would come, he must not find them on the mesa. Fear of her mother's angry spirit would not keep him from pursuing them if they were out in the open. It was the canyon that disturbed him, and although everyone in the Arboles Valley had heard that the Chumash Indians had once lived in caves hidden within the rocky cliffs, only those who had explored the canyon knew where they were. Even if fear did not keep John away, his ignorance of the canyon's secret places might help Rosa and the children elude him.

The rain made the climb down the switchbacks precarious. The children often stumbled, and Rosa grew hoarse encouraging them over the sound of the driving rain. She urged them along ever more swiftly, past the steep walls where cacti and chalk liveforever clung, past the waterfall that tumbled over rocky outcroppings into the Salto Creek. There, live oak trees provided some shelter from the storm, but soon the trail led them into the open again, deeper within the canyon but still far too close to the mesa. If John spotted them from above, he would pursue them. They had to be out of sight completely to have any chance of escaping him.

The way grew steeper, too steep for small hands and feet, so Rosa told the girls to leave their makeshift bags on the rocks. Unfolding the tarpaulin, she quickly flung it over their bags and baskets and held up one edge so Ana and Lupita could duck beneath it. "I'll be right back," she told them. "Don't move."

"Don't leave us!" cried Lupita.

"I'll be right back," Rosa repeated, bending to kiss them. Ana put her arm around Lupita's shoulder and tugged the tarpaulin over them.

Carrying Miguel, Rosa led Marta up to the cave she thought would afford them the best shelter — it was large enough for them to stand comfortably, the entrance was partially concealed by scrub and brush, and the path to it was visible only if one knew precisely where to look. When they reached the cave, Rosa handed Miguel to Marta and went back down for the other girls, leading Ana up first to get her out of the rain, and then going back for Lupita, the younger but stronger of the pair. When they were safe, she returned for their clothes and food and the valises, making several trips and often glancing to the rain-drenched skies, expecting any moment to hear angry shouts and see John glaring down at her.

At last they were all within the cave, too cold and miserable to speak or to do anything but sit and shiver and gaze out at the silver sheets of water streaming over the mouth of the cave. Rosa had matches but no dry wood to burn, no means to build a fire. Then she remembered her mother's quilts, and after wringing rainwater from her long hair, she told the children to change into dry clothes and gather around her. When they were all huddled together, she threw the quilts over them. "It'll be all right," she told them, forcing a confidence she did not feel into the words, as they shivered and watched the mouth of the cave and waited. "It will be all right."

"What if Papa comes after us?" asked Ana.

"He won't," said Marta, glancing up at her mother with a silent plea for confirmation.

"What about the horses?" Lupita chimed in. "We can't leave them in the rain."

"We can't bring them in here," Marta pointed out.

"They'll be fine on the mesa," said Rosa. "There's no lightning, and they don't mind a little rain shower."

"Papa will see them and know where we are," said Ana.

"The horses will be all right and so will we," said Rosa, but she could not promise them that John would not eventually come. Involuntarily, her gaze went to the two valises leaning up against the wall of the cave, the brown leather striped black from the rain. He would come for the money if nothing else. She remembered, too late, the third valise left behind in the hayloft, but at that moment it was less use to her than a pile of dry firewood would have been.

Gradually they grew warmer, but no more comfortable or less frightened. When the children grew hungry, Rosa fed them biscuits and cheese, and she almost wept from despair when Miguel promptly vomited. What was she thinking, fleeing across the mesa and cowering in a cave? Ana and Miguel could not endure the cold and damp long, and soon even strong Marta and bright Lupita would become listless and ill. But where could she go? She had no friends except Elizabeth, who had placed herself in grave danger by racing off to warn Lars. John had had a head start and a faster car, and he was armed. Even now Lars might be dead by John's hand, ambushed in the Jorgensens' garage or apricot orchards.

She clamped her lips tight to hold back a moan of grief and despair. She could not bear to think of Lars dead — Lars, the only man she had ever truly loved, the only man who had ever truly loved her.

From the time Rosa was a very young child, her mother had warned her never to trust a

Jorgensen, never to set foot on the lands they had unscrupulously wrested away from Rosa's great-grandparents, and never to speak to the Jorgensen children at school.

An obedient daughter, Rosa avoided the Jorgensen boys, but she could not resist studying them from a distance with apprehensive fascination — Oscar, a serious, towheaded boy two years younger than she, and Lars, his grinning, confident older brother, two years ahead of her in school. Quiet, diligent Oscar interested her less than his elder brother, who was popular and admired, given to pranks outside the classroom but intelligent and studious within it. He was quick to anger and quick to forgive, tall and fair-haired, with eyes as brown as a walnut shell and a smile that suggested that he found life endlessly amusing.

One spring day when Rosa was eight years old, two older boys followed her and Carlos home from school, taunting them with gibberish in a cruel imitation of Spanish. When she told the bullies to leave them alone, they laughed and knocked her books out of her arms. Suddenly Lars was there, seizing each bully by the scruff of the neck and pulling them roughly away. "Pick 'em up," he ordered, indicating the scattered books with a jerk of his head and shoving the bullies toward them.

Red-faced, the other boys scrambled to do as they were told.

"Now clean 'em up and give 'em back," Lars commanded.

The boys wiped off the dirt with their shirtsleeves and returned them to Rosa.

"Now tell her you're sorry."

As the humiliated bullies stammered out apologies and promises to leave her alone, Rosa clutched her books to her chest, seized Carlos's hand, and ran home without a word of thanks to their rescuer.

The next day at school, she ignored Lars as determinedly as ever, but at lunchtime, instead of joining his own crowd, he strolled over to the oak tree where she and her friends always sat, settled down on the grass beside her, and greeted all the girls with a smile. Inevitably they smiled back, but Rosa could only stare at him as he opened a paper sack and offered it to her. "No thank you," she said, turning away in disdain. "I don't want your candy."

"It's not candy," he replied, holding the bag so she could see the dried apricots within. "It's better than candy."

She hesitated, a refusal on her lips, but the sweet, enticing fragrance and soft orange color of the fruit proved irresistible. Lars's grin widened as she reached into the bag and took out a single apricot. Everyone said that the Jorgensens grew the juiciest, most delicious apricots in Southern California, and even dried, they retained every bit of their succulent sweetness, the very flavor of summer. One bite told Rosa that the praise was well deserved. "It is better than candy," she admitted, with a shy, delighted laugh.

"Have another," said Lars, pleased. "They're best fresh, right from the tree and warm from the sun. If your family comes out for the harvest, I'll prove it to you. My father always lets me pick some of the best apricots for my friends."

Rosa froze, her hand still reaching for the bag. Working the Jorgensen apricot harvest was a summertime tradition for families throughout the Arboles Valley, a festive, happy season of visiting with neighbors and picnicking in the orchard at noon, or so Rosa's friends had told her. Her parents had never joined in the harvest — nor would they want Rosa to accept gifts of apricots from Lars.

"Go on, help yourself," prompted Lars as she hesitated, holding out the bag. "There's plenty."

"I — I don't want any more." Her cheeks burned as she imagined her mother's re-

51

action if she could see Rosa sitting beside Lars in the schoolyard, not only sitting beside him but speaking with him and enjoying apricots that had grown on the land that had once belonged to their own family.

Lars waited for her to explain, but when she turned away from him, he shrugged and offered the bag to the other girls. Eagerly they passed it around the circle, sampling the fruit, thanking him, and exclaiming that they had never tasted sweeter, yummier apricots. For the first time, Rosa imagined her friends enjoying themselves at the Jorgensens' apricot harvest without her and resented missing out on all the fun.

She wished she had not refused to take another of Lars's dried apricots when he had first offered her the bag, because when it came back to her after being passed around the circle of friends, it was empty. Lars must have seen her disappointment, because he said, "I'll bring more tomorrow."

Don't bother, she almost retorted, but something made her hold back the words. Instead she nodded, and the next day he brought her a small bag of dried apricots all her own.

For the rest of the school year, Lars brought Rosa apricots at least once a week, and he would sit with her and her friends at lunchtime and entertain them with stories of his escapades on the ranch. On rainy days when the teacher held recess inside, Rosa and Lars would read together or play checkers, but their burgeoning friendship began and ended at the schoolyard. If they happened to see each other anywhere else, they would exchange a surreptitious glance of acknowledgment and then pretend not to know each other. If they were on an errand with their parents, which they usually were, they wouldn't risk even the glance.

As the years went by, Rosa's friendship with Lars blossomed, but in secret, like the delicate roses that climbed the trellis in the shade of her parents' house.

When Rosa was fourteen, the Arboles Valley School celebrated Valentine's Day with a party and gift exchange. Rosa had written Lars a clever poem, which she knew would make him laugh, and she had drawn a simple landscape of an apricot orchard to remind him of her promise to come to the Jorgensen ranch at harvest time someday.

When Rosa had returned after distributing her valentines to her classmates, she found a pink carnation on her desk, pink and white ribbons tied around the long stem, a small white card tucked beneath it.

"For my Spanish Rose," Lars had written inside in his familiar, orderly script, and he had signed it, "L. J." Glowing with warmth and happiness, she slipped the card into her valentine bag and suppressed a laugh. Lars knew all there was to know about apricots but he didn't know one flower from another. She didn't care. The pink carnation from the Arboles Grocery was as lovely to her as the most tenderly cultivated rose, because it was from Lars.

She walked home from school dreamily, smiling to herself and often raising the carnation to her face to inhale its delicate fragrance. She had watched Lars from the other side of the classroom as he had read her poem, and she had seen him throw back his head and laugh, just as she had hoped he would. The other boys demanded to know what was so funny, and one of the eldest — dark-haired John Barclay, who had taunted her and knocked her books from her arms years before — had dared to take it from Lars's hand, but Lars snatched it back again before John could read a single word. Then Lars's eyes met hers, and he smiled, and suddenly she knew that he would never have any valentine sweetheart but her. Warmth flooded her heart and spilled over until it filled every part of her from her eyes to her fingertips, and although she had never kissed Lars and was a little afraid to, she longed to kiss him then.

As soon as she arrived home from school, Rosa hid the flower in her bedroom, but Carlos, not meaning any harm, told their mother about it. With half-truths and red-faced silences, Rosa evaded her mother's questions about who had given her the carnation, guilt and disappointment stinging her with equal sharpness. She ought to be able to share her joy with her mother, her joy *and* her uncertainties, but her mother hated Lars — or rather, not Lars but the idea of Lars, and for that reason alone Rosa was forced to lie and to pretend that the happiest day of her life had been as ordinary and undistinguished as any other.

In the darkness of the cave, Rosa shivered and held her children close. Now the sweetness of first love was only a distant memory, and the man her childhood sweetheart had become had not called her his Spanish Rose in many years. He might, at that moment, be dead at her husband's hands.

Whimpering, Miguel eventually dropped off to sleep, and Ana and Lupita soon drifted off too, leaning against each other. Marta inched closer to Rosa and rested her head on her shoulder. "What are we going to do, Mamá?"

It was a question that Rosa had asked herself over and over as dusk stole over the canyon. "We'll sleep here tonight."

"And tomorrow?"

"We'll load up the wagon and leave the valley." It was the only choice.

Twilight descended, and as the cave grew colder and slipped into darkness, a gray, misty light lingered near the mouth of the cave. Despite the cold, Rosa was thankful for the cover of night. John would never brave the canyon after sunset, not with its steep paths and mountain lions. She shivered and wished again for dry wood. She wondered where John was now. Had he found Lars? Killed him? Had he returned to the adobe and ransacked it in a rage when he discovered she had taken the children away? Had he gone after Carlos, demanding to know where they were? What about Elizabeth? She knew where they had fled. What if John forced the truth from her?

Suddenly Marta stiffened. "What was that?"

Rosa heard nothing but the fall of the rain and the younger children's gentle breathing. "What was what?"

Marta sat up straight, staring into the

56

darkness outside the cave. "I heard something. A scraping sound. Rocks falling. Not big rocks. Little rocks, like the ones on the path."

Rosa held perfectly still, every sense alert. She waited, and listened, and heard nothing. "I think it's your imagination, *mija.*" The words had barely left her mouth when she heard the distant sound of a boot grinding gravel underfoot. A heartbeat later, a thin shaft of light illuminated the mouth of the cave.

Marta clutched her arm. "He's out there."

Rosa's heart was in her throat. "Stay here." Without a sound, she climbed out from beneath the quilts.

Marta seized her skirt "Mamá —"

Rosa hushed her with a quick gesture. Marta reluctantly released her and scooted deeper into the cave, closer to her sleeping brother and sisters, until she disappeared into the darkness. Rosa crept across the cold, pebble-strewn ground to the wall of the cave where she had left their belongings. She heard the scrape of leather on rock again just as she stumbled into her sewing basket. Swiftly kneeling, she groped blindly through the folded fabrics and spools of thread until her hand closed around her scissors. Grasping the finger loops like the hilt of a knife, she stole toward the cave entrance, heart thudding, eyes fixed on the dim, bobbing light that could only have been cast by a kerosene lantern carried by someone striding purposefully toward them. She heard more footfalls, and suddenly she glimpsed a dark figure through the rain, a grotesque silhouette against the sheets of water tumbling over the mouth of the cave, looming larger as he approached, and just as she raised her hand to strike him down, a man stepped through the falling water into the cave and raised the lantern, blinding her. Shielding her eyes with her free hand, she stumbled backward and nearly fell — and in that moment she knew from his height and light hair and thin build that the man was not John, not John at all but Lars.

"Rosa, thank God," he said when he saw her, the tense lines of his thin, weathered face easing. With a sob, she dropped the scissors and ran to him.

CHAPTER TWO

Lars barely had time to set down the lantern
before Rosa threw herself into his embrace.
"Thank God you're alive," she murmured,
burying her face in the warm, damp wool of
his sweater. After the barest hesitation he
wrapped his arms around her as if he were
afraid she would vanish like a mirage within
his embrace, but a moment later his arms
tightened and he held her as if no power on
earth could take her from him ever again.

"Thank God *you're* alive," he replied, his
breath warm against her ear. "I thought this
time maybe he'd killed you. The children
—"

"They're here. They're safe." They were
safe now. They were safe *for* now. "John went
after you —"

"I wasn't home," Lars said grimly. He
pressed his cheek against her forehead, and
she thought she felt the faint touch of his
lips upon her hair. "I'd taken a wagonload

of apricots over the grade to Camarillo. I got back to the ranch to find all hell breaking loose." He cleared his throat, released her, and glanced back into the darkness of the cave as if he had just remembered the children and was reluctant to say more within their hearing. Rosa followed his gaze over her shoulder. Just within the fading edge of the lantern's light, Marta and Ana sat huddled beneath the quilts, studying Lars solemnly but without fear.

"Hi, Mr. Jorgensen," said Ana in a small voice.

"Hello, Ana. Hi, Marta," said Lars gently. They smiled wanly, and as Rosa smiled back she felt Lars's hand on her chin. "Good God in heaven, Rosa," he said as he turned her face toward his. "What did he do to you?"

"Nothing he hasn't done before."

"You need to see a doctor." He stepped back to examine her, his hands still on her shoulders. "Why are you holding your side?"

She pulled away. "I'm all right."

"Rosa —"

She flashed him a look of warning, silently begging him not to make a fuss in front of the girls. They must not think of her as broken down, beaten, even if she were. Especially if she were.

"He'll never lay a hand on you again," said Lars. His voice was calm, but his mouth tightened and his eyes smoldered with silent fury. "You can't go back to him, not after this."

"I've already decided that I won't," said Rosa, shame and fatigue giving a sharp edge to her voice. "Is he searching for me? Is he coming after us?"

"That's the least of our concerns at the moment," said Lars, his gaze falling upon the girls again. "We can't stay here, not in this storm. The creek's rising past its banks. If we don't make the climb out now, we could be trapped here for days. My car's on the mesa. We can make it to Oxnard before midnight. I know a place we can stay for a while. They won't ask questions."

Marta threw off the quilts and bounded to her feet, but Rosa hesitated. "What about John? He's still out there looking for you, looking for us."

"No, he isn't." Lars lifted the lantern and eyed the baskets and bundles. "We need to move quickly. Can we leave any of this behind?"

"I didn't pack anything I didn't think we'd need. Lars, wait." She grabbed his arm as he stooped over to pick up the tarpaulin. "John wouldn't give up as easily as you seem to think. He's armed and he's looking for us."

Lars spared another glance for Marta and Ana. "No, he isn't, at least not right now. He's been arrested."

"What? But he didn't find you. Why would —" Rosa felt the blood drain from her face. "Oh, no. Elizabeth."

Quickly Lars grasped her by the upper arms, keeping her on her feet. "Elizabeth is fine," he said, quietly and firmly, his gaze locked on hers. "She's fine. I'll tell you what happened, but it'll have to wait. The creek's rising and we have to get out of this canyon."

She took a deep breath and nodded. "Marta, Ana, wake Lupita and come help us," she said. While Lupita yawned and stretched, clutching her doll, Lars spread the tarp on the floor of the cave, piled the sacks of clothing, their remaining food, and the children's other belongings into the middle, and quickly tied the bundle shut with a rope he took from his coat pocket. Marta picked up one of the valises and Ana the other. Rosa held Miguel, who rested his head drowsily upon her shoulder, and awkwardly lifted the sewing basket, the quilts piled on top.

"Stay close," Lars warned as he hefted the makeshift sack over his shoulder, raised the

62

lantern, and led them from the cave. The girls followed, although Ana threw Rosa a dubious look before stepping out into the rain, and Lupita balked at the mouth of the cave until Rosa gently nudged her with her hip to steer her forward. Covering her head and Miguel with her shawl, Rosa brought up the rear.

The gravel path had become slick with mud and rivulets of rainwater running off the cliff side. Rosa was soaked through in an instant, and as they made their precarious descent, a new roaring filled the air, loud and insistent. Miguel stirred beneath the shawl and lifted his head to peer out into the darkness. She murmured soothingly and rubbed her cheek against his until he rested his head upon her shoulder again, clinging to her blouse with his small fists. Lars glanced back often, offering a hand to Marta when she stumbled and lifting Lupita over a puddle. His eyes met Rosa's, and she managed a shaky smile to assure him all was well, but his expression told her that the worst lay ahead of them.

And then, just as they approached level ground, she spotted it — the creek, rushing and tumbling over its banks, higher than she had ever seen it. In the thin light cast from the lantern, she saw that the pool at the base of the falls had swollen to nearly twice its breadth since she and the children had passed by it before. A few yards ahead, a dark shadow moved over the path, and when Lars abruptly halted, she realized that the trail was submerged in water. "Wait," he called over his shoulder, shouting to be heard over the roaring of the falls.

Rosa drew the girls back, away from the floodwaters, and they watched as Lars waded ahead, stopping to catch his balance as the current swirled about him. The water nearly reached the tops of his boots, and when he held the lantern high, Rosa glimpsed the path appearing above the surface nearly eight feet beyond him. He forged ahead, his boots becoming completely submerged before he reached the other side. Dropping the tarpaulin bundle and setting the lantern high on a rocky ledge, he turned and waded back to them. By the time he reached them, the creek had risen past his knees.

"The current's strong," he told Rosa grimly, picking up Ana and taking Marta by the hand. "Wait for me here."

Rosa nodded and watched them cross, her heart pounding, holding her breath until they were safely on the other side. The water continued to rise, and Lars struggled against the current as he made his way back, the strain visible on his face as he forged ahead. Once, he stumbled, and Lupita shrieked as he disappeared beneath the swirling, black waters, but quickly he was on his feet again, water running off the brim of his hat. Rosa could not breathe until he had reached them. He paused only a moment to catch his breath, and then lifted Lupita, who flung her arms around his neck and hid her face within his collar. "Can you leave the basket?" he asked, his eyes on Rosa's.

She thought of her mother's quilts, rain-soaked but still precious. She thought of the Rodriguez and Diaz family photos, irreplaceable. She watched the waters swiftly rising, tore her gaze from Lars's, and shook her head, feeling foolish and stupid and stubborn, but she could not leave them behind.

Lars did not waste time in argument. "If you slip and go under," he said, taking Miguel from her, "for God's sake, let go of that basket and get to the surface. Nothing in it is worth your life."

Wordlessly she nodded, gripped the basket tightly, and followed him into the water, drawing in a sharp breath from the unexpected cold. The strength of the current caught her by surprise and she stumbled, but she quickly regained her footing and pushed on, her gaze fixed on Lupita's dark head on Lars's shoulder, her arms wrapped around his neck. One small hand clutched her wrist, the other held fast to her doll, which dangled by one foot down Lars's back. Rosa gasped as a surge of water flowed past her waist, and a few paces ahead of her, Lars halted and shifted the children's weight before forging on. Suddenly another surge of water tangled Rosa's skirts, and as she instinctively lifted the basket and stumbled forward, she glimpsed Lupita grabbing hold of Lars's coat with both hands. Her doll slipped from her grasp, struck the dark waters, and swept past Rosa too swiftly for her to seize it.

"Linda," cried Lupita. "Mamá, get her, get her, please!"

Rosa hesitated only a moment before she turned and went in pursuit, but the floodwaters carried off the doll faster than she could stride through the waist-deep water. She knew she would never close the ever-widening gap, nor could she seize the doll without first letting go of the basket. Behind her, Lars shouted for her to come back, and Lupita pleaded for her to go on, and the downpour blinded her and the roaring of the falls filled her ears. Numb from the cold, her teeth chattering, Rosa turned and pushed on through the water to the trail where Ana and Marta waited, where Lars was wading out of the shallows and staggering onto the muddy shore. As soon as he had carried Miguel and Lupita out of the flooded creek, Lupita wriggled free of his grasp and dashed to the water's edge, tears indistinguishable from rainwater on her cheeks, her sobs drowned out by the tumult of the surging water.

Lars handed Miguel to Marta and hurried back into the creek to help Rosa to safety. "I'm sorry, *mija*," Rosa gasped as she struggled free of the water. She set down the basket heavily beneath the rocky ledge where the lantern cast a thin circle of light around the shivering children. Ana flung her arms around her, but Lupita remained at the water's edge, weeping and gazing off after her lost doll.

"We can't linger." Lars squeezed Rosa's shoulder, strode over to Lupita, and scooped her up. He set her down beside her sisters and hefted the tarpaulin sack over his shoulder. "You can stop crying, little miss," he told her shortly. "Your mother is fine, and so are your sisters and brother, and so are you." He took Miguel from Marta. "Can you carry the valises?"

Marta nodded and seized their handles. Lars took the lantern from the ledge, and then they were on their way again, crossing beneath the cover of the scrub oaks to the foot of the trail leading up the canyon wall to the mesa. The climb was more slippery and treacherous than the descent had been, and to Rosa it seemed that hours passed before they reached the top, but at last they did, and the clamor of the falls and the swollen, rushing creek faded to a low murmur behind them. The horses whinnied in recognition as they approached, but Lars led their small party to his car parked just beyond the wagon. As Rosa loaded the children and their belongings inside, Lars strode off to check on the horses. He soon returned and assured the children that the horses were fine and that a little more rain wouldn't hurt them, since they were on high, level ground and there hadn't been a single rumble of thunder in the dark skies since the storm began. Ana and Marta seemed to take heart, but Lupita, sitting between them in the back, hugging her knees to her chest and sniffling, was inconsolable without her doll.

Lars took the wheel, and soon they were bouncing and jolting across the mesa. When they reached the road, Lars turned east, away from the Barclay farm. "I thought we'd take the Old Butterfield Road into Camarillo," he said.

"In this weather? At night?"

Lars shrugged. He knew the dangers, but it couldn't be helped. "We're less likely to run into anyone we know."

"If John's been arrested, why do we need to hide?"

"We don't know when he'll be released." Lars kept his gaze fixed on the road ahead, barely visible a mere two feet beyond the headlamps. "It'd be best if there's no one to tell him which direction they saw us go."

Rosa knew he was right, so she sank back into her seat, cradling Miguel and stroking his head until he drifted off to sleep. Before long, silence from the backseat told her that her exhausted daughters had fallen asleep too, but she was too nervous to speak while the car creaked up the narrow, winding road to the summit. Once they cleared the pass, she breathed a sigh of relief as the car rumbled down the road into the Camarillo Valley. As long as the brakes held, they were sure to make it the rest of the way to Oxnard safely.

She glanced over her shoulder to be sure the girls were still asleep, and then she turned to Lars. "Tell me what happened."

Lars hesitated, rubbing the stubble of golden beard on his chin. "Like I said, I was hauling a load of apricots to the packinghouse in Camarillo when John came after me. I didn't get home until hours after it was all over."

"After what was all over?"

His reluctance to tell her was evident in his pauses, and in the glance he gave her as they descended into the foothills. "My brother told me John showed up at the house, waving a pistol and demanding that they send me out."

"Didn't they explain that you weren't there?"

"I don't figure John was much up for a rational discussion of the facts, but Oscar shouted that I wasn't there and that he'd better shove off because Mother had called the police. Evidently John didn't believe him, because he shot out the window Oscar had been standing at only seconds before."

Rosa gasped. "Was he hurt?"

"No, he's fine. On account of the rain, everyone was inside — the family, the hired hands — so they decided to wait it out until the police arrived. Then what do they see but Elizabeth driving up to the house in my car."

"Oh, no."

"She's okay too," Lars quickly went on. "John fired at her, but she threw the car into reverse and sped off back the way she came until she was out of range. Then she turned the car to block the road, to cut off his escape."

"Did John go after her?"

"No, but he threatened to. For a while he paced in front of the house in the rain, shouting that they needed to send me out or he'd go after Elizabeth. As you can imagine, Henry wasn't about to let anyone harm his wife —" His voice broke off and he shot Rosa a quick, sidelong look, and Rosa felt herself diminished in comparison, a wife that a husband did not value enough to protect. Lars cleared his throat and fumbled for her hand, which he squeezed and held on the seat between them. "So. So Henry and Oscar and one of the hired hands — Marco, maybe you remember him — they slipped out the kitchen door. Oscar and Marco went around one side of the house, while Henry went around the other and snuck across the yard to my car."

Rosa took comfort in the warmth of his rough, callused hand around hers. It seemed a lifetime ago since they had last held hands in the shade of the apricot orchard, blissful in each other's company, the sun warm upon their shoulders, the air fragrant with spring blossoms. "And then?"

"And then Henry told Elizabeth to get out, or he pushed her out, or something, and while she took cover in a ditch, he drove the car straight at John."

Rosa knew John, and she knew he wouldn't have jumped out of the way. "John fired at him."

Lars nodded. "The bullet shattered the windshield. When he took aim again, Henry tried to swerve out of the way, but the car struck a rock and flipped on its side. Henry managed to climb out, but John had that pistol fixed on him and was coming closer, so Henry must have thought he had no choice but to charge him." Lars drew in a deep breath and slowly let it out. "John shot again, and that time he hit him. Close range, right in the chest."

"Dios mío."

"When they heard the gunshot, Oscar and Marco came running. They tackled John and wrestled the gun away from him. The police showed up shortly after that. One squad car took John to prison, and the other took Henry to the hospital."

"Do you know if he survived?"

Lars shook his head. "Elizabeth rode along with him, but last I heard, she hadn't yet called with any news. From what Oscar told me, Henry was wounded very badly. It'll be a miracle if he pulls through."

"Oh, poor Henry," said Rosa. "Poor Elizabeth. She has no one else in the Arboles Valley, no family, no money — what will she do?"

"She has work and a place to live," Lars reminded her. "My family will look after her. Don't worry. And don't write off Henry just yet."

Rosa nodded. For all their reserve, the Jorgensens were kindhearted people, more forgiving than her own family.

"By the time I got home, the police had taken everyone's statements and had left," Lars said. "Oscar filled me in and helped me get the car upright, and I headed straight to your place."

"By then I was already in the cave with the children."

"I didn't know that. I thought maybe he'd —" Lars cleared his throat and continued. "He never came after me like that before. I knew he must have finally figured out about the girls, or maybe you told him —"

"I swore I would never tell."

"I know that. You made me swear too. I thought maybe he . . . forced the truth from you." Lars flexed his hands around the steering wheel. "Rosa, I thought he'd killed you. I raced over there fearing I'd find you dead on the floor of the adobe, the children around you, sobbing —"

"Don't talk like that." Rosa glanced at the backseat, where the girls slept on. "Obviously he didn't kill me."

"Not for lack of trying, by the look of it," said Lars. "He's lucky he's safe behind bars, or I'd —"

"No, Lars. Don't even say it."

"I swear to God, Rosa, I'll never understand why you continue to protect him after all —"

"He's not the one I'm protecting," she snapped. "If you hurt him, you would end up in jail. What good would that do you? What good would you be to me or the children then?"

From the corner of her eye she saw a muscle work in his jaw. Long ago, he had promised her that he would not harm John, and she knew he would keep that promise and all others she asked of him from that day forward as atonement for the one promise he had broken, the one that had compelled her to marry John instead of him.

They drove along in silence across the valley, past rain-soaked fields of strawberries and alfalfa, past the large Queen Anne homes of prosperous farmers and small adobes like the one Rosa had left behind.

When Lars spoke again, the anger and frustration had left his voice. "You need to see a doctor."

The pain in Rosa's side had subsided to a dull ache, but the cuts and bruises on her face throbbed. All she wanted to do was find a safe, soft bed somewhere and sink into a dreamless sleep. "Ana and Miguel need to see a doctor more than I do."

"There's no reason why all three of you can't see a doctor. We'll go straight to the hospital."

"Not tonight, please," Rosa begged. "I can't face doctors and questions tonight."

Lars looked as if he might argue, but he glanced at her face and nodded reluctantly. "First thing tomorrow morning, then. I'll ask around and find someone who's good with children." He paused for a moment, lost in thought, and absently patted his coat above his heart. Rosa heard the faint rustle of paper within the inside pocket. "I collected a payment for Oscar at the packinghouse, but in all the excitement I forgot to give it to him. I guess what I'm saying is that I have money for the best doctors we can find. I know Oscar wouldn't mind."

"I have money too," said Rosa, suddenly

remembering the valises. "Oh, Lars, John is mixed up in something very dangerous. I don't know what exactly, or how long it's been going on, but he's been hiding guns and liquor and cash in the hayloft."

Lars shot her a curious look. "Cash and guns too?"

"Yes, four crates of tommy guns and three valises full of money. We — I took two of them."

"Why didn't you take all three? And why not a few of the guns for good measure? They might be handy in a tough spot."

It took her a moment to realize he was teasing her. "Lars Jorgensen, this is no joking matter. John's breaking the law." Suddenly something Lars said gave her pause. "You said 'cash and guns too.' You knew about the liquor? And you didn't warn me?"

"I suspected, but I figured you knew more about what was going on than I did."

"I didn't know anything about this until a few minutes before we fled for the mesa. Lupita saw John stashing the valises, and she showed me where they were." She studied Lars, bewildered. "What did you see that I overlooked? What made you suspicious?"

"Do you remember that day in June when Elizabeth and I came by to pick up the mail, and John and I got into it?"

"Of course I do," said Rosa, although she wouldn't have described the incident that way, since all the rage had come from John's side. John had been off on one of his mysterious errands when Lars and Elizabeth arrived, and while Marta and Ana led Lars off to play, Elizabeth came into the house to post a few letters to her folks back home in Pennsylvania and stayed to chat.

Then, suddenly, they had heard angry shouts from outside. John had returned and had flown into a rage when he discovered Lars playing with Marta and Lupita in the shade of the orange trees. John had seized the girls by the arms and was dragging them away from Lars, his face red with fury. "I told you to stay away from my family!"

Lars tried to calm him down, and when Rosa intervened, John knocked her to the ground. As Lars helped her to her feet, John shoved the girls into the house and returned a moment later clutching something in his right hand. Rosa heard Elizabeth cry out in alarm as he flung the object at Lars's chest. Instinctively, Lars caught it. Clear liquid sloshed inside the glass bottle.

"I remember what you are even if she doesn't," John had snarled. "Crawl back inside your bottle and leave us alone."

How Rosa had despised John at that moment, for frightening Marta and Lupita and bruising their arms as he dragged them away from Lars, for mocking Lars and the misfortunes of his past when he had struggled so hard to overcome them, for giving Lars the poison he could have used to destroy himself again. She had hoped that Lars would leave the bottle in the dirt before he drove away, but when she went out later to check, it was nowhere to be found. She assumed that he had taken it with him, awaiting the moment when he could slip off to some secluded corner of the Jorgensen ranch and drink it dry, but the next time she saw him, he had been as clear-eyed and levelheaded as ever, and had evidently not started back down the path that had once taken him away from her. She was so relieved that he had not fallen into his old ways that she never spared a thought for the bottle itself, and how John had come to have it. Liquor was not that difficult to come by, despite Prohibition, for a man who wanted a drink badly enough.

"That was a fairly pricey import, not some bathtub gin," said Lars. "Then, when I considered that flashy Chrysler John's been tearing around in, I put two and two together and it added up to trouble."

"Why didn't you warn me?"

He kept his gaze fixed on the road ahead. "What would you have done?"

"I don't know."

"You wouldn't leave him when he beat you. You wouldn't leave him when we had another child together. I didn't think you'd leave him over a few tenuous links to organized crime."

The implicit criticism stung. "You know why I couldn't leave."

"I know why you *said* you couldn't leave." When she made no reply, his voice lost its sharp edge. "Anyway, I didn't have much proof, just a bottle and my suspicions. So I turned the liquor over to the feds."

"You didn't drink it?"

She regretted her words the moment they left her lips. "No, Rosa," he replied evenly. "I didn't. It wouldn't have been much good as evidence if I had."

"Does John know that you reported him?"

"I don't believe he does, but it might not matter now anyway. When I went looking for you at your place, county deputies were already there, searching the entire farm for clues. By now they've surely found John's stash in the hayloft. He could be brought up on charges of racketeering as well as murder."

"Attempted murder," Rosa corrected him. She had to believe that Henry might somehow pull through.

"For his sake and Elizabeth's, I hope you're right." Lars fell silent for a moment. "I'm sure you know that I didn't report John to the Prohibition agents out of any deep and abiding admiration for the law. I did it hoping they would seize John and lock him up somewhere far away from you and the children. I understand that you don't want me for a husband, but for the love of God, Rosa, you shouldn't be with him."

Rosa stroked Miguel's soft, curly hair as he slept in her arms. "I know."

But she had wanted Lars for a husband. If he had been then the man he was now — sober, diligent, steadier — she would have married him despite her parents' objections.

They drove in silence the rest of the way to Oxnard. It was nearly midnight when Lars finally parked the car near the corner of Fifth and A Streets. "I'll be right back," he promised, and hurried off. In the backseat, the girls stirred sleepily, awakened by the sudden stillness. The storefronts closest to the car were dark, but light spilled from the windows of a few restaurants scattered down the street, and whenever a door opened, bursts of laughter and music punctuated the night as couples or groups of young men spilled out onto the sidewalk, holding umbrellas high if they had them, pulling up the collars of their coats if they did not. The men were loud and grinning and flushed, young and old and in between; the women were young, with short skirts and bobbed hair and high, teasing voices that rose into laughter or shrieks of dismay if they unwittingly stepped in a puddle. Rosa slouched in her seat and combed her long dark hair in front of her cheeks with her fingers, concealing her injuries, praying that the few passersby would be too absorbed in their gaiety to notice her. The sight of a woman with a bruised and battered face sitting in a car full of children downtown on a rainy Saturday night would surely linger in their memories should anyone come around asking questions later.

Exhausted, she closed her eyes and waited for Lars, but apprehension and dread kept her on edge. She had come to realize that John was not the only man who might be looking for her. The deputies who had searched the farm after John's arrest — surely they would have questions for the gunman's wife. They might assume she was John's accomplice and arrest her too. How could she prove she had not known her husband had become involved with bootleggers? Who would believe her? And what if the money she had taken was not John's payment for services rendered, but part of the cache itself? What if she had stolen from the mob? Gangsters wouldn't care that the police would have confiscated the valises anyway if she had not taken them. They wouldn't care that she had meant to take John's money, not theirs. If they tracked her down, they would punish her all the same.

Sick with dread, she sank lower into the seat — and bolted upright with a gasp when Lars suddenly rapped on her window. "I've taken two rooms at the Radcliffe Hotel," he said, opening the back door and picking up Lupita. With his free hand, he gently shook Marta and Ana awake. "We'll get you and the children upstairs first and I'll come back for your things."

Rosa nodded and climbed out of the car, resting Miguel's head upon her shoulder and wrapping her shawl around them both. The air was cool and misty and smelled of rain and sodden garbage and the ocean. Lars led them to a discreet entrance off the alley and inside a two-story brick building, up a narrow staircase, and along a dimly lit hallway. About halfway down, he stopped in front of a door, shifted Lupita to his other shoulder, and fumbled to fit the key in the lock. When the door stuck, Marta came forward to help Lars shove it open, but she recoiled from the smell of mothballs and old cigarettes that wafted from the room.

"Let's see what we have here," Lars said, leading them inside and groping for the light switch. Blinking as her eyes adjusted to the glare, Rosa took stock of the room and noted two beds, a wooden chair, a single window on the far wall, and a bureau stained with bull's-eye rings from old coffee cups. A narrow door to her right led to a bathroom with a toilet, a sink beneath a chipped mirror, and a clawfoot tub. That, at least, was a welcome sight.

Rosa drew the white eyelet curtains and set Miguel down on one of the beds. Without waking, he promptly rolled over onto his tummy, fists tucked into his chest, right cheek resting on the candlewick bedspread, rump in the air. Lars lay Lupita down beside him, but as he removed her shoes, she woke and sat up. "Where are we?" she said, the words fading into an enormous yawn.

"Someplace warm and dry and out of the rain," said Rosa, mustering up what she hoped would pass for brisk good cheer.

"When are we going home?"

"Not tonight."

"I'll be right back," said Lars, pocketing the key. "Lock the door and don't open it for anyone."

A small, wild laugh escaped Rosa as she nodded and locked the door behind him. If pursuers really did follow so closely behind them, they were already doomed.

She knew that if she sat down she would not get up again until morning, so she stayed in motion. Exhausted and drained, her head and rib cage throbbing, she draped her damp shawl over the bathtub to dry, helped Ana out of her shoes, and murmured responses to Marta, who had assigned herself the task of determining their sleeping arrangements.

When Lars returned from the car with the feed sacks full of clothing, Rosa sent Marta and Ana into the bathroom to wash their hands and faces and brush their teeth. A bath would have to wait until morning, she decided as she and Lupita took their turns at the sink. Miguel was down for the night and she had no intention of waking him. She had the girls change into their pajamas while Lars went back to the car for the rest of their belongings, and by the time he returned, she had tucked Marta and Ana in one bed and Lupita and Miguel in the other. Lars helped her shove the baskets and bags against the wall to leave a clear aisle from the beds to the bathroom, and then he took off his sodden hat, dug the room key from his pocket, and gave it to Rosa.

"I'll be right across the hall should you need me," he said, his hand on the door-knob. "I'll come back first thing in the morning. Don't open the door for anyone but me. I don't care who it is — innkeeper, chief of police, your husband, the devil himself."

Rosa promised she would not, and thus satisfied, Lars departed. Rosa had almost closed the door behind him when she suddenly pulled it open again. "Lars —"

He paused in the doorway of the room across the hall. "What is it?"

"I never thanked you. For coming after us, for seeing us safely out of the canyon, for bringing us here and finding us a room for the night — thank you. I'm ashamed I didn't say it sooner."

A brief smile flickered in the corners of his mouth. "It's all right. You're welcome." He stood watching her for a moment. "You know very well I'm not closing my door until you close yours and I hear that bolt slide into place, so you might as well go on and do it."

85

"Of course." She managed a smile. "Good night."

"Good night, Rosa."

She closed the door and locked it, and then, draining the last reserves of her strength, she changed into her nightgown and slipped into bed beside Lupita and Miguel. As she drew the covers over them, Lupita snuggled up to her little brother, thumb in her mouth. Rosa gently removed it, closed her eyes, and sank into sleep.

Rosa was sixteen the first time she woke to a soft rapping sound and discovered Lars standing outside her bedroom window, beckoning her to join him in the soft and misty night. Quietly she tiptoed past the rooms where her parents and brother slept and eased the front door open without a sound. Heart pounding from the fear of discovery, she let Lars take her by the hand and lead her away from the house, but they went only as far as the orange trees in the corner of the yard, where darkness offered scant concealment should her mother wake and peer out the window. Lars murmured her name as he tangled his fingers in her hair and kissed her, his lips warm and soft and insistent upon hers. Her head was spinning when she finally broke from him, and pushed him away, and breathlessly told him that she couldn't sneak out of the house in the middle of the night ever again. It was too dangerous. Her parents or a neighbor would spot them and it would all be over.

"If we don't meet like this, when will we ever see each other?" Lars asked, drawing her back to him. The arrival of summer recess had once meant that they would see each other rarely and only in passing until the new school year began, but not anymore. Lars had graduated the week before, and Rosa's heart sank whenever she thought of returning to school in September without him. Autumn would find her studying at her desk at the back of the classroom with the oldest students, while Lars would be hard at work on his father's ranch. He could not ride over to see her on a Sunday afternoon the way other young men visited their sweethearts, or have dinner with her family, or ask their permission to take her dancing at the Grand Union Hotel on a balmy Friday evening. It was unfair, and it was wrong, but as long as her mother's heart remained relentlessly hardened against the Jorgensens, Rosa and Lars would have to meet secretly under the cover of darkness or not at all.

The next time Lars came for her, she

quickly dressed, slipped soundlessly out the front door, and ran to the warmth of his embrace. Hand in hand, they stole away to a grove of live oaks out of sight of the house, and there they talked and kissed and held each other for hours until Rosa's apprehensions overcame her happiness. At any moment her mother, a restless sleeper, might wake, go to the kitchen for a drink of water, and check in on her children only to discover Rosa missing. "I have to go home," she murmured, her lips brushing his. Lars walked her back to her front door, where they parted with a long, wistful embrace.

"I love you, Rosa," he told her as she turned to go, still holding her hand. "I always will."

"I love you too," Rosa said, her voice breaking. She squeezed his hand tightly before going back inside.

As she crept silently to her bedroom, slipped into her nightgown, and climbed back into bed, she smelled Lars's scent upon her skin and wondered how she could be so blissful and yet so miserable at the same time, and how long she could endure it.

At least once a week Lars would knock softly upon her window in the middle of the night. After listening for a long, breathless moment to be sure he had woken no one else, Rosa would steal outside to meet him amid the orange trees. Sometimes they hastened away on foot to the live oak grove where he had tied up his horse; other nights Rosa climbed up behind him and clung to his waist as they galloped off to explore the valley by moonlight — the golden mesa, the scrub-covered foothills of the Santa Monica Mountains, the pebbled banks of the Salto Creek. They would talk and laugh, or dream aloud about a future they would spend together, or lie side by side holding hands and watching the stars until the ocean mists rolled in over the mountains and drew a soft veil over them one by one. Sometimes they lost themselves in caresses and kisses, and lost track of time too, until the brightening of the eastern sky sent them racing back to Rosa's house only moments before daybreak woke her family. Afterward Rosa would drift through the day half asleep, daydreaming of the previous night and of the next time Lars would come for her. Sometimes she nodded off at her desk in the middle of class, but her grades never faltered and everyone from her parents to her teachers would shake their heads and declare that she worked too hard. Guiltily Rosa would assure them that she really did not, but what they perceived as her modesty and diligence only made her rise in their esteem.

Sometimes Rosa would wake in the middle of the night longing for Lars, but when he did not appear at her window she would sink back into sleep, disappointed and lonely. Less frequently, but often enough to distress her, Lars would come to her with the smell of alcohol on his breath, talking louder than usual and more prone to boasting and silly jokes. Once, when she chided him for his drinking, he groaned and said, "Not you too. You sound like my mother."

Stung, Rosa retorted, "Maybe you should listen to her."

Lars laughed. "The way you listen to your mother?"

Rosa sat up, straightened her skirt, and picked leaves from her hair. "It's not the same. Do you really want me to obey my mother and never see you again?"

Of course he didn't, and although his words were slurred, his apology was sincere enough to mollify her, but she soon learned that although he was sorry for teasing her, he had no intention of mending his ways. A few weeks later, he showed up at her window long after she had stopped hoping for him.

Dawn was less than an hour away, and as she blinked sleep from her eyes she whispered through the window that she could not come out to him. It was nearly morning and the risk of waking her family was too great.

"Come back tomorrow," she implored, because she had not seen him for days and she missed him. "Come earlier, at midnight."

"I can't come tomorrow," he said, too loudly. "I'm here now. Come out and kiss me."

Alarm made her anger flare. "I told you, I can't," she whispered. "You should have come earlier."

"I couldn't come earlier. I was out with the boys."

And the boys had been drinking. She saw that now. Folding her arms over her chest and shivering from the chill, she said sharply, "You made your choice. Come back tomorrow, if you're sober."

He threw his head back and groaned. "Don't be a stick in the mud. You and John Barclay are a perfect pair. Both of you toe teetlers —" He shook his head roughly. "Both of you teetotalers, dull as dishwater and no fun at all."

Through the wall, she heard bedsprings

creak as her father turned over in his sleep, and she gestured frantically for Lars to be quiet. "If I'm as dull as you say, you shouldn't mind going home," she snapped. "Get drunk with your friends if that's what you call fun, but don't bother coming around here afterward."

He blinked at her, bleary-eyed and astonished. "Fine." He stumbled off, but when he was a few yards away, he turned around, snatched off his hat, and gave her a sweeping bow. "If you insist. I guess this is goodbye."

Rosa blinked back angry tears and watched him jam his hat back on his head and stagger off toward the oak grove. When the ocean mists closed around him and she could no longer make out his dark shadow through the gray, she sank back into bed, pulled the quilt over her head, and shook with silent sobs. He had never been so mean to her, and she had never seen him falling-down drunk before. The man he became when he drank frightened her, and not only because he grew careless and took stupid risks that could expose their precious, long-held secret. She had never wished Lars to be anyone but who he was, but at that moment she wished he would follow his friend John's example and forswear alcohol. It could not be that difficult. Her father never drank except for a sip of wine at Sunday Mass, which apparently was the limit of John Barclay's indulgence too. She had seen John at church, sitting in a pew near the front with his parents and elder sister, and if any trace of the childhood bully remained in him, he kept it well hidden. His father was fifteen years older than his mother and was in poor health, so at only twenty years old, John ran the family rye farm almost single-handedly, providing for his family faithfully and without complaint. Despite his greater responsibilities, John didn't need to blow off steam with a bottle of gin several nights a week. Why did Lars?

Lars did not come to her window the following night, and she was still angry enough not to miss him. Nor did she mind when he stayed away the next night, and the next. She imagined him nursing his aching head and bruised pride, and she planned what she would say to him when he finally returned. A week passed, and then another, and after a third, all thoughts of reprimanding him faded. Perhaps when he had said good-bye, he had meant forever. She could not bear to believe it, but every night he stayed away affirmed the same devastating conclusion.

She was seventeen, and she had loved Lars nearly half her life, and her heart was broken.

As the days passed, she tried to tell herself that it was all for the best. Her parents never would have accepted a marriage between them, and she could not bear the thought of marrying him without their blessing. Lars became someone she couldn't recognize and didn't like very much when he drank, and if he could not quit drinking for her sake, it was for the best that she had discovered that before she married him. And that was if the church would have permitted a mixed marriage. Lars had been baptized Protestant, but he was irreverent at best, irreligious at his worst, and he was adamantly opposed to converting just so she could marry within the faith. When she looked at the cold, plain facts, she had no choice but to admit that their love was not only forbidden but impossible, doomed from the beginning. She should be glad that he had abandoned her — and if she could not manage that, she ought at least to be relieved.

But she loved him, and she missed him, and she felt as if her heart had shattered, littering the empty places inside her with cold shards that stabbed her whenever she took a breath.

After a month and a day, she woke, disoriented, to the sound of rapping on her windowpane. Heart pounding, she flung open the window and clutched the sill, wordless and breathless, waiting for Lars to speak. He looked unhappy and ashamed and thoroughly sober. "Rosa, I'm sorry," he said quietly. His eyes and voice were clear again. "Before you tell me to go away, I wanted you to know that."

She shook her head. She had no intention of sending him away until he answered the question that had haunted her for weeks. "How did you do it?" she whispered. "How could you stop loving me so suddenly?"

"Rosa, I never stopped loving you."

"Then why have you stayed away so long? I told you to come back when you were sober." Suddenly Rosa had a terrible thought. "Do you mean you've been drinking every day since —"

"No. Not a drop since that night." His voice was firm, but his eyes were soft and pleading as he held out his hand to her, as if he thought she might take it and climb out the window and into his arms. "Rosa, I made a mistake."

"It wasn't a mistake. It was a choice."

"You're right, but maybe everyone should be allowed one bad choice in life that the

95

person they love will just forgive, without question, and give them a second chance. Maybe this can be mine."

She watched him, mulling over his words and struggling to settle her warring emotions. She was happy to see him, happy and relieved, but he had stayed away too long and the time apart had granted her both torment and insight. When hope faded into uncertainty in his eyes and his outstretched hand fell heavily by his side, compassion won out. She tore herself away from the window, threw on the dress she had worn the day before, and flew from the house as swiftly as silence allowed. When she caught up to him, he was trudging back to the oak grove, disconsolate.

"Lars," she called softly to him, but it was the sound of her quick footfalls on the dry earth that he heard, and when he turned, fierce joy lit up his sun-browned face. He ran back to meet her, and when he embraced her and murmured in her ear and kissed her, she felt as if everything that had been thrown into upheaval had fallen into place again, had been made whole and right.

He seized her hand and led her off at a run across the open field to the oak grove, where they quickly mounted his horse and galloped off. As they sped away, she clutched his waist, pressed her face to his back, and closed her eyes, not caring where they went, her dress pulled up past her knees and the wind in her hair. She and Lars were together again as they were meant to be, and that was all that mattered.

Even so, when Lars pulled the horse to a halt in front of the cabin her mother and grandparents and great-grandparents had once called home, she hesitated, gripping the saddle with both hands while he dismounted. Her gaze traveled from the shabby front porch to the bowing roof to the cracked and grimy windowpanes to the weeds growing through the boards of the front steps. She recognized the cabin from photographs in her mother's album, but in those days it had been a much-loved and well-tended home, not an abandoned relic from a bygone age.

She wished he had taken her almost anyplace else, but when he reached up to help her down from the mare's back, she swung her leg over the side and slid to the ground, and when he took her hand she let him lead her to the cabin. The wooden boards felt as if they would give way underfoot as they climbed the stairs and crossed the porch, and the hinges creaked a complaint when Lars pushed upon the door.

They entered a front room that filled the whole length and half the width of the cabin, with a kitchen on the right and a fireplace, a dilapidated chair, and a broken footstool on the left. She spotted two open doorways on the opposite wall, but it was too dark to see what lay beyond them. The air was hushed and stale, and she would have believed it had been undisturbed for centuries if not for the man's boot prints leading from where she and Lars stood to the room on the left. Lars gave her an encouraging smile as he led her in the same direction, and when he did she realized that he must have left the prints himself, perhaps only days before.

They entered a small room with a single window, a bureau, and a bed covered with a fresh, bright quilt that Lars must have brought over from the Jorgensen farmhouse. As they lay down upon it together and he took her in his arms, she wasn't sure whether to feel amused or indignant that he had been so certain she would forgive him, that she would come with him to this place. But there she was, lying in his arms again, his lips familiar and warm upon hers. She thought she felt the ghosts of her grandparents and great-grandparents watching over them in stern disapproval, but Lars's kisses soon warmed her until the ice of her worries melted and flowed off her summer skin, evaporating into the night air.

Later, as they held each other quietly, reluctant to part and all too aware that they must, Lars said, "Let me meet your parents. If they knew me, they wouldn't hate me."

"My father might not," Rosa acknowledged, "but my mother could never see you for who you really are. You're a Jorgensen, and that's reason enough to hate you."

"I'll change my name," he said. "Maybe she'll never know."

She laughed and slapped him lightly on the chest. "She'll know."

"She probably would," he said ruefully, and hesitated before continuing. "Rosa, we've talked about spending our lives together, but you won't even ask your parents if you can come to the ranch for the apricot harvest. Years ago you promised me you'd come someday, as soon as your mother realized I wasn't the devil and you could tell her about us. How is that ever going to happen if you won't even let me meet her?"

Rosa laced her fingers together, rested her clasped hands over her heart, and gazed up at a crack in the ceiling, jagged and splintered like a lightning bolt. "I don't know."

"Well, I'll tell you how. It won't happen at all."

Rosa knew he was right. "I don't know how to tell them about you without admitting I've been seeing you against their wishes." That, she knew, would make everything infinitely worse.

Silence fell over them, and as the minutes slipped past, the room grew lighter. Now the decades of accumulated dust on the limp eyelet lace curtains was readily visible, as was a steamer trunk in the shadows of the corner, and a sharp, diagonal crack dividing the cloudy mirror above the bureau. Rosa knew she should have been on her way home long ago, but just as she shifted to sit up, Lars's hand closed around hers.

"Rosa," he said, "when you turn eighteen and your parents have no power to prevent it, will you marry me, or do you mean for us to keep going on like this in secret forever?"

Her heart pounded, but she managed a weak laugh. "Was that a proposal?"

"Yes, I guess it was."

She slipped her hand free from his, sat up, and finger-combed her hair. "It wasn't very romantic."

"The wedding can be romantic, and the

honeymoon, and every day leading up to them and every day after, but right now I'm asking you a serious question and I want a serious answer." A single furrow appeared between his brows as he studied her. "Do you have any intention of marrying me, ever?"

"Of course," she said hotly. "Do you think I would sneak out of my house with you and — and lie in this bed with you if I didn't think we were going to be husband and wife someday?"

"Then either I'm going to have to meet your parents and win their blessing or we're going to have to marry without their approval," he said. "It can only be one way or the other. Which way is it going to be?"

Rosa desperately wanted to marry Lars in the church where she had been baptized with her family proudly gathered around them, but when she imagined introducing Lars to her parents, all she could envision was her mother's anger and her father's bewilderment, tears and shouting, accusations of betrayal and banishment from the only home she had ever known. "I don't know," said Rosa, her voice breaking. "I don't know what to do. I promise I will marry you someday, Lars. I want to with all my heart. I just don't know when and I don't know how. Don't you see how impossible this is for me?"

"I do, I do. Please don't cry." He put his arms around her. "I didn't mean to make you cry. Your promise is all I need. It's enough. We can figure out the rest later."

He embraced her gently, but although she held back her tears, she was not comforted. She wanted nothing more than to marry Lars and live with him happily for the rest of her life, but she could not see how to do that without losing her family. When she was younger, she had chosen her parents, and a few years later she could not have chosen between them, and now she had chosen Lars — but the severing of ties with her mother was a sacrifice she would delay as long as she could, as long as Lars was willing to wait for her.

Rosa woke to a soft rapping sound and light streaming through the gauzy curtains, and for a moment she was sixteen again, in the bedroom of her childhood home, warm and safe beneath a quilt her mother had made. Disoriented, she sat up and found herself in an unfamiliar bed with her two youngest children, and in a flood of awareness she remembered all that had happened the day before. The rapping came again, louder, and in the other bed Marta mumbled something, rolled over, and flung an arm around Ana. Rosa carefully climbed out from beneath the covers, but when she stood, the pain in her side stabbed so sharply that it left her breathless. Bracing herself against the edge of the bed, she waited for her head to stop spinning before she forced herself upright and went to answer the door. Her hand was on the bolt before she remembered the danger. "Yes?" she called through the door, low enough not to disturb the children.

"It's me," said Lars.

Quickly Rosa drew back the bolt and beckoned him inside. He carried a pink-and-white striped bakery box, which he set on the coffee-stained bureau. "I forgot milk," he said apologetically. He glanced at her and then looked away, as if he was embarrassed to be caught watching her in her nightgown. He had seen her in far less, but the last time had been more than five years before.

"That's all right," Rosa quickly said, smoothing over the awkwardness. "This will hold the children over until we can get them a proper meal." She lifted the lid, smelled sugar and pastry, and smiled. "Donuts. I never get them donuts."

"I could go out and find something else —"

"No, no, I only meant that this will be quite a treat. They deserve something special after all they've been through."

Lars grimaced, took off his hat, and sat down on the wooden chair, watching the children as they slept. He had showered but had not shaved, and he was clad in the same denim trousers, blue-checkered cotton shirt, and coat he had worn the previous day. He had brought nothing but the clothes on his back, Rosa realized, dismayed. Of course he had not packed for travel. He had raced to the adobe expecting to find her murdered, perhaps the children as well. He had not planned on an overnight stay — and the Jorgensens had surely expected him to return before nightfall. They were probably sick with worry, wondering what had become of him.

"You should call your mother and brother and let them know you're fine," Rosa said.

"I should do no such thing. No one can know where we are until I'm sure you and the children are safe, and I'm a long way from sure."

"Not even your own family?"

"They can't let slip what they don't know."

Rosa supposed he made a fair point, and

he would be seeing them again soon enough. A day or two of worry wouldn't matter in the long run.

The children stirred in bed, roused by their hushed conversation and the smell of donuts. Only Miguel seemed startled to see Lars there, and he reached for Rosa and buried his face in the collar of her nightgown when she picked him up. "Hungry?" she asked the girls, and passed the box of donuts. Delighted, they each took one, thrilled with the novelty of the treat and of eating in bed. Even Miguel overcame his shyness and took a few bites, but he refused to go to Lars when he offered to watch the children while Rosa bathed and dressed. Miguel climbed into bed beside Marta instead, and after Rosa warned the children not to bounce around with full tummies and make themselves sick, she took her things into the small washroom and drew a bath.

She avoided looking at herself in the mirror while she undressed, but as the chill of the tile floor crept into her bare toes, a morbid curiosity eventually compelled her to examine herself unflinchingly. She was a horror, she concluded, studying the mottled pattern of bruises and cuts on her face, shoulders, and side. It was a wonder the children didn't recoil from her.

She never should have let them become accustomed to seeing her in such a state.

She eased herself into the tub, sinking into the blissfully warm water. A bar of hard amber soap sat in a ceramic dish on a tile shelf above the faucet, so Rosa scrubbed herself clean of blood and dirt, treating her injuries as gingerly as she could. Stomach growling, she finished her bath, drained the tub, and refilled it as she dried off and dressed. Just as she was about to summon the girls, Ana knocked on the door and burst in without waiting for a response. Blinking back tears, Rosa stroked her head while Ana voided her bowels in an explosion of diarrhea. She was so thin that Rosa could count her vertebrae through her nightgown like pearls on a necklace. Frustrated and frightened, Ana sobbed all the while, and although Rosa soothed her and told her everything would be all right, she didn't know whether she spoke the truth.

A knock sounded on the door. "Mamá," called Marta. "Miguel has to go and he has to go *now*."

Hastily Rosa yanked open the door and, with Marta's help, managed to get Miguel's trousers off and set him on the toilet just in time. "He didn't throw up," Marta told her. "Not yet anyway."

Rosa nodded, but that didn't offer her much hope. She had nursed Miguel longer than any of her children, eighteen months, certain that he would be her last baby and longing to extend that precious time. For his first year, Miguel had thrived. He had smiled and crawled and talked and walked exactly when he should have, exactly like any other healthy child. But a few months before his second birthday, he had begun to steadily decline. She weighed and measured all her children vigilantly, and the numbers recorded in her notebook broke her heart: Miguel had lost weight since she had weaned him, and he had not grown in height at all in eight months. Once, he had run and played and found his way into all manner of mischief, but now all he wanted was for Rosa to hold him. And Rosa did, willingly, because she had already lost four children, four children she would never hold again, four children she would love and remember every day for the rest of her life.

She bathed Ana first and then Miguel, and as she carried him back to the bed to dry him off and dress him, she found Lars pacing by the window, stricken. "I shouldn't have brought sweets," he said. "I should have brought something simple, something plain, like biscuits or toast."

"Don't blame yourself," said Rosa, helping Miguel into a clean pair of trousers. "Biscuits and toast likely would have done the same. The only things Miguel and Ana manage to keep in their tummies are rice and tortillas and oranges, but they can't live on that."

Miguel suddenly perked up. "Tortilla, Mamá?"

"Are you hungry, sweetheart?" she asked, puzzled. He nodded. "Okay. Put your shirt on like a big boy and I'll see what we have." She stepped around Lars and knelt by the basket, hoping the rain had not ruined the food she had packed the day before. Luck was with her. At the bottom of the basket she found four corn tortillas wrapped in wax paper, still dry, but cold. She gave one to her son and watched with misgivings as he devoured it, expecting it to come right back up again. Instead Miguel beamed at her and asked for another, but Rosa told him he would have to wait rather than risk upsetting his tummy again.

"You didn't ask for my opinion," said Lars, "but if it were up to me, I'd take all of you to the hospital straightaway and not leave until you're patched up and someone can give us good answers about what's plaguing Ana and Miguel."

"As soon as the children are dressed and ready, we'll go." With John miles away and unable to interfere, with his arguments that they couldn't afford a doctor disproven by the small fortune she had discovered in the valises, nothing would prevent her from seeking a cure for her children's strange and sinister affliction, not while there was breath left in her body.

Within an hour they were on their way. Lars thought it would be too far for the children to walk, so they left the hotel through the same discreet alleyway entrance they had used the previous night, climbed into the car, and drove west down Fifth Street and turned north on F Street. On the way, they passed Plaza Park and a stately white building with Greek columns Lars said was the Carnegie Library. "Can we stop?" Ana begged, rising out of her seat.

"Ana, sit down," Rosa admonished.

"Can we? Please?" Ana said, promptly sitting down again. "They must have hundreds of books in such a big place."

"Maybe thousands," remarked Lars.

Rosa glanced at him, and when he nodded, she said, "All right. After we see the doctor."

Ana beamed as if she couldn't believe her

good fortune. The only library she had ever visited was the small bookcase in the Arboles Valley School, although she had seen photographs of other, grand and glorious libraries in far-off cities like San Francisco and New York.

"Can we play in the park too?" piped up Lupita.

"We'll see," said Rosa. The day had turned bright and sunny, with no trace remaining of the previous day's rainstorm, but Rosa could not shake the sensation that they were being hunted. She didn't want to frighten the children, but she would feel safer within the marble walls of the library than out in the open at a park.

Downtown Oxnard seemed busy and bustling to Rosa for a Sunday morning, but she rarely left the Arboles Valley, and for all she knew, there were fewer cars on the street and people strolling on the sidewalks than other days of the week. As a young woman she had traveled to Los Angeles to visit her aunt, a teacher, several times a year, but marriage had brought an end to her travels, since she could not take the children with her and she was reluctant to leave them at home alone with John, with his tempers and demands. Her last trip to Oxnard had been shortly after Maria died, to seek the aid of a *curandera* before she lost another precious child. The healer, an elderly woman who wore her white hair in a single long braid down her back, told her that the children's souls were frightened and lost, and unless Rosa found a way to bring balance and harmony to their spirits, their bodies would continue to suffer. She had encouraged Rosa to pray continuously and to nourish the children with the traditional foods of their ancestors. Rosa did, and it seemed that her remedies benefited the children to some extent, but their symptoms persisted. The *curandera* had urged Rosa to bring them back to see her in two months, but John, who referred to the old woman as a witch doctor and her treatments as a lot of hocus-pocus, forbade Rosa to see her again.

Before long they arrived at St. John's Hospital, a white, two-story building on the corner of F Street and Doris Avenue that looked to be about four times the size of the library. The children fell silent as they approached the imposing structure, and after Lars parked on the street nearby, Rosa had to coax them from the car with promises of visits to the library and the park and perhaps even the soda fountain Marta had spotted near the hotel afterward, if they were good.

Inside, Rosa asked the children to sit and wait while she spoke to the nurse at the admissions desk. The nurse, a plump, white-clad nun perhaps a dozen years older than herself, took one look at Rosa's face, shot Lars a cold and stony glare, and ushered her off to an examination room. "But my children —" Rosa protested, glancing back at them over her shoulder as the nurse briskly led her away.

"I'll see to them," Lars called after her, leaning over the desk to beckon another nurse who had just arrived.

The first nurse closed the door behind them firmly and instructed Rosa to sit on the examination table. After taking Rosa's temperature and inspecting the cuts and bruises on her face, she asked, "How did you come by these injuries? Take a bad fall, did you?"

"No." Rosa hardly knew what to say. Could there be any mistaking what had happened to her? Was the nun giving her the freedom to lie if she were too ashamed to tell the truth? "That is to say, I — I did fall, after my husband hit me."

"I see."

"I realize I look a fright, but I'm really more concerned about my children. May they see the doctor first?"

The nurse's mouth tightened. "Did your husband hit them too?"

"No — no, I mean, he spanks them when they misbehave, but he — he doesn't hit them the way he hits me. That's not why I brought them here today. Please, could the doctor see them first?"

The older woman's features softened. "We have several doctors, my dear. One of my sisters has already escorted your children to the pediatrics ward." She opened the door again. "Dr. Hayd will be in to see you shortly."

Alone, Rosa watched the door and wondered if she had made a terrible mistake in coming there. She should be with Ana and Miguel during their examination to answer the other doctor's questions and comfort them if they became frightened. Just as she was about to climb down from the table and go in search of the children's ward, the door opened and a tall, gray-haired man with round glasses entered. "Good morning," he greeted her, inspecting the notes on his clipboard. "Sister tells me you said you had a tiff with your husband. Is that so?"

Rosa clasped her hands together in her lap and studied them — the fingers slender, the nails uneven, the skin rough and dry from years of washing clothes and dishes

113

and children. "My husband hit me, yes."

Dr. Hayd glanced up, eyebrows raised. "Are you sure you didn't bump into a door or trip on a toy a child carelessly left on the bottom stair?"

"Quite sure." She sat up straighter and lifted her chin, irritated as much by the meekness in her voice as by his skepticism. "The injuries to my face you can see for yourself. I also have a cut on my head here —" She parted her long black hair. "And on my right side — I feel a sharp pain here whenever I draw a breath."

"Hmm." The doctor drew closer, inspected her face, examined her head, looked intently into her eyes one at a time, and pressed a stethoscope to her back and listened carefully as she breathed deeply in and out. "He seems like a good enough fellow. What did you do to provoke him?"

After a moment of bewilderment, Rosa realized the doctor had mistaken Lars for her husband. Stifling her instinct to defend him, she swallowed hard and said, "Whatever it was, I won't do it again."

"I'm glad you've learned your lesson. It's a pity to see bruises on such a lovely face." Straightening, the doctor frowned, nodded thoughtfully, and adjusted his glasses. "Well, you'll need a few stitches for the laceration in your scalp, but the scar won't be too visible thanks to your hair. I won't have to trim away any of those pretty locks to sew you up, so don't you worry about that. Afterward Sister Mary can clean and bandage the other cuts, which should heal fine on their own if you keep them properly dressed." He opened the door and spoke quietly to someone unseen outside before turning back to her. "Now for the bad news: It seems you have a fractured rib, but it's merely cracked, not broken clean through. I'll send you home with a rib belt, which you should wear regularly for six weeks, even while sleeping. Do you think you can remember my instructions or shall I repeat them to your husband?"

Humiliated, Rosa felt her eyes pricking with hot, angry tears, but she refused to let them fall. "There's no need. I can remember."

"That's a good girl."

At that moment, the plump nun returned carrying what appeared to be a broad elastic band and a small white box. "How are we?" she asked briskly, and Rosa murmured a vague reply. Sister Mary assisted the doctor as he cleaned the laceration, dabbed her scalp with ointment, and sewed the wound shut. Rosa could manage only a nod as Dr.

Hayd bade her farewell, instructed Sister Mary to tend to the rest of her cuts, and left the room.

Sister Mary's hands felt cool and dry against Rosa's flushed skin as she gently cleaned her wounds. "That wasn't so bad now, was it?" When Rosa made a scoffing sound and glanced toward the door, the nun set down the gauze and antiseptic, cupped Rosa's chin with her hand, and tilted her face upward so their eyes met. "I know what Dr. Hayd can be like. You mustn't let his thoughtless words trouble you."

Unbidden, a tear slid down Rosa's cheek.

"Marriage is a holy sacrament," said Sister Mary, "but I cannot imagine that our loving God would want you and those precious children to remain under the same roof as a man who would treat you so cruelly."

Rosa pressed her lips together to hold back a sob.

Sister Mary lowered her voice. "One of my sisters can keep your husband occupied with paperwork and I can bring the children to meet you at the back door. The parish house is nearby, and you'll find sanctuary there until you can find someplace safe to stay. Do you have anyone who can take you in — a mother, a sister, a friend, perhaps?"

"Oh, no, no," exclaimed Rosa. "The man

116

waiting for me — he's not the one who did this. He's not my husband. He's — a very dear friend. I've known him since I was child. He would never —"

Abruptly she stopped speaking. In her haste to defend Lars, she might reveal too much. Quickly she climbed down from the examination table, but the plump nun stood between her and the door, and she was studying Rosa's face carefully. "Are you sure, my child?"

"Absolutely sure." Surrounded by uncertainty though she was, she knew Lars would never hurt her — not intentionally, not again.

Sister Mary hesitated for a moment, but she let the matter drop. She explained how to wear the rib belt and how long to use it, and she advised Rosa to return in six weeks, sooner if she developed a fever or had trouble breathing, or if her pain worsened. "You may follow up with your own physician if you prefer," she added, and Rosa knew the kindhearted nun did not expect to see her again.

Sister Mary led her upstairs to the children's ward, where Marta and Lupita sat alone in the waiting room. "The nurse took Ana and Miguel in there," Marta said, breaking off the story she had been telling her younger sister to point down the hallway to the second door on the left. "Mr. Jorgensen went with them, but he told us to stay here."

Rosa quickly thanked her and hurried to join the others, her heart sinking when one glance over her shoulder told her that although Sister Mary had headed back toward the stairwell, she was still close enough to have heard Lars's name.

When Rosa entered the examination room, Lars and a younger, dark-haired man in a white coat broke off their conversation. "Mrs. Ottesen?" the man greeted her, and when he turned her way, she saw that he bore his weight on crutches and his right pant leg was sewn up at the knee.

She almost shook her head at his mistake, but a warning look from Lars stopped her just in time. "Yes," she said quickly. "I'm Mrs. Ottesen."

"No," said Miguel, sitting cross-legged on the examination table beside Ana. "She's Mamá." When Ana nudged him, he thrust out his lower lip at her. "Stop it."

The man smiled, but he seemed taken aback by Rosa's appearance. "I'm Dr. Russell. Your husband mentioned that you had an accident on the farm."

Involuntarily, Rosa's hand flew to her

bruised face. "Yes, but I'm going to be fine." She smiled at Ana and Miguel, praying they wouldn't contradict her.

"Then are you feeling up to a few questions? Your husband's told me about the children's affliction, but as the children's mother, you're probably more intimately aware of their symptoms."

"Of course," said Rosa. "Anything."

"Maybe Ana and Miguel should wait outside," said Lars, with a look that told Rosa he knew she would hesitate to tell the whole truth in their hearing. "Marta can keep an eye on them."

Rosa helped the children down from the examination table and asked Ana to take Miguel into the waiting room. After they were safely out of earshot, the long, painful tale of her children's mysterious illness poured out of her. She withheld nothing except for particular details that would betray the fiction Lars had invented to conceal their identities. Dr. Russell listened intently, nodding from time to time, prompting her with questions about the children's diet and the onset of their symptoms, their appearance, their growth, everything. When she finished, she felt as drained as if her heart had been wrung dry, but also, for the first time, she felt a small spark of hope. No other doctor had ever listened so long and so carefully when she spoke of the children, or with such determination to glean every relevant detail, no matter how minute.

But when Dr. Russell asked her to sit down, she braced herself for the worst. "Your children are suffering from malnutrition," he said simply.

"That doesn't make any sense," she said. "They have plenty to eat."

"Yes, they have food, but the chronic diarrhea and vomiting prevent them from taking any nourishment from it," he explained. "Their abdomens extended from gas, their general pallor and weakness, their poor growth — these are symptoms I would expect to see in children who have an inadequate diet due to poverty and neglect. As I've seen, however, your other two daughters seem perfectly robust and healthy, and presumably they enjoy the same nutritious meals as their siblings."

"They do," said Rosa.

Dr. Russell frowned thoughtfully. "You say Ana and Miguel have no trouble keeping down tortillas, rice, and oranges."

"Corn tortillas," Rosa clarified. "Flour tortillas don't agree with them. I haven't made those in years."

"Then I encourage you to feed them only tortillas, rice, and oranges until we get to the bottom of this," said Dr. Russell. "I realize that doesn't sound like a very well-balanced diet, but your most important duty now is to get some nutritious food into them."

"Of course." Rosa would have agreed to feed them bread and water ten times a day if Dr. Russell thought it might save them.

"When I was in the service, I worked with a physician who once described seeing a similar affliction in children in Chicago." Balancing on his crutches, Dr. Russell fell silent, thinking. "We lost touch after I was wounded and sent home, but I believe he's with Stanford University now."

"Could you consult him?" asked Lars.

"Certainly. It could take some time to verify his whereabouts and get in touch with him, but once we do, he may very well be able to advise me on how to help your children."

Dizzying relief washed over Rosa, but the doctor's unexpected words of hope did not lessen her sense of urgency. "Could you please try to find him now?"

"Of course, the moment I've finished my rounds."

"Could you find him *now*, please?" asked

Rosa, more insistently. "I realize you have other patients who need your care, but I've already lost four children, and if I lose Ana and Miguel while I'm waiting to hear from a doctor you knew in wartime nearly a decade ago, I won't be able to bear it." And if his former colleague could not help them, Rosa needed to know that too, so she could seek help elsewhere, so she did not let her hopes lift her up so high she would not survive the plummet back to earth.

"Very well, Mrs. Ottesen," Dr. Russell said. "If you and Mr. Ottesen would care to join your children outside, I'll see what I can do."

Lars's strong right arm steadied her as they walked back to the waiting room, where Marta was entertaining the younger children with a story about a bold prince and three valiant princesses who escaped the clutches of an evil sorcerer by transforming themselves into bears. Rosa cuddled Miguel on her lap and held Ana's hand as she waited for Dr. Russell to return.

The minutes passed with excruciating slowness, but at last the doctor appeared in the corridor, smiling as he swung toward them on his crutches. "Dr. Reynolds is with Stanford Hospital in San Francisco," he said. "He was in a lecture when I telephoned, so I had to leave a message with his secretary and wait for him to call back. Not only did he recall the cases in Chicago he had told me about years ago, but he's also currently treating several children afflicted with the same illness." His smile broadened. "He's observed excellent responses to a regimen created by a doctor in New York. He's going to tell me more about it, and I'll see if we can put your children on a similar course of treatment."

Rosa hardly dared believe what she was hearing. "There's a cure?"

"I don't know if it's fair to call it a cure when we haven't even identified the condition, but it does seem to be an effective treatment." Dr. Russell took a folded piece of white paper from his pocket and handed it to Lars. "Dr. Reynolds's credentials, as well as his address and phone number, should you have any concerns about his qualifications."

Rosa hadn't any; his status with the university hospital was enough to impress her, and she had no other options. "When can we begin treatment?"

"I'll need time to consult with Dr. Reynolds and to arrange the regimen. I think it would be reasonable for us to schedule an appointment a week from tomorrow."

Rosa's heart sank. She had hoped they could begin the next morning. With hopes of a cure within reach, how could she wait a week? How would she prepare rice and tortillas in the small rented room at the Radcliffe Hotel? How long would they need to remain in Oxnard while Ana and Miguel underwent treatment? What about school for Marta and Lupita? What about John, and the police, and the bootleggers, and anyone else who might be seeking them?

As they thanked Dr. Russell and left the children's ward, Rosa's mind worked furiously. "There must be something more we can do," she said to Lars, falling behind the girls as they led the way downstairs. "I can't bear to delay a week if there's a treatment that could help them now." Miguel was so light in her arms. Sometimes she felt that if she did not cling fiercely to him, he would drift free of her embrace, float away, and disappear.

Lars looked as if he were about to reply, but when they reached the lobby, he suddenly stopped short. "Girls," he called in an urgent undertone, and when they turned to look at him, he beckoned them to hurry back. Quickly he steered them down an adjacent corridor and around a corner. "Wait here." He ducked back the way they had come and returned a moment later. "We have to find another way out."

"Why?" Rosa imagined John pacing in front of the nurses' station. "Who's out there?"

"My brother, his wife, and Elizabeth." Quickly Lars looked up and down the branching corridor and led them off down the right-hand passage. "This must be where they brought Henry after he was shot."

"How did Elizabeth look?" Rosa asked, hastening after him, placing a hand on Lupita's shoulder to urge her forward more quickly.

"Upset, dazed — I only caught a glimpse of her, not enough for me to guess how Henry might be doing." Lars glanced down a hallway branching off to the left, and after a moment's hesitation, he led them down it. "Mary Katherine had her arm around her. She might have been crying. Oscar was speaking with a doctor."

Rosa held Miguel more tightly and quickened her pace. At the end of the corridor, she spotted a door with a small window through which bright sunlight streamed. Lars and the children saw it too, and as they raced toward it they narrowly avoided running into a man in a wheelchair emerging unexpectedly from a doorway. The nurse attending him shouted warnings after them, but they took no heed, and moments later, Lars shoved open the door and closed it behind them, silencing the scolding voice.

"Why," asked Lupita, catching her breath, "are we running from Mrs. Nelson? I like her."

"I should have thought of this," Lars berated himself as they hurried around the back of the hospital to the street corner, where they followed the sidewalk to the front parking lot. "I knew they'd taken Henry to the hospital, and of course St. John's was the best choice for them just as it was for us."

"It's all right," Rosa said. They reached Lars's car, climbed in, and drove off as soon as everyone was seated. "They didn't see us."

"They didn't this time," said Lars. "Next week we might not be so lucky. It's a miracle Henry survived that gunshot wound at all, and thank God he did, but we have to assume he won't be well enough to be discharged before we return to start the children's treatment. It won't be easy to sneak in and out of the hospital unnoticed."

You don't have to, Rosa almost said as he turned the car south onto F Street. Rosa must; she was their mother. Lars could — and should — return home to his family. He had seen Rosa and the children safely from the Salto Canyon to Oxnard, but she could not impose upon his kindness much longer.

When they turned east on Fifth Street, Rosa spotted a Chinese restaurant and asked Lars to stop. She had never eaten Chinese food before, but she knew they served plain white rice with their meals and that was good enough for her. While she puzzled over the menu, Lars stepped up to the counter and ordered two chicken dishes and one beef as if they were old favorites, but when or how he might have acquired a taste for it, she had no idea. There was so much about the man he had become that she did not know.

After a brief wait, the order came served in white cartons with wire handles. Rosa was glad to discover that the rice had been packaged separately. She intended to follow the doctor's instructions to the letter, and she didn't want a single drop of sauce to contaminate Ana and Miguel's food.

Returning to the car, they drove to Plaza Park and ate their lunches on the grass in the shade of a fig tree. Rosa expected Ana, and perhaps Miguel also, to protest when she served them only plain white rice while the other children sampled the new and exotic flavors of the dishes Lars had selected, but the visit to the hospital had left them quiet and subdued. They knew Rosa had lost other children — Pedro, the brother they remembered, and three other siblings they had never met. Miguel was too young to understand, but gentle, introspective Ana had always been remarkably perceptive for her age. The visit to the hospital had surely reminded her anew that she and Miguel might share their lost siblings' fate.

When they finished eating, Lupita bounded to her feet and begged to be allowed to play. Marta joined her, but Ana gazed at the white-columned library with such longing that Rosa wished she could take her inside.

"You two go along," said Lars, settling back against the fig tree. "I'll watch Marta and Lupita, and I'll play with Miguel, if he'll come to me."

Rosa hesitated, reluctant to let any of the children out of her sight. "I'm not sure that's a good idea. What if Oscar and Mary Katherine drive past on their way home? What if someone else from the Arboles Valley comes by?"

She was more afraid of gangsters and

police than of Lars's family or their neighbors, but she could tell from his expression that Lars understood. "If we're going to be out in public, we're probably safer splitting up," he reasoned. "Anyone looking for us would be searching for a woman with four children, and it's unlikely they'd look for you in a library."

Ana's crestfallen face immediately broke into a smile, and Rosa didn't have the heart to disappoint her. "Miguel, would you like to stay and play?" she asked. When he nodded, she tried to hand him to Lars, but at the last moment Miguel clung to her and turned his face away when Lars reached for him. "Okay. Do you want to go to the library with Mamá instead?" He nodded, so Rosa threw Lars an apologetic look and brought Miguel along as she and Ana walked hand in hand to the library. As they entered the front door and walked among the rows of bookcases, Rosa admired the elegant classical architecture and the well-maintained collections, but her gaze returned time and time again to her daughter's face, which she had not seen so lit up with happiness and wonder since her first day at the Arboles Valley School.

They couldn't borrow any books, but Ana was happy to browse the shelves, read aloud the titles on the books' spines, and open those that sounded most promising. Before long she chose a book, found a seat near a sunny window, and began to read, quickly and thoroughly captivated, while Miguel dropped off to sleep in Rosa's arms. An hour passed swiftly to Ana, lost in her book, and Rosa, content to watch her daughter's small and precious form bent over it. She hated to pull Ana away, but in the quiet of the library she had mulled over the hospital visit and had pondered her next steps. Now she realized with unmistakable certainty what she must do next. "Ana," she said softly, rising from her chair and shifting Miguel to her shoulder, "it's time to go."

Ana sighed wistfully as if she had known that the brief, delightful respite had been too bright and perfect to last. She returned the book to the shelf and slipped her hand into Rosa's, and as they left the library, she eagerly narrated the chapters she had read, describing the characters and settings so vividly that Rosa almost felt as if she had read the book herself.

At Plaza Park, they found Marta and Lupita laughing and squealing with delight as Lars chased them in a wild game of tag, darting just out of reach of his fingertips, shrieking when he bellowed like a bear and jumped out at them from behind a tree or a bench. Rosa marveled with astonishment bordering on alarm that Lars would so recklessly draw attention to themselves — and even more so, that he would throw himself so entirely into their play — but as she watched, her worries soon gave way to amusement. The girls' shouts woke Miguel, who rubbed his eyes sleepily and stared in utter bewilderment at Lars, who just then tripped and sprawled out upon the grass. The girls took the opportunity to tackle him, and as he watched, Miguel smiled bigger and bigger until he laughed aloud.

Lars looked up at the sweet, pure, happy sound, and his eyes met Rosa's, and in that instant she glimpsed him as he had been more than twenty years ago when she had fallen in love with him — so handsome, so confident, carefree and daring, so terrifying and exhilarating all at once that she could not have helped being drawn to him. She had loved him so completely, and yet it had all gone so terribly wrong.

His smile faltered, and she knew he read the memory of heartache in her eyes. Suddenly she felt exposed and vulnerable, as if everyone in the park were watching her and knew who she was. "Let's go," she urged Lars, picking up Miguel and motioning to the girls to head for the car. She wanted desperately to be behind the locked door of their hotel room, safe and unobserved.

The girls made a few token protests, reluctant to spend such a beautiful day closed up in a small hotel room, but beneath that, Rosa sensed an undercurrent of fatigue and a longing for quiet and calm. Back at the Radcliffe Hotel, they slipped inside through the alley door, and to Rosa's relief, Lars remained with them instead of going across the hall to his own room. His presence offered her a feeling of safety and security that even the locked door did not provide. Marta brought out her backgammon set, sat cross-legged on one of the beds, and invited Ana to play, while Miguel found his wooden train and began pushing it around the floor. Lupita looked at the pile of baskets and bags along the wall, and, watching her daughter's face and awaiting the inevitable, Rosa knew the exact moment Lupita remembered losing her doll to the floodwaters. Her eyes filled with tears, but without a word of complaint, she sat down on the floor between the two beds and tugged disconsolately at the buckle of her shoe.

Lars rose, put on his hat, and spoke quietly in Rosa's ear. "I'll go out and find her a new doll. There must be a shop open somewhere, even on a Sunday."

"Thank you. But wait," said Rosa, grasping his sleeve as he turned to go. "Just a moment." She opened one of the valises, counted out a few bills, and turned to find Lars staring at the valise in disbelief.

"How much do you have there?" he asked.

"I don't know. I haven't had a chance to count it."

"It must be thousands."

Rosa hoped so. She had no idea how long she would have to rely upon it as her only source of income. "Here," she said, placing the bills in his hand. "This should be enough."

Lars tucked the bills into his wallet. "More than enough. Is there anything else you want while I'm out?"

"Ice cream," Marta spoke up, moving a piece on the backgammon board.

"Yes, please," chimed in Lupita. "Ice cream, ice cream. We were good at the hospital, and you promised."

"Ana and Miguel can't have ice cream," said Rosa. "The doctor said so. It's not fair to get a treat that only some of us can enjoy."

"I don't really want any," said Marta quickly.

"I do," said Lupita. "Please?"

"It's okay, Mamá," said Ana quietly. "I'm not hungry anyway."

"I'm happy with oranges." Marta frowned at Lupita, but Lupita was looking up at Rosa beseechingly, oblivious to her elder sister's disapproval.

Rosa sighed, torn. "All right. If Mr. Jorgensen doesn't mind stopping for it, you can have a cone." To Lars she added, "Do you mind?"

"Of course not. Want anything for yourself?"

"Yes. A train schedule. We passed the station on our way into town last night, but I'm not sure how far away it is."

"It's only a few blocks down Fifth Street." His brow furrowed, and she knew he wanted to ask why she needed a train schedule, but he refrained. "I'll be back soon. Lock the door behind me —"

"And don't open it to anyone." She offered him a quick smile. "I know."

He smiled back, but with a faint grimace of concern. He suspected she was planning something, something he would not like. He was right.

As soon as he left, Rosa took inventory of the children's belongings, grateful that sensible Marta had packed so well. The children had plenty of clothes to suit them until Rosa could buy more, and she had even remembered socks and toothbrushes. Thus assured, Rosa set herself to counting the money she had taken from the hayloft. Intrigued, Lupita came over to help her while the other children looked on. If the bills had not been bundled into stacks the task might have taken Rosa all afternoon, but as it was, she finished counting and had repacked the cash in the valises by the time Lars returned an hour later.

Lupita brightened at the sight of the new doll and the ice cream cone, and she flung her arms around Lars's legs, speechless with gratitude. Gifts in hand, she climbed upon the other bed and happily cuddled her doll and licked her vanilla ice cream. Miguel tried in vain to climb up beside her, and Marta and Ana studiously ignored her, their gazes fixed on the backgammon board.

Lars eyed the neatly rearranged baggage, took a folded piece of paper from his inside coat pocket, and handed it to Rosa. "Mind telling me why you need a train schedule?"

Steeling herself, Rosa nodded. "Let's step outside." She asked Marta to keep an eye on everyone for a moment and led Lars into the hallway, leaving the door slightly ajar. She took a deep breath as Lars bent closer expectantly, his arms folded over his chest. "I can't wait until next week to start the children's treatment," she told him. "Ana and Miguel need help now. And what if after consulting with the other doctor, Dr. Russell realizes that he can't offer the same procedure for some reason? We'll have wasted seven days, and the children will be no closer to a cure."

Lars ran a hand over the golden stubble on his jaw. "What do you intend to do about it?"

"How can I sit here and wait when I know there's a doctor who's successfully treated this illness in other children? I'll wire Dr. Reynolds's office at the hospital to let him know we're on our way, and I'll take Ana and Miguel to see him." She indicated the train schedule. "There's a nine-twenty-six train tonight that would have us in San Francisco by half past nine tomorrow morning. I can afford a private car, and room and board in San Francisco for however long the regimen lasts." Or so she hoped. She had no idea how long the children would need to be treated.

Lars inhaled deeply, thinking. "All right then. We'll take the train. You and the children can wait here while I go out and buy whatever we'll need for the trip. First

I'll wire Dr. Reynolds at the hospital so he'll be expecting us —"

"Lars, I didn't think —" Rosa pressed her hand to her side as a sharp pain stabbed her. "You don't have to come with us. You shouldn't come. I can't ask you to leave your home, your family, the ranch —"

"You don't need to ask. I'm offering."

"But Lars," she said, at a loss, "I don't know when I'll be coming back. It could be months, years, if ever."

A muscle worked in his jaw. "All the more reason for me to come with you now."

"Lars —"

"No, Rosa." He held her by the shoulders. "I've kept my distance, and I've let John be a father to my daughters even though he did a spit poor job of it, because that's what you asked me to do. Now you're telling me that I might never see them, or you, again, and you think I'm going to just put the five of you on a train and wave good-bye from the station?"

"I suppose I didn't —" She couldn't look at him. She didn't know what to say.

"I'm coming along," he said emphatically. "You'll need my help, and there's nothing to keep me in the Arboles Valley if you and the children leave." He made a short, dry laugh. "Don't forget, I reported John to the

Prohibition bureau. Eventually some corrupt officer on the bootleggers' payroll will tell them who tipped off the feds, and they'll come looking for me."

Rosa pressed a hand to her mouth, stunned. She had not considered the danger he had placed himself into for her sake, to free her from John. He could not go home again, not now, not anytime soon.

"I have to disappear anyway." Lars managed a rueful smile. "I'd prefer to go with you and the children, so I could be useful, at least."

"Of course," said Rosa, in a voice barely above a whisper. She was suddenly profoundly glad that he would be coming with them. "Of course."

CHAPTER THREE

Rosa rejoined the children while Lars went out to wire Dr. Reynolds and to buy the supplies they would need for their journey. He returned an hour later with three secondhand suitcases, clothes and a razor for himself, a sleeve of paper cups, and a paper sack full of corn tortillas, stuffed peppers, white rice, and black beans, still hot. Rosa spread a blanket on the floor and filled cups with water from the bathroom tap. As she passed around the food, she announced that the meal was an indoor picnic to celebrate the exciting journey they would embark upon that night. The children brightened and chattered happily as they ate, querying Rosa and Lars about the towns they might pass through and what they might see along the way. Rosa answered their questions as best she could, keeping a watchful eye on Ana and Miguel and making sure only the corn tortillas and white rice passed their lips.

After supper, while Lars went to his own room to pack, Rosa transferred her and the children's clothing to the suitcases and refilled a single basket with the remaining food. As she worked, she said a silent prayer of thanksgiving when Ana and Miguel both kept their suppers down. Miguel had only a mild bout of diarrhea, which, Rosa told herself, could very well be a lingering symptom from the previous day rather than the onset of a new attack.

Just as she finished packing, Lars knocked on the door and beckoned Rosa into the hallway. "I didn't want to say anything in front of the kids, but we made the front page." He took a newspaper from his coat pocket, unfolded it, and gestured to a headline just below the *Oxnard Press-Courier* masthead.

"Oh, no," Rosa murmured as she began to read.

ARBOLES VALLEY RANCH HAND SHOT
Local Postmaster Terrorizes Neighbors
Wife and Four Children Missing

ARBOLES VALLEY, CAL., Sept. 14 — Local rye farmer and Arboles Valley postmaster

140

John Barclay is being held in the Ventura County Prison on charges of attempted murder after shooting and critically wounding a ranch hand who tried to disarm him during an altercation at the Jorgensen Ranch yesterday afternoon.

According to police investigators, Barclay brandished a firearm in front of the Jorgensen residence and demanded that the family send out Lars Jorgensen, elder brother of ranch owner Oscar Jorgensen. Lars Jorgensen, who was away from the ranch at the time, could not respond to the gunman's demands. Police would neither confirm nor deny rumors that Barclay accused Lars Jorgensen of having carnal knowledge of his wife.

The Jorgensen family phoned the police, but before officers reached the scene, Mrs. Henry Nelson, the wife of the shooting victim and a friend of Mrs. Barclay, arrived home. Barclay fired upon her car, but she put the automobile in reverse and drove out of range. Fearing for his wife's safety, Henry Nelson left the house through the kitchen door and attempted to sneak up on Barclay, but Barclay spotted him approaching and fired, seriously wounding Nelson in the left shoulder near the heart.

Oscar Jorgensen and another worker

subdued Barclay and restrained him until police arrived and took him into custody. While searching the Barclay farm for evidence, deputies discovered several large crates buried in straw in the hayloft. Inside was a stash of small arms, a valise full of cash, and more than fifty gallons of contraband liquor in bottles. According to a confidential source within the Prohibition Bureau, agents had received a tip that Barclay was involved with the illegal distribution of bootleg liquor, but they did not have enough evidence to obtain a warrant to search the property. The same source identified Lars Jorgensen as the informant, which offers another possible motive for Barclay's assault on the Jorgensen ranch.

Jorgensen's whereabouts are currently unknown. Also missing are Mrs. Barclay and the four young Barclay children. Investigators believe that Mrs. Barclay took the children to the Salto Canyon to hide from her husband, who beat her in a rage before departing to confront Jorgensen. Deputies found Barclay's team and wagon on the mesa, but Mrs. Barclay and her children were nowhere to be found. Mrs. Barclay is wanted for questioning, but it is feared that she and her children perished in the flash flood that swept through the canyon within hours of the shooting.

County Sheriff Tom Jeffries stated that depending upon the outcome of the investigation, Barclay could face additional racketeering charges. If Nelson does not survive, the attempted murder charge will be elevated to second-degree murder.

As of press time, then, John was in police custody, which meant he wasn't looking for them. The authorities suspected that Rosa and the children had drowned, so they were probably concentrating their search downriver from the canyon and might not investigate surrounding towns as thoroughly as they otherwise would have done.

Rosa was unsettled to read that she was wanted for questioning, but the report that she and the children were assumed dead gave her new reason to hope they could elude anyone searching for them, as long as they took every precaution to conceal their tracks. She folded the newspaper and returned it to Lars. "The police know you left home in your car, and they'll be looking for it. You should sell it and use the money to purchase a ticket for the express to Los Angeles."

His eyebrows rose. "I gather you want me to make sure I'm seen on the platform awaiting its departure too."

Rosa nodded. "If you can board the train and slip out just before it leaves the station, that would be even better. In the meantime I'll buy tickets to San Francisco for the six of us."

"All right," said Lars after thinking it over. "We'll do it your way, except I can't sell the car. It's not mine to sell. I'll take you and the children to the station, and then I'll find some out-of-the-way place, park the car, and walk back to the station. Eventually someone will notice that it's been abandoned and contact the police, and they'll send word to Oscar to come fetch it."

Rosa agreed. Lars's plan would also save them precious time. "Before we go to the station, do you think it would be safe to return to St. John's?"

"You want to get a second opinion from another doctor before we set out? I don't think we have time."

"No, that's not it. I want to leave some money with the kind nurse who treated me yesterday, enough to pay for Henry's treatment."

"Oh, Rosa." Lars sighed. "I admire your good intentions, but I hope I can talk you

144

out of it."

"I have nearly twelve thousand dollars in those valises, Lars." The amount seemed to startle him, but she hurried on before he could interrupt. "That's more than enough to pay our way for a long while. The Nelsons aren't wealthy people, and I want to help them. I owe Elizabeth that much. When I was unhappy and desperate, everyone else abandoned me, even my own brother, but Elizabeth became my friend."

"Not all of your friends abandoned you," said Lars mildly. "Some of us were told to keep our distance. Rosa, think about it. You're front-page news. How many people read the paper this morning and remembered seeing a distraught, injured woman with four children at the hospital yesterday? We can't do anything else to draw attention to ourselves, and offering a substantial amount of cash to settle another patient's bill is going to attract attention."

Rosa felt herself wavering. "What if you go alone?" she persisted. "You could take the money to Sister Mary. I'm sure she'd be discreet."

Lars shook his head. "Your heart's in the right place, but paying someone else's bills is going to stir up curiosity no matter who delivers the money. If anyone comes around later asking questions, we don't want the hospital staff to be able to give them a good description of me, or you, or the children, for that matter."

"I think it's a bad idea too," Ana suddenly spoke up. With a gasp, Rosa spun around to find Ana and Marta standing just inside the open doorway. How much had they overheard? "I like Mrs. Nelson but it's too dangerous to go back to the hospital. What if somebody sees you and takes you away from us?"

"*Mija,* no one could ever take me away from you."

"Then why are we hiding?"

Rosa hesitated. Lars had made his point and had nothing more to add, but Marta and Ana were shooting her pleading looks, and she knew she had lost the argument. "Very well," she said. They were right; even the slightest chance that the police or the bootleggers might be checking local hospitals for them posed too great a risk. The children needed her more than Elizabeth did.

She could not pay for Henry's medical care, but someday she would make it up to the woman who had befriended her and had given her reason to hope when so many other people she had known her entire life had turned their backs on her.

While Lars went down to the lobby to settle the bill, Rosa retrieved her shears from her sewing basket and took them into the small bathroom, where she balanced them carefully on a small ceramic shelf meant to hold a water glass and stared at her reflection in the cracked mirror. She had once been radiantly beautiful — dark, wide-set eyes fringed with long lashes; high, elegant cheekbones; full, red lips that curved gracefully into a beckoning smile. Worry and care had taken the glow from her skin and etched twin grooves from nose to chin around her mouth, which was usually either pressed into a hard line as it was now or twisted into a melancholy frown. Her eyes were haunted and shadowed, and she had become too thin, so the high cheekbones gave her face an almost skeletal cast. Her only remaining beauty of the many she had once carelessly taken for granted was her hair — long and thick, raven black with a sheen like obsidian, unmarred by gray. She wore it unfashionably long, braided into thick ropes and pinned up at the nape of her neck, and when she took it down at night, it cascaded down her back to her waist, a dark, silky waterfall. As the popularity of the bob had soared, her hair had become her most unique, admired, and recognizable feature.

She took a deep breath, removed every hairpin, and let her long hair tumble down. Swiftly and decisively, she braided the heavy locks into one long plait, took the shears in hand, and sawed through the braid at the nape of her neck. Immediately her head felt lighter, as if she had severed a chain tethering herself to the ground. Setting the braid on the edge of the tub, she finger-combed her hair into place and trimmed the ragged ends into a neat, smooth bob. When she was satisfied that from a distance she would resemble any other Southern California housewife, she set down the shears and cleaned up the loose snips of hair that had fallen lightly to the floor. If only she had some way to conceal the all too noticeable and memorable cuts and bruises on her face.

She considered throwing the braid away, but something compelled her to keep it. She left the small bathroom and knelt beside her sewing basket, where she exchanged the shears for two small lengths of a narrow ribbon, which she tied around the ends of the severed braid.

"Mamá," exclaimed Marta. "Your hair, your beautiful hair!"

Lupita gasped, her eyes wide with horror. "Mamá lost her hair!"

"No, I didn't," said Rosa, holding up the braid. "It's right here."

"Sew it back on," Lupita ordered. "You don't look like a mama. You look like a young lady."

Despite everything, Rosa laughed as she tucked the braid into the sewing basket. "Thank you, Lupita." She had spent the last twenty minutes studying herself in the mirror and she knew she looked every bit of her age and then some. She was digging into her overstuffed satchel for Elizabeth's tan cloche when a knock sounded on the door and Lars called out to let them know who was there. Clutching the hat, Rosa hurried to let him in, but he stood transfixed in the hallway, staring at her newly shorn head. "A good disguise, don't you agree?" She tugged the cloche over her dark bob. "If I'd answered the door with the hat on, you wouldn't have known me."

As he entered the room, he gave her a wry look that told her he would know her anywhere. "You'd fool a lot of people at first glance," was all he would admit.

It was time to go. With the girls' help, they carried their belongings downstairs in one trip, and they quickly loaded up the car and drove to the train station. Ocean mists had rolled in with the onset of dusk, and the children yawned and tried to make themselves comfortable in the backseat.

"Are we going home?" asked Lupita sleepily, where she sat between her older sisters holding her new doll on her lap in a fair imitation of Rosa holding Miguel.

"No, *mija*," said Rosa. "We're going to a city called San Francisco to meet a doctor who can help Ana and Miguel."

"Is Papa coming too?"

From the corner of her eye, Rosa saw Lars wince. "No, Lupita," she said. "He isn't."

"Why not?"

"He can't leave the farm," Marta spoke up tiredly. "Who would take care of the livestock and run the post office?"

Marta's reasoning must have satisfied Lupita, for she played quietly with her doll for the rest of the short drive. Lars parked and helped Rosa carry their luggage to the platform before climbing back into the car and speeding away.

"Girls, stay here and watch our things while I buy our tickets." Rosa picked up Miguel, who had squatted down to study a line of ants crawling along the wooden boards. In a lower voice, she added to Marta, "Don't take your eyes off those valises for a second."

"Isn't Mr. Jorgensen coming with us?" asked Marta.

"Of course," Rosa replied, with a reassuring smile for all of her daughters, who all looked equally anxious. "Aren't you excited for your first train ride? We're going to have a wonderful adventure."

Lupita beamed, but Marta and Ana managed only brave, pensive nods. Rosa promised them she would be right back and hurried to the ticket window to pay for a private car and six fares to San Francisco. On impulse, she also bought four lemonades from a vendor's cart and carried them carefully back to the children. "A treat to toast our journey," she said, handing each of her daughters a cup and helping Miguel with his. The girls brightened, and as they sipped their lemonade, they chatted excitedly about what it would feel like to sleep on a train. Rosa only half listened as she scanned the darkened streets and sidewalks for Lars, but there was no sign of him. "Done, Mamá," said Miguel, pushing his half-full cup toward her. Absently she took a drink, wondering how far Lars had gone, how quickly his long strides would bring him back to them.

No more than five minutes passed before

the train chugged into the station, white steam billowing from the smokestack. Clinging to her leg, Miguel watched, fascinated, his fingers in his mouth, while Lupita crouched behind the largest suitcase and covered her ears with her hands. A slow smile spread over Ana's face as the train came to a halt, and she watched, eyes shining, as passengers disembarked — men, women, children, young and old, dressed in smart suits and fine hats or in more humble attire, plain and durable but neat and proudly worn. As the conductor strode along the platform, calling out the destinations ahead, other northbound passengers began to board. Biting her lip, Rosa looked through the crowd in vain for a tall, thin, fair-haired and purposeful farmer, but Lars did not appear.

A porter approached and offered to help her with her luggage. She agreed, worried that refusal would make her more memorable. In any event, she thought as she followed the porter aboard and helped the younger children up the steps, she had to board. If Lars missed the train, she and the children had no choice but to travel on without him.

Suddenly she felt a pang of worry. What if he had been recognized as he hurried back to the station, and what if, even now, the police were interrogating him? Worse yet, what if John's mob colleagues had apprehended him instead? Her heart pounding, she followed the children into the private car and managed a polite smile as she tipped the porter. Perhaps, instead of parking the automobile, Lars had decided to keep driving, either home to the Arboles Valley or on to Los Angeles or off to some remote locale where he could lose himself among strangers. She could not blame him if he had. He was safer on his own.

Still he did not appear. As the children explored the train car and exclaimed over each novelty discovered — the bouncy leather seats, the clever washbasin, the bunks they could fold down when they wanted to sleep, if they could possibly sleep with so many marvels surrounding them — Rosa sank into a seat and gazed out the window. Outside the conductor passed, calling out a final warning to passengers who lingered on the now nearly empty platform bidding sad farewells to loved ones.

The whistle sounded. The train lurched forward and slowly began to pick up speed. Rosa stared out the window in crushing disbelief as they passed the ticket window, the lemonade vendor, and the end of the

153

platform, until they left the station behind. As the girls crowded around the windows to watch the city of Oxnard pass by, two quick raps on the compartment door drew Rosa's attention in time for her to see it swing open and Lars enter, breathless. She was so relieved to see him she couldn't speak, but the girls greeted him happily.

"Sorry to cut it so close," he said, removing his hat and dropping onto the seat beside her. He carried a few colorful pamphlets, which he showed her briefly before tucking them into his coat pocket. "I thought it might be prudent to let myself be seen looking over guides to Mexico."

"I thought maybe you changed your mind."

Lars folded his arms over his chest, closed his eyes, and settled back into the seat, panting as if he had sprinted across the platform and leapt onto the moving train. "That should've been the least of your worries."

Perhaps it should have been.

Before long the conductor came by to collect and punch their tickets. After he left, Lars lowered the bunks and stepped out into the hallway while Rosa and the children prepared for bed. In her exhaustion and worry she had not given any thought to their sleeping arrangements, but as uncomfortable as she was to share such a small space with Lars, she could hardly ask him to search for an empty seat in one of the passenger cars, where he would be forced to sleep sitting up or not at all. And that was if he found a vacancy, and if the conductor did not send him back to his ticketed car. So she put Ana and Marta to bed in one narrow bunk, and took Lupita and Miguel into her own, leaving one bed for Lars. She had drawn the curtain and turned out the lights before climbing under the covers, so when Lars returned, the car was dark. She heard him open his suitcase, undress, and climb into his own bunk, and then only the sounds of the train and Miguel's and Ana's soft, even breathing filled her ears. Lars was so quiet she knew he was still awake, and she wished that she could speak to him, to thank him for all he had done, to apologize for throwing his life into upheaval, but she didn't want to wake the children, so it was just as well that she couldn't find the words.

Lars's sacrifices and kindness were all the more extraordinary given that thirteen years before, she had broken his heart.

For a few months after she had agreed to marry him, Lars never appeared at her window with the smell of alcohol on his breath. He proudly told her of the money he was saving up and the gentle rise of the hill on the southern acres of the Jorgensen ranch where he planned to build them a house. Rosa cautioned him not to break ground just yet, and several times she had to remind him that she had no intention of marrying him on her eighteenth birthday but sometime after she graduated. To her relief he did not press her to be more specific.

In the weeks leading up to her birthday, he hinted that he wanted to buy her an engagement ring, but she begged him not to, because her parents would certainly notice a diamond sparkling on the third finger of her left hand. "But I won't ever want to take it off," she told him when he suggested that she wear it only when they were together in the cabin, and hide it when they were apart. She didn't tell him that she suspected her mother occasionally searched her room when she was at school. Rosa wasn't sure what she had done recently to raise her mother's suspicions, or what her mother thought she might find tucked away in her drawers or concealed under her mattress, but Rosa knew there was no place in her room she could hide a ring where her mother would not find it.

Then Lars suggested that she keep the ring in the cabin. "No one comes here but us," he said. "This is our place." And it was. Over time they had swept and scrubbed and improved the cabin with small comforts — pillows and sheets no one would miss from the Jorgensen farmhouse, a coffeepot and cups Rosa had picked up at a secondhand store — and while they both joked about "playing house," it almost did feel like a real home of their own. Since they intended to marry someday and felt almost married already, it became easier not to wait for marriage to be intimate. And one night they were. Lars was worried about hurting her and Rosa was worried about getting pregnant, but with each encounter such worries seemed less important until they disappeared entirely. Throughout her girlhood Rosa had overheard her mother and her mother's friends sharing countless confidences in hushed voices as they sewed or cooked, and they had inadvertently taught her how to count the days of her cycle to prevent a pregnancy. It did not always work, as Rosa had also learned from the older women, but it was the only preventative their faith allowed. Rosa resolved to be scrupulous and careful and take no unnecessary chances.

In June, Rosa graduated from high school and took a job as a bookkeeper and clerk at the Grand Union Hotel. She had always been good with numbers and she enjoyed the work as well as the bustle and excitement of the inn, but she regretted disappointing her mother, who had hoped Rosa would attend college and become something important, perhaps a teacher like her aunt. When her mother persisted, pleading with her at least to apply to the University of California and make up her mind after receiving her acceptance letter, Rosa explained that she loved the Arboles Valley too much to leave it. Her mother accepted Rosa's excuse with profound skepticism — and with good reason. It was not love for the valley that kept Rosa from going off to college, but love for Lars.

Rosa unwittingly disappointed Lars too. She did not realize that he had assumed she meant to marry him immediately after finishing school until he showed up at her bedroom window one night, red-eyed and slurring his words, full of lamentations and demands. Furious, she yanked the curtains shut and went back to bed, holding her breath for fear that he would wake her parents. Eventually he departed, and when he returned three nights later, sober and contrite, she only went to the cabin with him so that she could scold him. "I won't marry you until you stop drinking," she warned him, and he promised he would.

Weeks passed, and again he showed up drunk after a day at Lake Sherwood with his friends. She sent him away, and when he came back a few nights later, she warned him again that she would not marry him until he proved he could stay sober.

"You'll never marry me regardless," he told her, and strode back to his horse alone.

He stayed away a week, and as she had years before, she missed him and brooded over all that was wrong and impossible with their relationship, and she had almost decided to apply to college after all when once again he woke her with a soft knock on her window. He was sober, so she went off with him, glad and relieved. Later, as they lay side by side on the old bed in the cabin with the quilt drawn over them, she said, "I won't marry you until you stop drinking for good."

"I'll stop drinking when you marry me," he replied.

"How do I know that you mean it this time? You've promised before and you've let me down."

"Marry me and I'll prove it."

"If you can't stop before we get married, why should I believe you'd be able to after?"

"It's not that I can't," he said, an edge to his voice. "I could quit, if I wanted to. I could quit tonight."

"Then why don't you?" she persisted. "Why won't you, for me?"

"And leave you without an excuse to delay the wedding?" he retorted. "You wouldn't want that."

Mrs. Diegel, the young widow who had moved to the valley from Los Angeles to assume responsibility for the hotel when her father's health failed, certainly knew about their romance, but she was as discreet with her employees' affairs as she was with her guests'. She never failed to greet Lars cordially when he showed up at the office with a sack lunch or a basket of fresh apricots, but she never queried Rosa about him, except to note when they had returned late from an outing and to ask her to stay late to make up for it.

Perhaps Mrs. Diegel thought Lars was only one of several suitors, because he was not the only young man to visit Rosa at the hotel. John Barclay, whom she had rarely seen since he finished school four years ahead of her, had begun stopping by at least once a week to invite her to lunch or for a glass of lemonade after work. "I'm not a frivolous man, Rosa," he told her once, as if anyone would accuse him of that particular fault. Sometimes she found herself wishing that Lars could be half as diligent and steadfast as his friend and frequent rival without losing his passion and sense of fun. Sometimes, too, when she was angry with Lars for his drinking, she wished she could forget about him and fall in love with someone like John instead — or John himself. He certainly seemed fond of her. But although she cared about John, enjoyed his company, and cherished their friendship, she loved only Lars, and she longed for the day he would quit drinking, her mother would abandon her prejudices, and they could marry.

But that day seemed ever more elusive. She was twenty and Lars twenty-two, and he was tired of the need for secrecy and had become increasingly impatient with her interminable delays. Twice they broke off their engagement only to reconcile within the week. His drunkenness became more frequent and more ugly. When he was sober he was all that she wanted in a husband — a loyal, honest, kind, and loving man. When he drank, they argued and she despaired. How could she build a home and raise a family with someone so unreliable, so unpredictable? How could she live without the man she loved with all her heart?

One afternoon, after a rare pleasant lunch with Lars that had concluded with a long kiss good-bye over her desk, her mother suddenly appeared in her office doorway. "Mamá," Rosa exclaimed, bolting out of her chair and greeting her with a kiss on the cheek. Lars had left only moments before; her mother must have passed him on her way through the lobby. What had she thought? What had she guessed? Rosa felt her knees trembling as she offered her mother a chair. "What a surprise! Is everything all right?"

Her mother regarded her sternly. "No, in fact, something is very wrong." When Rosa sank into her own chair with the desk between them, stricken, her mother's expression softened. "I didn't mean to worry you, but *mija,* I am very troubled by your secrecy. I know — your father and I know — that you are in love. We think we know why you've been hiding this from us, but the time has come for you to tell the truth."

Shaking, scarcely able to breathe, Rosa clenched her hands together in her lap. "How long have you known?"

Her mother put her head to one side and

regarded her as if to say they had known for a very long time. "We waited as long as we could, hoping you would tell us on your own."

Rosa hesitated, bewildered by her mother's calm demeanor. "You aren't angry?"

"Because you have deceived us, yes, very. Because you have fallen in love, no. Never." Her mother smiled tenderly. "You're a beautiful, loving young woman, Rosa. If you've found the love of a good man, we're happy for you. We want to share in your happiness."

"I —" Rosa could not believe what she was hearing. "I didn't think you would approve. And I love him, but — I'm still not sure. He's a good man, but — it's just so hard to know what to do. There are things about him I wish he would change. I pray for him to change. Can I really love him if I want him to be different?"

"Oh, Rosa." Her mother rose and came behind the desk to embrace her. "Why did you keep your troubles to yourself for so long? I'm your mother. You can always talk to me about anything. You know I will always love you."

"And I will always love you." Rosa's vision blurred with unshed tears. "And I will always love him. I know I will. But that doesn't mean I should marry him."

Her mother straightened, her brow furrowing. "Has he asked you to marry him?"

Rosa nodded.

"He should not have done that without speaking to your father."

"You're right. I know that. But it's — well, you know how things are." Tentatively, Rosa added, "I'm surprised you're taking it so well yourself."

"There's no need for secrecy any longer," her mother assured her. "Invite John to join us for Sunday dinner. We need to get to know the man who wants to marry our daughter."

Rosa stared at her mother, as numb as if the air around her had frozen solid. As if from a very great distance, she heard herself say, "Invite . . . John?"

"Yes, and without delay," her mother replied.

Rosa could not take a breath or find the words for a reply. John. Her parents thought she loved John.

John courted Rosa for two years. Once a month he came to Sunday dinner at the Diaz home, and every other Saturday he took Rosa out on a date — a picnic, a dance at the Arboles Lodge, or a day at Lake

Sherwood with friends, outings from which one of his oldest friends, Lars, was conspicuously absent. The longer Rosa misled her parents and John, the more difficult it became to extricate herself from the tangled threads of her lie. One morning in the hushed gray hour before dawn, her mother met her at the door when she returned home after a night at the cabin with Lars. "Why don't you just marry him?" her mother implored, distressed and bewildered. Shaken, Rosa apologized for upsetting her mother, but she would not promise to stop slipping away at night. She knew she was moving inexorably closer to the day when she must elope with Lars or lose him forever, but as long as her mother believed Rosa went to John when she stole away from home under the cover of darkness, Rosa could defer that irrevocable choice.

And then, unexpectedly, the choice overtook her.

Her brother, Carlos, had finished school, and thanks to Rosa's recommendation to Mrs. Diegel, he had obtained a job as a handyman at the Grand Union Hotel. He had inherited their father's friendly, cheerful disposition as well as his gift for storytelling. One day in late July, Lars brought Rosa a basket of apricots fresh from the orchard, and to her relief, he did not remind her of her long-unfulfilled promise to come to the ranch for harvest someday. She savored the sweetness of one perfect apricot alone in her office and carried the rest home to share with her family. But her joy vanished the moment she entered the house and met her mother, who went impossibly motionless at the sight of the ripe fruit.

"Where did you get those?" her mother finally asked quietly, her dark eyes fixed on the basket.

"Mrs. Diegel gave them to me," Rosa said lightly, setting the basket on the kitchen counter too quickly, as if the woven slats had burned her palms. "She didn't want them, so she gave them to me."

A cold silence descended. Rosa was afraid to turn around and meet her mother's gaze, but she felt her accusing stare boring into her back.

"You will never see him again," her mother said in the same quiet voice.

Rosa whirled around to face her. "Mamá?"

"Marry John or don't marry him, but you will never see Lars Jorgensen again."

Shocked and dismayed, Rosa tried in vain to defend Lars, to defend herself for loving him, but her mother was resolute. Sick at heart, Rosa fled to her room, accidentally overturning the basket of apricots in passing.

Much later, Carlos knocked on her door and called softly to her, and when she allowed him to enter, he stepped cautiously into the room, white-faced and apologetic. He had not meant to divulge her secret; he had not even known she and Lars were in love. He had come home from work earlier than Rosa, as he often did, and when he told their mother about his day, he remarked that the Jorgensens' apricot harvest must have gone well, because he had seen Lars carrying a basket of the fresh, ripe fruit into the hotel office. He had joked that Lars had probably given it to Mrs. Diegel to pay off his bar tab. He never could have imagined that barely an hour later, Rosa would walk through the front door with that same basket in her hands.

Rosa did not blame him for unwittingly divulging her secret — but now they were all complicit in keeping the secret from their father.

Through August and September, Rosa managed to see Lars only twice, by leaving work early to meet him at the cabin. "Come away with me," Lars urged moments before they parted, taking her hands and clasping them to his heart. "We'll get married, and once it's done, everyone will just have to get used to the idea. Your parents will forgive you eventually. You know they will."

Rosa wanted desperately to believe him, but he was hung-over from another drinking binge and she could not bear the thought of exchanging marriage vows with him so haggard and shaking and ill. "If you can go two weeks without a drink," she said, "I swear I'll marry you the next day."

Elated, Lars vowed that not a drop of alcohol would touch his lips until they toasted each other with champagne on their wedding night. Since it was unlikely that she would be able to meet him each day to verify his sobriety, they agreed that he would light a lantern in the oak grove every night he kept his promise.

For five nights Rosa woke shortly after midnight, peered out her window, and glimpsed a pinprick of light like a distant star gleaming amid the oaks. On the sixth night, she woke to the sound of the wind stirring the curtains in the moonlight, threw off the quilt, and went to the window — but saw no glimmering light in the oak grove.

She took a deep breath, rested her arms on the windowsill, and stared into the shadows beneath the boughs. It was a windy night. Perhaps the shifting leaves and branches momentarily blocked the lantern from her view, and if she was patient, it would appear.

She waited.

Perhaps, she told herself, pulling her robe over her nightgown, the wind had put out the lantern. On bare feet she crept silently through the living room past her mother, who breathed deeply and steadily on the sofa. She eased open the front door and swiftly ran to the stand of live oaks where she had climbed upon Lars's horse and ridden off to the cabin on hundreds of other nights — but he was not there, nor did she find a darkened lantern, its flame extinguished.

The wind whipped her hair into her face as she turned back to the house. Unable to believe that he had failed her, she stayed awake all night at the window, hoping and praying that some unforeseen emergency on the ranch had merely delayed him. But the oak grove remained shadowed and still until the sunrise illuminated the valley.

Shame or gin kept Lars away the next two nights. The third night, exhausted from disappointment and heartache, Rosa slept until dawn. When she woke, for a fleeting moment she wondered if he had come, but then she remembered that it did not matter if she saw the distant flame the next night or the next or any other. Lars had broken his promise, he had made his choice, and she could not marry him.

On the morning of the fourteenth day, he came to see her at the Grand Union Hotel, his face pale, his eyes bloodshot, his hands shaking. He swore that he would never drink again, but she didn't believe him. She couldn't believe him. She told him it was over, and she told him good-bye.

She knew she had broken his heart and could not forgive herself for it. She confessed her sins to the elderly priest who had known her all her life and she did the penance he assigned, prayers and good works that seemed bewilderingly inadequate to atone for all the wrong she had done. As the days passed, exhaustion, worry, and guilt plagued her, and her appetite fled. At breakfast even her favorite dishes turned her stomach when her mother set them on the table before her, and although she would shut her office door against the aromas wafting from the hotel kitchen, her queasiness often did not dissipate until early afternoon, if at all.

Rosa was nearly eight weeks pregnant when she realized — first, with a steadily growing awareness intertwined with dread and denial, and then with a shocked dismay so intense and sudden it left her breathless — that she was carrying Lars's child.

She did not tell him. She did not tell anyone, though she knew it was a truth she could not conceal for long. For days her thoughts darted wildly, desperately, as she tried to stay calm and sort out what to do. The shame and humiliation she would bring upon herself, she would endure as the inevitable consequence of her poor choices and the just punishment for her sin. When she thought of her innocent child, however, and her parents, and her brother — then her heart broke again and again. Though they had done nothing wrong, they would share her disgrace.

Through all the turmoil and distress, Rosa had continued to let John court her. Lars's profound failure cast John's best qualities into a far more favorable light. John was pleasant company, and he was reliable and diligent. He did not drink. He would be a good provider. And then, when John came to Sunday dinner a week after Rosa discovered she was pregnant, her mother happened to remark that the Barclay farm had once been part of the old Rancho Triunfo, one of the sections the Norwegian immigrant who purchased it from Rosa's great-grandparents had sold off to his more recently arrived countrymen.

Suddenly Rosa realized how she could give her child a father, spare her family shame, and regain part of the land her mother had longed for all her life. It would mean losing Lars forever — but she had already lost him.

John had often hinted that he wanted to marry her, and always before she had replied with gentle discouragement, emphasizing how much she valued him as a friend. Now, with her circumstances entirely transformed, she responded with new warmth borne of desperation and hope. One evening she overheard her parents talking earnestly in hushed voices, and she knew John had spoken to her father. The following afternoon, John was waiting for her on the front verandah of the Grand Union Hotel as she left work. He took her hand and invited her to walk with him through the hotel's citrus grove, and when they were alone, he knelt in the middle of the stone path, took from his coat pocket a ring that had belonged to his grandmother, and asked her to marry him. Her thoughts flew to Lars, but she reminded herself what she owed her family and her unborn child, and she told John she would marry him.

Her parents rejoiced. Rosa and John met with their priest, and the banns were announced on the three following Sundays. Throughout that time, Rosa and her mother quickly planned the wedding celebration — but not without some bewildered protests from her mother that there was no need for such haste. Rosa braced herself for an outburst from Lars that did not come. Perhaps he did not know about the upcoming wedding. He was not Catholic, and so he wouldn't have heard the banns announced at Mass. Word of the upcoming nuptials spread from neighbor to neighbor, but slowly, and it was possible the news hadn't reached the Jorgensen ranch. Rosa didn't know, but she wondered.

As her wedding day approached, Rosa felt jumpy and unsettled and yet filled with a strange, fatalistic hope. She was fond of John and was confident she would grow to love him; she was determined to be a good wife and mother, inspired as much by love as the need for atonement. Successful marriages had been made from far less.

Rosa and John married in the church where she had been baptized, surrounded by her family and friends and his. She felt quietly content as he took her home to the small, cozy adobe amid the fields of rye along the mesa near the Salto Canyon, her mother's favorite vista. That night, she could not hide her tears after John made love to her, but he misinterpreted her grief and kissed her lovingly, assuring her that all would be well. She wanted to believe him, but apprehension had taken root in her heart, and she feared that a marriage founded upon a lie was doomed to failure despite all her good intentions.

Two nights later, she woke groggily to a furious pounding on the front door. "Rosa," Lars shouted, pounding again. "Rosa, come out!"

"What the hell is going on?" mumbled John, turning over in bed beside her.

Outside, Lars's voice broke and slurred. "Rosa, come out of there! You don't belong with him. You belong with me!"

Rosa felt a cold fist grip her heart. She sat up, heart pounding with dread, and when Lars persisted in shouting for her to come out to him, to run away with him, John sat up too.

"Is that Lars Jorgensen?" he asked, suddenly wide awake. "What does he mean, you belong to him? I know he was fond of you when we were kids, but you said that was over."

"It *is* over. Don't listen to him. He's drunk." More drunk than he had ever been, from the sound of it. Trembling, Rosa forced herself to lie down and draw the quilt up to her chin as if she meant to try to sleep through the tumult. "If we ignore him, he'll go away."

John threw off the covers. "If I get the shotgun, he'll go away faster."

"John," Rosa cried, seizing his arm. "You can't shoot him!"

"Of course I won't shoot him." John shook free of her grasp. "I just mean to scare him off."

As John climbed out of bed, they heard the rumbling of a truck over gravel. Another man's voice rang out, shouting for Lars to come away from the adobe. John went to the window and peered outside. "Oscar's come for him."

Quickly Rosa joined John at the window and watched with horrified dismay as Oscar dragged his shouting, weeping, stumbling brother to the truck and half shoved, half lifted him into the front passenger seat. Oscar did not spare a single glance for the adobe as he hurried around to the driver's side, climbed in behind the wheel, and sped off.

"I guess he heard about the wedding,"

John remarked, letting the curtain fall and guiding Rosa back to bed, his satisfaction unmistakable even in the darkness.

"I suppose so." Rosa sank into bed, sick at heart, wondering how Lars had heard the news. Despite their estrangement, she should have told him herself. To let him find out any other way, after all that they had meant to each other, was cruel.

She had been cruel and thoughtless and worse, but somehow he must have forgiven her, or he would not have rescued them from the canyon, nor would he have joined them on their pilgrimage.

The children woke early, and although Marta tried to keep her younger sisters and brother amused by watching the passing scenery, the novelty eventually wore off and they came to Rosa pleading hunger and boredom. When Lars suggested that they visit the dining car, the children seconded him so eagerly that Rosa didn't have the heart to refuse, despite her reluctance to abandon the security of their private car. She tugged Elizabeth's tan cloche snugly upon her head so that it pushed her short, dark locks forward, concealing some of her bruises. Even so, as she and Lars and the children seated themselves at two tables for four on opposite sides of the center aisle, a few other diners glanced at her face only to look quickly away again. She noted their reactions with grim satisfaction as she draped her napkin over her lap and encouraged the children to do the same. Perhaps, for the first time, people's inherent cowardice and reluctance to involve themselves in the aftermath of a woman's battering might protect rather than harm her.

The full-course meal of fried eggs, bacon, hash brown potatoes, toast with jam, and coffee would have been filling and delicious if Rosa had been able to relax enough to eat rather than glancing warily about for suspicious police officers and vengeful mobsters toting tommy guns. Nothing on the menu suited Ana's and Miguel's new diet, so after watching Ana glumly sit on her hands so she wouldn't be tempted to sample any of the tantalizing dishes on her plate, Rosa left Marta and Lupita to finish their lunch with Lars while she took Ana and Miguel back to their private car for another meal of cold corn tortillas. "I hate being sick," Ana confessed as she washed down another dull bite of tortilla with water.

"The doctor in San Francisco will help you," Rosa said, and for the first time, it felt like a promise she could keep.

Ana cheered up later when Lars returned with her sisters and offered to take them out to explore the train. Rosa was content to stay in the private car with Miguel, amusing him with games and songs, cuddling him while they watched the small towns and verdant farms pass by. Gradually the breathless fear that had squeezed her since John left the adobe to kill Lars lifted, replaced by sadness and grief and worry about what might lie ahead of them.

The train pulled into the Oakland station a few minutes after nine o'clock. After disembarking, they carried their luggage to the pier where they would board the ferry to San Francisco. Departing passengers climbed the steps they had recently descended, the conductor called for all to come aboard, the whistle blew, and in a cloud of steam, the train chugged out of the station. Minutes after it departed, another train passed on an adjacent set of tracks heading in the opposite direction, but it did not pause at the station.

"Is that the train we'll take home after Ana and Miguel see the doctor?" asked Lupita, craning her neck to watch as they walked along.

"No, *mija,*" Rosa said, shifting her sewing basket on her hip and holding tightly to

Miguel's hand so she wouldn't lose him in the crowd. "That's a freight train. See? There aren't any windows for people to look out of, no seats or dining cars. This train carries food and goods, but no passengers."

Lupita nodded and watched the train pass, intrigued, but Marta threw Rosa a quick, curious look from beneath raised brows, a single glance that told Rosa immediately that her eldest daughter had figured out that they were not going back to the Arboles Valley anytime soon, if ever. Rosa knew that eventually she would have to tell the others, but she dreaded that moment and had decided to put it off until after the doctor's examination. She didn't want to tell them they weren't going home until she could tell them where they *were* going, and she wouldn't know that until the doctor provided a diagnosis and recommended a treatment.

"There sure are a lot of freight cars," said Ana tiredly. She had slept poorly, woken throughout the night by the noise and jostling of the train and by stomach pains. Later, when she could not keep down the cornmeal mush she had eaten for breakfast, she confessed that she had tasted a few bites of chocolate layer cake at lunch the previous day when no one was watching. Rosa was greatly relieved that the cornmeal had not caused her illness, but not so relieved that she didn't scold Ana for disobeying the doctor's orders.

"I wonder what they're carrying," said Marta, watching the train cars pass.

"Maybe toys," Lupita guessed.

"Fruits and vegetables, more likely," said Lars. "Bound for markets throughout California and across the country."

Lupita seemed about to reply until she caught sight of the ferry. "Are we going on that?" she exclaimed, pointing.

When the children heard that they were indeed, they would have run ahead to join the queue if they weren't encumbered by luggage. They enjoyed the ride across the bay and seemed sorry when the ferry slowed and docked at the pier in San Francisco. They gathered their things and disembarked, and Rosa waited with them on the platform while Lars went off to make arrangements for a ride to the hospital.

"No need to hire a cab," Lars told Rosa when he returned. "A station clerk recommended a boardinghouse near the hospital, and a streetcar can take us almost to the front door. The fellow says the rooms are clean and the food is better than what we'll find elsewhere for the price. Sound all right to you?"

Rosa nodded. Although her first impulse was to make haste to the hospital, she reasoned it would probably be best to find a place to stay and make themselves more presentable first. With Lars's help she distributed the luggage among the six of them, and they followed Lars from the platform. The brisk streetcar ride up and down the steep hills of the city offered the children another adventure, and if not for Miguel's weakness and Ana's drawn face, Rosa could almost forget they were not an ordinary family out for a holiday — but they were far from ordinary, and although their lives would be forever intertwined, they were not a family.

They disembarked on a street corner a block away from the boardinghouse, a quaint, two-story residence in the Spanish style with stucco walls, a roof of curved red tiles, a deep front porch, and a patch of neatly mown green grass for a front yard. As they climbed the front stairs, they passed between two trellises covered with a deep, rich blush of climbing roses. Instinctively, Rosa glanced at Lars only to find him watching her, and although she quickly looked away, she knew he too was thinking of how, long ago, he had called her his

Spanish rose — in affection, in amusement, in longing, in exasperation, in the heat of passion, in the anguish of farewell. Now her bloom had faded and she was simply Rosa Barclay, his rival's wife.

Lars raised his hand to knock upon the front door, but then he hesitated and knelt down until he was eye level with Lupita. "Girls," he said. "We're going to play a game of Let's Pretend while we're here, all right?" Lupita nodded eagerly, Marta and Ana, with some caution. "I'm going to pretend to be your father, and your mother and I are going to use pretend names. You can call us Mama and Papa, okay?"

Lupita nodded, adding, "I want a pretend name too."

Before Rosa could urge him not to make matters more complicated than necessary, Lars said, "All right, Little Miss. What will your name be?"

"Maria."

Rosa felt a wrenching tug of heartache. "No, not that." Not the name of a daughter she had lost.

"Lupita is such a pretty name," Lars said, with a glance to Rosa that told her he understood everything. "It's perfect for a pretty girl like you. Why don't you keep it?"

Lupita's expression was a changeable sky,

her delight at the compliment hidden and revealed again by the shifting clouds of stubborn annoyance at being denied her own way. Eventually pride won out and she agreed to remain Lupita, so Lars nodded as if impressed by her good judgment and knocked upon the door. A gray-haired wisp of a woman in a faded calico housedress opened the door. "Yes?" she greeted them, her eyebrows rising at the sight of the four children and inching even higher at the sight of Rosa's bruised face.

"Good afternoon, ma'am. My name is Nils Ottesen and this is my wife, Rose." He put his arm around Rosa's shoulders and drew her forward, where she managed a smile and a nod. "Our family needs rooms for the night, possibly longer, and we've heard you run the most comfortable boardinghouse in town."

"Do you have any vacancies?" asked Rosa, shifting Miguel to her other hip, thankful that the children had chosen that moment to be quiet and well behaved.

"Well, I might." The woman's mouth thinned in suspicion as her gaze traveled from Rosa's bruised face to Lars's somber one. "But I can't have any trouble here or you'll have to leave at once."

"We won't be any trouble," said Lars,

"and we can pay up front."

The landlady needed only a moment to consider before she opened the door wider. "That's fair enough. I can give you two rooms, but the children will have to share beds."

"That's fine," Rosa said promptly, ushering the girls inside before the woman could change her mind. In the foyer, Lars signed the register with his alias and handed five dollars to the landlady, who introduced herself as Mrs. Sharon Phillips. She took two keys from a desk in the corner and led them, lugging their satchels and suitcases, upstairs, to two small rooms on opposite sides of a narrow hallway. She recited the hours and rates for meals and left them to settle in, but before she departed, her glance fell upon the quilts in Rosa's basket.

"Did you make these?" she asked, stooping over to flip over the edge of the one Elizabeth had called Arboles Valley Star.

"No, they're old family quilts." Rosa resisted the urge to nudge the basket out of the way so the landlady would stop pawing through her things. "My mother made the star quilt as a gift for me and — and Nils, and my great-grandmother brought the octagonal quilt with her when she came to California to marry my great-grandfather."

"They're charming." Mrs. Phillips straightened and regarded Rosa with new friendliness. "Old scrap quilts have so much character. It's good to see young people appreciating them. Nowadays everyone fancies quilts made from kits they get in the mail from back east, and that's if they bother to quilt at all. Can you imagine? That's cutting corners when they should be cutting templates, if you ask me."

Rosa didn't agree with the landlady's opinion, but in the interest of diplomacy, she made a noncommittal murmur and nodded.

Lars couldn't conceal his amusement. "Your quilts won her over," he said after the landlady disappeared down the stairs. "Maybe you should carry them wherever we go."

"Maybe," Rosa said, smiling, although she hoped she wouldn't need to win over anyone else.

They stowed their luggage, by unspoken agreement placing Rosa and the children in the larger of the two rooms and Lars alone in the other. Rosa took a moment to freshen up before washing Lupita's and Miguel's faces and brushing their hair, and instructing Marta and Ana to do the same for themselves. In the meantime Lars returned downstairs to ask the landlady for directions to the hospital. Before long they met him on the front porch and walked a few blocks to Clay Street, where they found the Stanford Hospital, a narrow, four-story building that appeared to have been fairly recently built.

Inside, Lars gave their assumed names at the registration desk and they settled in to wait. Not knowing when they would arrive in San Francisco, unable to linger in Oxnard until they received a reply to Lars's wire, Rosa and Lars had known they were taking a chance that Dr. Reynolds would be able to see them that day. As the minutes ticked past and the children grew bored and weary, Rosa began to worry that Dr. Reynolds might be too busy with other patients to see them, or too annoyed by her presumption at showing up without a proper appointment. If they were turned away now after coming so far —

She felt Lars's hand close around hers. "Rosa," he said in a low voice. "It's going to be okay. He's going to help us."

Rosa wished she could be so sure. She managed a smile and squeezed his hand in thanks. His hands were rougher than she remembered, callused and dry, but they were warm and strong and comforting. She wished she did not have to let go.

A nurse clad in a white cap and dress entered the waiting room carrying a brown clipboard. "Mr. and Mrs. Ottesen?" she inquired, looking around expectantly.

When Lars squeezed her hand and stood, Rosa quickly got to her feet, silently berating herself for forgetting their aliases. "Marta," she asked quietly, "will you please stay here with Lupita until we get back?" When Marta nodded, Rosa picked up Miguel, took Ana by the hand, and followed the nurse down a corridor to an examination room, with Lars close behind.

After settling Ana and Miguel side by side on the examination table, the nurse took their temperatures, weighed them, and listened to their heartbeats, smiling pleasantly all the while. Charmed by her friendliness, Miguel beamed and chatted with her, but Ana sat quietly unless asked a question, her expression tired, patient, and resigned. Rosa wished she could promise her daughter a cure and see hope light up her wan, pallid features.

Soon a short, stocky man with small, round glasses and a full, bushy black beard strode into the room carrying a folder of papers. Setting the folder aside, he smiled at the children and introduced himself as

Dr. Reynolds. "When Dr. Russell telephoned me yesterday, he left me with the impression that he intended to treat your children himself based upon my recommendations," he remarked to Rosa and Lars, his eyes twinkling. "I'm flattered that you made the long trip north to bring your children to see me instead."

His gracious humor put Rosa at ease, even as he commenced with the same tests and asked the same questions all the other doctors had. As Rosa described their symptoms and the progression of the mysterious ailment in the children she had lost, Dr. Reynolds nodded thoughtfully and examined Ana's and Miguel's eyes and throats and abdomens, drawing out more information from Rosa and from Ana too with peculiarly specific questions no other doctor had posed. At last he patted Miguel on the head, lifted him down, and handed him to Rosa. "Your children have celiac disease," he said, helping Ana down from the table. "They cannot digest sugars, starches, or fats. The resulting chronic, debilitating diarrhea causes malnutrition, and as you know, it can be fatal." The doctor smiled kindly, compassionately, and he rested his hand on Miguel's soft, dark curls. "However, I assure you that Ana and Miguel can avoid that fate."

Rosa drew in a quick, shaky breath. "You know of a cure?"

"I've heard of a treatment," Dr. Reynolds clarified. He glanced around for the folder he had set aside earlier, and he took from it a dog-eared medical journal. "Dr. Sidney V. Haas of New York City published a fascinating study in the *American Journal of Diseases of Children* last year. He's treated many children suffering from the same affliction as your son and daughter with great success. Simple but strict changes to his patients' diets resulted in a complete elimination of their symptoms and a return to vigorous good health."

"What sort of changes?" asked Rosa. "We'll do whatever we have to do."

Dr. Reynolds paged through the papers in his folder. "Dr. Haas discovered that ripe bananas have some essential property that enable them to break up starches and convert cane sugar into fruit sugars, which are more easily tolerated by the patient's digestive system. Once the problem of sugar and starch digestion is resolved, the proper digestion of fats follows. Consequently, patients are then able to take nourishment from the food they eat, and gradually attain good health."

Lars studied him, his glance falling upon the folder in the doctor's hands as if he wanted to read it for himself. "Bananas can do all that?"

Dr. Reynolds nodded. "We don't fully understand why, but they can." He went on to explain the specifics of what had come to be known as Dr. Haas's banana diet. Ana and Miguel should eat as many ripe bananas each day as they were willing to take, he emphasized, ideally between four and eight. They must avoid all breads, crackers, cereals, and potatoes, with rice being the only starch permitted. In addition to bananas and rice, the children could eat healthy amounts of cheese, oranges, vegetables, meat, and gelatin, and they could drink milk. Dr. Haas had observed improvement in his patients almost immediately after they had begun the banana diet, and most had been declared completely free of symptoms within three to six months. Even so, Dr. Reynolds noted, any deviation from the protocol after that time could result in a relapse.

As he spoke, Dr. Reynolds wrote down his instructions on a sheet of paper. "I'd like to examine the children weekly," he said as he handed the paper to Lars. "Especially in these early weeks, it's important for me to see how well they're responding to the diet. However, I realize you're a long way from home. If you prefer, I could write to your family doctor and he could take over their treatment."

"No," said Rosa firmly. They could not go home, but even if they could, she adamantly refused to entrust Ana's and Miguel's health to the doctors who had urged her to feed her children "wholesome white bread," something they should have scrupulously avoided. "You know more about this affliction than any other doctor they've seen. I want you to take care of them."

"Very well." Dr. Reynolds hesitated. "I'm mindful that you haven't been in San Francisco long. I should warn you that in the city, the cost of food and lodgings for a family of four could be prohibitive."

"A family of six," Rosa said without thinking, as a restless Miguel wriggled in her arms. "My other two daughters are waiting outside."

"You have two other daughters? Celiac disease often runs in families. Would you like me to examine them as well?"

"No, that's not necessary," Rosa quickly assured him, setting down Miguel but holding on to his hand. "They've never suffered the way my other children have."

"Hmm. Curious." The doctor pondered Rosa's words for a moment before setting the puzzle aside. "If the cost of keeping the entire family hereabouts for the duration of Ana's and Miguel's treatment is too much, you could admit them to the Stanford Convalescent Home. It's affiliated with Stanford University just as this hospital is, and it's quite close. Mrs. Ottesen could remain in the city to care for them, while Mr. Ottesen would be free to take your other children home."

"Thank you, Doctor, but we couldn't possibly split up," said Rosa. "We'll stay in San Francisco, all six of us, together. The separation would be a greater hardship than the expense."

"Of course. I understand." Even so, the doctor appeared no less worried as he turned to Lars. "But I'm sure you've left a job behind in Southern California. How likely is it that your employer will hire you back after such a long absence?"

"I worked my brother's ranch," said Lars. "He'd take me back in a heartbeat. He has to. We're family. In the meantime, I can find something here to pay the bills. Ranching and farming are in my blood, but I've held down other odd jobs from time to time.

Thank you for your concern, Doctor, but we'll get by."

"I apologize if I've overstepped my bounds." Dr. Reynolds smiled self-deprecatingly. "I've been told I have a tendency to do that. A hazard of the profession, I suppose."

"Not at all, Doctor." Lars rose and shook his head. "We're very grateful."

"Yes, thank you," said Rosa fervently, picking up Miguel again and taking Ana's hand. "Thank you for everything."

Dr. Reynolds accompanied them to the registration desk, where they scheduled an appointment for the following week. Before they parted ways, Ana peered up at the doctor solemnly and said, "Do you really think if Miguel and I don't eat bread and crackers and those other things, and eat bananas every day, we'll get better?"

Dr. Reynolds knelt down and looked her straight in the eye. "Ana, I promise you that if you follow the instructions I gave your mother, and if you never give in to the temptation to eat a cookie or a slice of toast, you *will* get better. You may get sick of bananas, but you won't be sick like you have been, not anymore."

Ana smiled up at him, speechless with

delight, her eyes shining with hope and happiness.

She found her voice after they left the hospital and walked back to the boarding-house. "He promised we'd get better," she said as they stopped at a market along the way to buy an ample supply of bananas, some ripe and ready to eat, others still green. "You all heard him. He promised."

Rosa and Lars exchanged a look, and Rosa knew he too hoped the well-meaning doctor would fulfill that promise. After so much false hope and disappointment, Ana's spirits would be crushed if this treatment failed, just as all the others had failed. Dr. Reynolds had said that the patients in New York City had begun to improve almost as soon as they started Dr. Haas's banana diet. Rosa might not have to wait long to see whether Ana and Miguel would regain the good health they had enjoyed all too briefly when they were babies.

When they told Mrs. Phillips about their visit to the hospital and the doctor's strict instructions, she assured Rosa that she would be happy to prepare special meals that would suit "the poor dears." True to her word, she served Ana and Miguel boiled white rice with sliced bananas on the side at suppertime, and kept the other guests' potatoes and pot roast and fresh bread well out of their reach.

By early evening, Rosa was so exhausted from travel and drained from the emotional turmoil of the day that she overruled the children's protests and put them to bed early. She tucked the three youngest children into the double bed — placing Miguel in the middle so he would be less likely to tumble out — while Marta took the small trundle bed and Rosa made the sofa more comfortable for herself with pillows and extra blankets she found in the wardrobe. When the children were settled, she kissed them good night, doused the light, and stood watching them in the semidarkness, thinking of their lost siblings until grief threatened to extinguish the new light of hope in her heart.

As the room darkened and the children's breathing became soft, steady, and even, she quietly stole into the hallway and knocked upon Lars's door. She heard bedsprings creak, footsteps muffled by a rug, and then the door swung open. "Rosa?" Lars asked, wide-awake and concerned. "Is everything all right?"

"I can't believe it was all a matter of what they were eating." Her voice shook with anguish and remorse. "Those doctors, they *told* me, they *said* I should feed them 'wholesome white bread.' I remember it precisely. I wrote it down to make sure I got it right. And now, now I discover —" Unable to go on, she lifted a hand and let it fall, helpless, trembling so hard that she had to brace herself against the doorjamb.

"Those doctors didn't know," said Lars, his voice gentle and full of compassion as he reached out to touch her shoulder. "They couldn't have known, and you couldn't have either. This research Dr. Reynolds referred to — that doctor in New York published it only last year."

"That should have been in time to save Pedro," Rosa choked out, tears gathering. "Not John Junior or Angela or Maria, but it could have saved Pedro. If I had taken him to the Oxnard hospital a year ago, he might have lived." He could be with her that very moment, a lively, mischievous six-year-old who loved to sing and peppered her with questions — about animals, the sky, what made cars go — from the moment he scrambled out of bed in the morning until she tucked him beneath his favorite Log Cabin quilt at night. He should be in the other room enjoying a soft bed and sweet dreams. He should have lived. They all should have lived.

"That's not your fault," said Lars. "John wouldn't let you take the children beyond the valley."

"I should have insisted! I should have defied him!"

Lars gently touched her bruised face. "I've seen what he does to you when he thinks you've defied him. You can't blame yourself for trying to find another way to get help and advice. How many letters did you write — dozens? Hundreds? You must have written to every doctor within a hundred miles of the Arboles Valley."

But not to the one doctor who could have helped her. "Why didn't I see it for myself?" The children never threw up rice or corn tortillas or oranges they plucked from the trees in front of the adobe. Why hadn't she detected the pattern? "I prepared every meal my children have ever eaten. Why didn't I realize what was making them sick?"

"How could you have?" Lars glanced down the hallway and pulled her into his room, shutting the door behind them. "Rosa, you've got to stop blaming yourself. You couldn't have known. If you served the children bananas and toast for breakfast and they got sick, you couldn't have known that the banana was good for them and the toast bad."

"I should have known." The effort to refrain from keening made her voice fracture through her clenched teeth. "I should have known. And if it turns out that it was all so simple, and that I could have saved all my precious babies, that none of them needed to die —"

She couldn't speak. She had no words, only tears. Lars drew her to him, and she buried her face in his chest and wept for the children she would have given her own life to save, but only now did she know how, and it was too late, too late.

Lars held her until she had no more tears, until grief and heartache wrung her dry. Then he kissed her gently on the forehead, led her by the hand to her own room, and made her promise that she would try to sleep. "Tomorrow Ana and Miguel will be better than they were today," he told her. "And the next day, they'll be better yet. Think of them, Rosa. Think of them and don't despair."

With a nod, she agreed to try.

The next morning after breakfast — for which Mrs. Phillips supplied Ana and Miguel with bananas and oranges and rice cereal in abundance — Rosa sent the children out to play in the backyard while she and Lars looked on from the patio and quietly discussed their circumstances. While the valises Rosa had taken from the hayloft were still comfortably full, travel expenses and the children's medical bills had already begun to deplete them with alarming speed. Lars wanted to find a job, but Rosa, ever mindful of the police and criminals likely searching for them, worried that he would be spotted. "I can't stay shut up in this boardinghouse for six months," Lars told her firmly. "I might as well earn some wages while we're figuring out what to do next."

Rosa eventually acquiesced, wishing she knew whether the police were closing in on them or if their search had stalled. Henry Nelson, too, was always in her thoughts, and she longed to telephone the Oxnard hospital and inquire about him. Rather than take that risk, Lars promised to pick up a newspaper the next time he went out. John's crimes and the suspected deaths of his family in the canyon were shocking enough that they might have caught the attention of local reporters.

The week passed. Every day Lars went out in search of work while Rosa took the children around the city. They rode cable cars and visited libraries; they climbed twisting streets to admire the view from the hilltops and watched ferryboats carry passengers across the bay. Rosa vigilantly monitored every mouthful Ana and Miguel consumed, constantly on guard as if their illness were an assassin that crept after them in the shadows, awaiting the moment when her back was turned to strike. With each passing day it seemed to Rosa that their eyes were brighter, they did not tire as easily, and a new rosiness had replaced their usual pallor. Every day without symptoms made Rosa's carefully guarded hopes rise in increments as fine as the soft wisps of chestnut brown hair she brushed away from Ana's face while she slept.

The day before the children's appointment, Lars was offered a job working in the stockroom of a department store on Union Square. The children cheered, but Rosa hid her misgivings as she congratulated him. Lars loved the outdoors, and she was certain he would soon become frustrated and claustrophobic shut within four walls all day. She wanted to tell him not to take the job, to wait until he could find a groundskeeper's position with the city parks department or something on the waterfront, but she knew he did not like being dependent — not upon his brother, not upon her, and definitely not upon John, or even John's illegal earnings. He would rather pay his own way doing dull, backbreaking work than treat their stay in San Francisco as a vacation at her expense.

Lars had also brought home a copy of the *San Francisco Examiner,* and while the children were distracted with their landlady's cat, he drew Rosa aside and showed her a small article on the sixth page. "Southern California Postmaster Charged with Attempted Murder," the headline announced.

Rosa murmured a prayer of thanksgiving that the charge was still only attempted murder and quickly read the rest of the article. While Henry Nelson's doctors confirmed that his condition was improving, he was still unable to offer his own account of the incident. Lars Jorgensen's automobile had been discovered parked behind a teahouse that Lars had been known to frequent years before, in its pre-Prohibition incarnation as a saloon. Lars himself was still missing, but a Prohibition officer praised him for upholding his civic duty at a time when far too few citizens were courageous enough to report bootleggers and smugglers. Federal agents had been tracking mob activity in Southern California for years, but until Lars's tip, they had lacked proof that the mob had enlisted the services of local farmers in their illegal liquor and weapons activities. Thanks to Lars, they were on the track of some highly placed figures in organized crime, and hoped soon to be able to put some of them away for good. One agent who spoke on condition of anonymity admitted he didn't blame Lars for disappearing. He'd have to be a fool not to lie low for the rest of his life, now that he had made himself an enemy of the mob. For all they knew, the mob had already found him and his bones were bleaching in the Mojave Desert.

With a shiver of apprehension, Rosa drove the image from her thoughts and read on. The previous afternoon, a child's rag doll had been pulled from the mud two miles downstream of the canyon's edge where Isabel Rodriguez Diaz had fallen to her death. Although an unidentified family member could not confirm that the doll belonged to one of the Barclay girls, it was believed to be, and therefore Rosa and her four children were presumed drowned.

"Lupita's doll," Rosa said, imagining her brother examining the mud-soaked doll, shaking his head, and handing it back to a police officer. She tore her gaze from the paper and fixed it upon Lars. "They think we drowned. Do you think this means they'll stop searching for us?"

"I think they might concentrate their search in the mud where they found the doll."

"And when they don't find our remains?"

Lars shrugged. "I doubt they'll resume looking for you elsewhere. Even if they do, by that time, the trail will be stone cold."

Rosa fervently hoped so. She finished reading the rest of the article only to discover that John was considered a flight risk and was being held without bond. She felt faint with relief knowing that he could not pursue her. If only someone at the prison would think to question him about his mother-in-law's suspicious death, which had occurred at the same place where his wife and children had likely perished — but Rosa doubted anyone would. If John were convicted, whatever punishment he received for the attempted murder and racketeering charges would have to suffice for her mother's murder as well, as profoundly unfair and inadequate as that would be.

A thick blanket of fog cast a gray, chilly pall over the morning, but Rosa's spirits had not been so bright in years. Ana and Miguel had not had a single recurrence of their symptoms since they began the banana diet, and

Rosa was sure they had put on weight. Although she did not dare say the words aloud, in case she had imagined improvement where none existed, she trusted that the doctor would give them good and welcome news that day.

Later, she almost wept from joy when Dr. Reynolds confirmed what her mother's heart had already known. Ana and Miguel had gained weight, their pulses were stronger, and they would almost certainly continue to improve as long as they remained on the banana diet. Rosa could not let her vigilance slip, not for a single cracker or cookie, not for a single crumb of bread or cake.

"Before you go," Dr. Reynolds added as Rosa and Lars thanked him profusely and the children beamed, "I took the liberty of inquiring about a place for you, Mr. Ottesen."

"Thank you, Doctor," said Lars, "but I've already found work."

"I think you'll want to at least consider this," the doctor assured him, and Rosa touched Lars's arm, a silent plea to hear him out. "I grew up on a farm, and I know how it feels to be in love with the land. Neither the passing of the years nor the devotion to another profession will ever strain the soil from my blood." His gaze grew distant for a moment, as if he were looking down from a hilltop upon the acres he had worked in his youth. "When you mentioned you were a rancher, I remembered a conversation I had not long ago with a patient and former neighbor of mine, a man named Dante Cacchione. He and his wife, Guiditta, are third-generation winemakers from the Sonoma Valley, but as you can imagine, they've fallen upon hard times in recent years because of Prohibition."

Rosa nodded, and Lars remarked, "I imagine there's not a lot of money in winemaking these days."

"They've managed to keep their vineyard going by selling wine grapes, but they aren't earning enough profit to pay for field hands. Their only help comes from their children." Dr. Reynolds looked from Lars to Rosa and back, earnest. "I won't pretend you'll earn a fortune, but the Cacchiones are willing to offer room and board for your entire family and a modest wage if you agreed to work for them through the harvest next fall." He nodded to Rosa. "They'd appreciate your help as well during the busiest parts of the season, Mrs. Ottesen, if you can spare time away from the children."

"My eldest girl can watch my younger

children if I'm needed." Not for the first time, Rosa wondered how she would get by without sensible, reliable Marta, her strong right arm. "But what about bringing Ana and Miguel to their weekly appointments?"

"It's a quick train ride between here and Santa Rosa, and the fares are quite reasonable," Dr. Reynolds assured her. "It would be much less expensive than renting a place in the city, and you'd have all the benefits of the country air for the children's recuperation."

"What about schools?" asked Lars. "We would need to enroll Marta and Lupita right away, and Ana, when she's ready."

"I'm ready now," Ana piped up.

Rosa smiled and stroked her daughter's soft, chestnut brown hair, which seemed to have grown thicker in the past week. "As soon as you've regained your strength," she promised.

The doctor smiled. "I attended Santa Rosa public schools, and I received a fine education, if I do say so myself."

Lars folded his arms over his chest, nodding as he mulled it over. "It sounds like a good opportunity. What do you think, Rose?"

His use of her alias gave her a momentary start. "I — I think it sounds wonderful."

The children would thrive in the fresh air and sunshine of the countryside, far from the din and frenzy of the city and the press of the crowds. She knew Lars would much prefer laboring in a vineyard than placing boxes on shelves in the windowless back room of a department store. As for herself, she understood completely the doctor's inherent love for the land, and felt herself longing for broad, tilled vistas and fresh fruit warm from the sun with greater urgency the longer she spent her days surrounded by steel and concrete.

"Would you care to discuss it privately for a moment?" the doctor asked, turning toward the door.

Rosa and Lars exchanged a look. Lars raised his eyebrows in a silent question and Rosa quickly nodded. "I think we've already made up our minds," said Lars, reaching out to shake the doctor's hand.

CHAPTER FOUR

Mrs. Phillips was disappointed to learn of their imminent departure, but she wished them well and invited them to visit whenever they returned to San Francisco. The next morning, she treated them to a sumptuous breakfast, including rice porridge with brown sugar and bananas for Ana and Miguel, hearty bacon and eggs and biscuits for the adults, and as a special birthday treat for Lupita, waffles with strawberries and whipped cream. Lupita smiled radiantly and basked in the attention when Mrs. Phillips led all her guests in singing "Happy Birthday" to her. It occurred to Rosa that as a middle child between a responsible eldest sister and two chronically ill siblings, Lupita was rarely the center of attention, and she was grateful that their landlady had made her birthday special.

But in the midst of all the excitement, Lupita forgot the new rules and offered to share her birthday waffles with her siblings. As Ana declined with a rueful shake of her head, Marta suddenly shouted a warning and pointed across the table to Miguel, who was digging eagerly into Lupita's breakfast. With a gasp, Lupita snatched the fork from his hand before he could take a bite. He stared at her, thoroughly disappointed and speechless with bewilderment, his lower lip quivering. "I'm sorry, Miguel," Lupita apologized. "I forgot." She shot Rosa a look of stark horror through eyes misty with tears, realizing how close she had come to making her little brother sick again. Rosa assured her that no harm had been done, but it was a good reminder to all of them that they had to be especially careful with Miguel. He was too young to understand what he could and could not eat, so they had to be aware for him.

The sobering reminder diminished some of Lupita's birthday joy, but Lars cheered her up with the promise of an exciting day ahead full of new places to see and unexpected surprises. "And presents?" Lupita asked, bounding out of her seat. When he assured her that there would most certainly be presents, she clapped her hands and impulsively hugged him. Lars's startled expression softened into tenderness as he awkwardly returned her hug. Rosa was so moved she had to look away.

They packed up their belongings, settled the bill, bade their landlady good-bye, and rode the cable car to the ferry, where they crossed the bay to Sausalito and boarded a train to Santa Rosa on the Northwestern Pacific line. Rosa and Lars exchanged amused glances over the children's heads as they took their seats, enjoying their excitement and sense of adventure. Before long, the whistle blew, steam drifted past the front windows, and the train lurched forward. As it chugged away from the station, Lupita suddenly bounced in her seat and declared, "I know what one of the unexpected surprises is."

Rosa smiled, her heart warm with affection. "What's that, *mija?*"

"We're going home to see Papa."

"Oh, no, Lupita, we aren't," said Rosa, dismayed. "We're going to live on a grape farm for a while. We have to stay near the city so Ana and Miguel can visit Dr. Reynolds every week. Don't you remember? I told you last night before bed and again this morning at breakfast."

"But . . . maybe that was just a pretend story so I wouldn't guess the surprise."

"No, *mija,* it's the truth."

"Will Papa meet us at the train station?"

"No," said Rosa. "No, he won't."

"Is he coming later?"

"No, Lupita. He won't be joining us at all."

"But it's my birthday."

Rosa took a deep breath and said, with utter truthfulness, "I know he remembers, and I'm sure he's thinking about what a big five-year-old girl you are today." What she could never tell her precious daughter was that John would remember the day but only to curse Rosa for betraying him.

Lupita looked so crestfallen that Rosa handed Miguel to Lars and pulled Lupita onto her lap. "You'll like it there, I'm sure," she said, kissing her on the cheek and stroking her thick chestnut brown hair off her neck. "Remember the pictures Mrs. Phillips showed us? Didn't she tell us that the Sonoma Valley is one of the most beautiful places in California?"

"She said the world," Lupita corrected her glumly. "One of the most beautiful places in the world."

"Well, that's even better, isn't it?"

Lupita sighed and rested her head on Rosa's shoulder. "I guess so."

Patting her comfortingly on the back, Rosa caught Lars's eye and gave him a small, perplexed shake of the head. John had never paid much attention to Lupita when they were all together at home in the adobe, nor had he ever made a fuss over any of the children's birthdays, nor had Lupita seemed overly fond of the sullen, mercurial man she knew as her father. Rosa was at a loss to explain why Lupita apparently missed him so much. It seemed impossible to believe that she had any fond memories of him, for he had never treated her with any particular tenderness. By the time Lupita came along, John's capacity for affection had been eroded away to nothing by grief, betrayal, and resentment.

And that too was Rosa's fault.

Six weeks after their wedding, a month after Lars pounded on the door of the adobe and begged Rosa to come away with him, Rosa told John that she was expecting a child. He was surprised but proud and pleased, and as the winter passed and he eagerly built a cradle and considered names, Rosa convinced herself that he would be a good father and that she had made the right choice. Her parents were elated, and her mother happily set herself to work on a Four-Patch quilt for the baby. Rosa was grateful beyond measure for her mother's joy and reassurances, which comforted her in the midst of a constant swirl of guilt and grief and worry. Lars had not tried to see her again, but Rosa had heard rumors that he had nearly killed himself with liquor that night, and in the weeks since he had not left the Jorgensen ranch — and some said he had not left his bed. No one knew whether he was drinking himself into an early grave or drying out, but everyone was astonished that he had been driven to such extremes over a marriage between his two childhood friends. Distressed, Rosa prayed for him, for their baby, and for herself, that she would be a steadfast wife, a devoted mother, and eventually, if it were ever possible, a good friend to Lars. She had so much to atone for.

The winter passed, and with regret, Rosa arranged to see her mother less often. Whenever she went to the grocery store or church, she endured innocent teasing from well-meaning neighbors who beamed as they declared that she was enormous for so early in her pregnancy and surely must be carrying twins. She feared that her mother, who knew her secrets, would take one look at her and guess the truth. As spring approached and John turned his attention to the rye fields, she longed for her mother's practical advice and cheerful help around the house, but she dared not reach out to her, not yet. She would ask John to fetch her mother as soon as she felt the birth pangs beginning. When that moment arrived, the comfort of her mother's presence and her reassuring confidence with babies would be more important than concealing her secret shame.

But on that sunny spring day when Rosa's contractions began and rapidly intensified, John, who could count to nine as well as the next man, raced off to summon the doctor, frantic in his belief that his child would be born two months too early. Thus Rosa spent most of her labor alone in the adobe longing for her mother. John returned with the doctor in time for the birth, and when the doctor delivered her beautiful baby girl, rosy and pink and crying indignantly, perfectly healthy and obviously full-term, the doctor bathed her, swaddled her in a soft flannel blanket, and declared with forced heartiness that for an infant born two months premature she was as robust as they could have hoped, which surely spoke to Rosa's vigorous constitution.

Tears slipped down Rosa's cheeks as she held her daughter, oblivious to the doctor's hushed conversation with John just outside the door. Eventually John came to her bedside and wordlessly took the baby in his arms. He held her for the longest time without speaking, swaying gently from side to side, and punctuating the silence with slow, deep breaths like gusts of wind heralding an approaching storm.

"What should we call her?" said Rosa tentatively when he would not speak, exhaustion roughening her voice. "Do you still want to name her Mildred after your grandmother?"

Only a few days before he had insisted upon it, but now he frowned and returned the baby to Rosa's arms. "It doesn't suit her. Call her anything else. Call her whatever you like."

Abruptly he turned to go, and in a sudden swell of alarm, Rosa called after him, "John?"

He paused in the doorway, his back to her. "Yes?"

"Are you —" She swallowed back her tears and held her daughter close. "Are you angry? Did you hope for a son?"

He was silent a long moment, and when he spoke, his voice was low and subdued. "I prayed for a healthy child of our own."

Her deep pool of grief and remorse, so long contained, spilled over under the pressure of his gaze. "I should have married Lars," she choked out, bowing her head and rocking back and forth. "I should have married him, and maybe everything would have been —"

"No." John sat down on the bed and grasped her shoulders. "You couldn't have brought an innocent child into the world with that — that drunk. Rosa, I love you. You're my wife. I'm this child's father. That's the way it is. That's the way it'll be. Do you understand?"

Bewildered and dazed, Rosa took a deep, shuddering breath and nodded, her gaze fixed on her daughter's sweet, delicate features. Dark eyes, a thick cap of soft, dark hair, and a precious rosebud mouth — already Rosa loved her more than she had ever loved anyone, and she knew she would give her own life to protect her.

John gripped her shoulders so tightly it pained her. "Then we'll never speak of this again."

Again Rosa nodded, swallowing hard, her heart welling up with gratitude. She had wronged John terribly, but he had forgiven her without anger, without recriminations. For the rest of her life, she should need no more proof of his love and goodness than that.

Surely she had made the right choice — for herself, for John, and for their daughter.

Rosa and John named the baby Marta, after Rosa's paternal grandmother — or rather, Rosa suggested the name and John agreed that it would do. Rosa knew her father would be proud and pleased by their choice, and she looked forward to telling him. She missed her parents desperately, and as the days passed, it seemed very strange that they did not come to meet their new granddaughter.

Marta was three weeks old on the day John came in from the rye fields carrying a large basket covered with a small Four-Patch quilt. "They came," Rosa exclaimed, recognizing her mother's handiwork. As John set the basket upon the kitchen table, Rosa flew to the front room to welcome her family. But no one waited there. She flung open the front door, wondering why they had not followed John inside, only to find the yard empty except for a feral cat prowling for mice near the barn.

Rosa slowly shut the door and returned to the kitchen, where John was unpacking the basket. She stroked the soft folds of the quilt, bewildered. "Did they leave the basket on the doorstep? Why didn't they knock? Were they afraid to wake the baby?"

"It was just your mother, and she didn't come up to the house." John took a flat bundle wrapped in cheesecloth from the basket and lifted back one edge. A waft of steam emerged, and Rosa smelled corn tortillas. "I met her on the road."

Perplexed, Rosa watched him take a covered dish from the basket. The tantalizing aroma of her mother's tamales drifted to her, evoking memories of her *abuelo* mixing *masa* at the kitchen table and instructing Rosa patiently so that one day she would be able to make the Christmas delicacy as well as he did. Everyone else who had been fortunate enough to taste her *abuelo*'s tamales declared that they had no equal, but Rosa loved her mother's best. "My mother spent hours in the kitchen preparing these foods and weeks making the quilt, she carried this heavy load five miles from home, but she wouldn't go the last few hundred yards to the house? That doesn't make any sense."

"Rosa —" John sighed heavily and set the dish on the table. "She was in a hurry. I told her Marta was napping and she said she'll meet her another time."

"Why didn't you tell her to come in anyway?" Rosa cried. "Marta doesn't have to be awake for my mother to see her. If she's in that much of a hurry, you can drive her home."

As she turned to leave the kitchen, John caught her by the arm. "Rosa, no. Don't."

Rosa struggled, but she could not free herself from John's firm grasp. "I won't be gone long. If Marta wakes up, just rock her until I get back."

"Rosa, stop it." An unfamiliar grimness in his voice brought her to a halt. "She doesn't want to see you."

Rosa stared at him, shaking her head. "You're not making any sense."

"Your parents don't believe that Marta was born two months early," he said, his voice bitter and cutting. "You've disgraced the family, and they want nothing more to do with you. Your father insists."

Rosa couldn't breathe. It was exactly what she had feared in those frightening early weeks of her pregnancy. Her parents might indeed disown her over such a terrible, mortal sin, but a small voice in the back of her thoughts whispered a protest. Her gaze fell upon the basket and her mother's gifts. "Why would my mother bring me this beautiful quilt and my favorite foods if she and my father have renounced me?"

"To soften the blow, I guess."

Drawing in a long, shaky breath, Rosa

sank into a chair and rested her head on her arms upon the table. As her tears began to fall upon the tabletop, John was suddenly standing behind her, rubbing her neck and shoulders. "It's all right. You have me and Marta. You don't need them."

But she did, she did.

Eventually, time and the duties of new motherhood wore the edge off Rosa's grief. She found comfort, even pleasure, in making a home for her husband and daughter, and when she sat with Marta on a quilt in the shade of the orange trees, she would gaze out upon the fields of rye where her husband labored and feel an overwhelming rush of thankfulness. She could not have borne her family's abandonment alone.

In those early weeks, John was as dutiful a father to Marta as if she were truly his own child. He seemed, sometimes, to have convinced himself that she was. Lars stayed away, long after the news of Marta's birth surely must have reached him. Rosa concluded — sadness inexplicably tainting her relief — that evidently he too wanted the world to believe that John was Marta's father. His absence convinced Rosa that she had made the right decision, and she strengthened her resolve to forget Lars and be the wife John deserved.

But before long, she began to wonder whether instead John had become the husband she deserved.

Marta was almost three months old when Rosa took her along on a trip to the Arboles Grocery. As she carried Marta past bins of dark green asparagus and bright red strawberries, she stopped short at the sight of a familiar, beloved figure in the next aisle — her mother, picking out a chicken for Sunday dinner. Cautiously, heart pounding, Rosa summoned up her courage, and said, "Mamá?"

Her mother whirled around. "Rosa."

Rosa offered her a tremulous smile, expecting her mother's startled expression to harden into righteous indignation. Instead Isabel rushed forward to embrace her, her eyes widening in wonder at the sight of the baby in her arms, snuggled in the Four-Patch quilt she herself had made. "Oh, my darling," she gasped, her hands trembling as she tentatively reached for her granddaughter. "Oh, what a perfect angel."

Rosa blinked back tears and gently placed baby Marta in her mother's arms. She watched as her mother gazed with open adoration upon her granddaughter as if she were soaking in every detail — her sweet baby scent, her long eyelashes, her tiny nails on tiny fingers. Her mother's rapturous expression, as unexpected as it was welcome, emboldened Rosa to speak. "Thank you for the quilt," she said hesitantly. "And the tortillas and tamales. They were delicious."

Isabel held the baby close as if some small part of her feared Rosa would snatch her away. "I wanted to do so much more."

Rosa wished she had. "I've missed you. I — I understand why you stayed away."

Her mother glanced up from Marta long enough for Rosa to read new puzzlement in her expression. "I stayed away because you asked me to. Otherwise I would have been there, every moment."

Rosa shook her head, bewildered. "I never asked you to stay away."

"Your husband passed along your message."

"No. You must have misunderstood him. He wanted you to reconsider. He told me that you and Papá had disowned me when you heard about Marta, about when she was born —" The shock in her mother's eyes abruptly silenced her, and then, after a moment of confusion, Rosa understood. John had lied. Her mother had not known until that moment the truth about Marta's birth, and Rosa had unwittingly given herself away.

Slowly her mother said, "Marta was not born early."

Rosa dropped her shopping basket and quickly took Marta back from her stunned mother. "I have to go."

"Rosa —"

"Tell Papá I'm sorry." Rosa fled from the store, Marta in her arms.

Dazed, she walked down the street to the hardware store, where she found John conversing with the storekeeper as he browsed the tools. "Rosa," he said, surprised. "I thought I was supposed to pick you up at the grocer's later. Are you all right?"

"I — I'm not feeling well." She spoke the truth; she felt faint and dizzy and needed to sit down. She couldn't bring herself to confront her husband then, with her head swimming from shock and the storekeeper looking on. "Can we go home, please?"

John quickly made his purchases and escorted her out to the truck. As they drove home, Rosa held her sleeping daughter and tried to find the words to tell John that she had discovered his lie, but every time he glanced over at her, she found herself unable to speak.

"I heard some interesting news at the hardware store," John remarked later as he pulled up a chair to the table and tucked his napkin into his collar. "A few weeks ago, Lars Jorgensen asked his father to give him his inheritance early so he could strike out on his own."

"Isn't his inheritance the southern half of the ranch?" asked Rosa, filling John's plate and setting it before him. Anxiety stole over her again at the mention of Lars's name, which John had made her promise never to speak in his presence.

"That's right." John gave her an appraising look. "I guess I shouldn't be surprised you knew that."

Rosa kept her voice steady as she spooned a small portion of potatoes and apples onto her plate. "Everyone knows that, or they ought to be able to figure it out. What else could Mr. Jorgensen fairly do but divide the ranch between his two sons when he passes on?"

"Lars apparently can't wait that long, and he must have made a convincing argument because his father agreed to give him his share." John allowed a meaningful pause as he took his fork in hand. "Of course, we both know Lars can be persuasive when he wants something badly enough."

Disconcerted, Rosa almost let the pitcher slip from her grasp as she filled their water glasses. "I don't see how working half of the same land he's always worked is striking out on his own," she said as indifferently as she could manage.

"It wouldn't be, which is why he's sold it."

Rosa stared at him in disbelief. "Sold it? He sold off half of the Jorgensen ranch?"

John nodded. "To some family from Iowa — Frazier, I think they're called."

Rosa set down the pitcher and sank into her chair, stunned. "I can't believe his parents allowed it."

"They couldn't very well prevent it once old Jorgensen signed over those acres to him. They were his, free and clear, to do with as he wished. Still, I bet old Jorgensen didn't know Lars meant to sell them or I doubt he'd have gone along with it." Shaking his head, John cut himself a thick slice of bread and put it on his plate, setting the long knife on the wooden cutting board with a clatter. "Frank Johnson heard from one of Jorgensen's hired men that as soon as Lars pocketed the cash from the sale, he packed a rucksack, climbed on his horse, and rode out of the valley without looking back."

"Where did he go?"

"Why do you care?"

"I don't," Rosa replied, too quickly, clenching her hands together in her lap. They were ice cold, despite the balmy weather. "I'm just curious."

"Frank didn't say and I didn't ask." John took a bite of his dinner, nodded in satisfaction, and took another. "Anyway, he's long gone now, and I say, good riddance. This is delicious, honey."

"It's your mother's recipe," Rosa murmured. As John turned the conversation to the farm, she picked up her fork and moved the food around on her plate, but her stomach was in knots and she knew better than to try to eat.

Lars had left the Arboles Valley, left her, without even saying good-bye, without meeting his daughter. That should have been what Rosa wanted, but with no idea where he had gone or when he might return, she felt as shocked and bereft as the night he had failed to light the lantern in the oak grove.

But there was nothing she could do, no comfort to be found except in loving Marta.

The next Sunday, John, Rosa, and Marta went to early Mass instead of the midmorning service they usually attended. As the parishioners filed out of the church afterward, Rosa passed her parents and brother in the aisle. A greeting died on Rosa's lips as her father gazed through her as if she and the baby in her arms were as insubstantial as vapor. Behind her father's back, Carlos and her mother shot her furtive, sympathetic glances before they too turned away, without a single word for her, without a loving kiss for her baby. She had never felt more alone, and with nowhere to turn, no safe refuge, she dared not confront John about his lies or his inexplicable determination to drive Rosa and her mother apart.

In anguish, she sought counsel from her parish priest, who had heard her confession and absolved her of her sins before her marriage and again shortly after Marta's birth. He expressed sorrow when, after reciting her venial sins, she confessed that she still thought of Lars often and worried about him, wherever he was. The priest urged her to concentrate on prayer whenever her thoughts strayed to Lars, and reminded her that in all things she must accept the will of God and submit to her husband. As Rosa left the confessional, the priest added that if her father should come to see him, he would remind him that the Lord called all Christians to forgive others as they wished to be forgiven, and this included wayward daughters. "Don't lose hope, my child," he told her, and his compassion brought tears to her eyes.

If Rosa's father did hear the good priest's message, it failed to sway him.

One afternoon, Rosa was pushing Marta in her stroller after running an errand at the bank for John when she heard someone call her name. She turned to see her mother dashing across the street toward her, and after a quick, tearful embrace, they hurried off together down a side street where fewer eyes would see them. There her mother cuddled her granddaughter and delivered the devastating news of her father's decree: Rosa was dead to him, and her mother and brother must disown her as well.

"You're speaking to me now," said Rosa hollowly.

Her mother shifted Marta to her shoulder, defiance flashing in her eyes. "You're my daughter and I could never abandon you. I see no good whatsoever in your father's command that I renounce you or in your husband's attempts to keep us apart. And so I see no reason to obey them."

Rosa felt long-dormant hopes stirring. "Do you mean that you'll see me again, me and Marta?"

"Of course, *mija,* but we must meet somewhere far from prying eyes." Isabel stroked Marta's soft, dark locks, thinking, and then her face lit up. "The mesa, our picnic spot near the canyon. Would you be able to slip away and meet me there without raising John's suspicions?"

Rosa assured her that she could. A few months after their marriage, John had taken a second job as the Arboles Valley postmaster, and once a week he went to the train station to collect the mail. If Rosa left soon after John departed, she could take Marta to the mesa and visit with her mother, and return home before John arrived. He would never know that his wife and daughter had been away.

They agreed to meet on the mesa once a week if the weather was fair and if their husbands did not unwittingly intercede. Mindful of the waning afternoon and the men waiting for them at home, they embraced and parted with tearful, hopeful smiles.

A year passed. Rosa devoted herself to her family, finding happiness in the minutiae as well as the milestones of Marta's childhood — first words, first steps, first hugs and kisses — and it seemed to her, day by day, that John grew happier, more confident, more content. She had never seen a prouder man than the day he held his firstborn son in his arms. "We'll name him John Junior," he declared, cradling the baby tenderly only minutes after his birth. Watching them together from where she lay resting in bed, Rosa was overwhelmed with love, and joy, and hope. Their daughter Angela was born a year and a half later, and for a while, Rosa believed that despite the sorrow of her continuing estrangement from her father and brother, God had heard her prayers, and she and John would be happy together.

Then, only a few months after Angela was weaned, she fell seriously, chronically, incomprehensibly ill, plagued by diarrhea and stomach cramps that left her listless and bloated. A few months later, John Junior began to suffer from the same symptoms. Only Marta thrived, glowing with robust good health as she sweetly tried to help her mother care for her younger siblings.

Angela died in March 1917, John Junior seven months later, a mere few weeks after Ana was born. As the household plunged into grief, John seemed to conflate Ana's birth and her elder siblings' deaths. He never warmed to her, never held her unless Rosa urgently needed him to, offered no suggestions for her name. On the morning of her christening, Rosa reminded him that they had to have a name before the ceremony. John replied, "My son is dead. Call her whatever you want." Rosa chose Ana Maria, in the desperate hope that the Blessed Mother would protect her namesake.

The sunny hours spent on the mesa with her mother and the children were Rosa's only respite from the grief that pervaded her home, offering her solace even on the anniversary of John Junior's death. Wind swept the mesa as Rosa and Isabel sat near the canyon's rim watching five-year-old Marta amuse Ana, who had grown into a lively toddler. Despite the melancholy anniversary, Rosa had to smile as Marta threw handfuls of golden grass into the air around her younger sister, who squealed and laughed as she tried to catch them. But it was a wistful smile, since Isabel had just finished telling Rosa how she had spent the morning laying flowers upon her grandchildren's graves. Rosa had never visited the cemetery after John Junior's funeral; it would be more than she could bear to see headstones engraved with her beloved children's names. Marta and Ana were as healthy and happy as any two girls in the Arboles Valley, and the child within Rosa's womb seemed to be growing steadily, but sickness and death seemed to lurk in every shadow. Her daughters' vitality seemed a cruel illusion, and she no longer expected to see them reach adulthood. With no future to hope for, she had learned to be content with every moment, and that was enough to endure each day.

Then Isabel, gazing upon her grand-daughters at play, said, "They're so full of joy and light. I don't see anything of John in them."

With a jolt of recognition, Rosa knew then God had sent her an opportunity to redeem herself by telling the truth, even if it meant that her mother too would renounce her, and her last refuge would disappear.

"Mamá," she said softly, "there's something to what you say."

Her mother turned her head sharply, her gaze keen. "What do you mean?"

There Rosa's courage faltered. "There is something of John in the girls, though you might not want to see it because you despise him."

Her mother studied her for a long moment. "I do despise him," she admitted, turning her gaze back to her granddaughters. "I think I understand his grief, though I've never lost a child, but I can't forgive him for lashing out at you. You should be able to draw comfort from each other in your mourning. Instead John seems to blame you."

Rosa laughed shortly. "He's not the only one."

"Ignorant people, whispering cruel rumors," her mother said in disgust. "Pay them no mind."

Marta proved to be as devoted a big sister to Maria when she was born in the winter of 1919 as she had always been to Ana. John and Rosa were blessed with another son in the spring of the following year, and for a brief, precious time, all four children thrived. The perpetual scowl left John's face, and he treated Rosa with kindness he had not shown since the early months of their marriage. Then Maria fell ill, and then Ana, who had so long eluded the strange sickness that had claimed her siblings that her parents had begun to hope that, like Marta, she would avoid their fate. Soon after John Junior passed away, in a rare display of tears, John confided to Rosa that his eldest sister had died in childhood after suffering from a similar affliction. "We must resign ourselves to the will of God," he had choked out, roughly brushing away his tears with the back of his fist. Then he had bitterly added, "At least we'll still have Marta when all the others are dead and buried."

Distressed and angry, Rosa poured out her heart to her mother. "You mustn't give up searching for a cure, no matter what your husband decides for himself," Rosa's mother said staunchly, embracing her with one arm and cradling baby Pedro in the other. "And I will help you. I've heard of a powerful *curandera* in El Paso, someone I haven't consulted before. I'll write to her today."

Reluctant to tear herself away from the comfort of her mother's company, Rosa lingered on the mesa longer than she should have. When she finally arrived home with the children, she found John sorting mail in the front room. "You're home early," she said breathlessly, managing a smile in passing as she took the children to their bedrooms and put them down for a nap.

John met her in the kitchen as she was tying on her apron. "Where were you?"

"Out for a walk."

"You were gone a while. Long walk for such little girls."

"We didn't go far. We stopped to play on the mesa." Rosa suddenly remembered that she had once told him that the mesa was her mother's favorite place in the Arboles

Valley, and she hurried on before he had too much time to ponder the implications.

"Did you meet your mother there?"

"Would that be so wrong?" she asked. "The girls ought to know their grandmother. You forbade me to invite her here, but you never said I couldn't see her elsewhere."

"Well, I'm saying it now. I don't want you seeing her anymore."

"She's my mother," Rosa protested.

"She disowned you!"

"My father did. She didn't." A vivid image sprang into her mind's eye, John unpacking the quilt-draped basket of delicacies her mother had prepared so lovingly and telling her that her mother never wanted to see her again. He had lied to her, and she still did not understand why. "She never disowned me and she never will. But even if she had, she obviously wants the girls and me in her life now. Why are you dead set against it? What has she ever done to offend you? You were the one she preferred. You were the one she wanted me to marry. She never hated you the way she hated Lars —"

John slapped her across the face, sending her reeling back against the kitchen table. "I told you never to mention his name," he thundered, clenching his fist so close to her eyes that she could make out the black hairs against his tanned skin on the back of his hand. "Is that why you married me? Because you couldn't marry him?"

"You were my friend, and you loved me, and I thought we could be happy —"

He seized her by the shoulders again and shook her until her head swam. "Answer the goddamned question!"

"Yes," she choked out. She shouldn't have married him. Better to bear a child out of wedlock than to endure a lifetime of misery and deception. But it was a lesson learned too late.

He stared at her for a long moment, red-faced from rage, breathing heavily. "You are a filthy whore," he said flatly, releasing her. "I've raised that girl as my own daughter, and this is how you repay me, by going behind my back, plotting against me."

"I took the girls to see my mother," Rosa said, incredulous, clutching the back of a chair for support. "How does that hurt you?"

He shook his head slowly, a warning. "Don't make me hit you again."

"If that's what you want to do," she snapped, "is there anything I could say that would prevent it?"

This time, his closed fist knocked her

sprawling to the floor. As she lay there, stunned, he came upon her so swiftly that she instinctively rolled onto her side and curled protectively around the child in her womb. But the kick she was expecting did not come. "Don't try to see her again," John said without emotion, and walked away. She heard his boots striking the floor as he crossed the front room, the door open and shut. Only when she heard the tractor start up and knew he would not soon return could she take a deep, shuddering breath, drag herself into a chair, and rest her throbbing head in her arms on the table.

Week after week, Rosa's distress escalated as she imagined her mother sitting alone on the old quilt she spread on the grass of the mesa, waiting and waiting without fail, hoping Rosa and the children would come. Rosa wanted desperately to send her an explanation through mutual acquaintances when they came to the Barclay farm to pick up their mail or post letters, but John was always hovering nearby, rendering it impossible for her to exchange more than a few pleasantries.

As spring blossomed into a glorious, warm summer, the rye grew tall in the fields surrounding the adobe and fruit ripened on trees throughout the valley. Neighboring farmers cheerfully predicted a harvest more plentiful than in decades, but the promise of abundance did not touch Rosa, who felt herself fracturing under the strain of Ana and Maria's illness, John's coldness, and her interminable isolation. She had not fully understood how much her weekly visits with her mother had sustained her until they were gone.

In late July, Rosa was hanging wash on the clothesline when a dark, unfamiliar automobile slowly crawled up the gravel drive from the main road and parked between the house and the barn. Pinning one last sheet to the line before going to see who the visitors were, Rosa glanced over her shoulder and spotted two grim-faced men emerging from the car. Her heart plummeted when she recognized the sheriff and the young, red-haired priest who had replaced her old confessor. "I'm afraid we have some bad news, Mrs. Barclay," the sheriff greeted her solemnly. "May we come in? Is your husband home?"

Her mouth dry, she nodded and led them into the front room, where they waited while she went to ring the triangle to summon John. They waited for her to be seated and for John to come in from the fields before they told her that earlier that day, her mother's body had been found at the bottom of the Salto Canyon.

"We found no signs of foul play," the sheriff said. To Rosa it seemed that his voice came from very far away. Her ears rang and her vision seemed dimly unfocused. Her mother, dead? It was impossible. Impossible. "From the condition of her remains, we believe she fell from the top of the canyon. Do you have any idea why she might have been out that way alone?"

Everyone waited for Rosa to speak, but when she said nothing, John cleared his throat and said, "My mother-in-law walked on the mesa often. She enjoyed taking in the view of the canyon."

The sheriff nodded. "Then we have no reason to suspect her death was anything but a tragic accident."

"Of course it was an accident," said the red-haired priest firmly. He moved to the sofa beside Rosa, and in a gentler tone, added, "Your father and brother are making arrangements for the funeral mass on Thursday. I understand that you've been estranged, but I thought you'd want to know."

"Thank you, Father," Rosa murmured. Tears filled her eyes, blurring the men's faces. She understood then why the priest had emphasized that her mother's death was surely an accident. Isabel had been a faithful, devout Catholic all her life, but if she had committed suicide, she could not be buried in sacred ground.

The sheriff, the priest, and John quietly discussed the investigation while Rosa stared into space, insensible. She roused herself enough to bid the visitors good-bye when they left, and to thank the priest for his promised prayers. When she and John were alone, he held her for a moment and told her he was sorry for her loss, and then he returned outside and resumed his work. Momentarily alone, Rosa could almost believe that the sheriff and the priest had never been there, that the terrible event they had come to tell her about had never happened. Life not only went on, it had barely paused to mark her mother's passing.

Marta and Ana clung to Rosa and wept when she told them that their *abuela* had gone to heaven. Maria was too young to understand, but she knew that her mother and sisters were sad and so she was too. Rosa assumed she would have to beg John to let her attend her mother's Mass of Christian Burial, but he decided that the entire family must go. "If we don't, people will talk," he told her the night before the service.

"People will talk anyway." She saw it in their eyes as they came to the farm to pick up their mail, heard it in the undertone that ran beneath their solemn, gentle words of condolence. She realized she was probably the only person in the Arboles Valley who believed her mother's death was an accident, but she had grown accustomed to being alone in all the different ways a woman could be alone, and their doubt did not weaken her certainty.

The funeral mass was solemn and poignant. Rosa could not bear to look upon her mother lying in repose in her coffin, so she fixed her gaze on the back of her father's head, grayer than she remembered and bowed in grief. Rosa, John, and the children had seated themselves near the back of the church rather than in the front pew where the closest family belonged, and after Mass when the mourners gathered at the grave site, they made sure to be among the last to arrive so her father would not notice them. Rosa and John had agreed that they would quickly slip away as soon as the final prayers were spoken, but in the press of the crowd leaving the churchyard, Rosa suddenly found herself face-to-face with Carlos.

"Rosa," Carlos murmured, hesitating before he embraced her. He nodded to

John, and a flicker of a smile appeared on his face as his gaze lingered upon his nieces and nephew, whom he had never met. Before Rosa could speak, their father came upon them. Distracted by sorrow, he did not immediately recognize her, but when he did, his eyes widened and he stared in wonder at his four grandchildren.

"Papá," Rosa greeted him tremulously, pained to see him muddled by grief and loss, aged beyond his years. "This is Pedro," she said, nodding to the baby in her arms. "John's holding Maria, and here we have Ana and Marta, my eldest."

He gazed at each of his grandchildren as she named them, his watery, red-rimmed eyes filling with tears. Then he patted Marta on the head, cupped Ana's cheek with his hand, and reached forward to offer Pedro a finger to grasp. Suddenly his arms were around Rosa, and he bent to rest his head upon hers. Motionless from astonishment, she felt his tears falling upon her hair as he held her, swaying slightly as he shifted his weight from foot to foot. She drew in a breath, and as her lungs filled with her father's familiar smell of wool and tobacco and cedar, she felt the strange sensation of the weight of years of unhappiness falling aside. "Papá," she said, resting her cheek upon his shoulder and closing her eyes. "I've missed you so."

Just as suddenly as he had embraced her, he let her go. "You broke her heart," he choked out. "You broke her heart and now she's gone."

"Papá —"

"Don't. Don't speak to me." He shook his head and pushed past her. Carlos went after him, throwing her an impassioned look over his shoulder, a warning not to follow. Shocked into silence, Rosa stared after them as they disappeared into the crowd of mourners, her father's words of rebuke and condemnation ringing in her ears.

John saw her swaying and managed to steady her before she collapsed. He handed Pedro to Marta and helped her to the car. "He blames me," she murmured. "He thinks she took her own life, and he blames me."

"It was an accident," John said, "but let's face facts — she wouldn't have been on the mesa that day if not for you."

Rosa felt as if a cold wind had swept her last hopes away. Her teeth chattered violently and she clutched her arms to her chest, shivering. She thought she might never be warm again.

She had no safe refuge anymore. Her

mother was dead and her father had rejected her.

She wept for her mother — and for herself. She could not leave John now.

More than five years had passed since that desperate hour, but Rosa had finally left him.

The train sped north, carrying Rosa and her children and Lars away from John, away from the adobe, and for Rosa and the children at least, away from the only lives they had ever known. Her gaze went to the luggage racks above their seats where the two precious quilts Elizabeth had rescued — one a cherished family heirloom, the other the last gift from her beloved mother — sat neatly folded among their few belongings.

Somewhere, in some faraway town Rosa had never seen, in a home she could as yet only vaguely imagine, she would spread the quilts upon warm, snug beds and her children would sleep peacefully beneath them, safe and sound at last. Rosa would have her brave and loyal friend Elizabeth to thank for whatever happiness they found there.

With each passing mile, as city blocks and streetcars gave way to rolling hills and farmers' fields, Rosa felt John's stranglehold upon her imagination loosening. He was in prison and likely to remain there for a very long time. The police believed that she and the children were dead; perhaps John believed it too, if jealous suspicion had not prompted him to conflate Lars's disappearance and her own.

If there were any justice in the world, John would be convicted of her mother's murder as well as Henry Nelson's shooting, but it was not to be.

When a sudden surge of anger swept through her, Rosa turned her face to the window so the girls, enjoying a game of backgammon with Lars while Miguel dozed on her lap, would not notice. John had pressured her to blame herself for her mother's death, when he knew Isabel had perished at his own hands. Rosa felt a spiky, cold shiver down her spine when she remembered the aftermath of her mother's accident. Nothing in John's manner, not his words or his deeds or even the slightest, betraying flicker of emotion in his expression had implicated him. She was shocked and bewildered enough to think that he had taken her mother's life; that he showed not a wisp of regret or remorse terrified her.

She recalled a day not long after her mother's death when John had come home from an errand pale, clammy, and trembling. Alarmed, she had questioned him, but he rebuffed her until she threatened to summon the doctor. He wasn't having a heart attack, he had insisted roughly, he had just taken a fright. On his way home he had crossed the mesa, and for a moment he had thought he had seen Isabel walking along the edge of the Salto Canyon. "She stopped in her tracks and stared right at me," he had said, shaking as he paced the length of the front room, clenching and unclenching his fists.

"It must have been someone else," Rosa had replied, refusing to believe even for a moment that her mother's unquiet spirit haunted the mesa. "Or perhaps it was a tree blowing in the wind. The sunlight streaming through the mists can play tricks on the eyes."

"That was no tree," John had retorted. "Trees bend or break, but they don't walk. Someone was out there."

"Whoever it was, it wasn't my mother," Rosa had said sharply, and John set his jaw and never spoke of it again. Now Rosa looked back on the bizarre exchange with new insight: Her mother's ghost had been a figment conjured up by his own guilty conscience. To Rosa, his fearful avoidance of the mesa thereafter was as good as a confession.

They disembarked in Santa Rosa, and as Lars and Rosa stood on the platform in the midst of the bustling crowd making sure that all children and luggage were accounted for, a young, dark-haired man worked his way through the throng toward them. "Mr. and Mrs. Ottesen?" he asked. He looked to be about sixteen years old, and wore his tie loosened and his gray flannel hat set at a jaunty angle.

"Yes," Lars replied, shaking his hand. "I'm Nils and this is Rose. You must be Vincenzo Cacchione."

"Please call me Vince," he said, smiling as he tugged on the brim of his hat and nodded to Rosa. "Ma'am."

Lupita scowled. "She's not *Rose.*"

Marta nudged her, too late to do any good.

Vince feigned astonishment. "She's not? Then who is she?"

"She's Mamá, of course," said Lupita indignantly.

Vince burst into laughter, and nervously Rosa joined in. "Thank you so much for coming to meet us, Vince," she said.

"My pleasure." Vince seized the handles

of Lars's suitcase and one of the valises. "The wagon's over this way if you'll come with me."

Quickly they snatched up the rest of their luggage and followed Vince from the platform, through the station, and outside to a wagon hitched to a pair of sturdy brown draft horses with black manes and tails. Rosa rode beside Vince on the wagon seat holding Miguel on her lap, while Lars piled in back with the older children and their belongings.

"Ma said to take you to the pickers' cabin to unload your things before bringing you up to the house," Vince explained with a grin as he took the reins and chirruped to the horses. "She's going to put you to work right away."

"That's fine," said Lars. "We can settle in later."

For Rosa, Vince's words immediately evoked memories of the dilapidated cabin on the Jorgensen ranch, and she wondered with some trepidation what the pickers' cabin would be like. She also wondered what sort of work Mrs. Cacchione had in mind for their first day. Rosa would prefer to work in a garden or in the vineyard, although she knew nothing about tending grapevines. She and the children had been too long sitting indoors and strolling paved sidewalks. Fresh air, sunshine, and the rich, earthy smell of overturned soil would do them all good.

As they passed through Santa Rosa, Vince asked the children their names and pointed out important places along the way — the bank, the post office, the pharmacy with the best soda fountain for miles. "Everyone's looking forward to meeting you," he said, glancing over his shoulder to grin at the children. He reeled off the names of his seven brothers and sisters too quickly for Rosa to remember them all, but she gathered that he was the third eldest, with an older brother and sister and several younger siblings around the same ages as Ana and Marta. Rosa hoped they would become fast friends. They would be far less apprehensive on their first day at their new, unfamiliar school if they had already befriended a few of their classmates.

They left the streets of the small town behind and traveled south along a wide dirt road over gently rolling terrain. The hills framing the valley in the distance reminded Rosa of home, although deep green pines and leafy redwoods covered the peaks rather than soft green scrub and sage. The sun shone in a clear, blue sky, as if it had burned away all the damp chill of the fog-shrouded city they had departed that morning. The breeze was warm and fragrant and carried an unfamiliar fruity, woodsy perfume; Rosa inhaled deeply, savoring the enticing scent. They passed farms with fields of overturned earth giving evidence of the recent harvest, orchards busy with pickers climbing ladders and filling buckets with apples and plums, and vineyards with low, neat trellises covered in grapevines, the leaves awash in the changing colors of the season — green, gold, and scarlet.

"Is the grape harvest over for the season?" asked Lars. Only then did Rosa grasp what he had immediately observed, that no pickers moved among the vineyard rows, and the autumn tints of the grape leaves heralded their demise.

Vince nodded. "You missed the crush too."

"The crush?" asked Marta.

Vince threw her a grin over his shoulder. "Sure. You know that wine comes from grapes, don't you? Well, we have to crush the grapes to get the juice that turns into wine." His searching gaze traveled the vineyard rows and settled for a moment upon a white Victorian house on a distant hill. Rosa wondered who lived there. "The crush used to be the busiest, most important few weeks in the Sonoma Valley. When I was a kid, at this time of year, these roads were filled with wagons and trucks bringing in the crops or hauling grapes from vineyards to wineries. Everyone was in a hurry to get the work done. The crushers rumbled and growled as ripe grapes were dumped into them by the basketful, and men shouted to be heard over the din — calling out orders and sizing each other up and querying one another about who'd already finished their crush and who was still picking and which lazy souls had yet to get started. The air was so heavy with the sweet smell of grape juices that you'd have thought you could drink it. But nowadays —" Vince shrugged, making a rueful face. "You'd hardly know the crush was happening at all."

"But the crush doesn't happen at your vineyard anymore, isn't that so?" asked Rosa. "Dr. Reynolds said that you grow and sell wine grapes now rather than making wine."

"I didn't say *we* were crushing," said Vince quickly. "That would be illegal."

As Vince fell silent for the first time since they had left the station, Rosa glanced over her shoulder at Lars, raising her eyebrows.

Lars, bemused, gave her a small shrug in return.

About five miles south of Santa Rosa, Vince slowed the horses as they approached another lush vineyard basking in the sun. "This is home," he announced proudly. "Sixty acres of the most beautiful, fertile land in God's creation."

"It's so pretty," breathed Ana.

Rosa couldn't have agreed more. She shaded her eyes with her hand and admired the hundreds of orderly rows of low, sturdy trellises etching the level earth with green and gold. In the distance, a grand two-story redwood residence commanded the view from the heights near a grove of walnut trees. Through the foliage, Rosa glimpsed the golden tan of another redwood building some distance beyond the house, which she supposed could be the winery. She wondered if it had been abandoned since Prohibition had begun or if it had been put to another purpose.

Lars squinted in the sunlight as his gaze came to rest on the far hills. "What are you growing in that orchard?" he asked. "Pears?"

"Prunes," Vince replied.

"Don't you mean plums?" asked Rosa, smiling. "You harvest plums. It's only after drying that they become prunes. Isn't that so?"

Vince smiled back. "I suppose that's so, if you're a stickler for accuracy. We call 'em prunes whether they're dried or still green on the trees."

Rosa resolved to do the same, even though the idea of harvesting prunes conjured up images of fruit left on the trees far too long. To do otherwise would mark them as outsiders.

A road broad enough for two wagons to pass easily wound up the gradual slope toward the residence, but instead of taking it, Vince shook the reins and ordered the horses onward until they reached a second, narrower lane, with well-worn wheel ruts along the edges and a wide thatch of tough grass growing down the center. Vince slowed the horses to a walk as the wagon swayed and pitched along. Rosa clutched Miguel tightly upon her lap with one arm and grasped the seat with her free hand to brace herself. "It won't be much farther," Vince assured them, and at that moment the redwood shakes of a roof came into sight, and as the wagon rumbled over a low rise, the rest of the cabin appeared in a hollow shaded by oak and walnut trees. It was larger than Rosa had expected, with solid walls of redwood logs, a broad front porch, glass windows, and a chimney of smooth, round river stones. The breeze carried to her the burbling of an unseen creek and the sweetness of grapes. Captivated, Rosa held her breath, half fearing that Vince would steer the wagon past the cabin and take them farther on down the road to an as yet unseen, dilapidated shack reminiscent of the one on the Jorgensen ranch, but he pulled the horses to a halt and offered to help them unload.

Delighted, the girls scrambled down from the wagon, which prompted Miguel to wriggle and squirm on Rosa's lap, eager to follow. "Marta, would you please take your brother?" she called out, struggling to keep hold of him. Marta hurried back and reached up as Rosa handed him down from the wagon seat. With Miguel clutching Marta's hand, the children ran to the cabin, bounded up the three low steps, and knocked on the door. Laughing, Vince called out that they should just go on in, since it was their place now and no one was there to answer their knock anyway.

As Rosa, Lars, and Vince carried their luggage to the cabin, Rosa heard the girls squealing with joy over whatever it was they had discovered within. Suddenly Ana appeared in the doorway, breathless. "There's an attic, Mamá," she exclaimed. "With six beds. Six!" Just as quickly, she darted off again.

"They've grown accustomed to sharing beds," Rosa explained to Vince as she followed him across the threshold, a valise in one hand and her other arm wrapped around the sewing basket with the precious quilts folded on top.

"The previous tenants did too," Vince replied, setting the other satchel and Lars's suitcase on a braided rag rug just inside the front door. "They had ten children, all boys."

"My goodness, what a handful," Rosa replied, smiling to conceal an unexpected pang of grief. She should have eight children running through the cabin, eight children, not four, calling out to one another as they explored its every nook — five girls and three boys, each of them brown-eyed, dark-haired, and beloved.

She felt Lars's hand on her shoulder, his gentle, sympathetic squeeze, and she knew he had read her thoughts. "Why don't you take a look around while we unload?" Lars said quietly, and when she nodded, he headed back out to the wagon with Vince.

Quickly Rosa walked through the cabin,

taking in as many details as she could. Their luggage sat on the smooth redwood planks of a front room that seemed spacious and charming after a week spent in the boarding-house bedroom. A large stone fireplace occupied one wall, with comfortably worn chairs drawn up in front of it. Sunshine streamed through the windows, the rays illuminating dust motes as they fell upon a faded sofa set against the back wall. A doorway on the right led to a kitchen, where Rosa noted a deep double sink, an older but tidy stove, and a rectangular wooden table with two chairs on the ends and long benches along the sides — plenty of room for all. There was no icebox, but a door on the far wall revealed stairs leading down into a dark root cellar, and the air that wafted from it was so chilly that goose bumps prickled her arms. Another door revealed an ample pantry, but the shelves were bare except for a broom propped up in the corner, a dusty can of peaches, and a tin of sardines. Glancing around at the cupboards, Rosa hoped they were better stocked, with pots and pans and dishes and cutlery.

Returning to the front room, Rosa glanced warily upward at the sound of the children's footsteps pounding overhead as they sprinted from one end of the attic to the other. "Seems sturdy enough," she murmured when the ceiling didn't cave in. She pushed open a door that stood ajar near the foot of the staircase. White eyelet curtains were drawn over the two windows, but enough sunlight peeked through for Rosa to make out a double bed with sheets and blankets folded in a pile at the foot, a tall wardrobe, a shorter bureau with a chipped china pitcher and dish set upon it, and a redwood rocking chair, a jumble of straight lines and level planes. The air was stale and still, so Rosa drew back the curtains and opened the windows, welcoming the freshening breeze inside.

Leaving the room, she climbed the stairs to the attic and found the children bounding from one twin bed to another, talking and laughing and flinging themselves upon the mattresses experimentally to find the softest and most comfortable. The ceiling sloped so that she had to stoop unless she stood where the sides came to a peak in the middle. Someone had made up the small beds with sheets and pillows, but although Rosa looked around for blankets or quilts, she found none. Perhaps she would find some in the bedroom below, tucked away in the bureau or the wardrobe.

Mindful of the time and the duties awaiting them at the big house, Rosa gathered the children and ushered them back downstairs and outside, where Lars and Vince waited in the wagon. "It's lovely," she murmured to Lars as Vince shook the reins to prompt the horses. "It's more than I hoped for."

"Seems mighty nice," Lars admitted just as quietly. "I was expecting —"

"Something more like our old cabin," Rosa interrupted, smiling at her fears. "So was I." Her words hung in the air between them — *our old cabin* — and she felt a rush of heat and embarrassment. Mercifully, Lars merely nodded and turned his practiced farmer's gaze upon the vineyard, as if he were more interested in assessing their fecundity than interpreting her brief, thoughtless lapse into misplaced nostalgia. Perhaps he truly was.

Retracing the wagon's path, they soon came to the road leading up the gentle hill to the Cacchione residence. Lilies and jasmine bloomed in the front garden, and as they drew closer, Rosa heard voices, adults as well as children, joined in animated discussion punctuated by laughter. As they passed the house, several outbuildings came into view — a carriage house, a barn, and several others — and suddenly a group of boys and girls raced from the barn toward them, calling out Vince's name. As he pulled the horses to a halt, they caught sight of Rosa's children and stopped short, and the two groups of young people studied each other in bashful silence.

From the height of the wagon seat, Vince regarded his younger siblings with comic affront. "I bring you a wagonload of new friends, and you don't even say thank you?"

"Thank you, Vince," they chimed in unison, grinning at the newcomers, who smiled shyly back. Vince and Lars helped the girls down from the wagon, but Miguel buried his face on Rosa's shoulder and held fast to her dress with his small fists. Patting him reassuringly, Rosa told the girls they could go without him, and the older children promptly ran back to the barn together. Vince drove the wagon into the carriage house, and as he unhitched the horses and led them off to the stable, he called over his shoulder that his parents were in the barn, and that Rosa and Lars were welcome to walk over and introduce themselves.

As Vince disappeared around the corner, Lars offered Rosa his arm. "Let's go meet our new employers and get to work." Rosa hesitated a moment before slipping her hand into the crook of his elbow. They were supposed to be married. They couldn't very well meet their new employers separated by the careful distance of strangers.

Together they crossed the yard to the barn, but they stopped short in the doorway. Within, all was bedlam — children of all ages running and shouting, women in calico work dresses laughing and scolding as they swept the broad plank floor and raised clouds of dust and showers of hay, men grunting as they hefted long trestle tables and benches into rows at one end of the vast space. Lars caught a young, dark-haired boy by the shoulder as he darted past and asked him where Mr. Cacchione could be found. "Pa's over there," the boy replied, pointing to a group of men wrestling an enormous oak barrel into the far corner.

Overwhelmed, Rosa hung back, but Lars folded his callused hand around hers and led her through the throng. They reached the corner just as the men finished setting the barrel in place and began congratulating one another in a cheerful mixture of English and Italian. "Mr. Cacchione?" Lars broke in, raising his voice to be heard above their laughter.

A short, powerfully built man with salt and pepper hair and a neatly trimmed goatee broke off his conversation and turned toward them. "I'm Dante Cacchione."

Lars reached out to shake his hand. "I'm Nils Ottesen and this is my wife, Rose." He placed his other hand on Rosa's back, and she stepped forward and managed a smile, though the alias fell like a heavy yoke upon her shoulders. "Thank you for taking us on. We're grateful for the work. You won't be sorry."

"I'm glad you could join us on such short notice." Dante Cacchione's voice was deep and rich, and he shook Lars's hand heartily, and then Rosa's, as the other men drifted off to other tasks. "When Dr. Reynolds said you needed work and a place to stay — well, he's not a man I can say no to with a clear conscience."

A woman came up alongside him then, tucked her hand beneath his arm, and rested her other hand on his shoulder. "Dr. Reynolds saw our entire family through the influenza epidemic. We'd do anything for him."

Rosa surmised that the woman must be Mrs. Cacchione; the fondness in her eyes as she exchanged a smile with Mr. Cacchione was unmistakable. Like her husband, she looked to be in her mid-fifties, her eyes merry, her face and hands browned from the sun. She wore her hair, so dark it was nearly black except for a patch of white at the crown, pulled back in a loose knot at the nape of her neck, and the lines around her mouth and eyes gave evidence to a ready smile. She was a good three inches taller than her husband, with a solid, sturdy frame that conveyed strength and comfort. Rosa liked her immediately.

"Vince was supposed to take you by the cabin," Mrs. Cacchione continued. "Did you have a chance to settle in?"

"We dropped off our things and took a quick look around," said Rosa. "But we wanted to get right to work."

"Oh, very good. We always welcome diligent workers around here! I hope you and your children will be comfortable in the cabin. I always found it cozy, if a bit small." She glanced around as if hoping to pick out the new arrivals from among the throng of boys and girls, but she soon smiled and shook her head, giving up. "You'll have to introduce me later."

"Of course, Mrs. Cacchione. I'd be happy to, and I look forward to meeting your children as well. The others, I mean. We've already met Vince."

"Oh, goodness, please call me Guiditta." She patted her husband on the shoulder. "Perhaps you can find something for Nils to do while I put Rose to work?"

Dante agreed, and Rosa and Lars had time for a quick, parting glance before Guiditta whisked her away, found an idle broom, and set her to helping the other women sweep the floor. They were curious and friendly, having heard only that the Cacchiones had been expecting friends from San Francisco just in time for the party. Rosa felt inexplicably warmed and happy to hear herself named a friend by a woman she had not even met at the time the claim of friendship had been made, perhaps because Rosa had so few friends. As they tidied the barn, there was a flurry of names exchanged and histories shared and familial ties recounted, and Rosa tried in vain to catch and hold them all. Some of the women made their homes at neighboring farms and others on vineyards scattered around the Sonoma Valley, and all had been invited to the Cacchiones' home for their annual harvest celebration, the most anticipated event of the autumn aside from the crush and far more relaxing than that.

The most difficult preparations had already been completed before Rosa's arrival, and soon the barn was swept clean and aired out, the tables and benches and chairs arranged. Most of the other women hurried off then to freshen up and change into party clothes, but Rosa was obliged to make do with a surreptitious visit to the powder room in the big house, where she inspected herself in the mirror, smoothed the wrinkles from her traveling dress with her hands, ran her fingers through her new bob, and pinched her cheeks to bring some color to them, hoping that would suffice. She was among the first of the women to return to the barn, but before long her new acquaintances appeared in pretty dresses and lipstick, and soon other guests from near and far began to arrive, and a band comprised of neighbors and friends set up their instruments. By twilight the party was well underway. The barn had been transformed by music and revelry into a dance hall that, as one guest observed, for fun alone rivaled any of the fancy resorts along the Russian River. The band played popular tunes and old favorites, polkas and foxtrots and the occasional Italian folk song, to which many of the guests sang along. Enough of the words were similar to the Spanish spoken in her childhood home that Rosa was able to grasp the meaning of the heartfelt lyrics, stories of love of family and sweethearts and home.

When Rosa wasn't checking in on her

children, who were perfectly happy among their new friends and neither wanted nor needed her hovering nearby, she was helping Guiditta or meeting her new neighbors. She chatted at length with Salvatore and Beatrice Vanelli, a gentle, childless couple in their early sixties who for nearly four decades had grown acres of lush Zinfandel grapes that produced excellent wines celebrated for their anise, blackberry, and pepper notes, although the couple had been obliged in recent years to tear out most of their vines and replant table grape varietals and prune trees. Sal and Bea owned forty-five acres in a small town called Glen Ellen between Santa Rosa and Sonoma, right next to the Beauty Ranch, where Jack London's widow, Charmian, still lived. Sal had once been good friends with the famous writer and adventurer, but they had had a falling-out over Jack London's repeated offers to buy Sal's land and Sal's adamant refusals.

When Miguel found a playmate in the two-year-old son of Alegra Del Bene, the strikingly beautiful, Italian-born second wife of a widowed vintner, she and Rosa struck up a quick and cheerful friendship as they chased their children around the party in a valiant attempt to keep them out of trouble. Alegra's husband, Paulo, a longtime Santa

Rosa vintner who had been fortunate enough to secure a sacramental wine permit soon after Prohibition began, was more than twice her age. When they were first introduced, Rosa assumed Paulo was Alegra's father, but the couple were so amused by her mistake — which apparently was not uncommon — that Rosa was not embarrassed, and she listened with interest as they took turns telling the story of how they had met. After his first wife died, Paulo had mourned her deeply, but after a time he had written to family back in his native Italy and asked them to find him a new bride, someone hardworking and pleasant who would be a good mother to his four children. His sister-in-law made it her mission to find a suitable woman, and a few months later, Alegra arrived on one of the so-called "macaroni boats," speaking no English and wearing a ribbon tied around her neck from which dangled a cardboard sign with the words "Paulo Del Bene — San Francisco" printed on it. "Imagine my delight," Paulo told Rosa as Alegra smiled and blushed, "when this beauty descended the gangplank!" It was love at first sight, and seven years and three children later, it was obvious that they adored each other still.

It was Alegra who insisted Rosa sample a

glass of wine from the barrel in the corner. "The Cacchiones, they make the most marvelous vintages," she pronounced, linking elbows with Rosa and steering her around the dance floor to the other side of the barn. Rosa, who in all her life had only tasted sips of Communion wine at weekly Mass, was unprepared for the richness and flavor of the Cacchiones' wine, which Alegra explained was a Burgundy. "You will learn to taste all the flavors in a wine," she promised, pleased by the obvious pleasure Rosa took from her first drink.

Her head felt pleasantly light when Guiditta summoned her to help serve the harvest feast. Nearly all the wives joined in the procession from the residence's grand kitchen to the barn, carrying enormous bowls of steaming hot pasta topped with luscious red tomato sauce fragrant with herbs; crocks of rich, savory meat stews; crusty loaves of bread; platters heaped with sausages and salami; bowls of pungent pickled cucumbers and asparagus, both sweet and sour; dishes of sugared almonds; and huge platters of a cornmeal, cheese, and butter dish Beatrice told her was called polenta, perfectly delicious and perfectly safe for Ana and Miguel to eat. Desserts followed — peach cobblers and a variety of pies: apple, blackberry, and strawberry — topped with as much thick, rich cream as anyone could desire. Keeping a watchful eye upon Ana's and Miguel's plates, Rosa ate until she was satiated, but then found she had room enough to accept another glass of wine from Dante himself.

When everyone had eaten their fill, empty dishes were cleared away and what few desserts remained were arranged on a table pushed up against the wall for anyone who might work up an appetite dancing. Without waiting for Guiditta to ask, Rosa found an apron in the Cacchiones' enormous kitchen and dove into washing dishes alongside a charming and chatty dark-haired young woman who turned out to be the Cacchiones' eldest daughter, Francesca. When Rosa mentioned her hopes to enroll Marta, Ana, and Lupita in school as soon as possible, Francesca assured her that the grammar schools in Sonoma County were as modern and instructive as any to be found in San Francisco. Rosa was pleased to learn that the bus picked up Francesca's younger brothers and sisters at the foot of the hill where their driveway met the main road, so Rosa's girls would not have far to walk, nor would they have to wait at the bus stop alone.

It was nearly midnight when the last dishes were washed and dried and put away. Reinvigorated by the sounds of music and laughter, Rosa and Francesca left the house together, crossed the starlit yard, and returned to the barn, where they parted company, Rosa to join her family, Francesca to seek out her friends. Many of the children had found their way up the ladder to the hayloft and had fallen asleep in a bed of scattered, golden straw, and Rosa found Lupita, Ana, and Miguel among them, her son nestled close to Alegra's. Smiling, Rosa descended the stairs and watched the dancers, her toes tapping in time to the music, and spotted Marta beaming with pure delight as Vince whirled her about.

"He's four years older than she is," Lars said in her ear, coming upon her so suddenly she was unaware of him until he spoke.

"They're only dancing," Rosa replied. "He's just being friendly."

"Of course he is," Lars scoffed. "I'm going to keep my eye on that one."

Rosa laughed, charmed by how easily he stepped into the role of the protective father and yet wistfully aware of how long he had been denied the privilege. "I'm sure he's fine."

"He'll be fine as long as I'm watching him." As the band struck up the first familiar notes of "I'll See You in My Dreams," Lars held out his hand to her. "Care to dance? Don't tell me your feet are too tired, because I know for a fact you haven't danced a single step."

She hadn't, but she had been on her feet all night serving and clearing away and washing dishes and chasing children, and yet she would not let sore feet keep her from dancing now that he had finally asked. She nodded, gave him her hand, and muffled a sigh of contentment as he put his arms around her. They circled the dance floor without speaking until the last notes of the song faded. Lars did not release her, nor did she pull away, so when the band began another tune, they resumed dancing. It took Rosa a moment to recognize the melody, but when she did, she let out a rueful laugh.

Lars recognized it too. "The one I love," he said conversationally in time with the music, "belongs to someone else."

"Yes," she replied, "that's the name of the song, all right."

His eyebrows rose. "You don't care for the melody?"

"I don't care for the title. It doesn't suit me."

"I don't like it much myself."

He drew her closer to him, and after a fleeting moment of hesitation, she relaxed and let her cheek rest against his chest. He smelled of hay and salt, earth and fresh air.

It was after midnight when the party began to draw to a close. Rosa offered to stay and help tidy up, but Guiditta assured her she had already done more than her share and the rest could wait until morning. After Rosa and Lars gathered up the children, Dante offered them lanterns and directed them to a shortcut back to the cabin, a quarter-mile walk that wound past the old winery and through the vineyard, a much shorter journey than the route they had taken in the wagon earlier that day.

"That was the best birthday party ever," Lupita mumbled drowsily as Lars picked her up and carried her from the barn. She clasped her slender arms around his neck and promptly fell asleep on his shoulder.

Rosa laughed softly, nuzzling Miguel's soft curls with her lips as he dozed in her arms. Cool mists had rolled in from the distant ocean, blotting out the stars, so they made their way back to the cabin carefully along the well-worn path. Marta and Ana led them, clutching lanterns and reliving the evening in quiet voices, their heads close together. Lars carried the third lantern, and Rosa stayed close to his side so she could remain within the circle of light it cast.

Rosa's heart and head were full of the events of the day. "I can't believe our good fortune."

Lars made a noncommittal grunt. "Neither can I."

"You think it's too good to be true?"

He gave her a sidelong glance. "Don't you?"

She had been desperately unhappy so long that she might be expected to look upon an unexpected shower of blessings with a cynical eye, but the opportunity for friendship and prosperity she had observed among the Cacchiones and their neighbors seemed wonderfully real. "The Cacchiones seem like good people."

"They haven't told us everything that goes on here."

"Of course not. There wasn't time because of the party. We'll learn more about what they expect of us tomorrow."

"That's not what I meant." Lars lowered his voice and slowed his pace, allowing Marta and Ana to pull farther ahead of them. "That was a mighty big barrel of wine in the barn, set out in plain sight for all to see."

"I know. I tasted it."

"Yes, I saw. You seemed to be enjoying yourself."

Rosa resisted the impulse to ask him if he had indulged too, reluctant to appear as if she doubted his resolve. "They weren't trying to hide it, so it must be all right. Perhaps it was left over from before Prohibition. Wines are supposed to age, aren't they?"

Lars shrugged and shook his head, uncertain. "I suppose that could be it. But I spotted a lot of wary glances thrown our way until folks saw that the Cacchiones trusted us."

Rosa hadn't noticed. "Well, we are strangers in town, and this seems to be a close-knit community. Everyone seemed friendly enough to me." But his worries sowed seeds of doubt. "Do you really think they're hiding something?"

"I think time will tell, but in the meantime we should be careful."

"We need to be careful anyway," Rosa reminded him. "We're the ones who aren't being perfectly honest with our new acquaintances, *Nils*."

Lars snorted dryly and quickened his pace to catch up with the girls, and Rosa fell into step beside him.

Before long they reached the cabin, a snug

273

and welcome haven in a night that had grown cooler since they left the barn. Marta and Ana climbed the attic steps wearily, and Rosa followed close behind, Miguel in her arms. Lars carried Lupita upstairs, placed her still sleeping upon one of the beds, and returned downstairs for the children's belongings before bidding the girls good night and leaving the attic. After tucking in the children, Rosa returned downstairs to check the master bedroom for extra blankets and found Lars peering through the doorway and eyeing the bed. He looked up at the sound of her footsteps. "I'll take the sofa."

She nodded and brushed past him, feeling a flush rise in her cheeks as she searched the bureau and wardrobe for extra blankets. Finding none, she made up her bed with the folded sheets but carried the blanket to the front room, where her mother's quilts still rested on top of her sewing basket. She gave Lars the blanket as well as the quilt Elizabeth had called the Arboles Valley Star, and took the Road to Triumph Ranch quilt for herself. Then she wished Lars good night, went off to the bedroom, and shut the door.

She wondered if he would notice the intertwined initials her mother had embroidered upon the quilt and puzzle over their significance.

As she drifted off to sleep to the gentle music of the brook, the wind in the oak boughs, and the soft, occasional creak of bedsprings overhead, she drew her great-grandmother's wedding quilt up to her chin and hoped the children would be warm and comfortable in the attic. As autumn waned, the nights would likely grow colder, and the children would need quilts for their new beds. Closing her eyes, Rosa envisioned herself sitting by the fireside piecing scraps into cozy quilts, one for each of her beloved children. For Miguel she would stitch a quilt using the Railroad Crossing pattern, in hopes that he would sleep as peacefully beneath it as he had in her arms on their journey north, lulled by the music and motion of the train. For Lupita she would make a Happy Home quilt, a symbol of her wistful prayers that her little girl would be content wherever their journey led them, and not miss too much the unhappy, broken home they had left behind. Ana, her little scholar, would cherish a Schoolhouse quilt, and as for Marta, the Loyal Daughter block suited her so perfectly it could have been named for her.

She hoped that as long as they resided

within the cabin, and wherever they dwelt thereafter, quilts sewn with love would offer her children warmth, comfort, and a sense of home.

CHAPTER FIVE

The next morning, Rosa woke to the sounds of the children's footsteps overhead and muffled laughter. Pulling a robe on over her nightgown, she padded down the hall to the bathroom to wash up before returning to her bedroom to dress for the day, her thoughts already running through the many tasks awaiting her. The first, of course, was breakfast. The children would be hungry, and although Mrs. Phillips had packed them an ample lunch for the train the previous day, little remained left over to portion out among six people. Rosa would have to ask the Cacchiones for a ride to the market later that day, or else borrow staples from their pantry until a more convenient time arose. Rosa disliked depending upon someone else for transportation and was reluctant to put herself in debt to their new employers on their first full day of work, but there was no way around it. They had to eat, and it was absolutely essential that they replenish their stock of bananas.

She heard the children scrambling down the attic stairs, and when she joined them in the front room, she found them gathered around Lars, peering into a large picnic basket in his hands. "Someone left this on the front porch," he said, smiling a welcome. She returned his smile, and her gaze fell upon the blanket and quilt neatly folded on the sofa. She hoped he had slept well there. With a pang of embarrassment, she realized she should have taken a bed in the attic with the children and given him the bedroom. She would suggest the change to him that evening, although she suspected he would insist she keep the most comfortable room for herself.

"What's inside?" she asked, bidding her children good morning with fond hugs and kisses.

"Breakfast, I gather," Lars replied, handing her the basket. "Strawberries, cream, a bottle of milk, and a loaf of bread."

"Didn't I say the Cacchiones were good people?" she teased.

"I never said they weren't," he protested mildly.

She laughed and carried the basket into the kitchen. When she unpacked it, she also found a paper sack of prunes, a jug of olive oil, sugar, polenta left over from the party, and a note addressed to Rose. "I hope your first night in the cabin passed well," Guiditta had written. "Polenta makes a delicious breakfast. Cut slices, fry them up in hot oil, and serve with cream and sugar. Come up to the house whenever you're ready. Bring the children, of course! They can all play together while we show you and Nils around."

Delighted, Rosa searched the cupboards for a frying pan and soon had breakfast underway. In the meantime, Marta found plates, cups, and cutlery on the shelves, rinsed and dried them, and set the table. They chatted as they worked, slicing strawberries and pouring milk, and although Rosa felt somewhat awkward moving about the unfamiliar kitchen as if it were her own, the customary rituals of tending to her family reassured her, as if nurturing those she loved performed a transformative magic upon her surroundings, changing any setting, however strange and new or unanticipated, into a home.

The polenta was as delicious as Guiditta had promised, the strawberries fresh and sweet. The children ate heartily, chattering about what the day might bring, well rested and cheerful despite staying up so late the previous night. Occasionally, Rosa and Lars exchanged amused glances from opposite ends of the table, and at certain moments it almost felt as if they were a family, complete and contented in a home of their own. Wistfully Rosa realized that it was only an illusion, and like all illusions it could not last, but that did not mean she would not take what consolation from it she could.

After breakfast, Marta washed the dishes while Ana dried and Rosa swept the floor, and soon they were ready to follow the sunlit path through the vineyard up to the Cacchiones' grand redwood residence. When they arrived, they found Vince and his older brother, Dominic, in the yard between the garage and the barn, peering beneath the hood of a Mack AC delivery truck with "Cacchione Vineyards" painted in large, white script letters on both sides of the covered bed. The impression Rosa had formed of the Cacchiones' eldest son when they met at the party was that he was as serious as Vince was merry, although according to Francesca, the brothers were equally hardworking and responsible. Though Dominic was only twenty-two, he had been married for more than a year to Mabel, a vintner's daughter from Healdsburg, and the happy couple had made their home within the Cacchione residence and were expecting their first child. The younger Cacchiones were playing tag nearby in a clearing framed by walnut trees, and after promising to look after Miguel, Rosa's girls ran off to join them. Miguel trotted off happily, holding one of Marta's hands and one of Ana's, sometimes lifting his stout little legs so they would swing him in the air between them.

Dominic told Rosa and Lars that his parents were in the kitchen lingering over breakfast and that they should go on inside. They found their new employers seated at the corner of a large wooden trestle table, papers spread out before them, forgotten cups of coffee pushed aside and growing cold. The snatches of conversation Rosa overheard from the doorway seemed hushed and earnest, and when they broke off at the sound of the door closing behind Rosa and Lars, the strain on their faces was evident. Even so, Guiditta's smile was genuine and warm as she rose to greet them and offer them coffee. They gladly accepted, and as Guiditta took two cups from the drying rack beside the sink and filled them with a dark, strong brew, Dante gathered up the papers with a sigh and tapped them into a neat pile.

"Bills," Guiditta said, handing the steaming cups to Lars and Rosa and gesturing to the cream and sugar on the table. She emptied her and her husband's cups into the sink and refilled them.

"You may have come in the nick of time," Dante said, thanking his wife with a smile as she handed him his refreshed cup. "I'm considering ripping out our vines and planting apricot trees in their place."

"Surely not all of them," protested Rosa. The long, level plains would seem barren and desolate in the wake of the destruction of so much beauty, no matter what was planted in its place.

"No, not all," he admitted with a rueful grimace. "I exaggerate the need. These vines have flourished here since before I was born. My grandfather planted them, and it would be like tearing out my own heart to uproot them. But if we're going to keep this land in the family for generations to come, we'll need to find another source of revenue." He nodded appreciatively to Lars. "That's why, when Dr. Reynolds mentioned your experience growing apricots in Oxnard, I jumped at the chance to take you on. This morning I'd like you to walk the fields with me. I've picked out a few places where I might establish an apricot orchard, and I'd like your opinion on which is the best."

"I'd be glad to help," said Lars, taking a sip of coffee. "But I'm not confident apricots would thrive in this climate."

"We won't know unless we try," Dante replied. "It's an experiment, and one that might fail, but if it succeeds, eventually it'll pay for itself and then some."

Rosa glanced from Dante to Guiditta as she stirred cream and sugar into her cup. "I gather that growing wine grapes isn't as profitable as winemaking once was."

"It was, at first," Guiditta said. "In the early days of Prohibition the demand for wine grapes was so overwhelming that some of our neighbors enjoyed their most profitable seasons ever."

"As did we," said Dante. "But our success encouraged many other growers to jump in, not only in the Sonoma and Napa valleys but elsewhere in California and in Europe as well. Overproduction led to a glut in the market, and prices plummeted."

Guiditta shook her head, frowning. "Grapes have been left to rot on the vine because it would cost more to hire pickers to harvest them than a grower could sell them for."

"Not here, though," Lars remarked. "Your vines look exceptionally well tended to me."

"They are. I couldn't mistreat my vines any more than I could hurt one of my own children." Dante took a deep drink of coffee, set his cup on the table, and fixed it with a distant, brooding stare. "My grandfather came to this country in the middle of the last century, beckoned, like so many others, by the promise of gold in the California hills. But he was clever, and he soon realized that most of the ambitious young men who toiled in the mountains and streams would have nothing to show for their adventures later in life except for entertaining stories, debts, and regret. He chose a more reliable, though less romantic, path to earning his fortune."

"Making wine?" Rosa guessed.

Dante grinned and shook his head. "Not yet. Instead of buying picks and pans and surefire maps to secret mother lodes, he bought a few acres of arable land and grew fresh vegetables to sell to the miners."

Eventually, Dante told them, his grandfather saved enough money to buy thirty of the acres the family cultivated to that day. He cleared the land, cutting down enormous redwood trees and tall oaks. He wrestled stubborn stumps from the ground with chains and horses, and he carved furrows in the soil with a plow borrowed from a sympathetic countryman who had settled in the Sonoma Valley a decade earlier. His parents had grown Zinfandel and had made their own wines in their small village in the hills above Rome, and when Dante's grandfather observed how well grapes thrived in the soil and climate of Sonoma County, he built trellises, bought cuttings from the Franciscan priests at the Mission San Francisco Solano de Sonoma, and cultivated more than a thousand grapevines. In the years that followed, he planted more vines, built himself a sturdy redwood cabin in a picturesque walnut grove by a cool, fresh creek, married the kindest and wisest daughter of his generous neighbor, and created wines of such magnificent flavor and depth that they were coveted by the finest hotels and restaurants in the growing metropolis of San Francisco, sixty miles to the south.

"When my grandfather was ready to retire, my father took over the vineyard. In time he added twenty acres to the property and built this house." Dante gestured appreciatively to the four walls around them and ceiling above. "Our vineyard thrived, but not without toil and hardship. The worst trial struck in 1892."

"A plague of phylloxera," said Guiditta with a shudder, crossing herself as if to ward

285

off another such disaster.

"A voracious, relentless pest," said Dante with distaste. "A louse that feeds on the sap of grapevine roots, poisoning them with every bite so they cannot heal. Starved of nourishment, the vines become stunted and deformed and prone to fungal infection. My grandfather — and most of the other wine-makers throughout the valley — were forced to tear out their vines and replant resistant stock, at an enormous cost."

"Not only in money but also in time," Guiditta added, crossing the kitchen to stand beside her husband's chair. "Grape-vines need at least three, perhaps as many as five, years to establish themselves and come to full bearing. In all that time, there could be no harvest, no crush, no winemak-ing. As you can imagine, it was quite a setback, but the Cacchione family endured it."

Dante inhaled deeply, his mouth twisting into a bitter, angry frown. "To think my father and grandfather saw our winery through that hardship, only for me to lose it now, all because of a stroke of a Washington bureaucrat's pen."

"You haven't lost it yet," Guiditta re-minded him earnestly, placing a hand on his shoulder. "And we won't."

Dante patted her hand. "From your lips to God's ears, *cara mia*." To Lars and Rosa, he added, "You have to understand, even when the debate grew heated, none of us thought Prohibition would come to pass. It was all politics, just so much noise and chatter, the Wets and the Drys and their ceaseless arguments."

"Early on, the Drys insisted that Prohibition was necessary due to the wartime emergency," Guiditta said, sitting down beside her husband. She gestured for Rosa and Lars, still standing by the counter, to join them at the table. "To conserve grain for the soldiers."

"Apparently no one told them grapes are not grain," said Dante in disgust.

"When the Great War ended, we thought that would be the end of it," Guiditta continued. "No war, no wartime emergency, no need to conserve grain — or grapes. We couldn't have been more wrong."

"As for the temperance movement, we didn't consider ourselves the target of their complaints. They condemned saloons and all the vices they spawned, not —" Dante gestured to his own kitchen table, his dark eyebrows drawing together. "Not what we do here, providing a family with a good glass of wine to enjoy with their supper. How could our livelihood, our tradition, our craft, go from being a time-honored profession to a criminal act in a single day?"

Guiditta patted his hand and regarded him with affectionate sympathy. "When the law passed," she explained to Rosa and Lars, "we were taken aback, but we assumed Prohibition might last a few months, perhaps a year at most, and then lawmakers would see the folly of it and everything would return to normal."

"That was where you went wrong," said Lars dryly. "I try never to assume too much common sense on the part of lawmakers."

Dante let out a dry laugh. "That wasn't the only place we went wrong. Our customers, though, they knew better. In the weeks leading up to the moment the act would become law —" He shook his head, still amazed by the memory. "People desperate to buy wine came at us like — like ants on a watermelon at a picnic. Like bees on a honeycomb."

"They wanted to go into Prohibition with fully stocked wine cellars," said Guiditta. "Local folks bought all they could afford, or as much as they could carry off in their cars and wagons."

"The roads between the Sonoma and Napa valleys and San Francisco were choked with delivery trucks," Dante added. "They sped off to hotels and restaurants and homes of the wealthy with full loads and returned empty. It was a mad dash just to keep up, and the whole time we kept one eye on the calendar. We sold as much wine as we could as the deadline approached."

"And all the while," Guiditta said, shaking her head at their folly, "we hoped and prayed that something would happen at the last minute to spare us — the wartime emergency would be declared over, or common sense would prevail, something."

Rosa knew well that deliverance had not come. She thought back to the beginning of Prohibition — January 17, 1920 — and remembered wondering if Lars, whom she had not seen in six and a half years, would at last find the sobriety that had eluded him when they were young and in love. Later, on the rare occasions when she had considered the new law, she had felt relief for the families who would be spared the tragic consequences of alcoholism and wistful regret for herself and Lars, for whom Prohibition had come too late. But by that time she had already lost John Junior and Angela, gentle Maria was approaching her first birthday, and she was six months pregnant with Pedro. John had turned bitterly cruel, and she and her mother and the children had been reduced to furtive visits on the mesa. She could be forgiven, she hoped, for not sparing much worry for the unfortunate winemakers whose lives had been overturned by Prohibition.

"What about the wine you couldn't sell before the law went into effect?" asked Lars, with a note of irony Rosa suspected the Cacchiones did not know him well enough to detect. "What happened to it? Did you have to break open the casks and pour the wine out onto the ground?"

Even as she observed Dante wince at the very thought, Rosa remembered the barrel of wine at the harvest dance and knew that Lars was well aware that the Cacchiones had not destroyed all of their wine. Dante and Guiditta exchanged a look, and after a long moment, Guiditta nodded, agreeing to an unspoken question from her husband. "Come," Dante said, abruptly rising. "I'll show you."

Quickly they finished their coffee and followed Dante and Guiditta outside. They crossed the yard, where the two brothers still wrestled with engine parts beneath the hood of the truck and the younger children ran and shouted beneath the walnut trees. They followed a cobblestone path to the low, elegant redwood building Rosa had glimpsed through the foliage as they had gone by in the wagon on their way to the cabin the previous day. Passing beneath one of the archways, they entered through the front double doors into a single large room where all manner of winemaking implements and trellises in need of repair sat idle, although someone apparently cared about them enough to make sure they did not gather dust. Dante led the way down a broad staircase into the cool depths of a cavernous room that seemed larger than the structure above it. The tan earthen walls of the subterranean cavern were smooth and straight, curving elegantly where they bowed to meet the high ceiling. They were lined with large oak barrels arranged on their sides upon thick, solid shelves, but as Rosa drew closer, she saw that they were trapped behind a cage of chicken wire that ran from the floor to the ceiling.

Dante swept his arm in a broad arc. "This, my friends, is what happened to our wine." He strode across the floor and struck a heavy padlock that bound two sections of the wire barricade together, sending it swinging back and forth with a rasping complaint as it scraped against a sharp, protruding edge. "Prohibition officers took inventory of our wine before locking us down, and each year we have to pay for a federal permit to keep our wine in storage. You might say we're buying the privilege of not profiting from our years of backbreaking labor and patience."

Frowning thoughtfully, Lars tested the thickness of the chicken wire with his fingers. "Padlock or no, this shouldn't be too difficult to get around."

"Perhaps not," said Guiditta, tucking a loose strand of dark hair back into her bun with a sigh, "but agents come around from time to time, unannounced, to check that not a single gallon has gone missing. If they discovered we'd broken the law, we would lose everything."

"We might lose everything anyway," said Dante grimly.

"We won't," said Guiditta, more firmly than before. She walked along the row of entrapped barrels, marking off several dozen with the span of her hands. "These casks contain our finest quality wines," she told Rosa and Lars. "These vintages can age for ten to thirty years, becoming ever more palatable and therefore more valuable. This is our long-term investment. Our future lives within these casks." She turned to the remaining barrels, the vast majority. "These barrels — well, worrying over them has given me many a sleepless night. Their quality will last three to eight years, but after that, the wine will turn. It will be sour and utterly worthless, unsuitable even to make vinegar."

"What about those barrels over there?" asked Rosa, indicating a few barrels shelved on the far wall, unencumbered by wire.

"Empty." Then Dante promptly corrected himself. "Empty of wine. Since we can't fill them with new wine, we fill them with water instead, to prevent the wood from going bad."

"So then you do have some hope," Rosa said, "that someday you'll be allowed to make wine again."

"Some of your friends continue to make wine now," remarked Lars. "I met one of them last night — Paulo Del Bene. He makes sacramental wines for churches and synagogues. Couldn't you as well?"

Dante folded his arms over his chest and shrugged as if he had considered doing so many times. "Perhaps if I had followed my good friend Paulo's example early on I could have, but we don't make the type of wine churches and synagogues prefer. It would be an enormous expense to replant my stock and wait years for the vines to mature. I've already replaced some of my Zinfandel vines with Alicante Bouschet. The wine they make isn't as good, but the skins of the berries are thicker and so they're less likely to bruise or rot during shipment. I can't tear out those vines, since those are the grapes that are selling, and it would break my heart to uproot my best Zinfandels. The older those vines get, the deeper into the earth their roots go. They draw up minerals from deep within the earth and give my wine its magnificent flavor." He shook his head. "I can't uproot any more vines to plant something new. I just couldn't."

"Dante would also have to apply for a special license through the Prohibition Department and receive approval from the church," said Guiditta. "Paulo Del Bene and the bishop are good friends, so that wasn't an obstacle for him."

"Obstacles," said Dante. "I'll give you obstacles. Winemakers with sacramental wine permits already produce more wine than the entire country's churches could possibly use, and they all have a head start on us. Even if we started today, the effort would likely bankrupt us before we earned a single dollar from sacramental wines."

Lars shook his head in sympathy. "Doesn't

sound like you have a lot of options."

"I don't want options. This is the wine I make," said Dante with fierce, protective pride, spreading his arms as if he would embrace all the barrels arranged before them. "This is the wine my father and grandfather made. This is what I know." He fixed Lars and Rosa with a piercing, challenging look. "You tell me. How can my life's work suddenly be wrong when it was never wrong before?"

Rosa had no words for him. She could only shake her head in helpless, stricken sympathy.

"Scores of vineyards in the Sonoma and Napa valleys have closed since that law was enacted." Dante gazed at the wire-bound casks as if they were a beloved burden. "Thousands of grape growers and winemakers have lost their livelihoods. But it's not only us. Think of it — jobs for migrant pickers are scarce. Brewers, bottle makers, coopers, hops growers, wagon drivers, deliverymen, and on and on — all have been thrown out of work. We may be next."

"We won't be," said Guiditta softly, but with less conviction than before. "We'll find a way."

Rosa wished she could offer them words of comfort, but they needed help, not cheerful platitudes. Lars was right. The Cacchiones had indeed been hiding something — their uncertainty, their fears, their precarious toehold on the edge of bankruptcy.

"You understand now, don't you?" asked Guiditta, taking her husband's arm. "Our harvest dance last night wasn't a celebration of our abundance, although of course it's always proper to be grateful for one's blessings. It was a commemoration of our very survival. We're still here. Despite the attempts to ruin us, we're still here, and we'll still be here when this madness ends."

Dante's eyes shone as he placed his hands on her cheeks, gazed at her with naked admiration, and kissed her full on the lips. It was such a tender, intimate moment that Rosa had to look away.

"Ma," a young man shouted down the stairs from above.

Dante and Guiditta separated. "Yes, Mario," Guiditta called back.

"There's a bunch of tourists out here, on their way home from one of them resorts on the river. They want to know if they can gather some walnuts for the drive back to the city."

"One of *those* resorts," Guiditta corrected automatically. "Why, yes, of course. Fetch them some baskets and show them the way.

I'll be right there." She turned a look of resignation upon Lars and Rosa. "And this is how we'll stay afloat until Washington comes to its senses."

Rosa managed an encouraging nod in response, but she had balanced the books for the Grand Union Hotel back in the Arboles Valley, and it was obvious that the Cacchione Vineyard was a far more complex venture. She doubted the sale of a few pounds of walnuts to passing tourists would suffice to keep it afloat.

Rosa accompanied Guiditta to the walnut grove while Dante and Lars set out to inspect the different sites Dante was considering for an apricot orchard. After the tourists paid for their walnuts and set off in a roadster that bore an unsettling resemblance to John's, Guiditta showed Rosa around the kitchen, garden, and outbuildings where in the weeks to come she would spend her days working side by side with the Cacchione family.

Rosa soon realized that she and Lars were very fortunate that Dr. Reynolds had recommended them to the Cacchiones, because she couldn't have asked for a more ideal place to live and work while Ana and Miguel underwent treatment. She liked the

Cacchiones, from the youngest to the eldest, and the beautiful vineyard was as pleasant as their company. Although the days were long, the work was no more difficult than what she was accustomed to — if anything, the routine farm chores seemed easier because they were shared, and she no longer toiled in isolation. She enrolled the girls in school and started sewing quilts for the children's beds and turning the cabin into a proper home. Lars began planning the apricot orchard on a sunny hillside on the northern hills of the property, but he also worked alongside Dante and his sons in the vineyard, determined to learn all he could about cultivating a crop very different from what he knew.

Every Wednesday morning, Rosa, Ana, and Miguel rode the train into San Francisco to meet with Dr. Reynolds. Ana grumbled about missing school and spent the entire ride sitting with her knees pulled up to her chest and her nose in a book, but Miguel enjoyed the trips, peering out the windows to watch the passing scenery and studying the train's features with awestruck fascination. With each examination, Dr. Reynolds noted marked improvement in their health, with one exception — the day after Alegra Del Bene brought her young son over to play, and the well-meaning, generous boy shared half of his jelly sandwich with his new friend. Dr. Reynolds assured Rosa that the effects of Miguel's lapse would not last, as long as he resumed the banana diet immediately. "Eat only what your mother says you may. No more mistakes," he warned his patient, and Miguel held his tummy and nodded solemnly.

One week their examinations ended early, so Rosa decided to visit Mrs. Phillips before catching the train back to Santa Rosa. Their former landlady greeted them with delight and marveled at how healthy and robust Ana and Miguel had become since she had last seen them. She served the children bananas sliced on pretty china plates and milk in teacups, offering scones and tea with honey to Rosa. As they chatted, Rosa noted with some satisfaction that not once did Mrs. Phillips refer to them as "poor little dears."

As they were leaving, Rosa spotted a newspaper folded on an armchair in the parlor and on an impulse asked if she might borrow it to read on the train. "I'd like to see if there's any news from home," she explained.

Mrs. Phillips clucked sympathetically. "You must miss it terribly. Well, from the look of things —" She paused to beam at the children. "They'll finish their treatment soon and you'll be able to return home. Of course you may take the paper. Would you like me to keep an eye out for stories about Oxnard from now on? I'd be happy to save them for you until your next visit."

Rosa gladly accepted her offer — adding, as an aside, that she had family in the Arboles Valley and would be interested in news from there too — and promised to stop by again soon. Tucking the paper into her coat pocket and taking each of the children by the hand, she bade Mrs. Phillips good-bye, promising to bring her some walnuts on her next visit.

The excitement of the day had worn out Miguel, and he slept most of the ride home, resting his head on Rosa's lap while she read the newspaper above him. As she skimmed the pages, a bold headline suddenly caught her eye: "Attempted Murder Charges Against Postmaster Dismissed."

Her heart plummeted. *"Dios mío."*

"What is it, Mamá?" asked Ana.

"Nada, mija," she said, shifting the paper so Ana would not glimpse her father's name and demand the truth. Dubious, Ana returned her attention to her book as Rosa read the article, her hands trembling so much that the words on the page blurred

and ran together. Despite the presence of irrefutable witnesses and the testimony of shooting victim Henry Nelson, prosecutors had been forced to drop attempted murder charges against John Barclay due to a technicality. He remained in custody on charges of racketeering, but his lawyer said he intended to plead not guilty and was confident that he would prevail in court.

Rosa carefully folded the paper and set it aside as if nothing were amiss, and then she held herself perfectly still, staring straight ahead, scarcely able to breathe. A technicality. There was no question that John had shot Henry and had threatened to kill Lars, and yet if not for the contraband the officers had found in his hayloft, he would be a free man. Her blood ran cold with shock and fear, and not even the welcome news that Elizabeth's husband was evidently on the mend offered her any solace.

Until that moment, Rosa had not realized how much her hopes for a safe and happy future for her children had depended upon John being confined to prison for the rest of his life.

She dared not speak and allow her shaking voice to betray her fear and disbelief. Ana too was quiet, but Rosa assumed she was engrossed in her book until, just as they passed through the El Verano station, she marked her place with her finger and closed her book on her lap. "Mamá?"

"Yes, *mija?*"

"We aren't really going home after Miguel and I are better, are we?"

Rosa considered her words carefully. "No, *mija,* we aren't."

"Are we ever going back?"

Rosa did not see how they would ever be safe to do so. "I don't think so. I'm sorry."

"No, that's fine. I don't want to," Ana said quickly, opening her book again. "I like the cabin better. My new teacher's nicer than my old teacher. I like the Cacchiones and I like Mr. Jorgensen."

"I like them too." And she desperately wanted to keep them out of danger.

She put her arm around her daughter's shoulders and Ana snuggled up closer to her, smiling with contentment as she lost herself in her book again. The train steamed ahead, but their destination no longer felt like a safe haven to Rosa.

She inhaled deeply and stroked Miguel's hair, willing herself to remain calm. She could not allow herself to be swept away by the flood of fear that crashed down upon her. She must hold fast and let it wash over her and back out to sea, as she had done before when danger and despair threatened.

When Isabel died, Rosa might have succumbed to that undertow of grief were it not for her children, whose needs outweighed her own.

Like their siblings before them, Ana and Maria had seen every doctor in the Arboles Valley to no avail, and John refused to allow Rosa to take them beyond the valley. Frustrated, Rosa nonetheless remained undaunted. She remembered that a guest had left behind a Los Angeles business directory at the Grand Union Hotel, so she borrowed it from Mrs. Diegel and wrote to every doctor listed, describing the children's symptoms and begging them for advice.

One day, she was out back weeding the garden and puzzling out how she might obtain similar directories for Oxnard and Santa Barbara when she heard a car approaching the front of the house. "Marta, please watch your sisters and the baby until I get back," she called, brushing the soil from her hands and glancing into the bassinet where Pedro slept peacefully. Tucking a stray lock of hair back underneath her kerchief, she rounded the corner of the adobe and spotted the Jorgensens' Model T parked near the barn. The driver emerged, tall and thin, with fair hair visible beneath his hat. For a moment she wondered who Oscar's new hired hand was; a heartbeat later, she recognized Lars.

Riveted in place, she watched, scarcely able to breathe, as he crossed the gravel driveway to come to her, his worn boots kicking up clouds of dust.

He looked weather-beaten, thin and weary, as if he had aged far more than the seven years that had passed since she had last seen him. When he was still a couple of yards away, he halted, removed his hat, and regarded her somberly. "My condolences on the loss of your mother," he said, his voice rougher than she remembered and yet achingly familiar. "I came as soon as I heard."

Where had he been, she wondered, that it had taken six weeks for word to reach him? Or had he gone so far abroad that he had needed all that time for the journey home? "I'm sure your family was happy to see you," she managed to say. As far as she knew, Lars had not returned to the Arboles Valley since his departure seven years before, not once. In all the time he had been away, the Jorgensens had never sent him a letter through the Arboles Valley Post Office, nor had she seen his familiar handwriting on any envelope she had sorted into the Jorgensens' mail bundle. Either Lars and his family had not exchanged a single letter throughout his long absence, or they had found another way to correspond, one that did not require the Barclays' involvement.

"They were, and I was glad to see them," Lars replied. "How are your father and Carlos bearing up?"

"I don't know." Their eyes met for a moment, but Rosa quickly dropped her gaze. "They don't speak to me." She was surprised his brother had not told him. Everyone in the valley knew of the longstanding estrangement, even if they misunderstood the cause.

"I'm sorry." Frowning, Lars put his hat back on and eyed the rye fields, thick and golden beneath the warm August sun. "Where's your husband?"

"At the hardware store, picking up a part for the harvester." She took a deep breath to marshal her courage, and as she exhaled, she said in a rush, "Do you want to meet Marta?"

Immediately Lars returned his gaze to Rosa's face. "Marta's your eldest."

Rosa bit her lips together and nodded.

"Yes," he said. "I'd like that very much."

Rosa led him around to the back of the

house. Near the garden, Marta knelt beside the bassinet, tickling Pedro's chin with a long blade of grass gone to seed. Even from afar Rosa heard his happy squeals and saw his plump legs kick with delight. Nearby, Ana and Maria lay on their backs gazing up at the sky, inventing names and histories for the aerial creatures they spied in the clouds. Marta looked up as they approached, beaming and beautiful, and she tilted her head in friendly curiosity at the sight of Lars.

"That's Marta," Rosa murmured, urging Lars forward with a nod. He cleared his throat and continued on beside her until they reached the garden. "Girls, this is Mr. Jorgensen."

"No, he isn't," said Marta. "I've seen Mr. Jorgensen at school when he comes for Annalise, and this isn't him."

"This must be the other Mr. Jorgensen," said Ana, studying him. "Not the grandpa, the one who went away."

Lars nodded. "That's right. The Mr. Jorgensen you know is Oscar Jorgensen, my brother."

"How do you do?" asked Ana politely, standing up, straightening her dress, and offering him her hand to shake.

Rosa would have sworn she saw the corners of Lars's mouth quirk in a smile as he shook her hand formally. "I'm doing fine, thank you." He nodded to Maria, shyly peeping up at him from her seat in the grass, and offered his hand to Marta. "You must be Marta."

"How did you know my name?" she asked, smiling as she shook his hand.

"Your mother told me." He closed his other hand around hers. "I've wanted to meet you for a very long time."

Marta's brow furrowed in puzzlement. "Really? Why?"

"This is Ana," Rosa broke in, "and Maria, and the baby is Pedro." She stooped over to tickle his tummy to cover the tears that suddenly sprang into her eyes. Straightening, she said, "I should fetch your mail so you can be on your way."

Lars tore his gaze away from his daughter. "Of course, yes, I should take the mail." He smiled briefly at Marta and squeezed her hand before releasing it. "It was nice meeting you children."

"It was nice meeting you too," said Marta, and Ana chimed in her agreement, while Maria covered her eyes with her hands and watched him through her fingers and Pedro waved a chubby fist at his sisters.

Quickly Rosa led Lars back around to the front of the house, where he waited outside while she went to retrieve the Jorgensens' mail. She had so much to tell him, so much to ask, but she was afraid — afraid of what he might say, afraid of what John might do if he came home and found Lars there.

"She's a beautiful girl," Lars said when she returned outside, his voice thick with emotion. "You've done well with her — with all of them — you and John both have."

"Thank you," Rosa replied stiffly. Was this his way of telling her that she had done the right thing in marrying John? She never would have expected him to make such an admission, and she doubted he would have if he knew the sort of man his old friend and rival had become. "I've buried two other children, you know — a son and a daughter."

She did not know what had prompted her to say that, but as she felt her face flush in embarrassment, Lars nodded, his expression mirroring her heartache. "I know, and I'm sorry." Suddenly he reached out and placed his hand on her shoulder, a gesture of understanding, of brotherly compassion. "I'm sorry for all the losses you've suffered, and for any unhappiness that you might have endured on my account. If there's anything I can do to make things right, you know you only have to ask."

Rosa pressed her lips together and nodded. "Thank you." Briefly she lay her hand upon his, and then she stepped away, and his hand fell to his side. He studied her for a moment, then nodded and turned away, striding back to his brother's car with the mail bundle tucked under his arm.

"Lars," she called after him as he opened the car door. "How long will you be visiting?"

"It's no visit," he replied. "I'm home to stay."

A hundred questions sprang to her lips, but she held them back. "John goes to the train station every Monday at noon to pick up the mail," she said instead. He had resumed his regular schedule shortly after Isabel died. "You could come back sometime, if you want. If you'd like to see Marta."

In response, Lars nodded and climbed into the car. A few minutes later he was gone, leaving behind only a faint, low cloud of yellow-brown dust lingering above the road — and questions, so many questions, for which she ached to know the answers.

For the next four days, Rosa wondered with a mixture of hope and dread whether Lars would return. When Monday noon came and John departed for the train station, she distractedly began and abandoned several chores, checking the clock often, straining her ears for the sound of a car approaching, and peering out one window and then another just in case her ears had deceived her. Finally, disgusted with herself, she put a drowsy Pedro down for his nap, sent the girls out to play, pulled her hair back into a kerchief, and began the weekly laundry, dragging the washtub into the sunshine before filling it so that she could enjoy the fair weather and keep an eye on the children while she worked. As soon as she was up to her elbows in soapsuds, she heard the clatter of the Jorgensens' Model T coming up the drive.

Quickly she snatched up a towel and dried her arms, leaving John's filthy overalls to soak in the tub. She waited until Lars parked the car before crossing the yard to meet him. "Come for the mail?" she asked, as if he were any other neighbor.

He nodded and took a small paper sack from his coat pocket. "I brought a little something for the girls too. Pedro is probably still too young to have any, but I'll let you be the judge of that."

Her heart leapt as he handed her the bag, for even before she opened it, she knew what it held. The sweet fragrance and bright color of the dried apricots vividly illuminated long-shadowed memories, and for a moment she was a child in the schoolyard again.

"Go on," Lars urged as she closed her eyes, inhaled deeply, and sighed, enjoying the familiar mouthwatering scent. "There's plenty for you too, and more where that came from."

Smiling her thanks, Rosa took an apricot from the bag and savored the delicious sweetness. "Better than candy," she said, repeating their old joke, and Lars grinned. Curious, the girls abandoned their play in the shade of the orange trees and hurried over to see what was going on. When they learned that Lars had brought them a treat, they thanked him happily and clamored around Rosa for a taste. Rosa allowed them to have two pieces each, but decided to save the rest for another day.

"I'll bring more next week," Lars promised, with a questioning look for Rosa. She nodded, unable to keep from smiling as she turned and went inside for his mail bundle.

His visit lasted all of ten minutes, but it brightened her day, and his promise to return gave her something to look forward to throughout the week whenever she was feeling especially exhausted and worried and lonely. The following Monday, Lars arrived earlier and stayed longer, and to the girls' delight, he remembered his promise to bring them more apricots. When the girls ran off to play, carrying the paper sack as if it held a hard-won treasure, Rosa and Lars lingered in the yard, chatting about the girls, the weather, and the plentiful harvests both families were in the midst of bringing in. When he left, Rosa was sorry to see him go, and sorrier still that she had not been bold enough to ask him where he had spent the previous seven years, why he had returned to the Arboles Valley, what had become of his inheritance, and how he was, really, behind the perfunctory greetings they had offered one another.

Week after week, Lars returned every Monday without fail, with apricots for the children and kind, gentle words for Rosa. Even after school resumed in September and he no longer had the opportunity to see Marta, his visits continued. Eventually, tentatively, their conversations evolved from the safe niceties of acquaintances into the shared confidences of friends. At last Rosa learned that in his seven-year, self-imposed exile, Lars had traveled throughout the western United States, settling down briefly in Los Angeles, Portland, Seattle, Denver, and Albuquerque, with shorter stays in smaller cities throughout California. He had spent the profits from the sale of his inheritance on several failed business ventures and had returned home penniless and, like the Prodigal Son, had thrown himself upon the mercy of his family. Oscar, who in Lars's absence had married and had accepted responsibility for the day-to-day operations of the ranch from their ailing, aged father, welcomed his brother home with open arms and hired him as his foreman. Unlike his biblical predecessor, then, Lars had not been restored to his birthright, but he had three square meals a day, a roof over his head, the company of his family, and gainful, worthwhile employment he had failed to appreciate in his youth.

As for his persistent struggles with alcohol, he professed that he had lost all taste for gin after drinking himself nearly to death "that one night back in November 1912," as he carefully referred to the night shortly after Rosa's wedding when he had pounded on the front door of the adobe and begged her to run away with him. Prohibition made alcohol more difficult to come by and helped him stay on the straight and narrow. He admitted that even though he had remained sober for eight years, he was wary of testing his resolve, so he would not allow himself even a tiny sip of liquor lest he fall back into his old, destructive ways. Rosa was glad to hear it, but her congratulations were tinged with melancholy. She could not help wondering how differently their lives might have turned out if only he had found sobriety eight years earlier.

"Why did you come back?" Rosa asked him one Monday in early December when cool rains fell and they sat in the kitchen drinking coffee while Marta was at school and Ana read her younger siblings a story in the front room.

"I heard your mother died," he said, mildly surprised, for he had told her so upon his first visit.

"After seven years away, you came back just to express your condolences?" Rosa asked, skeptical.

"I thought you might need some comfort." He hesitated, and then he shrugged. "I didn't intend to stay, but my mother and Oscar talked me into it."

She watched him for a long moment in silence as he absently stirred his coffee. "I'm glad they did."

He smiled briefly, set down his spoon, and reached across the table to squeeze her hand.

It was good to have a friend again, one

who didn't judge or condemn or doubt. With Lars she felt as if she were no longer the careworn farmwife and grieving mother but the bright young beauty with a promising future she had once been. They lingered at the table long after their cups were empty, until Lars noticed the time and said he had to be on his way. As reluctant as Rosa was for him to go, she was more unwilling for John to find him there, so after seeing Lars to the door, she hurried back to the kitchen to wash their cups and the coffeepot and return everything to its proper place.

But in her haste, she had not taken care to conceal all signs of Lars's visit. As she was preparing supper, John came into the kitchen carrying the paper sack of apricots Lars had brought for the girls to share. "I found this outside on the grass beneath the orange trees," John said, eyeing it before he tossed it on the table, his dark, thick brows drawn together in puzzlement. "It's half full of apricots."

"Only half full?" Rosa shook her head, heart pounding with apprehension she hoped he wouldn't detect. "I told the girls they could have one piece each. They were supposed to bring the bag back inside afterward. I hope this won't spoil their suppers."

"Where'd they come from?" John clarified since she had ostensibly missed the point. "They look like Jorgensen apricots."

"How so? I wouldn't know one apricot from another." That was no lie. "The Arboles Grocery carries dried apricots, and they're still reasonably priced this time of year." Also not a lie, since she didn't claim she had bought them there. "Why? Is something wrong?"

John had already turned to leave the kitchen. "Just don't let them waste food like that, leaving the sack outside on the ground. Money doesn't grow on trees."

"Of course. I'll tell them."

When he was gone, Rosa snatched up the bag and stashed it in the side cupboard. She would have to be more careful or she would lose her only friend.

A few days later, John was working in the barn when Betsy Frazier came by to mail a letter and pick up a package from Sears, Roebuck & Co. Rosa was busy in the kitchen canning orange marmalade, so John took care of Betsy, bringing the letter into the house and carrying the parcel out to her car. A few minutes later, Rosa happened to glance out the window and was surprised to find them still chatting. John tended to be abrupt with customers, sending them on their way and returning to the work they had interrupted as soon as their business was done.

After a bit she heard Betsy drive away, and then the front door opened and shut. "You'll never guess what Betsy Frazier just told me," John said as he entered the kitchen. "Lars Jorgensen is back in town."

"Yes, I know," Rosa replied nonchalantly. It would do no good to feign ignorance. "He returned in August. He stopped by to express his condolences."

"For what?"

"For the death of my mother, of course," said Rosa, incredulous.

John studied her, his eyes narrowing. "Why didn't you tell me he was here?"

Ladling marmalade into sterile jars, she managed a shrug. "You've forbidden me to mention his name."

"Don't get smart." When she made no reply, he pulled out a chair and sat down at the kitchen table. "He squandered his entire inheritance, and now he has to live off his brother's charity. How pathetic."

Rosa didn't know what to say, but John was watching her, waiting for a response. "I suppose there's a lesson in that for us all."

"What exactly am I supposed to learn

from Lars Jorgensen?"

"I — nothing." Rosa wished she had simply agreed with him that Lars was pathetic. That was all John had wanted to hear. It shouldn't matter that she didn't believe it. "I only meant that we should all take care not to repeat his mistakes."

Suddenly John bolted to his feet and seized her wrist. The ladle flew through the air and clattered upon the table, spattering John's face with hot marmalade. He swore, wiped his face with the back of his hand, and yanked her closer until their faces were only inches apart. "You burned me!"

"You grabbed my wrist. I didn't mean to —"

"How stupid do you think I am?" He struck her across the cheek.

"Please, John, it was an accident!"

Her protests died as he struck her again and again. Shielding her head with her arms, she backed away from him while he rained blows upon her. Suddenly her lower back collided with the edge of the sink and she crumpled to the floor, her legs bent painfully beneath her. He tangled his fingers in her hair and yanked her onto her side. "Don't try that again," he said, and stormed out of the kitchen.

Closing her eyes, Rosa lay on her side and

held perfectly still, listening, catching her breath, feeling the sting of each blow, tasting blood. Her cheek was damp against the linoleum, but from blood or tears or both, she would not know until she sat up, pulled herself to her feet, and examined her face in the mirror. But she was not ready to do so yet. Not yet.

"Mamá?"

Muffling a groan, she sat up as quickly as she could to find Ana, pale and tearful, lingering in the doorway. "Yes, *mija?*"

"Did Papa hit you?"

What a fool Rosa had been to think she could shield her children from John's ugly brutality. "Yes, Ana."

Her chin trembled. "He shouldn't do that."

"No, he shouldn't." Rosa tried to stand but fell back against the cabinet beneath the sink, head spinning. Ana flew to her side and helped her to her feet. Rosa thanked her and turned on the tap, splashed her face, and felt for loose teeth with her tongue. A sharp sting as the water hit her cheekbone, warning of a cut, and she gingerly probed it with her fingers. It was not deep, and perhaps it would not leave a scar.

Rosa managed a wan smile for Ana to assure her she was all right, and then sent her off to check on her napping siblings. Alone again, she cleaned herself up, put on a fresh apron, and finished the marmalade. Before long a dozen glass jars were lined up neatly on the counter, catching the afternoon sunlight that streamed through the windows and glowing as if they contained the essence of summer itself. Anyone who entered her kitchen at that moment would think she had spent a pleasant, industrious day in her happy home. How easily the truth was swept away like the bits of orange rind that had fallen to the floor.

When Marta came home from school, she gasped in shock at the sight of her mother's face. Rosa braced herself for questions, but the telltale signs of John's violence were easy enough for Marta to interpret. Rosa was thankful that Marta still had the presence of mind to be angered by John's cruelty, that Ana could still voice her conviction that he was wrong to hit her. If they ever accepted his behavior as normal, as something that they too should expect when they were old enough to marry, Rosa would have failed them utterly.

That evening, sore and exhausted, Rosa went off to bed as soon as she tucked in the children and kissed them good night. John woke her when he climbed beneath the covers a few hours later, and although she feigned sleep, he stroked her arm and kissed her neck so persistently that she couldn't pretend to sleep through it. She had dreaded and expected this. On days he hit her, his lovemaking started out gentle, almost as if he meant to apologize or comfort her, but it grew more aggressive as he went along, until for her it was always uncomfortable, sometimes painful. He wanted her to desire him, but through the years, every blow had driven out a little more of her affection for him until none remained. She couldn't bring herself to pretend she enjoyed his attention, but she would not humiliate and anger him by rejecting him. All she could do was submit, as her wedding vows bound her to do.

Her thoughts floated free of her bruised and aching body and she was back at the Jorgensen cabin again, safe and beloved in Lars's arms.

As the weekend passed, Rosa longed for Monday, but that morning she woke before dawn to the sound of retching from Pedro and Maria's bedroom. Quickly snatching up her robe, she raced next door only to find that Pedro had vomited all over himself, his quilt, and his crib. "It's all right, *mijo*," she murmured, carrying him to the kitchen, where she quickly undressed and bathed him before taking him back to his room. As soon as she had him in a clean diaper and pajamas, she heard the unmistakable sound of diarrhea. Pedro had quieted down, soothed by the comfort of Rosa's voice and the warm bath and soft, clean clothes, but at this he began to cry again. "It's okay," Rosa said as she changed his diaper a second time. "It's okay." But as she carried him around the front room, rocking him gently in her arms and whispering a lullaby, a too-familiar dread stole over her. Pedro was only six months old. The other children had been granted at least a year of good health. It was too soon, it was too soon, it was desperately unfair —

"Mamá?"

Rosa turned to find Marta padding into the front room, blinking and yawning. "Oh, Marta. Did Pedro wake you?" When Marta nodded, Rosa sighed and said, "He's quieting down now. Go back to bed, *mija.*"

Practical Marta promptly realized something Rosa had forgotten. "I'll hold him while you change his sheets," she said, crossing the room and reaching for her baby brother.

"You need your sleep," Rosa protested,

but she let Marta take him.

"So do you, Mamá." Marta cradled her baby brother and murmured soft baby talk to him in a sweet falsetto. "I'd rather hold you than clean up your crib, you know that, baby brother? You know why? Because you are a sweetie pie, but throw up is yucky."

Rosa managed a wan smile before hurrying off to strip Pedro's mattress, wipe down the bars of his crib, and put on fresh sheets. When she returned to the front room, Marta was sitting in her father's favorite chair, Pedro asleep in her arms. "Don't tell Papa," she implored as she carefully passed the baby to her mother.

"Never," promised Rosa solemnly. "Now, off to bed. Thank you, *mija.* I don't know how I'd manage without you."

Marta offered her a proud, drowsy smile and went to her room.

Rosa put Pedro down in his crib with a kiss and a whispered prayer, and then returned to her own bed, where John slept or pretended to. Listening and alert, she had trouble falling back asleep and doubted that she would be able to or even that she should. Hours later, she woke with a start to find the sun hidden behind gray storm clouds, John gone, and the aroma of brewing coffee in the air. Pedro must have slept the rest of the night through, she realized as she threw off the covers and hurried to him. She found Ana kneeling on the floor beside the crib, one arm extended through the bars so she could entertain her brother by dancing his teddy bear around. "He needs his diaper changed really, really badly," Ana reported when she heard her mother enter.

"I could tell from the hallway," Rosa replied, forcing a wry tone to disguise her worry. More diarrhea. She had seen this before and she knew what the rest of the day would hold, what the next months and years would bring, if God granted her baby so much time. She muffled a sob, asked Ana to go and set the table for breakfast, and changed Pedro's soiled diaper, silent tears of anguish slipping down her cheeks.

She carried him into the kitchen and set him in his high chair while she prepared breakfast. "Pedro was sick last night," she told John when he came in from the barn and pulled up a chair to the table.

He frowned, resigned, as she set his plate of bacon and eggs before him. "I guess we knew that was coming. The Lord giveth and the Lord taketh away." Rosa felt an iron hand constrict her throat. Without a word, she went to the icebox for butter for John's toast, and as the girls came to the table, she busied herself pouring them glasses of milk so she would not lash out at him.

Gray sheets of winter rain began to fall soon after Marta left for school and John for the barn, muttering about the broken tractor he had been unable to repair. Ana and Maria were listless and tired, despite her attempts to coax them into cheerfulness, so she told them stories and taught Ana how to make paper snowflakes out of old newspapers while Maria played with her doll. All the while Rosa struggled to feed Pedro, or at least get some milk or water into him, but everything came back up, and he went through two diapers an hour until he was utterly empty. He had a fever, which was unusual, but it did not seem dangerously high. She felt herself straining from the effort of maintaining a calm, reassuring demeanor for the children's sake while inside she felt as if she were gasping for breath and screaming for help in a silent void.

When John came in for lunch, she beseeched him to stop by Dr. Goodwin's house on his way to the train station to fetch the mail. "There's no sense in asking him to come by," John replied. "He'll only say it's the same thing the older kids get and he won't have anything for it."

He left for the station. Rosa put the children down for their afternoon naps, tidied the kitchen, and tried to calm her frantic thoughts with the familiar routine of household tasks, but nothing worked. A knock on the door startled her so much that she jumped, and when she answered it, she was surprised to see Lars standing there, rain dripping off the brim of his hat. In all her worry, she had forgotten that he might come.

"Rosa," he said, his brows drawing together in concern. "What's wrong?"

Everything was wrong, everything. "Pedro's sick," she said before words failed her. If she let out one drop of her anguish, she knew it would all come pouring out of her, and she could not risk unburdening herself with the children in the house where they might overhear. She tugged on her boots, which she had left by the front door after going out to feed the chickens. Stepping out into the rain, she shut the door, seized Lars's hand, and dashed through the mud to the barn. Once inside, she dropped his hand, sank heavily upon a bale of hay, and fought back tears, oblivious to her rain-soaked clothes and hair and the cold seeping into her bones.

"What is going on?" Lars demanded. He

shrugged out of his coat, shook the rain off of it, and draped it over her shoulders. "Good lord, what happened to your face?" Before she could try to conceal her bruises with her long hair, he sat down beside her and cupped her chin in his hand, turning her face toward him. Steadily his anger rose as he took in the cut on her cheekbone, her bruised jaw, the black eye. "Christ almighty, I'll beat the hell out of him for this."

"No." She turned her head to free her chin from his grasp. "You'll just make everything worse."

"Is this the first time he's hit you or does this happen a lot?"

"Lars, listen to me. That's not important now —"

"Like hell it isn't. Rosa, you shouldn't live this way. It's not good for you or the children."

He would never understand that she had no choice. "Pedro's sick," she blurted. "He's had diarrhea for half a day, and he throws up everything I try to feed him. It's too soon — it's not supposed to happen so soon! He's only six months old. I don't understand how this can be. Each of the other children thrived for at least a year before they fell ill, and it didn't strike Ana until she was five. He's still just a baby. Why is this happening now?"

"Rosa." Lars put his arms around her and she fell against his chest, sobbing. "Rosa, it's okay. It's going to be all right."

She shook her head, clutching his wool sweater with both hands. It was never going to be all right. She could not lose another child. Her heart couldn't withstand it.

"Rosa." His voice was calm in her ear. "Listen to me. Pedro has diarrhea and he's throwing up. Does he have a fever too?"

"Yes."

"Well, so does my niece."

Her breath caught in her throat. "What?"

"Annalise had to stay home from school today sick with the same stomach bug it sounds like Pedro has. A few of her friends had it last week. It's been working its way through the school all month."

Rosa took a deep, shuddering breath. Could it be as simple as that, a common illness spread from child to child? She desperately wanted to believe it, but fate was never kind to her children and spared them nothing. "Pedro doesn't go to school, and Marta isn't sick, so she didn't give him anything."

"Maybe, maybe not. Maybe Marta had a mild case, so mild that neither of you realized she was even sick. Maybe someone brought it here when he came to pick up his mail. Maybe I'm that someone, in which case, I'm terribly sorry."

"Do you really think that's all that's troubling him?" she asked, sitting up and blinking away her tears.

He nodded, his hands lingering on her shoulders. "Rosa, sometimes children just get sick. I'm sure he'll be fine in a few days. Don't be afraid and don't lose hope." Gingerly he brushed a lock of long dark hair away from her face, tucked it behind her ear, and traced the line of her cheekbone and jaw with a fingertip just above her skin so that she felt the warmth of his hand although he did not touch her cuts and bruises. "Pedro will be fine, but you, Rosa, you need to do something about this. This can't go on."

He leaned forward and kissed her gently on her cut cheek, and then near the tender bruise around her eye, and then he stroked her hair again and pulled her close to him so that her cheek rested on his chest. She could feel his heartbeat through his sweater, and as she closed her eyes, his arms slipped beneath the borrowed coat so that he could embrace her. She clung to him for a long moment, listening to the pounding of his heart, and then, still dizzy from relief and overwhelmed by a sudden rush of memories

— the touch of his hands, the scent of his skin — she raised her face to his and he met her with a kiss.

As the rain crashed upon the barn roof, the years fell away and Lars was holding her once more and loving her as he had so many nights so long ago when they had stolen away to the abandoned ranch cabin near the apricot orchard, when the promise of lifelong love seemed within reach, and grief and heartbreak were only indistinct shadows on the horizon.

Afterward, Rosa lay quietly within the circle of Lars's arms, his coat drawn over them for warmth. She could not believe what she had done.

"You should leave," she said softly, sitting up and brushing loose hay from her hair and dress. "I need to go inside too, to check on the children." They were probably still asleep, but she didn't want them to be afraid if they woke and called for her and she didn't answer.

He caught her by the arm as she rose and straightened her dress. "You aren't still worried about Pedro?"

"Oh, I'm worried about him. He's a sick little boy. But I'm not as terrified as I was before you came." She managed a tremulous smile and clasped his hand. "Thank you."

He stood, brushed hay from his clothes and hair, and gave his coat a good shake. "But you're still upset. What's wrong?"

"What's wrong?" she echoed, feeling tears gathering. "I'm married, Lars, and not to you."

"Not for lack of trying on my part."

"You didn't try hard enough when it counted," she reminded him. She felt flushed and dizzy. She pressed her icy hands to her burning cheeks and sat down heavily on the hay bale. "We can't ever tell John. He can't ever know."

Lars stared at her in disbelief. "You mean you're going to stay with him?"

"Of course," she said numbly. "We're married. He's my husband. What are you suggesting — divorce? You know I could never —"

"Rosa, you're miserable with him. He hits you."

"Only when he's upset." All the more reason for Lars to leave immediately. She stood too quickly, waited for the room to stop spinning, and started for the barn door. "I can't talk about this now. You have to go. Please."

Grimly he drew in a deep breath and nodded. Snatching up his hat from the floor, he wrapped his other arm around her waist and pulled her closer for a deep, soft, lingering kiss. Despite her apprehensions, she melted into him all over again. Then she pulled herself together and pushed him away. "You have to go."

"I'm coming back, you know."

"Next Monday." She squeezed his hand in farewell and then tore herself away. Perhaps by Monday she would know what to do. She couldn't think now, with Lars's smell on her skin and Pedro sick in the adobe and John on his way home. She couldn't believe what she had done. Already the past hour seemed like a dream, vivid in slumber only to fade upon waking.

She dashed to the adobe without looking back. She heard the roar of the car as Lars started the engine, the sounds muffled by the rainfall and fading as he drove away.

The week passed. As Lars had predicted, Pedro soon recovered and was restored to his usual sweet, happy self, but Rosa's relief was tempered by her memory of what she and Lars had done. Guilt stabbed at her at unexpected moments throughout the day. Another woman might have been secretly glad to betray an unkind, unloving husband, and consider the brief, illicit bliss small recompense for the pain and misery he inflicted upon her. She might look forward to another encounter the next time her husband was away, and she might even consider running away to be with her lover. But not Rosa. In Lars's arms she had remembered what it was like to be loved and cherished, and her heart ached with loss now that the fleeting moment had passed and would not come again. It could not. In one forbidden act she had broken every vow she had made to her husband, to God, and to herself.

It took all her courage to tell John that she needed him to watch the children while she went to confession, and that it could not wait, but he revered the church enough to accept that whatever was troubling her was between her and God. The young, red-haired priest who had been so kind when her mother had died a suspected suicide was stern and unyielding when it came to adultery. In the past, Rosa had left the confessional feeling freer, lighter, more capable of living a good Christian life, and eager to fulfill the penance assigned to her by the compassionate elderly priest. Now, many years and many failures later, his young successor made her feel disconsolate and alone.

Monday came. Soon after John left for the train station, Rosa watched through the kitchen window as the Jorgensens' Model T pulled up to the barn and came to a halt. Lars emerged with the customary paper sack in his hand and called out a greeting to Ana and Maria, who played with their dolls on a quilt beneath the orange trees. Lars tousled Ana's hair, tickled Maria beneath her chin, gave them the sack of dried apricots, and chatted with them for a bit before heading for the adobe. Rosa quickly left the window so she could meet him at the front door.

"Rosa," he greeted her simply, taking off his hat and studying her face as if he were looking for new injuries as well as clues to the workings of her mind.

"Come in. Please." She opened the door wider, breathless from anxiety. "I'll get your mail."

"There's no rush. How's Pedro?"

"Much better, thank you. He's napping at the moment." Blinking away tears, she retrieved the Jorgensens' bundle from those lined up against the wall and handed it to him. Instead of taking it from her, he placed his hands over hers so they both held it together.

"What have you decided?" he asked, his solemn gaze locked on hers.

"What happened last week can never happen again," she said in a rush.

He uttered a short, dry laugh as he took the bundle and tucked it under one arm. "Rosa, if I had known you had no intention of leaving your husband, it wouldn't have happened last week either."

"I can't leave him."

"Do you love him?"

She couldn't bear to say the words aloud, the admission that she had failed utterly in everything she had resolved to do when she married John and chose him to be her child's father. "He's my husband. The church forbids divorce."

"Because it's better for a woman to stay married to a man who hits her."

"I have nowhere to go. No way to provide for the children."

"Come live with me," he urged. "I'll take care of you and the children. We'll fix up the cabin and make it a proper home."

She laughed, helpless. Lars barely had enough to provide for himself, and he wouldn't have even that small portion except for the generosity of his brother. "I can't tear the children away from the only home they've ever known, and I can't live in sin with you."

"Then you and the children can have the cabin," he shot back, exasperated, "and I'll stay in the farmhouse with my family, same as now. The point is you can't stay here. Every week that I come by, I see that a little more of the Rosa I fell in love with has died. You're Catholic but Jesus wouldn't want you to be a martyr."

His tone made her bristle. "You don't know anything about my faith or what the Lord would or wouldn't want me to be. He would tell me to go forth and sin no more, and that is what I'm going to do."

Lars watched her for a long moment in silence. "I see you've made up your mind."

"I have, and I ask you to help me. Don't ever tempt me again. Please." Not with kisses, not with the promise of compassion and affection, not by offering her an escape from the purgatory she had created for herself. Enduring the life she had chosen, the life she had inflicted upon herself, and Lars, and John, and the children, was the only way she could atone for all the wrong she had done, including what she had done the week before in a moment of weakness that must never come again.

"I won't." The undercurrent of anger and frustration in Lars's voice was unmistakable. "I'll never again ask you to do anything you're not prepared to do, unless I think your life is in immediate danger. And then

336

you'd better believe I'm not going to stand by and let John kill you."

"He wouldn't do that."

"I'm not so sure." Lars frowned and shifted the mail bundle to his other arm. "I hope he proves me wrong. I'm going to keep coming here week after week, every Monday like clockwork, to see if you're okay. You don't have to talk to me if you don't want to, but know that I will be here."

"Of course I'll talk to you," she said, pained. He was her only friend. How could she not?

"Then I'll see you next week." He nodded good-bye and left. As her eyes filled with tears, she heard him call his farewells to the girls, start up the car, and drive away.

He kept his promise, showing up every Monday without fail through the Christmas holidays and into the New Year. At first their conversations were stilted, polite, perfunctory, but gradually their old affection and fondness and the habits of their long, shared history wore down the wall she had hastily built between them. They chatted fondly over cups of coffee at her kitchen table; he brought apricots for the children and city directories from places he traveled to on ranch business for her. If she sometimes felt a sad yearning for him or let her thoughts wander to what might have been, she admonished herself for entertaining such dangerous, careless ideas and put them aside.

She had wanted desperately to forget that illicit, fleeting moment in Lars's embrace, to put it behind her, to be a good and faithful wife from that day forward.

She had yet to discover how utterly impossible that would prove to be.

In the cabin later that evening after putting the children to bed, Rosa showed Lars the newspaper Mrs. Phillips had given her. She gnawed the inside of her lower lip as she watched him read, his expression growing stormier with every line. "John's still locked up," Lars said quietly when he finished. He folded the paper and tossed it onto the sofa.

"On racketeering charges," Rosa pointed out, bending to pick up the paper, determined to keep it out of the children's sight. "And for how long?"

Lars took her by the shoulders and fixed her with a steady gaze. "If he's found guilty, he could be locked up for years," he said, with reassuring certainty. "And if some other technicality crops up and he's released on account of it, he still has no idea where we are. He doesn't even know where to

338

begin to look. You'll only make yourself sick from worry if you keep on like this."

Rosa knew he was right, but she could not completely banish her fears.

As the weeks passed, Mrs. Phillips saved several newspaper clippings for Rosa, but none mentioned John, so she assumed he remained in prison awaiting trial. She was struck by the realization that John had almost certainly never returned to the adobe after his arrest. He would not know that she had taken the strongbox with the deed to the farm and all their other important papers when she fled. She imagined her kitchen under a layer of dust and wondered if a generous neighbor had come by to harvest the rye fields and feed the livestock in John's absence. Perhaps her brother had. It pained her to think that Carlos needlessly mourned his nieces and nephew, and maybe even his estranged sister. She wished she could send word to him that they were safe, but the risk of discovery was too great.

Rosa and Lars and the children fell into the familiar, comfortable rhythm of farm life, school, and weekly visits to the doctor. Nils and Rose had become essential members of the household, although Rosa noticed that Dante and Guiditta, perhaps unconsciously, kept some tasks within the family. No one but themselves and their three eldest children ever entered the winery unescorted, and Dante carried the only key to the tall double doors, which were always locked, in his pocket. Every Thursday, Dante and Dominic — and Vince too when school wasn't in session — set out early in the morning to make deliveries and returned just in time for a late supper. Although Lars offered to accompany them, they assured him they were so used to working together that they could manage fine on their own. "At least let me help you load the truck," Lars said, determined to prove his worth to his new employers. Dante replied that if anyone had to stumble out of bed an hour before sunrise and shoulder heavy loads, it ought to be Dominic and Vince, who had all the stamina of youth and none of the responsibilities of parenthood, and therefore could manage on fewer hours of sleep. "I guess when Mabel has her baby, I'll offer again," Lars told Rosa privately, and she suspected they would gladly accept his help at that time.

On other occasions, at the end of the day when the supper dishes were washed and put away and Rosa and Lars sat on the back steps watching the children climb the walnut trees or play on the banks of the creek, Lars expressed other doubts. "It doesn't add up," he would say, shaking his head. Wine grape sales had been poor that year, as carloads of fresh, plump, ripe fruit, in perfect condition when the train departed the station in Santa Rosa, arrived at the markets in New York utterly worthless, having spoiled at their destination when repeated delays prevented them from being unloaded — or so the brokers insisted, dubious claims the Cacchiones had no way to verify. Tourists occasionally stopped by, wanting to buy lunch or fresh eggs or walnuts or prunes, and Guiditta always sold them what they wanted, but fewer travelers had passed by as Christmas approached, and Rosa couldn't imagine Guiditta earned very much from their modest purchases. "I can't figure it out," Lars said, brow furrowed in puzzlement. "At this rate, they should have gone bankrupt years ago."

Paradoxically, Lars's doubts offered Rosa a glimmer of hope. Perhaps the Cacchiones had misjudged their financial circumstances. Perhaps they were not as close to bankruptcy as they believed. Years before, when Rosa had first begun working as the bookkeeper for the Grand Union Hotel, she had found an error in Mrs. Diegel's receipts that had spared her from overpaying her creditors several hundred dollars. If Rosa went over the Cacchiones' ledgers with the same painstaking scrutiny, she might discover a hidden windfall in their accounts.

But Guiditta graciously refused her offer. Rosa persisted, promising that she would keep whatever she discovered in the strictest confidence. She wouldn't alter a single line of the vineyard's accounts, but would instead make her notes lightly in pencil in the margins so that Guiditta or Dante could look over them before she made any changes to the original records. Still Guiditta refused, pleasantly but with a decided firmness that made it clear she did not want Rosa's help.

Rosa pretended that she understood, but the rebuff stung. Either Guiditta didn't believe Rosa was up to the task, or she didn't trust her. Either way, it didn't bode well for Rosa's future with Cacchione Vineyards — not that Rosa expected to stay forever, or to move up in the company as Mrs. Diegel had always promised her she could at the Grand Union Hotel. Perhaps the Cacchiones were interested only in Lars's knowledge of apricot cultivation and had found work for Rosa as a diversion. Perhaps they didn't really need either Rosa or Lars, but had kept them on out of obligation to Dr. Reynolds, who had saved their lives during the influenza epidemic.

Lars thought she worried unnecessarily. "All this means is that the Cacchiones don't want you to see their books."

"Why not?" Rosa asked. "Why wouldn't they? I'm honest, and I could help them."

Lars admitted he couldn't think of a reasonable explanation except that he and Rosa were mere employees, and new employees at that, and the Cacchiones ran a family business with family secrets. In time, Guiditta might trust Rosa enough to accept her help with the books, just as Dante might allow Lars to help with the weekly grape deliveries.

A few days before Christmas, the two eldest Cacchione brothers rose even earlier than usual to load the truck for what was expected to be one of the largest deliveries of the year. The truck was long gone by the time Rosa and Lars walked to the residence to begin their workday. Rosa spotted tire tracks in the yard, which had been softened into mud from the previous night's rain showers, and the narrow traces of the carts the brothers had used to haul the bushels of grapes from the old wine cellar, which Rosa had heard the Cacchiones mention but had never seen for herself. Out of sight of the house and yard, it lay an eighth of a mile beyond the newer, modern winery and was accessible only by a narrow, overgrown footpath. Although Dante's father and grandfather had once stored all the wine the vineyard produced in the old cellar, Dante used it only to keep surplus grapes chilled until they could be sold.

That day, Dante, Dominic, and Vince had not returned from their rounds by the time Rosa and Lars went home at the end of the day. That was not unusual, so Rosa thought nothing of it as she prepared supper for Lars and the children and took care of her housekeeping chores before putting the children to bed and climbing wearily beneath the covers herself.

She had been asleep for an hour, perhaps two, when a pounding on the door woke her. She leapt from bed, snatched up her robe, and fled into the front room, her heart racing, her imagination darting wildly. Lars reached the door first, and when she joined him she discovered not the police or gangsters or her husband on the doorstep, but Dante.

"The truck broke down a mile up the road," he said grimly. "We need your help unloading it. We could use both of you, if you can leave the children alone."

"Give me five minutes to dress," Lars said.

"I'll come too," Rosa said, stopping by the kitchen to scrawl a note for Marta before hurrying off to the bedroom to change. Within minutes she, Lars, and Dante were in the car rumbling over the rough path from the cabin to the road, where Dante gunned the engine and sent the car hurtling forward into the night. As they jolted along, Rosa reached for Lars's hand, and when his eyes met hers, she knew he too wondered what needed to be unloaded with such haste at that hour of the night — empty fruit crates? It made no sense.

Before long, they spotted the Cacchione Vineyards delivery truck pulled over by the side of the road. The front was jacked up on the driver's side and a punctured tire lay on the ground nearby. Guiditta was already there with the wagon, holding the horses' reins as Dominic and Vince heaved something into the back. As they approached, Rosa realized that they carried small wine barrels and jugs, apparently empty but still a bulky, cumbersome load.

Without sparing time for explanations, Dante parked the car and joined his sons, transferring empty wine barrels and jugs from the back of the truck into the wagon. Lars and Rosa fell into place beside them, and when the wagon was full, Guiditta chirruped to the horses and rode off toward home. Everyone else stayed behind to fill the back of the car with the few casks that remained, and just before they squeezed into the seats and sped off after Guiditta, Vince snatched a worn tapestry bag from the cab of the truck and locked the doors.

No one spoke on the drive back to the vineyard, or when they arrived and joined Guiditta in carrying the empty casks up the hill and into the old wine cellar, where the walls were lined with large barrels like the one Dante had tapped at the harvest dance. As they raced back and forth between the wagon and truck and cellar, Rosa saw enough to understand that even if she had time to spare for a thorough search, she would not find a single grape in the old cellar, unless she counted the crushed liquids that were aging into wine in the hundreds of neatly arranged barrels filling every available space in the cool darkness of the cavern.

The Cacchiones were bootleggers.

CHAPTER SIX

After the last empty cask was stashed in the old wine cellar and the door locked and bolted, Guiditta shivered in the cool night air and offered to make them something to eat while they sat in the warmth of the kitchen and talked. "The boys are exhausted," Dante said, shaking his head. "Explanations can wait until morning." Lars took Rosa's arm and led her along the narrow, overgrown trail to the yard, where they parted ways with the Cacchiones and continued carefully down the vineyard path to the cabin.

They went inside, and Lars shut the door behind them and leaned heavily against it. Their eyes met, and Rosa saw her own bleak uncertainty mirrored in his.

"Maybe there's a logical explanation," she said.

"There is, and I know it," said Lars grimly. "They're selling wine."

"I meant a different logical explanation." One easier to accept, one that exonerated them of all wrongdoing.

Lars sighed and ran a hand over his jaw. "They'll have all night to invent a good story."

But Rosa didn't want a reassuring lie. She wanted the truth.

In the morning, Rosa saw Marta and Ana off to the school bus stop before walking with Lars and the younger children to the Cacchione residence. Guiditta met them at the kitchen door and beckoned them inside, as she often did, for a cup of coffee before beginning the day's work. As Rosa and Lars helped themselves, Guiditta treated Lupita and Miguel to fresh milk and bananas fried in honey and sent them off to play with her younger children. When Dante came in from his morning chores, he greeted Rosa and Lars with a nod, poured himself a cup of coffee, and sat down at the head of the table with a sigh of resignation. Guiditta took the chair at his right hand; Rosa and Lars sat down across from them and waited.

Dante was silent for a long moment, his gaze fixed on the cup resting on the table before him, his tanned, weathered hands encircling it for warmth. "What can we do to persuade you not to turn us in?"

"We're not going to turn you in," Lars answered for them both, although they had not discussed it. "We're in no position to judge you. It's none of our business how you run your affairs."

"It is your business now," said Guiditta. "We'd hoped to keep this from you, but now you know, and if we're caught, you could go down with us."

"We'll say we knew nothing about it," said Rosa.

Dante regarded her skeptically. "Even under oath? Even if your testimony against us is the price you have to pay for your own freedom?"

"I —" If Rosa were locked away as John was now, and all she had to do was tell the simple truth of what she knew to be released and reunited with her children . . . If the moment came, she did not know what she would do.

Dante nodded as if her silence confirmed his fears. "The less they know, the better," he said to his wife.

She touched him gently on the forearm. "They already know enough to ruin us if they want to. Nils says they aren't going to turn us in, and I believe him. Since they've learned what we do, they might as well know why."

The Cacchiones had resumed selling wine only out of necessity, Guiditta explained, not avarice, not willful disregard for the law. Their luscious, vibrant wine, the result of years of toil and patience, was the family's most valuable asset, second only to the land itself. The law required them to pay taxes on their sixty acres regardless of how much or how little it had profited them in a given year. They were required to buy an annual permit to store the wine they were not permitted to sell. They could not earn enough to pay those expenses by selling walnuts and prunes and lunches to infrequent tourists. If they hadn't resorted to bootlegging, they wouldn't have survived.

"I sell wine. I've always sold wine," Dante broke in. "As a winemaker, I was a man of dignity and I won the respect of other dignified men. I earned a decent, honorable living. The politicians who made the laws forced me to abandon my livelihood — not only my profession but my very way of life. They've never met me. They've never visited Sonoma County. They know nothing about wine, this magnificent gift of God and nature and man working together in harmony. They care nothing for the families whose lives they've devastated. They care only about winning their next election and pleasing the influential people who can help them stay in office."

The Cacchiones had never abandoned winemaking, at first because they believed Prohibition would be repealed eventually and they would need to have mature wines ready to sell, and later, because they could not afford to stop. When Lars had examined the padlocked wire fencing in the wine cellar and noted that it was hardly an impenetrable barrier, he had been entirely correct. In the far corner, partially concealed by the water-filled barrels, Dante and Dominic had exploited a weakness in the enclosure, creating a low, narrow passage at the bottom just large enough to roll a wine barrel through. They filled the smaller casks and growlers with mature vintages, then refilled the empty barrels with new wine and wrestled the barricade back into place. It was a truckload of these casks, not crates of wine grapes, that Dante, Dominic, and Vince delivered to San Francisco each week, bribing the car ferry's fire security officers so they could cross the San Francisco Bay unimpeded.

The daylong, hazardous journey to the city and back demanded constant vigilance, as federal Prohibition agents patrolled the city streets and the back roads of the countryside searching for bootleggers and smugglers. Until they unloaded their illicit cargo at various hotels, restaurants, and speakeasies throughout the city, they were in jeopardy, hunted by officers and gangsters alike. One summer evening gangsters masquerading as federal agents had hijacked them just north of Petaluma. They were driving south when suddenly two sedans pulled out from a side road and blocked their way, forcing Dante to slam on the brakes. Three men in dark suits brandished guns, ordered Dante and his sons out of the truck, and declared them under arrest. The Cacchiones complied and stood with their arms raised above their heads on the side of the road, expecting to be slapped into handcuffs and hauled off to prison, but instead two of the men returned to the sedans, the third climbed into the cab of the truck, and all three sped away, leaving the Cacchiones staring in stunned bewilderment after them. The truck was later found abandoned outside of San Rafael, its entire cargo missing. When the officers who contacted the Cacchiones and helped them recover their vehicle asked why Dante had never reported the theft, Dante lied and insisted that he had, blaming the lack of a police report on misplaced paperwork.

The incident left the Cacchiones shaken, but they did not, they could not, forswear bootlegging. Instead they changed their schedule so that they left home in the morning and caught an earlier ferry into the city, but although this allowed them to avoid gangsters, it risked exposing them to more scrutiny by the police. They had to buy the silence of an entirely new shift of fire security officers so they could cross on the ferry, and they had to find new customers willing to accept deliveries in broad daylight. Although they took every precaution to avoid the attention of Prohibition agents, they lived under the constant threat of discovery, and the strain upon their nerves was almost crippling. That was why, when the delivery truck broke down the night before, they could not have waited until morning to unload the empty casks they had collected from their customers. If a police officer or Prohibition agent — or for that matter, a curious tourist or suspicious neighbor eager to profit from a reward — happened by and peered into the truck, the Cacchiones would have been undone.

"This isn't how we want to live," Dante said. "Who would live this way if he had any other choice? We know we risk arrest, imprisonment, and ruinous fines. We could be raided and be forced to watch agents break open our barrels and casks with axes and spill the wine out upon the ground. But what else can we do? We can choose the risk of losing all we own in a federal raid or the certainty of losing our home and property. Nearly every winemaker in Sonoma County has made the same choice. What would you do?" He looked from Lars to Rosa and back, raising his chin in defiant challenge. "You have four children. What would you risk to keep a roof over their heads? What would you do to keep them fed and clothed and safe?"

The kitchen rang with expectant silence as Dante waited for an answer.

"You're breaking the law," said Lars, "but as I said before, we're not going to turn you in. You've given us work and a place to stay, and we're in your debt."

"Your secrets are safe with us," promised Rosa. Guiditta's eyes filled with tears.

Someday, Rosa suspected, she might need Guiditta to preserve their secrets in return.

For a long time afterward, Dante's words lingered in Rosa's thoughts. What would she do to ensure her children's happiness and safety? What sacrifices would she demand of Lars for their sakes?

What had she already done, and what had

she failed to do?

In January 1921, the Santa Ana winds had brought summer out of season to the Arboles Valley. Strong, warm gusts from the eastern deserts flew across fields and hammered upon farmhouses, sending tumbleweeds bounding across roads, rattling windows, snatching laundry down from the clotheslines, and filling eyes, hair, mouth, and nostrils with dust. Everyone who visited the post office grumbled about the weather and hoped for a return of winter rains to fill the Salto Creek and cover the mountaintops with snow that would melt in spring and assure plentiful water come summer. Rosa too yearned for a change in the weather. The hot, relentless winds left her breathless and dizzy and disoriented, nauseous and tired. Then the winds shifted. Clear skies and bright sunshine and ocean mists and pleasantly cool breezes once again blessed the valley, but Rosa felt no better. It did not take her long to figure out why.

At first she said nothing to anyone. The loose dresses she wore around the house concealed her condition for the first two months, but she had borne many children and she knew it would not be long before she began to show. Before her body gave away her secret, she told John. As she had expected, he sighed heavily and told her that perhaps this time God would bless them with a healthy child. "I hope so," she told him tightly, forcing a smile to conceal a surge of anger. God might bless them with a cure for the beloved, imperfect children she had already borne if John would allow them to travel beyond the valley for treatment. John had responded the same way with each pregnancy after John Junior died, as if the children they had buried and those yet living within their home had profoundly disappointed him. She should be used to it, but his reaction had not lost the power to wound her.

She dreaded telling Lars and deferred the inevitable as long as she could, past the point when postal customers started giving her midsection surreptitious, curious looks and a few bolder neighbors had inquired whether she was "in a family way." She avoided the subject for so long that Lars brought it up. "You're looking well," he remarked one Monday afternoon as she refilled his coffee cup and topped off her own. "You were getting a bit thin, if you don't mind my saying so, but it looks like you've put on some weight."

"I have." She returned the coffeepot to

the stovetop and settled back into her chair, cupping her suddenly icy hands around her cup for warmth. "I'm expecting a baby."

Lars watched her in perfect stillness for a brief moment that to Rosa seemed to stretch out for an eternity. "Congratulations," he finally said. He didn't look surprised. "When?"

"September."

He drew in a slow, deep breath, and she knew he was counting the months backward. "Then the child could be mine."

She nodded.

"Do you know for sure?"

"No, I don't."

He reached across the table and took her hands. "Rosa, think carefully. How likely is it that the child is mine?"

"I don't know," she said, pronouncing each word distinctly.

"If this baby *is* mine —"

She slipped her hands from his grasp and knotted her fingers together in her lap. "Either way, John will be his father, or her father, just as he has been Marta's. It's the only way."

"It's not the only way," said Lars, incredulous. "It's not even the best way. You love me. I love you. That's never going to change. John mistreats you, and it's not good for the children to see that. You can't expect me to let him raise my child, not this time, not when I'm sober and perfectly capable of —"

"It's equally likely that it's John's baby," she countered, lowering her voice and glancing toward the front room where Ana was reading Maria a story. All morning Maria had rested listlessly on the sofa, weak and exhausted after a difficult bout of illness that had begun before dawn. "What would you have me do? Tell my husband that the child I'm carrying may be yours, but just in case it's his, he shouldn't throw me out of the house?"

"If he threw you out of the house, you'd be better off."

"Not without my children, I wouldn't be." He didn't seem to grasp that leaving John meant abandoning her children. She had committed adultery. In the eyes of God, the law, and the community, she was an unfit mother. She knew how a judge and jury would see matters. John would be cast as a wronged husband, a devoted father even to the offspring of his wife's premarital adultery, a landowner and a good provider. If Rosa left John, no judge would grant her custody of the children, not if John fought for them, and he would, if only to spite her.

What would become of them without their mother? What tales would John invent to explain why she did not come home, why she had not taken them with her? How long would it take before he taught them to despise her? And what of Ana and Maria, chronically ill and in the care of a man who had given up searching for a cure? What of sweet baby Pedro, if he too became sick someday?

Lars pushed back his chair and stood, shaking his head slowly in disbelief. "I can't go along with this. I just can't."

"Please, Lars," Rosa implored, tears of anguish and remorse welling up and spilling over before she could hold them back. "The child may be John's, in which case none of this — nothing that we're arguing about right now — none of it will matter."

"It all matters, Rosa."

Wordlessly she shook her head. Nothing she said would make him understand. Lars had known John longer, but Rosa knew him better. Staying with John and concealing her tryst with Lars was the only way to keep her children. It was the only way.

Lars paced the width of the kitchen. "You're thinking only of how to get through the next few months and not of what might happen years down the road. Let's say the baby is mine and you don't tell him. What do you think will happen when John figures it out on his own?"

"He never has to know," said Rosa. "He'll never know unless we tell him."

Lars halted and regarded her, his face drawn in compassion and frustration. "Rosa, he'll know. Forgive me, but if the baby turns out like Marta, if this child doesn't get sick, he'll know."

Her heart plummeted as the truth of his words sank in. Suddenly she heard the familiar rumble of John's truck coming up the gravel drive. With a gasp, she snatched up the coffee cups and dropped them into the sink, where lukewarm dishwater and soapsuds concealed them. By the time John opened the front door, Rosa and Lars were in the front room with Ana and Maria, and Rosa was handing Lars his mail bundle and offering her best regards to his family.

John watched them from the doorway for a moment, his hand on the doorknob, the gray U.S. Mail bag slung over his shoulder. Then he came inside, but he left the door open, and he strode past them to set the heavy bag on the floor beside his desk with a dull thud.

Rosa was too upset to speak.

"Hello, John," Lars greeted him easily.

"I heard you were back in town." John glanced at the bundle in Lars's arms. "You came too early. If you'd come a couple of hours later, you'd have this week's mail in your bundle as well. I don't have time to sort it now, so you'll have to wait until tomorrow at the earliest."

"I don't mind making another trip." Lars put on his hat, nodded to Rosa, and headed toward the door.

John's gaze shifted to Rosa, and she quickly fought to compose herself, hiding her distress beneath a placid mask. "You know," John mused, addressing Lars but keeping his eyes on Rosa, "this is the first time I've seen you pick up the mail since you came back. Now that I think about it, I can't recall the last time I've seen anyone from your place around here, and yet your family's bundle is picked up once a week like clockwork."

Lars halted at the door and turned around, his face expressionless.

"Most people pick up their bundle on Tuesday afternoon or Wednesday morning," John continued, his voice thoughtful with a thread of anger running through it. "They know I fetch the mail from the train station on Mondays and sort it on Tuesday mornings. But you —" John's steely gaze shifted to Lars. "You knew my schedule too, didn't you? And you planned accordingly."

Lars fixed him with the same easy, self-assured grin that used to charm Rosa into forgetting all his faults. "Well, John, if I'd known how much you missed me, I would have come on Tuesday afternoons."

"John, please," Rosa murmured, mindful of Ana watching silent and wide-eyed from the sofa, the book forgotten on her lap, her sleeping sister's little hand curled in hers.

John's eyes narrowed as he looked from Lars to Rosa and back. "I think you've upset my wife."

"I'm fine," said Rosa, but her voice shook. "Lars was just leaving."

As Lars put his hand on the doorknob, John barked, "Don't come back. Send your brother or one of the ranch hands for the mail from now on, but don't you come back around here. Don't you ever set foot on my land when you know I'm away and my wife is home alone."

"She's in no danger from me," Lars said, his grin disappearing like the sun slipping behind a thundercloud. "It's you she's afraid of."

John clenched his fists and took a step toward him. "Come near her again and you'll be sorry."

"Hit her again and *you'll* be sorry."

"John, Lars," Rosa broke in. "Please stop it. Not in front of the children. Lars, please just go."

"I will," he said, glaring at John. "I'll go away and I'll stay away, Rosa, if that's what you want. Is that what you want?"

"Yes," she cried. "Yes, that's what I want. Please go away and don't come back. Please. It's for the best."

Lars took a step backward as if her words had struck him in the chest. For a moment he looked as if he might argue, but just then Ana gasped and he looked her way as if he had forgotten she was there. He offered her a rueful smile and a shrug that managed to make the whole scene appear harmless and comical, a misunderstanding between grown-ups, easily settled and forgotten. He left without another word, without a parting glance at Rosa.

"Let's hope that's the last we see of him," John said as they heard the car start up and drive away.

Lars did as she asked. Others from the Jorgensen ranch came each week to pick up the family's mail, and although at first Rosa hoped someone would pass along a message from Lars, no one ever did.

The months went by. Ana, usually the

most reasonable of the children, began refusing the wholesome diet of white bread and milk the doctor had recommended and stubbornly insisted upon eating rice, beans, and corn tortillas or nothing at all. Rosa found a certain logic in her finicky habits; if she were going to be sick anyway, why shouldn't she eat her favorite foods? John, who hated waste and required the children to clean their plates at mealtimes, objected whenever he caught Rosa indulging a picky eater. "You're only going to spoil her," he warned when he found Rosa putting beans in to soak for the fifth night in a row.

"I'm going to make pot roast, potatoes, and bread for the rest of the family, so it shouldn't bother you that Ana wants something different," Rosa pointed out. "I don't mind the extra effort, nothing will go to waste, and she'll clean her plate, so what's the harm?"

"Children need to be obedient and eat what's set in front of them," John argued. "She's going to grow up to think she's always going to get her own way."

"As long as she grows up," Rosa replied quietly, putting the lid on the pot of beans.

Privately Rosa worried about the consequences of disregarding the doctor's orders, but as the summer passed, Ana's symptoms lessened, and it seemed to Rosa that her limbs fleshed out a bit and her bloated abdomen receded somewhat. Perplexingly, Maria followed the doctor's prescribed diet to the letter but grew progressively weaker. Rosa was tempted to put her on Ana's adopted diet too, but she was reluctant to ignore the most up-to-date medical advice she had been given. She wished one of the many doctors she had written to had replied with something else to try, but she suspected none of them wanted to overrule a local physician who had actually examined the children.

In late September Lupita was born, and when Rosa held her for the first time, she thought she imagined a striking resemblance to Marta, but she quashed the faint stirrings of anxiety their similarities evoked. She saw more of herself in their dark eyes and hair and skin than either John or Lars. No one would doubt Lupita was John's child — no one but Lars and Rosa herself. But she could not help brooding over the inescapable flaw in her plan Lars had detected: If, as the years passed, Lupita remained as vigorous and healthy as her eldest sister, John would realize that Rosa had betrayed him.

He had forgiven her once before because

he loved her and wanted her for his wife. He would not forgive her a second time, and Rosa could not blame him.

She buried her guilty secret deep in her heart and resolved to forget that Lars had ever returned to the Arboles Valley. For her family's sake, it had to be as if he were still hundreds of miles away.

A year passed. Lupita took her first steps. Ana started school, and never before had Rosa seen a child more eager to learn. She devoured books and spent hours scribbling stories of her own on scrap paper while most of her classmates were still mastering the alphabet. Rosa exhausted every likely contact in the last of her city business directories, but came no closer to a remedy for the children since John forbade her to hazard a trip beyond the Arboles Valley. John, mercurial as ever, was kind to her one week and indifferent the next, but even the worst of his indifference was preferable to his rage. In all that time Rosa saw Lars only once, from a distance, when he rode by on horseback one summer afternoon while she played on the mesa with the children. She didn't know if he even saw them, and if he did, whether he recognized them.

Winter came, with long stretches of clear, cool, sunny weather occasionally interrupted by billowing gray clouds and chilly rains. On such a gloomy day in February, an unexpected visitor knocked on the adobe door — her brother, Carlos, haggard and grim. She had not seen him since their mother's funeral and knew immediately that he would not have sought her out at home if their father were still living.

He had died the night before of a heart attack, Carlos told her, glancing around the adobe uncomfortably as if worried that even this necessary errand was a betrayal of his father's wishes that he disown his sister. The funeral mass would be in two days, and if Rosa and her family attended, Carlos wanted them to sit in the front pew beside him. Rosa thanked him and told him they would come, and after he left, she wondered if his small gesture were the overture to their eventual reconciliation. Carlos had not embraced her, he had declined her offer of coffee, and he had remained standing throughout his brief visit, but she decided to interpret his invitation to sit in the family pew as the extending of an olive branch. Time would tell.

Her father's funeral was less upsetting and grueling than her mother's had been, since Isabel had died so unexpectedly and under such suspicious circumstances. And yet it was sadder in its way, for with her father's passing, Rosa was forced to abandon her long-held hopes that he might someday forgive her. As she mourned for her father, she silently lamented the years he had wasted in estrangement and the potential for love and joy he had needlessly squandered in refusing to acknowledge his grandchildren. She felt sorry for her children that they would never know their grandfather, but she felt sorrier still for him.

Five weeks after the funeral, Rosa gave birth to a son. Moved by compassion and sorrow, inspired by fond memories of much happier days long ago, she named her newborn Miguel after his late grandfather. It was a tribute to the memory of the Papá she had known as a child, the man who had loved and cherished her.

Less than six months after Miguel was born, Maria died.

All summer long Maria had grown weaker and weaker until she had spent most of her waking hours lying prostrate on the sofa, clutching her stuffed bunny. After her precious girl was gone, Rosa descended into a black pit of despair deeper and more impenetrable than any she had fallen into before. It was all she could do to force herself out of bed every morning to fix breakfast for her family and change Miguel's diapers and see Marta and Ana off to school. She washed the dishes and did the laundry mechanically, as if her spirit had fled and some unseen, relentless puppeteer mercilessly pulled the strings that kept her in motion. Soon thereafter, Pedro — her happy, chubby, mischievous Pedro — showed his first symptoms of the terrible affliction that had taken his brother and sisters.

Rosa was convinced that if she had to bury another child, she would go mad. She would go mad and go to the mesa as her mother had done and hurl herself from the rim of the Salto Canyon until she struck the unyielding earth and quiet oblivion absorbed all her pain.

But as the dark thoughts flew about her like blackbirds in the rye fields, she would remind herself that her mother had *not* taken her own life, she had fallen, and Isabel would not approve of the despairing turn her daughter's thoughts had taken. Rosa would remember that the five living children God had thus far let her keep still needed her, and would need her for many years yet. So she persevered. Prayer was an insufficient balm for her shattered heart, but her children — Marta, Ana, Pedro, Lupita, and little Miguel — they offered her their pure, innocent love, and the sight of their sweet faces and the music of their voices gave her reason enough to keep living.

Thus when Pedro passed away one afternoon shortly before his fifth birthday, Rosa chose not to follow quickly after. She made the funeral arrangements and buried another son and tried to comfort his frightened and unhappy surviving siblings.

"We must accept the will of God," John said stoically as they drove home from the parish cemetery, clad in mourning black, their faces pale, their eyes red with tears, their minds and hearts numb from pain.

"God's will?" echoed Ana from the backseat, bewildered. "Why does God want us to die?"

"He doesn't," Rosa said, her voice rising until it took on a note of hysteria. "Your brother's death was not God's will. God has blessed us with the means to purchase a car that can carry us to towns beyond the Arboles Valley, and he has blessed doctors in those towns with knowledge and skill that might help us if only —"

"Shut up, Rosa," John barked.

Rosa knew if she spoke another word she would break down entirely, so she gazed out the window at the rolling hills and the farmers' fields and tuned out John's voice as he launched into an explanation of the problem of evil he probably recalled from his catechism days. The children listened dutifully, but they seemed unsatisfied.

John was responsible for the deaths of their children, Rosa thought as they drove home. John had refused to seek out a treatment that might have saved them. She didn't blame God, or her sins, or evil let loose in the world. She blamed John.

That night he tried to seek comfort in her arms, but she rolled onto her side, her back to him. He placed his hand on her hip, but she brushed it off with a murmured "No." He rolled onto his back and sighed heavily, but he left her alone, perhaps too surprised by the novelty of her demurral to protest. The next two nights he approached her again, and she again refused. After that he stopped trying. Rosa expected him to demand her submission, but to her astonishment, he did not argue or cajole or force himself upon her.

The relief and liberation she felt upon his tacit agreement to leave her alone startled her with its intensity, but she did not expect him to tolerate rejection forever. When he changed his mind, he would do so with a vengeance, but for the moment she had gained a small measure of peace, a respite from living a lie.

For two years Rosa and John lived in the same home, shared the same bed, ate together, ran the farm and the post office together, raised their children, spent nearly every minute of the day, waking and sleeping, within sight or earshot of each other. And yet with each passing day, the chasm dividing them grew until to Rosa it seemed as deep and as broad and as difficult to cross as the Salto Canyon. Like the place where her mother had perished, her marriage's outward appearance of tranquil beauty concealed treacherous dangers.

But Rosa knew the enduring, strained peace between her and John could not last. For Lupita thrived. She grew and blossomed and bloomed with such inexhaustible, graceful vigor that Rosa was certain the mysterious illness that had tormented her siblings would never afflict her. And with each passing year, the moment when John would no longer be able to overlook that fact, that striking, unmistakable similarity to Marta, drew inexorably closer.

And now the dreaded day had come and gone, and Rosa would have faced it alone if not for Elizabeth Nelson. A newcomer to the Arboles Valley unencumbered by the longstanding fears and prejudices of her neighbors, she befriended Rosa when everyone else shunned her, denounced John's brutality when everyone else looked away — and perhaps most significantly, though she had been unaware of their entangled pasts, she had warned Lars of Rosa's ongoing unhappiness and had drawn him into her life again. He had resumed his visits to the Barclay farm, he had met Lupita for the first time, and he had given Rosa hope and friendship and had asked for nothing in return. Rosa had even, at long last, kept her promise to him, and had come to the apricot harvest on the Jorgensen ranch. She and the children had enjoyed a picnic lunch with Lars in the shade of the orchard as if they were any other neighbors and not a family stalked by suspicion and death.

And then John had seized upon the truth and everything had come crashing down around them, but Elizabeth had been there too, to help Rosa make the final break from John and flee, and as a consequence, Elizabeth's husband lay in a hospital bed recovering from a gunshot wound, and Lars had left his home and family behind, perhaps forever.

Elizabeth and Lars had both sacrificed much for the sake of her and her children, more than Rosa could ever ask of a friend, but the children were safe, and for that, she owed them everything.

Although Lars and Rosa had given their word not to betray the Cacchiones, Dante and Guiditta seemed no less apprehensive than before. Even so, when Christmas arrived a few days later, the two families celebrated together at the Cacchione residence. At first their holiday was strained and formal, with a thin veneer of merriment put on for the younger children's sake, but before long the joy and peace of the season filled their hearts, and a sense of forgiveness and acceptance descended upon both households.

In the week between Christmas and New Year's Day, friends and acquaintances visited the Cacchiones daily, bringing gifts of sweets, bottles of olive oil, and the fruits of their own harvests. In return the Cacchiones gave their guests jugs of fine wine, which they quickly nestled into the bottom of their baskets and covered with packages of dried figs, sugared almonds, and biscotti. On New Year's Eve, the Cacchiones again swept the barn clean and invited their friends to a celebration Dante and Guiditta called La Festa di San Silvestro. The guests celebrated the waning hours of 1925 with music and dancing, laughter and jokes, and a delicious feast featuring many dishes made from lentils, which in the Italian tradition represented riches, abundance, and good fortune in the New Year. Spicy sausages, stuffed pork, pasta, gnocchi, and sweet cakes for dessert completed the menu. Rosa was not surprised to see that every course was accompanied by the Cacchiones' renowned wines, as well as grappa, a strong brandy distilled from the pulpy, fermented residue of grapes pressed in the crush of winemaking.

Alegra Del Bene, her husband, Paulo, and their children were among the guests. Rosa was happy to see her friend again, but although Alegra embraced Rosa and smiled warmly when she arrived, it seemed to Rosa that she became somewhat tired and withdrawn after their sons ran off to play together. Concerned, Rosa asked her if she was unwell, but Alegra shook her head and said it was nothing, only that she would be glad to put the troubles of 1925 behind her. Rosa nodded sympathetically, surprised by the implication that the Del Benes too were struggling. She had assumed that their sacramental wine permit had spared them from the financial worries their neighbors had been forced to shoulder. She thought of the valises full of cash hidden in the wardrobe back in the cabin, and she wished she could offer enough of it to ease Alegra's worries. But she glumly recalled Lars's warnings and knew she couldn't risk it, just as she could not have risked paying Henry's bills at the Oxnard hospital for Elizabeth's sake. She could not help feeling that she was putting her own safety and comfort above her friends', but her safety and comfort was also her children's. As much as she hated to admit it, she knew she could not dispense gifts of cash to her friends in need without drawing the wrong sort of attention to her family. Someday, she vowed, it would not always be so.

Rosa soon learned that Alegra was not alone in her readiness to leave the old year and its many woes behind. During supper, Rosa and Lars sat at the end of one long trestle table with Salvatore and Beatrice Vanelli, the former winemakers from Glen Ellen who had switched from creating lush Zinfandels to growing table grapes and prunes. Salvatore acknowledged that although their new crops had earned them a modest profit over the past year, he missed the old days and prayed every night for Prohibition to end so they could resume winemaking, his passion and calling for more than thirty years and his father's before him. But when Salvatore rose to refill his glass from the barrel in the corner of the barn, Beatrice nearly broke down in tears as she confessed that Salvatore was ever the optimist, and that as for her, she did not know how much longer she and Salvatore could hold on. "We've considered selling the land and starting over somewhere else," she said, but then fell abruptly silent as her husband returned to his seat beside her.

Everywhere Rosa looked around the table, she saw hardworking men and women persevering in the face of ever worsening misfortune, refusing to abandon hope as they mourned their lost, beloved way of life. She wished with all her heart that the New Year would bring them all the prosperity and peace they deserved, but when she pondered all that the future might bring, she could not see an end to their troubles.

For most of January, the weather mirrored their uncertain, unfathomable future. A thick, impenetrable fog smothered the valley, hoarfrost clung to tree limbs and fences and windows, and the temperature often dropped below freezing at night. Landslides closed roads through the mountains to the coast and the customary tasks of that time of year were postponed until the unusual brutality of the weather eased.

Later in the month, news spread through the Sonoma Valley of a fatal shootout between two policemen on a busy street in downtown San Francisco. As the policemen fired upon each other, mothers with children had fled the scene in terror and pedestrians had cowered behind parked automobiles to avoid the hailstorm of bullets. Miraculously, no bystanders were injured in the shocking gunfight. The policeman who died had accused his assailant of bootlegging, and their fatal duel was the culmination of years of accusation and mistrust between them, or so the surviving officer explained from the hospital bed where he was recovering from his wound.

For a while afterward, Guiditta forbade Vince to accompany Dante and Dominic on their delivery runs into the city, but eventually she relented, because they could not manage without him. Until then, Rosa had lived in dread that Lars would volunteer to take Vince's place, but to her relief, he did not. She could not bear to think of him exposing himself to such dangers. Just as Dante could not get along without Vince, Rosa had discovered that she could not get along without Lars.

With each passing day that Rosa, Lars, and the children lived beneath the same roof, sharing meals and helping with homework and arguing and laughing together, they became more like a family, drawing closer like a wound knitting together, the pain of it easing as the scar formed. The girls had become so accustomed to calling Lars "Pa" in front of the Cacchiones that they no longer reverted to "Mr. Jorgensen" when they were alone. Miguel went to Lars willingly now, and showed him more smiles and affection than he had ever offered his true father, who had too often frightened him. He had become an active, mischievous boy, eager to laugh at a pratfall or a silly song, reluctant to see the day end and go to bed at night, even to sleep beneath the colorful, scrappy Railroad Crossing quilt Rosa had made for him.

"Will you make mine next?" asked Lupita eagerly the night Rosa put the last stitch into the binding of her brother's quilt. Lupita knew that as the next youngest, it was rightfully her turn.

"I'll begin as soon as I mend these shirts for Pa," Rosa promised, rising from her chair near the fireplace and brushing loose threads off the quilt, studying her handiwork with a critical eye.

Lupita thrust out her lower lip. "But I've been *patient.*"

"I know, but I'll need you to be patient another few days."

"And that's just until Mamá can start it," Ana pointed out. "You'll need to be patient for weeks longer while she makes it."

Rosa muffled a sigh, wishing that Ana didn't always feel compelled to be sure everyone understood the whole truth.

Lupita's cheeks flushed scarlet. "I want my quilt now."

Rosa raised her eyebrows at her youngest daughter. "Lupita, *mija,* what has gotten into you?"

"The shirts can wait," said Lars mildly from the sofa, regarding them over the Santa Rosa *Press Democrat.*

"No, the shirts can't wait," said Rosa, with a warning frown for Lupita. She wished Lars hadn't spoken. They could not reward Lupita's willfulness. "You can't wear them when they're missing buttons and the cuffs are torn."

"I can take care of Pa's shirts," offered Marta, rising from her seat on the floor near the hearth.

"Stop calling him that!" Lupita thrust her arms straight down by her sides and balled her hands into fists. "He's *not* our *pa!*"

"Oh, he is too, Lupita," snapped Marta. "Just shut up. He is too our father, yours and mine. Don't be such a stupid little spoiled brat. Mamá will make your quilt as soon as she can."

Lupita burst into angry tears and fled for the attic. Ana stared at her eldest sister, and then her gaze traveled from Rosa to Lars and back again, her mouth opening slightly in shock. Feeling faint from dismay, Rosa could only stare wordlessly at Marta until she felt a tug on her skirt. "Pa's my pa too," Miguel said anxiously. "He's my pa too."

Wordlessly, Rosa stroked his soft curls and threw Lars a helpless look, stricken. Lars cleared his throat, folded the newspaper, and set it aside. "How long have you known?" he asked Marta quietly, leaning forward to rest his elbows on his knees.

Rosa saw in her eyes that until that moment, Marta had only suspected. "I don't know. A while. I figured it out. I mean, Lupita and I have never been sick, and Ana and Miguel and the others . . ." She shrugged and gestured, a quick wave of the hand, as if to say it had only been a matter of time, since she was nobody's fool, and of course, she was absolutely right.

"Marta, *mija,*" Rosa began shakily, "there's so much you're not old enough to understand —"

"Can we not talk about it, please?" pleaded Marta, inching toward the attic stairs. "Not right now?"

Rosa nodded, and Marta bit her lip and darted off upstairs. A moment later Rosa heard her murmuring gentle apologies to her weeping sister. Ana dragged herself to her feet and, ducking her head to hide the tears in her eyes, she crossed the room to give Lars a quick hug before hurrying after her sisters.

"Mamá?" said Miguel, clinging to her leg.

Rosa bent to pick him up and hugged him to her heart. Her eyes met Lars's, and even if she were blind she would have sensed the love and compassion and regret in his gaze.

In all their hushed debates about whether to tell the children and how to tell them, they had never imagined them coming to the truth in such a clumsy, careless manner.

But now, at last, they knew, and even as Rosa ached for them in their pain and confusion, even as she dreaded the tearful questions that were sure to follow in the days to come, it was an immeasurable relief that the lie no longer divided them.

At first the girls pretended that the revelation had never happened. Marta and Ana were respectfully distant to Lars, while Lupita fiercely ignored him, and he wisely gave her a wide berth. Miguel, too young to understand, was happy, believing the conflict had been resolved because no one was shouting anymore. Rosa knew that she would need to unsnarl the tangled threads of their family for him again when he was older. Marta seemed relieved to have the truth out at last, perhaps because she was the eldest and most mature, perhaps because she had figured out the truth on her own instead of having it hurled at her in a moment of anger, perhaps because she had feared and despised John for years and was fiercely satisfied to learn that he could claim no part of her. Ana, solemn and quiet, lost herself in her books. All six of them were frustrated and hurt and angry and lost to some degree, and they cared about one another. Their pain would not be so great, Rosa realized, except that along the way, they had somehow become a family.

Ana was the first to approach Rosa with difficult questions. "Did you ever love Papa?" she asked, not meeting her mother's eyes. Rosa knew that what she meant was, "Do you love me and Miguel as much as you love Marta and Lupita?" The answer to both questions, spoken and unspoken, was a heartfelt, sincere yes, and Ana seemed content with that.

Marta was the first to grasp that Rosa had given birth to Lupita — Lars's child — while still married to John. The knowledge mortified her, and for a time she looked askance at Rosa and was too embarrassed to talk to Lars, but eventually she resolved her conflicted feelings, or perhaps she decided to set them aside until she could better understand them.

Eventually the household settled back into something resembling their former comfortable familiarity. Lupita still refused to address Lars as Pa or Papa or even Mr. Jorgensen, but referred to him, when she had to, with the appropriate pronoun. Lars took it in stride, careful to treat the children as he always had and to require nothing more from them than the respect Rosa had taught them to offer every other adult they knew. As the days passed, the girls seemed to remember how much they had liked him when he was simply Mr. Jorgensen, their mother's friend and the generous neighbor who once brought them dried apricots that were even better than candy. Now they knew he meant much more to them than that — and that they meant much more to him than they had ever suspected.

A break in the weather at last allowed impatient grape growers throughout Sonoma County to properly tend their vines. January was the time for pruning and cleaning up, a daunting amount of work that required everyone, young and old, to contribute. Lars followed Dante, Dominic, and Vince closely to learn how to cut back the previous year's growth, leaving the structural vines intact and trimming away the dead wood and weak branches. When Rosa remarked that it seemed they were cutting back the vines to barely a fraction of their former abundance, Dante explained that fewer, well-spaced buds would mature into fewer, but much higher-quality grapes. "The secret to an excellent wine isn't the richness of the soil or even the skill of the winemaker but the quality of the grape," he emphasized, cutting a twisted, dead twig from the structural vine with proud satisfaction.

While the men pruned the vines, the women weeded the soil so that no predatory growth could siphon away nutrients from the grapes. Darting in and out among the rows, the children gathered up the uprooted weeds and pruned vines and tossed them onto a pile in a clearing on the edge of the vineyard. At suppertime they gathered around the long table in the Cacchiones' kitchen and devoured a hearty supper of beef stew, pasta, and polenta, which Rosa and Francesca had helped Guiditta prepare.

At dusk Dante set the enormous pile of clippings ablaze. Thrilled, the younger children watched the flames lick the wood, squealing and jumping when a sudden pop and shower of sparks startled them. As the fatigued adults found places to sit and discuss the work accomplished that day and the unfinished tasks they would need to complete in the days to come, the children ran around searching out dead twigs and dried leaves to throw upon the bonfire. Smoke rose into the evening sky and drifted over the still, shadowed trellises, wafted aloft by gentle breezes from the south. Guiditta reminisced aloud about a time in the not too distant past when a multitude of bonfires at vineyards throughout Sonoma County would fill the air with white smoke and the scent of burning. She had learned to associate the smell of burning grape wood with anticipation for spring on the vineyard. The old, dead vines had been cut away to make room for new growth and new vintages, and throughout wine country, grape growers and vintners prepared for a new season, fresh and full of hope. But now only a scattering of bonfires sent plumes of smoke rising into the skies above Santa Rosa, and only the most optimistic and determined among them believed that their spring toil would guarantee a bountiful harvest come autumn.

But even those with lowered expectations and diminished hopes labored vigorously in their fields and vineyards throughout the waning days of winter, holding on until better days could come.

Spring brought unbroken sunshine and tranquil breezes to Cacchione Vineyards. The return of temperate weather lifted Rosa's spirits despite the strain and worry that lingered in the aftermath of the secrets discovered and revealed over the winter.

Fair weather also heralded the return of tourists to Sonoma County. Several times a day, the sight of a roadster churning up a cloud of dust as it turned off the main road toward the winery summoned Guiditta from her chores to fetch the visitors walnuts, prunes, fresh eggs, lunch, a tour of the vineyard — whatever they wanted. After Mabel gave birth to a daughter in mid-April, Guiditta was often too preoccupied caring for her grandchild and daughter-in-law to greet visitors, so Rosa and Francesca would see to them instead. Unlike Guiditta, however, they were too nervous to offer guests glasses of wine with their lunch or after a tour. Rosa had been startled the first time she witnessed Guiditta produce a jug of wine and distribute glasses to three couples enjoying eggplant caponata, bread, cheese, and olives on an old, soft quilt spread on the grass in the shade of a stand of oaks. "Did you know," Guiditta had inquired conversationally as she filled the glasses, which the picnickers held up eagerly, "that despite Prohibition, it's perfectly legal for families to make up to two hundred gallons of wine each year for their own use?" She never claimed that the Cacchiones produced no more than that amount, nor did she explain how serving wine to paying guests fit within the definition of a family's own use. The tourists were either too busy enjoying their wine to parse her logic, or they understood and were more than willing to play along.

Once a wealthy San Francisco couple traveling to their summer home on the Russian River cajoled Guiditta into selling them an entire cask of the vintage they had sampled. "Dante would get in a lather if he knew I'd done that," she confessed to Rosa as the couple drove away. Rosa had spotted her selling casks a few other times too, but only when Dante was away from the vineyard, and Dominic and Vince, who would have told him, were nowhere in sight. When it fell to Rosa and Francesca to entertain tourists, they offered nothing stronger than iced tea, lemonade, and ice water. Word must have spread about the differences in hospitality, because over time, tourists and summer residents began asking specifically for Guiditta, and they often drove away without a bite of lunch or basket of prunes when they were informed that she was not available.

In the last week of April, Guiditta, Francesca, and Rosa were out among the trellises training new vines when they heard the sound of car wheels churning on gravel. Guiditta, intent on the task at hand, sent her daughter to see what the visitors wanted. Francesca hurried off and returned about twenty minutes later to report that two gentlemen had only wanted directions to Highway 101, but she had persuaded them to buy a dozen prunes before they left.

"That's my girl," Guiditta praised her. "They wandered a bit out of their way, didn't they?"

Francesca nodded. "They said they came in from San Francisco this morning, but one of them mentioned something about Los Angeles, as if he'd lived there until recently." She nudged Rosa and grinned. "He looked so much like your husband that when I first saw him from a distance, I thought that's who he was."

Rosa felt her stomach turn over. "My husband?"

"Yes, although the resemblance isn't that striking up close. He and Nils could be brothers, but not twins. They both have the same blond hair, though this fellow had more of it. He was a bit younger than Nils too, but shorter and heavier. Not chubby, I don't mean that. Just as if he's eating well at home."

"I imagine Nils eats well at home too," replied Guiditta, a gentle reproach in the sidelong look she gave her daughter. "I know he eats well when the Ottesens join us for dinner."

"He certainly does. We all do," said Rosa, managing a shaky laugh although her heart thudded in her chest. Her husband — of course Francesca had meant Lars. Francesca's description did not resemble dark-haired, muscular John in the least — but suddenly Rosa realized that it described Oscar Jorgensen all too well. Could the visitor have been him? Could Lars's younger

390

brother have traced him so far? No, it couldn't be. They had left no trail to follow when they had fled Oxnard, except for the false leads pointing pursuers south to Mexico, and like John, Oscar would have had no idea where to begin searching.

Francesca got back to work and Rosa quickly did too, her momentary terror fragmenting under the weight of cool reason. If the visitor had indeed been Oscar, he certainly wasn't looking for his brother particularly well, since he hadn't mentioned him or shown Francesca his photograph. Nor was it likely, Rosa realized with some amusement, that the diligent, responsible Oscar would have left the Jorgensen ranch to his hired hands in the middle of such an important season, not unless he knew exactly where to find Lars and believed him to be in mortal peril. A search unlikely to bear fruit was a task for the doldrums of winter, if ever.

Seven months had passed since Dr. Reynolds had first examined Ana and Miguel at the Stanford Hospital, and in all that time, Rosa had scrupulously kept them on Dr. Haas's diet, contriving variations on bananas and polenta so that they would not grow bored with a monotonous menu and be tempted to stray. Although Rosa sometimes feared her eyes deceived her and that such simple changes to their diet could not possibly have brought about the miracle she had prayed for, Ana and Miguel seemed perfectly healthy, lively and vigorous, with no sign of the symptoms that had once tormented them. Even so, when Dr. Reynolds pronounced them fully recovered from the symptoms of their illness, Rosa was stunned. She had borne the certainty of her children's inevitable early deaths for so many years that she had long forgotten what it felt like to look forward to watching them grow up. Rosa stammered her thanks, wishing she could express to the generous, attentive physician the depths of her gratitude. A handshake and prompt payment of their bills seemed a perfunctory and indifferent response to the man who had saved her children's lives.

She promised the doctor she would keep Ana and Miguel on the diet so they wouldn't suffer a relapse. She promised herself she would never take a single day with them for granted.

Before catching the train home, she and the children paid one last call on Mrs. Phillips. Rosa had brought her a basket full of asparagus, rhubarb, and spinach from the garden she had planted in a sunny spot near the cabin. Mrs. Phillips accepted the gift with delight and lamented that all she had to offer Rosa in return was tea and cookies and a newspaper clipping. Torn, both wanting and dreading news of John and Henry with equal measure, Rosa forced herself to wait until she and the children were on the train bound for home to read the article. After Miguel fell asleep with his head resting on her lap and Ana became engrossed in a library book, she took the clipping from her purse, smoothed out the creases with shaking hands, and read that John had been found guilty of racketeering and had been sentenced to five years in federal prison.

Rosa folded the paper, tucked it back into her purse, and took a deep, shuddering breath. Five years seemed an alarmingly brief span of time. And if John chose to become a model prisoner, he could be released even sooner than that on good behavior.

That night after the children fell asleep, she told Lars the news and was not surprised when it left him unperturbed. He was not afraid of John, not the way she was, and he found it highly unlikely that anything John might report to his old mobster friends upon his release, whether five years hence or half that, would help them hunt him down. "He doesn't know where we are," Lars told her as he had so many times before. This time he took her hands and pulled her close to him. She rested her head on his chest and listened to the reassuring sound of his steady heartbeat until her own heart stopped racing from fear. Then she pulled away from his embrace, unwilling to meet his gaze although she kept her hands in his. It was dangerous to let him hold her too long, for it made her yearn for their old intimacy. She could never divorce John now, and after what Lars had said to her the day Lupita was conceived and as they danced at the harvest celebration, she was ashamed to suggest that she would be willing to take him as a lover while she was married to someone else. She didn't feel married to John anymore — her marriage vows had been damaged when John beat her and when she had betrayed him, and they had been shattered beyond repair when he murdered her mother — but Lars still saw her as married. And so, she was forced to admit, she *was* still married, whether she felt that way or wanted to be or not.

She couldn't ask John for a divorce without coming out of hiding and endangering them all, and Lars understandably didn't want to be with someone else's wife. He cared about Rosa, but he had fled with them because he couldn't bear the thought of never seeing Marta and Lupita again. He remained with them, pretending to be her husband and fulfilling the role of father for his children as well as John's for their sake, not hers.

It was a brutal, bitter truth, but she had to accept it. To deny it now, as she and Lars were growing closer, would be to confront inevitable heartache later.

A few days later, Rosa was in the vineyard helping Francesca train the last of the new vines when she glanced up at a sound from the road and saw a dark sedan approaching the residence. Guiditta was in the house caring for the baby while her exhausted daughter-in-law slept, so Rosa brushed debris from her hands and said to Francesca, "I'll see to them. You got the last one."

"Thanks. Don't take any wooden nickels," Francesca advised cheerfully.

Rosa laughed and hurried back through the rows of trellises, lush and green with new foliage. When she reached the yard, she spotted a black-suited man striding back and forth beside the dark sedan, a gray flannel hat on his head, his hands on his hips.

When he removed his hat and mopped his brow with the back of his hand, she stopped short, taken aback by his resemblance to Lars. When the stranger glanced her way and nodded, she roused herself and went to welcome him. This surely was the man who had bought prunes from Francesca once before, and he did indeed look enough like Lars that he could have been a third Jorgensen brother.

"Welcome to Cacchione Vineyards," she called breathlessly as she approached. "What can I do for you?"

"I'd like to speak with Guiditta Cacchione," he replied, glancing past her toward the house. "Are you her?"

"No, I'm Rose. I work for Mrs. Cacchione."

"Nice to meet you, Rose. I'm Dwight Crowell. Could you go fetch Mrs. Cacchione for me? There's a particular purchase I'd like to make, and I hear she's the one to ask for."

"I'm afraid she's busy at the moment." Rosa gestured over her shoulder to the residence, smiling apologetically. "Her daughter-in-law had a baby girl a few weeks ago, and like any proud grandma, Mrs. Cacchione is always on call. But I'd be happy to help you if I can. Would you like some lunch, or perhaps some more prunes?"

Mr. Crowell's eyebrows rose as if he had not expected Rosa to know that he had visited the vineyard before. Indeed, if not for his resemblance to Lars, Rosa wouldn't have known, because Francesca wouldn't have bothered to describe him. "I guess another half dozen prunes would be about right."

Rosa smiled and beckoned him to follow her up to the front porch, where she showed him to a comfortable redwood chair and told him she would be right back. She hurried inside to the kitchen, descended into the refreshing coolness of the root cellar, and carefully placed six perfect, sweet prunes into a paper sack. When she returned to the front porch, the chair was empty but the sedan was still parked in the yard. Rosa searched for Mr. Crowell and found him wandering by the winery, peering in through the windows and testing the double front doors. Uneasy, Rosa halted in the middle of the yard and called, "I'm afraid they're locked."

"So I found out myself," he replied, grinning easily as he stopped tugging on the doors and came to join her. "I guess there's not much use for this old building anymore."

"On the contrary, the wine cellar's full," said Rosa. "The Cacchiones have a storage permit, but the wine's out of reach behind a very strong padlock."

Mr. Crowell planted his hands on his hips and turned slowly in place, squinting as he took in the winery, the residence, and the main outbuildings. "Seems like a waste to pay to store wine they can't sell."

"I've heard Mr. Cacchione say the same on more than one occasion." Rosa found herself wishing that Dante would appear, or Dominic or even young Vince. Something about Mr. Crowell made her uncomfortable, something that had nothing to do with his superficial resemblance to Lars. "I think when he considers all the work his family put into the creation of those wines, he can't bear to destroy them."

Mr. Crowell nodded thoughtfully, his gaze returning to the winery. The longer Rosa studied him, the more differences between him and Lars she noticed. Mr. Crowell had a thin white scar running from his right ear-lobe to his jaw, and there was a look of arrogance in his eyes that would never appear in Lars's. Rosa thrust the bag of prunes toward him and named her price. He took the bag, dug some coins out of his pocket, and placed them in her hand. As she thanked him, he said, "It's a mighty hot day, Rose, and I'm parched. I don't suppose I could refresh myself with a glass of wine before I hit the road?"

Rosa assumed a tragic expression. "I'm so sorry, but we aren't allowed to sell wine anymore. Would you like some lemonade or iced tea instead?"

He fixed her with a piercing stare, but she did not flinch. "Lemonade, please." She smiled, nodded, and hurried back into the kitchen. When she returned, he accepted the glass, sipped the sweet coolness, and leveled his gaze at the vineyard. "Mind if I have a look around?"

"Of course not," said Rosa brightly, falling into step beside him as he headed off to the barn, although it was obvious that he had intended to go alone. As they walked, she recited a history of the vineyard and noteworthy facts about each building they passed, having memorized the standard tour she had overheard Guiditta deliver so many times.

Time and time again, Mr. Crowell's gaze returned to the winery. "You say the Cacchiones can't sell me any wine, but folks say they're still making it."

"Well, of course," said Rosa innocently, wondering which folks he meant. "But no more than two hundred gallons for their own use. That's the law. They can and do sell wine grapes, though. Would you be interested in a bushel?"

Mr. Crowell shook his head and handed her his empty lemonade glass. "No, thank you." Frowning thinly, he strolled back to his sedan, opened the door, and touched the brim of his hat to her. "Thank you for the refreshments, Rose, and the tour. What did you say your last name was?"

"I don't think I did. It's Ottesen."

"Ottesen," he repeated thoughtfully, and climbed in behind the wheel.

Disconcerted, Rosa nonetheless smiled and waved as he pulled away, but as soon as he drove out of sight, she let all pretense of hospitality drop. Mr. Crowell resembled Lars, but he reminded Rosa of John. Both men shared an almost tangible determination to get whatever they wanted.

When Rosa next saw Guiditta later that afternoon, she took her aside and told her about Mr. Crowell's return visit to the vineyard, how he had wanted to speak to Guiditta personally, and how he had wanted to buy wine. "Did you sell him any?" Guiditta asked.

"Why, no," said Rosa, taken aback. As far as she knew, except for a few jugs the family kept in the cellar of the residence to drink with meals, all of the Cacchiones' wine was locked away in the winery and the old wine cellar. If Rosa wouldn't dare serve glasses of wine to jolly picnickers, Guiditta ought to know she wouldn't sell an entire barrel to a lone stranger. "He bought another half dozen prunes and looked around a bit. I gave him the usual vineyard history and a glass of lemonade."

"Why didn't you come find me so I could unlock the old wine cellar?" Guiditta asked cheerfully. "Was Dante watching? If that's the case, good girl and well done."

"No, that wasn't it." Guiditta's apparent lack of concern bewildered Rosa. "I didn't want him to know you sell wine. He said that he heard that you did, but he didn't bother to name the person who had told him, so I insisted that you sell only wine grapes. Something about him bothered me. He was too . . . curious."

For a moment Guiditta's expression grew troubled. "Did you take him past the old wine cellar on your tour?"

"Of course not," said Rosa. "He barely glanced that way, thank goodness. I don't think he even saw the footpath." If he had, Rosa didn't know what she could have done to prevent him — grabbed his arm and pointed out interesting sights in the opposite direction? Pretended to sprain her ankle so he would have to help her hobble back to the house? "It really wasn't much of a tour. I just followed him as he wandered around. Guiditta, do you suppose he could have been a Prohibition agent?"

Guiditta frowned, mulling it over. "I doubt it. They're much more aggressive. They love to flash their badges and order people around. If he were an agent, he could have commanded you to go get me, forced me to unlock the winery, and poked around to his heart's content instead of rattling locked doors and peering through windows."

"I suppose," said Rosa, dubious.

Guiditta patted her on the shoulder reassuringly. "Please don't worry. He asked for me, not Dante, and I bet a Prohibition agent would ask for the man of the house. Most likely, Mr. Crowell got my name from a satisfied customer and all he wanted was to take some good wine home to his wife. He probably hoped that if he wandered around long enough, he'd find me or someone else willing to sell him a barrel since you wouldn't. But just in case, I'll have Dominic and Vince move some brush to hide the foot of the trail. I doubt he'll return, but if he does, I'll take care of him myself."

"If he comes back, I don't think you should sell him any wine."

Guiditta smiled. "Because you don't want to be caught in a lie?"

"Because I don't like him," Rosa countered. "It's only one barrel of wine. Can't you let this one customer go, just in case he isn't really a customer?"

"Only one barrel of wine, you say, but one barrel of wine well appreciated might lead to another, and sales add up." Guiditta sighed, her gaze traveling the length of the vineyard from the rows where they stood to the road. In the distance, the sun in its decline nearly touched the tops of the mountains sheltering the valley. "But it wouldn't hurt to be cautious. If Mr. Crowell returns, and I doubt he will, I'll try to find out where he heard that we have wine for sale. If he can't name our mutual friend, I won't sell him a drop. Will that satisfy you?"

"Not entirely, but it'll do," said Rosa, and Guiditta laughed, throwing Rosa a smile that was both fond and teasing. She thought Rosa worried too much, and perhaps she did. From time to time, and almost always in jest, Guiditta made distinctions between the passionate, headstrong nature of the

Italian Cacchiones, and the more cautious, stoic temperament of the Norwegian Ottesens, no matter how often Rosa reminded her that she was of Spanish heritage. Unfortunately, Rosa's mistrust of Mr. Crowell fit too well into Guiditta's assumptions about Norwegian reserve to be entirely credible.

By the middle of May, tiny buds resembling miniature clusters of grapes appeared within the lush, green foliage throughout the vineyard, and Dante announced that it was time to begin suckering the grapevines. Just as pruning the dead or extraneous wood from the vines promoted better, stronger growth, so too did removing unnecessary leaves and shoots allow the strength and vigor of the plant generated from sunlight, earth, and water to flow into fewer, but healthier grapes with a superior taste.

Dante taught Rosa and Lars how to identify the most dominant shoots on the vine, those that had sprung from the prominent buds left behind during winter pruning. The dominant shoots would be left to grow into strong, vigorous clusters of grapes evenly spaced along the vine, while all others would be plucked away. Excess leaves should be removed as well, so that those remaining would be evenly exposed to the sunshine and dispersed enough to allow fresh breezes to circulate through them, helping to prevent the growth of fungus and mildew upon the clusters. As the grapes developed, they would gain better, more uniform exposure to the sun, enhancing their flavor and allowing them to ripen more evenly. At first Rosa and Lars worked under Dante's watchful eye, but before long they gained his confidence and he allowed them to thin the shoots and leaves unsupervised. Knowing how much Dante treasured his vines, Rosa was proud to have earned his trust.

One beautiful Thursday afternoon, Rosa was in the vineyard thinning shoots alongside Guiditta and Francesca while others labored along more distant rows. Lars was off planting saplings in the burgeoning apricot orchard on the sunny northern hills, and Dante, Dominic, and Vince were off on their weekly delivery run to San Francisco. Chatting with the other women while they worked, Rosa kept one ear tuned to the walnut grove where Lupita, Miguel, and the other children too young to attend school played under the watchful gaze of Mabel, who sat upon a faded quilt in the shade cuddling baby Sophia. Rosa glanced up at the sound of a car turning onto the gravel drive from the main road and spotted a dark sedan making its way up the hill.

"I'm off to earn my butter and egg money, or maybe my walnut and prune money," Guiditta joked as she went to see what the visitors wanted. "Save some shoots for me."

"We'll be sure to," Francesca promised. She and Rosa continued with their work and conversation, but not fifteen minutes later, the sound of automobiles speeding along the main road interrupted them. As they stood amid the trellises shading their eyes with their hands, they watched with rapidly increasing concern and bewilderment as two more dark sedans and a police wagon pulled off the main road onto the Cacchiones' driveway and raced up to the residence.

"Oh, no," Francesca breathed, dropping her pruning shears and running toward the house. "Papa and the boys. There must have been an accident."

Her heart in her throat, Rosa quickly hurried after her.

"What is it?" Mabel called frantically as they passed. "What's going on?"

"I'll find out and come right back," Rosa promised breathlessly as she ran by. She caught up with Francesca just before they reached the back of the winery, and when they rounded the corner and approached the rear of the house, she spotted the two sedans parked in the yard alongside the one that had arrived earlier. The police wagon pulled to a halt nearby with a screech of brakes and a cloud of dust. A few dark-suited men milled about as a pair of uniformed officers climbed down from the cab of the police wagon with weapons drawn. As Francesca came to an abrupt halt, Rosa too froze in place and watched in horror as Mr. Crowell emerged from around the front of the residence propelling Guiditta before him, her wrists handcuffed behind her back. She threw them a look of utter desperation as she stumbled toward the police wagon.

"Ma," Francesca shrieked. She darted forward and tried to tear Guiditta from Mr. Crowell's grasp, but another dark-suited man leapt forward, seized her by the shoulders, and pulled her away.

Rosa hurried after Guiditta. "What are you doing?" she cried, keeping herself between Mr. Crowell and the police wagon in a vain attempt to slow his progress. "Where are you taking her?"

"Mrs. Cacchione is under arrest for violating the Volstead Act," he barked, shoving Guiditta to the side when Rosa blocked his way. "I'm taking her to the courthouse in

Santa Rosa, where she'll be arraigned and held over for trial."

"On what grounds?" Rosa felt hands close around her upper arms as another dark-suited man seized her from behind, but she tore herself free and darted out of reach. "She's done nothing wrong. Let her go!"

"Frannie," Guiditta called shakily as Mr. Crowell forced her into the back of the police wagon. "Please meet Mario and Gina when they get off the school bus. Tell your brothers and sisters I'm fine and I'll be home soon." She flinched when Mr. Crowell snorted derisively, and then an officer slammed the doors behind her and she was gone from sight. With a groan the engine started and the wagon began to rumble down the gravel driveway.

The man restraining Francesca suddenly released her as the other men climbed into their cars. "Stop," she screamed, sprinting after the police wagon, but it sped away from her onto the main road, and eventually she stumbled to a halt, gasping. Rosa caught up to Francesca and put her arms around her, and Francesca clung to her, shaking and sobbing.

Lars reached them just as the cars were disappearing down the road toward Santa Rosa. "What happened?" he demanded, catching his breath after his hard sprint. Rosa quickly explained, and the grim look he gave her over Francesca's head told her that his worst fears had been realized. "I'll follow them and see what can be done. Francesca, can you fetch me the keys for your father's car?" Wordlessly, Francesca nodded, wiped her eyes with the back of her hand, and fled back to the house. When she returned with the keys, it was quickly decided that Francesca would accompany Lars to the courthouse, while Rosa would stay behind to meet the children at the school bus and tell Dante what had happened as soon as he returned from the delivery run.

After Lars and Francesca raced off, Rosa returned to the walnut grove and quietly gave Mabel the dreadful news. "I knew it," Mabel murmured bleakly, her face ashen. "I always knew something like this would happen someday. I warned Dominic, but he —" She pressed her lips together and shook her head, her eyes full of tears.

Although her heart pounded with frantic worry, Rosa took a deep, shaky breath and returned to the vineyard, hoping to calm herself with the distraction of familiar tasks. But her thoughts raced as she thinned shoots from the vines. She had known all along that Mr. Crowell couldn't be trusted. What had Guiditta done to prompt the arrest? What would become of her? Would the officers return later for Dante, Dominic, and Vince? Suddenly Rosa felt a chill of dread. What if Dante and his sons had already been apprehended on the way to San Francisco?

When Rosa spied the school bus approaching, she hurried off to meet it. She told the young Cacchiones in a voice ringing with false nonchalance that their mother was away on an errand, and she called all the children together into the Cacchiones' kitchen, where she and Mabel fixed them a snack and sent them back out to play. Then Rosa and Mabel waited, watching the road anxiously, keeping an eye on the children playing in the yard, passing the baby back and forth and alternately speculating quietly about what could be happening at the courthouse and reassuring each other that all would be well.

Suppertime approached with no word from the courthouse and no sign of their absent loved ones. Rosa and Mabel were too anxious to eat, but they prepared a simple meal of pasta, salad, and bread for the children, who happily enjoyed the novelty of sitting around the kitchen table together with no grown-ups to remind them to mind their manners. Only the eldest children, Marta and Ana among them, eventually noticed Rosa and Mabel's distraction and began watching them anxiously, gradually realizing that there was something strange and disturbing about the absence of their parents and eldest siblings.

At twilight, long after Rosa and Lars ordinarily would have taken their own children home to the cabin, Rosa gathered all of the youngsters around her in the Cacchiones' front room and was telling them a bedtime story when suddenly she heard the delivery truck rumbling up the driveway. Breaking off in mid-sentence, she hurried outside to meet them and told Dante all that had happened that day. Stricken, he ordered his sons to unload the empty casks and hide them in the old wine cellar. Rosa joined in, and as soon as the last cask was hidden away, Dante leapt back behind the wheel and sped off down the road toward the courthouse. Dominic had wanted to accompany him, but just as he was climbing into the truck beside his father, Mabel returned from checking on the baby and begged him not to go. Rosa read the terror in her eyes and knew that Mabel feared that if the Cacchione men set foot in the courthouse, they would not be allowed to leave. Reluctantly Dominic agreed to remain behind, and as Dante raced off in the delivery truck, Mabel fell into her husband's arms and began to weep.

The hour had grown late, the children were tired and curious, and Rosa knew she had to take them home. Vince promised to run down to the cabin as soon as they had any news, so Rosa hugged Mabel, gathered up her children, and headed off down the path through the vineyard. Miguel fell asleep in her arms moments after they set out, and Lupita clung to her hand, yawning and dragging her feet. Marta and Ana walked a few paces ahead with the lantern, talking in hushed voices and glancing over their shoulders at Rosa from time to time, their sweet faces drawn in puzzlement and worry.

Later, after Rosa tucked them into bed, she sat alone in the front room, gazing out the window into the darkness and straining her ears for the sound of an approaching car. She heard the attic stairs creaking and glanced around to find Marta tiptoeing downstairs in her nightgown. Rosa held out her arms and Marta climbed onto her lap as if she were as young as Lupita again. "Mamá," she asked, resting her head on

Rosa's shoulder, "where's Pa? Where's Mrs. Cacchione, really?"

Gently Rosa told her that Mrs. Cacchione had been arrested but assured her that Lars, Mr. Cacchione, and Francesca were doing all they could to gain her release. When Marta asked if Mrs. Cacchione had done something wrong, Rosa told her in all truthfulness that she wasn't sure what in particular had prompted the arrest.

To Rosa's surprise, Marta nodded knowingly. "The Cacchiones are selling wine, aren't they? Mario told me they do."

Rosa sighed, smoothed Marta's chestnut hair away from her face, and kissed her on the top of the head. "Mrs. Cacchione has sold wine from time to time."

"But that's against the law. It's wrong."

Rosa hesitated. It was against the law, but whether it was wrong, she was not entirely sure anymore. "If being against the law is enough to make it wrong, then yes, it would be wrong."

Marta peered up at her, curious, a question on her lips, but before she could speak, they heard boots on the front porch and the front door swung open. "Pa!" Marta exclaimed, leaping up from Rosa's lap and flinging her arms around Lars's waist. He hugged her and glanced over her head to

Rosa, shaking his head, grim and exhausted.

"Is Mrs. Cacchione home?" Marta asked.

Lars hesitated. "Yes, Mrs. Cacchione is safe at home," he said carefully. "She's very tired and I'm sure she's climbing into bed this very moment, and bed is where you should be too." Visibly relieved, Marta nodded, gave Rosa one last kiss good night, and tiptoed back up to the attic. Rosa and Lars both listened for the sound of creaking bedsprings, and when all was quiet overhead, Lars beckoned Rosa to follow him into the kitchen. There he removed his hat, splashed his face with water, and settled wearily into a chair, resting his elbows on the table. Rosa offered to make him a cup of coffee or something to eat, but he declined, saying that all he wanted was a good night's sleep. Gesturing for quiet, he said, "Guiditta and Francesca are home, but Dante's still down at the courthouse."

"What?" Rosa exclaimed, lowering her voice to add, "Why?"

"He convinced the judge that Guiditta was only following his instructions and that he should be arrested instead. The judge agreed to the exchange since, as he said, it would be a great hardship for the children if their mother were locked up."

Rosa sank into a chair across the table

from Lars. "And it won't be a hardship if their father is locked up?"

"It's what Dante wanted. It's what any man would do for the woman he loves, the mother of his children."

Their eyes met, and involuntarily Rosa held his gaze until she couldn't bear it any longer and let her eyes fall to her hands, clasped tightly in her lap. "What's —" She cleared her throat and tried again. "What's going to become of Dante?"

"There'll be a trial, and he'll be sentenced. With any luck the judge will hit him with a stiff fine rather than a few years in jail. At least then he'd be free to provide for his family, though obviously not in the way he has been."

Rosa pressed a hand to her forehead, dizzy. Although immeasurably better than a prison sentence, a stiff fine might still be enough to ruin the Cacchiones. "Oh, Lars. This is terrible, just terrible."

"It is, but they made their choices, Rosa, knowing the consequences."

"What choice did they ever really have?" she countered. "They couldn't give up their vineyard. You're a farmer. You know what it means to lose land your family has held for generations."

415

"Yes, I know," he replied quietly. "As do you."

They sat silently for a moment, each lost in thought, each longing for beloved acres, rolling hills and tilled fields and rich soil, the promise of spring and the abundance of harvest. Rosa understood why the Cacchiones had taken such risks to hold on to their land, defying the law and courting danger rather than letting their cherished ranch slip from their grasp. She might have done the same in their place. She would have done the same.

The next morning, Lars rose before dawn, bolted down his breakfast, and hurried off to the Cacchione residence to check in with Guiditta and Dominic before heading out to the orchard. Rosa saw Marta and Ana off to the school bus and hurried after him as soon as she could, Lupita and Miguel in tow. The yard was empty and hushed, the usual bustle of a spring morning on the ranch oddly absent. Unsettled, Rosa found the Cacchione children playing with jacks and wooden trains on the front porch and sent Lupita and Miguel running off to join them while she went inside to the kitchen. There she found Guiditta, pale and drawn, sitting with a cup of coffee cooling in her grasp, a plate of eggs, buttered toast, and ham untouched on the table before her. Mabel and Francesca sat on either side of her while Vince paced nearby, scowling and muttering under his breath. They greeted Rosa with bleak, wordless nods, all except Guiditta, who stared straight ahead at nothing, her face hollow and gray, dark circles beneath her eyes, her lips almost colorless.

Dominic had already left to meet with the family's lawyer, Francesca told her, and with occasional worried glances at her mother, she explained what had happened the day before to provoke Guiditta's arrest. Mr. Crowell had asked for another half dozen prunes and lunch, and Guiditta had offered him a glass of wine with her usual intimation that it was from the family's two hundred gallon supply for their own personal enjoyment. When Mr. Crowell praised the vintage and asked to purchase a jug to take home to his wife, she remembered Rosa's warnings and cautiously demurred. But Mr. Crowell persisted, promising to pay top dollar and mentioning a neighbor who, he claimed, had assured him Guiditta had excellent wines to sell. Guiditta knew the neighbor he named, and thus reassured, the lure of the astonishing price Mr. Crowell offered proved too great a temptation.

Guiditta sold him a jug of wine for five dollars, unaware that his colleagues from the Prohibition bureau were watching the scene unfold through binoculars, awaiting his signal to swoop in and arrest her.

"He said Clifford Clarkston sent him," Guiditta said numbly when Francesca finished. "He had a name. I believed him. And now we're ruined."

They all hastened to assure Guiditta that she should not lose hope, that the judge had shown mercy in allowing Dante to take her place and that he might be more merciful still throughout Dante's trial. But Guiditta was not comforted, and in the two weeks leading up to Dante's trial, she sank deeper into despondency.

The proceedings were swift and methodical, retold in exacting detail in the Santa Rosa *Press Democrat* and followed closely by everyone in Sonoma County — and with apprehension by Dante's fellow grape growers, many of whom were themselves bootleggers. As testimony proceeded, it came out that Mr. Crowell had not chosen Clifford Clarkston's name at random merely to lend credibility to his story, but rather that the neighbor had fired off an angry letter to the "lazy" Prohibition bureau to report the Cacchiones and to demand that the department "step on them" and help make Sonoma County dry and sober once and for all.

Arriving home after a grueling day in court, a bewildered and exhausted Guiditta told Rosa that she couldn't understand why Clifford Clarkston had reported them. Their families had always gotten along well enough, except for one incident about five years before. Clifford and Dante had exchanged heated words after Clifford had let his fence fall into disrepair and his cows had wandered onto the Cacchiones' property, destroying a half-acre of the Cacchiones' oldest and most prized Zinfandel vines before the herd could be rounded up. But that had been years ago. Clifford had paid for the damage and the Cacchiones had put the matter behind them. They assumed Clifford had too, but evidently he had nursed a grudge all the while, and had at last found a way to satisfy it.

The Cacchiones' lawyer put forth a valiant defense, but eventually Dante was found guilty and sentenced to a one-thousand-dollar fine and two years in prison. As the sentence was handed down, the crowds packed into the courthouse burst into catcalls and angry jeers, Guiditta's anguished cry ringing out above the uproar. Dante merely lifted his chin stoically and allowed the bailiff to lead him away in shackles.

But the family's punishment did not end there. Two days after Dante was sentenced, Mr. Crowell again led a team of Prohibition agents and police officers to Cacchione Vineyards, but this time someone tipped off the press and a team of photographers and reporters accompanied them. Rosa, Lars, and the children stood with the Cacchione family behind the residence as Crowell led a group of officers and agents to the winery. Flash pans burst and reporters jotted notes. Crowell paused a few paces away from where Guiditta stood at the top of the back stairs and ordered her to unlock the heavy redwood doors.

"I seem to have misplaced my husband's key," Guiditta replied in a clear, steady voice.

Crowell squinted up at her. "You sure about that?"

Guiditta nodded.

Crowell studied her for a moment, then craned his neck and shouted to a pair of officers waiting by the cars. "Tell Donaldson to bring the axe."

Another uniformed officer promptly hurried over, his beefy fists clenched around the thick wooden handle of an axe. Crowell waved him ahead to the winery doors. The officer raised the axe over his right shoulder and took a careful practice swing. He planted his feet, raised the axe again, and —

"Wait," Guiditta called, digging into her dress pocket and producing an iron key. "I found it."

Unamused chuckles and mutterings went up from the men gathered in front of the winery. Her chin held high, Guiditta crossed the yard and unlocked the doors, and the waiting officers immediately swept past her into the winery. As the photographers and reporters swarmed near, Guiditta pushed through the crowd and retreated to the safety of the back steps. Rosa put her arm around Guiditta's waist, and only then did she realize Guiditta was shaking.

The Cacchiones and their employees and children watched, motionless and silent and powerless, as the agents hauled the barrels up from the wine cellar, knocked out the bungs, and poured the rich, red wine onto the ground. At first the dusty earth drank it in, but as thousands and thousands of gallons spilled out into the yard, puddles formed, and then pools, and then a river of wine flowed down the hill. The agents laughed and joked as they jumped out of the way; reporters and photographers, engrossed in recording the scene, cursed as the cascade splashed over their leather shoes and soaked the cuffs of their trousers. Crowell and some of the other agents posed for photographs with the wine barrels before they knocked out the bungs; Rosa knew those photos would run in papers across the country alongside warnings to other bootleggers that eventually the law would catch up with them as it had the Cacchiones.

Suddenly Guiditta choked out a sob, but she caught herself, drew in a quick breath, and watched as the officers brought out a barrel of the Cacchiones' best vintages, one that could age for ten to thirty years, the wine Guiditta had called their long-term investment. Rosa and Francesca stood on either side of her, their arms around her, keeping her on her feet when she wavered. A photographer turned their way, but just before the flash pan exploded with light, Rosa ducked her head and allowed her hair to fall in her face. She glanced Lars's way and saw that he had stepped behind Dominic and turned his head just in time. Rosa's heart pounded as other photographers and reporters crowded around, shouting over one another to be heard as they fired questions at Guiditta, at Dominic, at any of them who might respond.

Francesca shrank back, but Guiditta stood her ground, looking defiantly into the cameras although she did not answer the questions shouted at her. "Would you take the children inside?" she asked Rosa in an undertone. Eager to avoid the cameras, Rosa nodded, gathered the children, and ushered them through the back door into the kitchen.

Just as she was about to follow them indoors, she felt a hand close around her elbow. "Well, Mrs. Ottesen," Crowell addressed her, a triumphant gleam in his eye. "Were you aware that it's against the law to lie to a federal officer involved in an investigation?"

"Only if you're aware that you're doing so," Rosa countered, yanking her arm free of his grasp. "Isn't it against the law to pressure someone else into breaking the law? If it isn't it should be."

Crowell smiled faintly. "I asked around, and you want to hear something interesting? I didn't find any Nils or Rose Ottesen in state or federal tax records going back ten years. Nor do either of your names appear on any voter registration lists, city directories, or the register of live births." He nodded to the kitchen windows, where

Rosa's children and Guiditta's alike were peering through the glass, wide-eyed, tearful, and worried. "Your children were born in Oxnard, weren't they? Mrs. Cacchione said that's where you're from."

Rosa's heart plummeted. She wondered what else Guiditta might have casually let slip as she had served Crowell his lunch that fateful day. "You must have overlooked something."

"On the contrary, I was very thorough." His mouth curved in a mocking grin. "Very thorough."

"Not thorough enough, obviously." Rosa yanked open the back door. "You were looking in the wrong place. We're not from Oxnard. We're from Stavanger. Since you apparently don't have anything better to do than to snoop around into other people's lives, you might as well start digging there."

"I will," he assured her, touching the brim of his hat as if to thank her for her assistance.

Without another word, Rosa went inside and shut the door in his smirking face before he could glimpse the dismay in her eyes. She knew he would not let the matter rest.

Another two hours passed before the officers finished emptying the wine barrels in the yard and searching the outbuildings for more. Eventually all the Cacchiones retreated inside, but Guiditta, Dominic, and Francesca were often drawn to the windows, where they would watch the officers and agents at their work, shake their heads bleakly, and turn away. A frisson of apprehension filled the residence as everyone waited for some black-suited agent to stumble upon the footpath to the old wine cellar Vince had concealed behind a pile of brush, which only at first glance appeared to have been arranged by nature. But the searchers did not venture far beyond the outbuildings. Perhaps because they had found so much wine padlocked behind the chicken wire, they assumed that there could not possibly be any more to find. They had spilled more than 120,000 gallons of wine that day in a river that continued to flow from the front of the winery through the grapevines and downhill to the creek. The wine-soaked air was heavy with the fragrance of berries and black pepper, and throughout the yard, empty barrels lay abandoned on their sides as if scattered by a violent windstorm.

Eventually the agents and officers must have decided that their work was done, for they climbed back into their cars and police wagons and drove off. With nothing interesting to detain them, the reporters and photographers soon followed. At last the ranch was still. Dominic and Vince were the first to step outside and survey the damage the men had left behind, but the others soon joined them, except for Mabel, who remained inside to watch the children. The ranch had been thrown into utter disarray. Tools had been torn from their hooks in the barn; the winery was a mess of twisted chicken wire and splintered wood; the yard was a swamp of red-hued mud buzzing with bees drawn by the enticing scent of wine; and the livestock had been neglected all day. Rosa and Lars helped the Cacchiones restore the ranch to some semblance of order, breaking only for a hasty supper of bread, cheese, and prunes. Only the children mustered up much of an appetite.

At dusk Guiditta wearily announced that they had done enough for one day and could finish up in the morning. She blinked back tears, but her voice was steady as she thanked Rosa and Lars for their help. "You're true friends and loyal neighbors," she said, embracing each of them in turn, and Rosa couldn't help thinking of the neighbor who had informed on them. She imagined his narrow, bitter face lighting up with vengeful glee as he pored over the Santa Rosa *Press Democrat* the next day, his thin lips moving silently as he read each painful detail of the Cacchiones' downfall, his eager gaze lingering on the photographs of the spilled wine and ruined family.

The photographs. Rosa felt a chill of dread as she and Lars and the children picked their way along the muddy footpath toward the cabin. Although they had tried to avoid the cameras, there was no way to be sure they had succeeded. If they had been captured on film, their photographs might appear in newspapers throughout California and across the nation, divulging their location and their new identities. Anyone could find them — and their pursuers would find an eager accomplice in Crowell if their search led them his way.

As Rosa, Lars, and the children reached the cabin, the forlorn scent of spilled wine wafted on the breeze. Suddenly Ana seized Rosa's hand. "Look, Mamá," she cried, pointing. "The creek!"

Rosa halted, transfixed by the sight of red, foaming liquid spilling over the smooth stones of the creek, where clear waters had sparkled only hours before. A river of wine flowed past their cabin home, each drop representing years of toil and patience wasted, as it carried a family's lost hopes and prosperity to the ocean miles away.

CHAPTER SEVEN

Word of the raid on Cacchione Vineyards spread swiftly through Santa Rosa and throughout Sonoma County. Friends and neighbors came by, bringing casseroles and sympathy and offering their support. Clifford Clarkston was denounced by one and all so vehemently that it seemed to Rosa he would have been well advised to pack his bags and leave town, for he had few friends left in Santa Rosa. It seemed to Rosa that everyone wanted to know, but none dared ask, what Guiditta planned to do next.

Alegra and Paulo Del Bene were among the first to visit. Paulo, proving himself a staunch friend, attended Dante's sentencing and visited him in prison at least once a week. The Del Benes took up a collection to pay Dante's fine, and Rosa overheard Paulo promise Guiditta that the Del Benes would help the Cacchiones however else they could. Privately, Paulo told Lars that the Del Benes' sacramental wine permit had not shielded them from Crowell's relentless scrutiny. Before Crowell had revealed himself as a Prohibition agent, he had come nosing around their place, insisting he had it on good authority that they regularly sold wine to San Francisco tourists and demanding that he be included on their list of trusted customers. Since Guiditta's arrest, he had inspected their winery every week, determined to find evidence of criminal activity. He so intimidated Alegra that she had taken to hurrying inside with the children whenever she heard a car approach. If business called Paulo away from the vineyard, she would remain indoors all day with the curtains drawn, pretending no one was home. Paulo had complained to the Prohibition bureau, but Crowell's superiors apparently concluded that the Del Benes wanted him to back off because they had something to hide, and the frequency of his visits increased.

Naturally Lars told Rosa, and Rosa, troubled and indignant, urged Alegra to bring the children to the cabin for the day whenever she felt unsafe at home alone. Or, if Crowell showed up to bother her, Alegra should call the Cacchiones and Rosa would come right over.

To her surprise, Alegra's cheeks flushed and she demurred. "I didn't mean to worry Paulo — or anyone else," she said quietly, her eyes downcast. "I shouldn't have complained. Mr. Crowell's a nuisance, but I'm sure he'll eventually tire of this game and leave us alone. We haven't done anything wrong. We have a sacramental permit and we sell our wine only to the diocese and not a drop to anyone else. Mr. Crowell can search our property all he likes, he can nag me until he runs out of breath, but it won't do him any good. He won't find any evidence against us because there isn't anything to find."

"In that case, I wouldn't put it past him to invent something," Rosa said darkly, but when Alegra blanched, she quickly apologized, regretting her gallows humor. Alegra managed a strained smile and told her there was no harm done.

A week after the river of wine flowed downhill from the winery and stained the creek red, Rosa received a letter from Mrs. Phillips. She had read about the raid in the *San Francisco Examiner,* and she had enclosed the article. "I'm sorry to see that your family has been caught up in these troubles," she wrote. "If you ever need a place to stay, remember that my door is always open to you." Though Rosa was touched by Mrs. Phillips's concern, any comfort she might have found in the offer of sanctuary immediately vanished when she unfolded the newspaper clipping. A photograph of Crowell surrounded by his agents as he knocked the bung from a barrel appeared next to a picture of an officer posed in front of the winery doors gripping the unnecessary and unused axe. Beneath those was a photo of the Cacchiones standing behind the residence, stricken and angry as they watched the agents and police at work. Among them stood Rosa, hair in her face and Miguel on her hip, and Lars, half hidden behind Dominic. Although their faces were partially concealed, Mrs. Phillips had still recognized them. Granted, she knew they worked for the Cacchiones and would have made a point to look for them in the photos, but someone who knew them well might be able to identify them from as little as a casual glance at the newspaper.

But what was done was done. Rosa and Lars could not erase their images from the newspaper. The question that haunted Rosa was what they should do next.

They could continue on with their new lives in Santa Rosa, taking a chance that the people searching for them would never see the photo, or if they did, that they would not think to question the caption that identified those pictured as members of the Cacchione family. Or they could flee without a trace, without telling any of their new friends where they intended to go, and start over somewhere else. Rosa knew that would be the most prudent course, but she couldn't bear to uproot the children again and she couldn't imagine where else they might go. Nor did she wish to leave. She cared about her new friends, she found solace in the beauty of the northern California countryside, and, despite the struggles that afflicted grape ranchers throughout Sonoma County, she enjoyed working on the vineyard. The alchemy that transformed luscious grapes into rich wines fascinated her, so whenever she had the opportunity, she queried Dante and Guiditta about wine-making — how variations in sunlight affected the flavor of the fruit, how barrels made from one species of oak or another imparted different tastes and aromas to the wine stored within them. The making of a truly magnificent wine seemed both an art and a science, with a dash of faith and magic thrown in for good measure. Rosa wished she could try her hand at it, and she often thought about asking Dante for cuttings so she could plant a few grapevines on a small plot of level ground east of the cabin. But then she gazed upon the acres of trellises the Cacchiones cultivated, and she considered how generations of their family had plowed their hearts and souls into the arid soil from which their grapevines sprang, and her fond wish seemed an insensitive lark, especially with Dante behind bars for refusing to abandon the vintner's craft he so cherished. Who was she to think she could fare any better than the Cacchiones had, especially in such troubled times?

But then a spark of defiance would flare up and she would think, well, why couldn't she? Certainly not yet, and perhaps not for a long while, but why couldn't she try her hand at winemaking? The law permitted households to make up to two hundred gallons for the family's personal use, and she wouldn't want to make even that much, since Lars wouldn't drink it. Perhaps someday, if she had a few acres to call her own and Prohibition ended and if her vintages were good enough, she could even open her own winery to the public.

But those dreams, as far off into the future as they were, bound her and the children to the northern California wine country. But Lars didn't need to stay — and shouldn't stay — now that their photo had been plastered on the fifth page of the *San Francisco Examiner* and reprinted in an unknowable number of other papers across the country.

She told him so one night after the children had gone to bed, as they sat on the front porch talking and listening to the creek and the wind in the oaks.

"You're free to go your own way," she said quietly, cupping her half-empty wineglass in her hands. "You probably should."

"I'm aware of that," said Lars mildly. "How could I not be, considering how often you tell me so?"

"It's dangerous for you to stay with us. It always was, but it's even more so now that our picture was in the paper. What if John's gangster friends see it?"

"What are the odds that they will?"

"I'd rather not gamble that they won't," Rosa retorted, frustrated by his inability or unwillingness to recognize the danger. "Not when your life is at stake."

"Some rather unpleasant folks are looking for you too, but you're staying put."

"The only people who want to find me are John and the Arboles Valley police. John's locked up and it'll be years before I have to worry about him showing up around here. The police want me for questioning, nothing more, and they think I'm dead. The people looking for you want to kill you —" Rosa choked up, composed herself, and pressed on. "I couldn't bear that."

"Rosa." Lars sighed, took the wineglass from her, set it on the floor, and took her hands in his. "They aren't going to kill me. They aren't even going to find me. Anyway, you're the one who took their money. You're in just as much danger as I am. Either we all leave, or we all stay, but we're going to do it together — you, me, and the children."

The children. Of course. They were the link that bound Lars to her. "I know you can't bear the thought of leaving the children unprotected. You have to believe I'll keep them safe."

"I know you will," he said, his brow furrowing. As many times as she had reminded him that he was not bound to them, she had never pressed him so urgently, and she knew he didn't like it. "But you won't have to bear that responsibility alone. I'm not going anywhere, Rosa, not without you and the children."

"Be practical, Lars. You ought to think of your own safety."

"I'm their father. It's my duty to think of their safety before my own."

"You're Marta and Lupita's father."

He studied her, incredulous. "Do you really think I care any less for Ana and Miguel?"

"I — I didn't mean that the way it sounded. I know you'd miss them — all four of them — and they'd miss you too. I know you love them —"

"Rosa, I love *you*," he broke in. "Yes, I love the children, but I also love you. If we had no children, I would still love you, and I would still stay with you. I'm where I want to be — with you. Don't you realize that by now?"

"I — you loved me once, long ago, but —"

"I love you still," he said firmly, tightening his grip around her hands. "That hasn't changed. Come on, Rosa. You've always been the smartest girl in school. Think about it. Do you really think I've stayed out of obligation or out of love for the children but not because I also love you?"

As he spoke, Rosa tried to blink away her gathering tears. "I can't divorce John," she choked out. "I would if I could, but the moment I file the papers he would know where we are. Everyone would know who we are. It's too great a risk."

"I know that, Rosa." Lars stroked her hair

away from her face and caressed her cheek. "I know you're married. I know you can't marry me. I love you anyway. That's not going to change. I'm going to love you, cherish you, honor you, and be faithful to you as long as I live. Maybe I won't ever be able to make those vows standing beside you before a priest or a justice of the peace, but that doesn't mean I consider them any less true."

"It's too much. I can't ask that of you."

"That's fine, since you didn't ask. You didn't need to."

"But it's not right for you to promise me so much when I have so little to offer you in return."

He studied her for a moment, searching her face for the secrets of her heart. "Are you really going to sit there, look me in the eye, tell me you don't love me, and expect me to believe it?"

"I do love you," she said, her voice an ache in her throat. She should have told him sooner or not at all. "Of course I love you. I love you with all my heart."

"Then what's all this nonsense about having nothing to offer me?" He looked pained, bewildered. "Your love is everything to me, Rosa. Of all the things I've lost in my life, your love is the only one I know I can't live without." He glanced away, cleared his throat. "I'm staying, Rosa. Stop telling me I should leave you."

She choked out a laugh. "That never works anyway," she said, smiling through her tears. "Every time I tell you to go away, you always come back."

"And I always will," he said, "but just the same, I'd prefer it if you'd stop asking."

She laughed again and agreed, nodding and wiping the tears from her eyes. Then his arms were around her and his lips were touching hers, and she knew that whatever dangers lay ahead, they would face them together.

Two weeks after Dante's sentencing, Guiditta asked Rosa and Lars to join the Cacchiones for supper. Dante's absence cast a pall over the gathering, but the meal was excellent as always, the roast chicken and tender pasta and vegetables fresh from the garden as full of flavor as the wine Guiditta poured. Afterward, the younger children ran off to chase fireflies in the vineyard while their elders lingered at the table, refilling their glasses — all except Lars, who abstained despite the teasing and cajoling of his hostess. They savored the vintage wistfully, for when it was gone, they might not make any new wine to replace it. It was risky enough to steal away to the old wine cellar and retrieve a cask for the family's use, never knowing who might be observing them through binoculars from a distant hill or when Crowell might suddenly appear for an impromptu inspection. When harvest came, they could not risk a crush. They would have to sell the entire crop as wine grapes, or try to, praying that the market would not be saturated that autumn, that their carloads would be unloaded immediately upon arrival at the train station in New York, and that they would avoid the multitude of other hazards that might befall them — frost, insects, hail, flood, drought.

But when Guiditta sighed, rested her elbows on the table, and regarded each of them steadily and with new fire in her gaze, Rosa knew she had no intention of relying upon wine grape sales alone. "Thanks to the Del Benes, and to all our friends who threw money into their hat, we're able to pay your father's fine," she said, looking at her children but then including Rosa and Lars with a nod. "However, we have nothing left over to see us through the harvest."

"We can still sell prunes, walnuts, and lunches to passing tourists as we always have," said Mabel, shifting baby Sophia on her lap. "We can add eggs and plum preserves to the list too, and instead of waiting for customers to come to us, we can sell to some of the markets in Santa Rosa. If we economize, we'll be all right."

"What about selling those twenty acres we talked about?" Dominic asked his mother. "The timber alone would fetch us a good price."

"No, son," said Guiditta, shaking her head. "We've discussed this, and I haven't changed my mind. I won't sell any of the Cacchione family land except as a last resort. Your father entrusted Cacchione Vineyards to us while he's away, and when he comes home, I want him to find it whole and thriving." She made it sound as if her husband were merely away on a long but necessary journey from which he would soon return. "The old wine cellar is still full of wonderful vintages, but they won't stay wonderful forever. We can't wait. We have to sell it now before it turns, while we still can."

Stunned, Rosa sat back in her chair as Mabel and Francesca exclaimed in astonishment. Dominic said nothing, but a muscle worked in his jaw as if he had been expecting and dreading his mother's announcement. Vince leaned forward, his face alight with eager determination, and said, "Now you're talking."

"How can you suggest such a thing after all we've been through?" protested Mabel. Startled, baby Sophia whimpered on her lap. Mabel patted her soothingly and added in a gentler voice, "That Crowell wretch is watching us every moment. We'll get caught, and we'll join Papa Dante in prison."

"Not every moment," said Francesca, although she looked apprehensive. "He spends a lot of time over at the Del Bene place pestering poor Alegra."

"Crowell has never come out our way before ten o'clock in the morning," said Guiditta. "I can't imagine he'll suddenly start showing up before dawn. We can have the truck loaded and ready to go well before then, as we always have. He'll never know."

"There are other Prohibition agents and police out there who keep earlier hours," Dominic reminded her, "and other dangerous fellows on the roads between here and the ferry to San Francisco."

"I'm in," declared Vince. "I can make three deliveries a week if you need me to, Ma, and I can start first thing tomorrow. Our customers might need a bit of sweet talking at first, since we left them in the lurch."

"They ought to understand that wasn't

our doing," said Dominic. "We didn't have any warning ourselves. We should have. We've paid enough in bribes."

Guiditta nodded, frowning thoughtfully. "Vince is right. It's been a few weeks, and most of our customers have probably found other suppliers for the meantime, but they surely read the papers and know what's been happening here. Our wines should win them back, but if that fails, knock something off the price to sweeten the deal. Not too much, mind you. We need to sell as much of our wine as we can, as soon as possible. I want every barrel in the old wine cellar empty by winter."

"I can't believe we're even considering this," said Mabel, shaking her head.

"We don't have any choice," Guiditta countered. "It's sell the wine or sell the land, and I'll be damned if I'll sell a single acre without your father here to tell me that's what he wants."

"We'll sell all the wine, and we won't hold anything back," declared Vince. "We'll make a bundle and be done with bootlegging once and for all."

Mabel sharply glanced his way, and then looked to Guiditta. "Is that true? After we sell all the wine, we can get out of the bootlegging business once and for all?"

Guiditta smiled sadly. "Once we sell all our wine, we'll have no more to sell, will we?"

"You should still crush grapes this fall," Rosa broke in. "Forgive me. I realize this is a family matter, but shouldn't you make at least a small amount of new wine? Or hold back some of your younger vintages just in case?"

"In case of what?" asked Vince.

"In case Prohibition is repealed." Rosa looked around the table and noted the range of expression from thoughtfulness to incredulity. "It could happen, and you ought to be prepared."

"Our license to store wine was revoked," Guiditta reminded her. "If Crowell or any of his ilk discovers more than two hundred gallons of alcohol on our property, we'll be punished to the fullest extent of the law. Dante's case generated too much notoriety. No judge would show mercy for a second offense from the infamous Cacchione family."

"Then make two hundred gallons and not a pint more."

"I realize that sounds like a lot of wine," said Dominic, "and it is, for a single family's household use, but that's not nearly enough to keep a winery in business."

"Two hundred gallons is better than no wine at all," Rosa persisted. "The day Prohibition is repealed, customers will come from miles around to buy every drop of wine you have in your cellar. But that's only if you have wine to sell. You'll earn exactly nothing from every barrel of wine you decide not to make."

"She's right," said Vince. "We should keep back two hundred gallons of the vintages that'll age well and sell everything else. That way we'll be prepared."

"We should clear that cellar of every barrel, cask, and growler and not even think about replenishing them until it's legal to do so," Mabel countered. "And that day may never come. As long as there's a Republican president in the White House, Prohibition will be the law of the land, no matter how many families it bankrupts, no matter how many gangsters it enriches. They don't care what happens to people like us, as long as they get their share."

"Let's all take a deep breath," advised Dominic. "In the end, it's Ma's decision, and we'll abide by what she says."

"No, that's not how I want this to be," said Guiditta. "If we do sell our wine, we'll all take on the risks involved, so we should all share in the decision. That's why I've included you in this discussion, Nils and Rose, for all that Rose insists that it's a family matter."

"Well, you all know how I feel," said Mabel wearily. "I think we should sell all the wine and be finished with bootlegging once and for all. We shouldn't crush this fall or make any new wine until and unless it's legal to do so. We can still grow and sell wine grapes. We still have prunes and walnuts, and in a few years we'll have apricots. That will have to be enough."

"Even if we're tightfisted, that probably *won't* be enough," said Vince. "The feds don't know about the old wine cellar and they don't ever have to find out. We should go on as we have been — except no more selling glasses of wine to passing tourists, Ma. We'll sell to the hotels and speakeasies in San Francisco and nowhere else. As for new wine, I think we should make all we want. No two-hundred-gallon limit for me. Might as well be hanged for a sheep as for a lamb."

"Better not to be hanged at all," said Francesca with a shudder. "I think we should keep all the wine in the old cellar locked up good and tight, and not crush this fall. I don't think Pa would want any of us to join him in prison."

"We won't get caught," scoffed Vince.

"Ma got caught."

"We won't repeat her mistakes."

"No, we'll make fresh new ones, especially now that the police are watching us more closely than ever."

"Children, please," said Guiditta. "Don't bicker."

"What do you think, Nils?" asked Dominic.

Lars folded his arms across his chest, weighing his words carefully. "I think you should keep two hundred gallons of the vintages that will age well, so that you'll have inventory on hand to sell should Prohibition end. Dump the rest of the wine and make no more."

"Dump it?" exclaimed Rosa. "Think of all the years of hard work and time and patience that wine represents. How would your family feel if apricots were suddenly declared illegal and Crowell and his men emptied out your drying sheds and ordered you not to grow any more? Would you cut down every apricot tree on the Jorgensen ranch?"

Abruptly she fell silent, realizing she had said too much even before Lars shot her a warning look. "Apricots are not wine, and it's a fallacy to compare the two," he said.

447

"I'm not suggesting the Cacchiones should uproot their grapevines. They can still grow and sell wine grapes. Anything else is too risky considering they're known bootleggers."

"Find me a grape grower in all of Sonoma County who isn't a bootlegger," said Vince.

"The Del Benes and the Vanellis, just to name two," said Francesca. "We should take a page from their book. How do they get by?"

"With the help of a sacramental wine permit in one case and table grapes in the other," said Dominic. "We don't have those options."

The debate wore on until late in the evening, when everyone ran out of arguments and Guiditta said that she would sleep on it and let them know her decision in the morning. It seemed to Rosa that everyone left the table worried and dissatisfied in varying degrees. There was, simply, no perfect resolution for the problems they faced, and any path they chose would lead them through hazardous terrain.

For her part, Rosa remained incredulous that Lars thought the Cacchiones ought to dump their precious stores of wine, but she shared his belief that it would be dangerous and imprudent to resume bootlegging. Rosa thought they should instead keep the old wine cellar well stocked with their best vintages, dumping wine under the cover of night only if it turned. They could make two hundred gallons of new wine each year, remaining within the legal limit, and as they emptied barrels taken from the old wine cellar, they could replace them with the new vintages stored in the winery. That way they would continue to replenish their hidden stores as older vintages failed, but an outside observer would never find more than the legally permitted amount of wine in their main cellars. When Rosa suggested this to Guiditta, however, Lars pointed out that her plan depended upon the old wine cellar remaining a carefully guarded secret. If Crowell or another agent strolled merely a few paces beyond the yard, he would stumble upon the footpath that would lead straight to the old wine cellar. The Cacchiones were fortunate that it had escaped notice thus far, but Lars doubted their luck would hold. If and when the old wine cellar was discovered, it must hold no more than two hundred gallons of wine, or the Cacchiones would be undone.

The next morning, Guiditta waited for Lars and Rosa to arrive before announcing her decision. She intended to resume deliveries to San Francisco, selling as much wine as they could as quickly as possible, reserving only the finer vintages whose quality would improve rather than diminish with a few more years to age. As for the autumn crush, Guiditta would discuss their options with Dante the next time she visited him and defer her final decision until a few weeks before harvest. Considering how their shipment of wine grapes had been allowed to rot in a train car parked at the station the previous year, she was reluctant to rely too much upon those estimated profits and would prefer to make new wine.

Later, when Rosa and Lars could discuss matters privately, they discovered that they had both reached the same conclusion: They sympathized with the Cacchiones, but bootlegging obliged them to venture into the same circles as the police and the mob, the very people whose attention Rosa and Lars dared not draw. The longer they remained at Cacchione Vineyards, the more likely they were to cross paths with someone who could connect Nils and Rose Ottesen with Lars Jorgensen and Rosa Diaz Barclay.

Then, two days after Dominic and Vince resumed their deliveries to the city, a letter arrived at the vineyard addressed to Rosa Barclay in care of Guiditta Cacchione.

When Guiditta showed it to her over their morning coffee, Rosa went cold. "That 'E' looks like an 'A,' but the name could be Rose," Guiditta said, puzzling over the words scrawled on the outside of the envelope. Rosa did not recognize the block printing, but one glimpse of the Ventura County postmark sent shock and fear coursing through her veins. "But 'Barclay'? Does this mean anything to you, Rose?"

"Barclay is my maiden name," said Rosa faintly, taking the envelope and tucking it quickly into her pocket. It was all she could do to sip her coffee and discuss the day's work with Guiditta, Francesca, and the others rather than bolting from the kitchen and tearing open the envelope where no one could observe her — or compulsively flinging it unread into the fire.

It was midmorning before she could slip away unnoticed to the barn, where she opened the envelope and found a newspaper clipping within. Even before she unfolded it she knew it would show the photo taken behind the Cacchione residence on the day of the raid.

Scrawled beneath the image in pencil, written with such force that the strokes sharply embossed the newsprint and almost tore it, were the words, "Damn you both to hell."

John had not signed the note, but she recognized his handwriting, and even if she had not, no one else hated her and Lars enough to have sent that message.

Her stomach lurched. She staggered away from the barn, fell to her hands and knees, and vomited into the bunchgrass and yarrow. Head spinning, she sat down hard and fought to catch her breath. John had found them. He could not reach them, but he knew where they were, and he could tell anyone — the police, his gangster friends, anyone.

She was not sure how long she sat there, dazed and reeling, before she heard someone shouting her name. She pushed herself to her feet, brushed dirt and grass from her dress, wiped her mouth with the back of her hand, and walked unsteadily around the barn. She found Guiditta and Francesca standing in the yard, shading their eyes with their hands and calling for her. Francesca saw her first and touched her mother's arm, and then they hurried toward her. "Rose!" exclaimed Guiditta. "You're as white as a sheet! Are you ill?"

The sun seemed unnaturally harsh and bright, the air still and stifling. "I — I'm not feeling well."

"You should go home at once and lie down. Francesca, walk her back to the cabin."

Francesca nodded, but Rosa gestured feebly toward the house. "I have to fetch the children —"

"They'll be fine here until the end of the day," Guiditta said firmly, studying her with concern, her brows drawn together over her dark eyes. "They're all playing so nicely together and Mabel's keeping an eye on everyone. Nils can bring them home when he's done for the day. I'll send him with a bit of supper so you don't need to fix anything."

Tears sprang into Rosa's eyes. "You're too kind."

"Nonsense. I'm just the right amount of kind." Guiditta smiled briefly and shooed Francesca forward. Francesca took Rosa's arm, and Rosa, still dizzy, leaned on her as they walked slowly through the vineyard to the cabin, a blessedly cool sanctuary in the shade of the oak and walnut trees. How much longer would it remain their safe haven?

When Francesca left her at the cabin door, Rosa slipped inside and lay down on the sofa that doubled as Lars's bed. Her last thought before she sank into a restless doze halfway between sleeping and waking was that she wished she were bold enough to ask him to share her bed. What a comfort it would be to feel safe in his arms once again, to feel less alone, when night came and fear and worry enveloped her.

"Rosa?"

She opened her eyes to find the cabin dim and Lars kneeling beside the sofa, alone, gazing down at her with urgent concern. Distantly she heard the children shushing one another on the front porch.

"Rosa," Lars said again, gently brushing a lock of dark hair out of her face. "Guiditta said you were ill. What's wrong?"

She took a deep, shaky breath, sat up, and took the envelope from her pocket. He opened it warily, his face darkening as he read the scrawled curse, its every word sharp with hatred. "He's still behind bars," Lars said tightly, as he returned the clipping to the envelope and slipped it into his pocket. It was a relief to have it away from her, out of sight.

"But he knows where we are," said Rosa.

"We'll have to move on."

Her heart sank, although she had reached the same unhappy, inevitable conclusion.

454

"Where will we go?"

Lars shook his head, frowning. "I don't know. We were planning to leave Cacchione Vineyards anyway. It's too dangerous for us here."

She nodded, drawing her knees up to her chest and gazing around the cabin, missing it already. "We've been happy here. I hate to leave."

"Me too." Lars hesitated. "Maybe we don't have to go far, just far enough to throw him off the trail, John and anyone he might send after us."

She shuddered, imagining dark-suited men pursuing them, fedoras pulled low over their eyes, tommy guns held at the ready. "In other words, as far away as we can go, as fast and as soon as we can."

He placed a hand on her leg as if he thought she might bolt from the sofa and start throwing clothing into suitcases. "Not necessarily, and we aren't going to run off without a plan. We need to think this through."

"We'll need to think quickly," she told him, as the door burst open and the children rushed in, breathless and sweetly concerned for Rosa's health and hungry for the supper Guiditta had packed in the basket Marta carried.

■ ■ ■ ■

More bad news awaited them when they arrived at the Cacchione residence the next morning. Several days earlier, Salvatore Vanelli, whom Rosa had met at the harvest dance and at several other gatherings at the Cacchione home, had suffered a heart attack while working in his vineyard. Although his condition was serious, he was recuperating at home and his doctor expected him to pull through.

"I wish I had known sooner," fretted Guiditta as she packed an enormous basket with bread, fruit, preserves, hard cheese, and wine. "Bea and Sal weren't blessed with children. They're all alone on that remote place except for their foreman and the hired hands. Good people, all of them, but they aren't family." She regarded Rosa, Francesca, and Mabel with affectionate pride. "I'm off to see how I can help. I know I can trust you to look after things while I'm gone."

"Of course, Ma," said Francesca.

"Don't worry about us," said Mabel, holding out baby Sophia for a quick kiss. "We'll tend the vineyards, we won't sell any wine to anyone, we'll fix lunch and supper for everyone, and we'll be perfectly cordial to Mr. Crowell should he rear his ugly head."

"Maybe not perfectly cordial," Rosa amended. "I think we could manage to be coolly civil."

"That's good enough for me," said Guiditta, hurrying off.

As soon as the door closed behind her, Francesca turned to Rosa. "And how are you feeling this morning?"

Aside from the lingering dread evoked by John's note and the heartache of knowing that she must soon uproot her children and leave her new friends, she was fine. "Much better, thanks."

Francesca and Mabel exchanged a quick glance. "Really?" asked Francesca. "Even this early in the morning?"

Rosa looked from one eager sister-in-law to the other before it dawned on her what they were thinking, and she had to laugh. "If you've been waiting for a big announcement of a blessed event, I'm sorry to disappoint you."

"I told you so," said Mabel, swatting Francesca lightly with a dish towel. "It was just the heat after all."

Rosa nodded, relieved that they had found their own explanation. As Mabel teased her sister-in-law and Francesca protested that her first guess had been perfectly reasonable, Rosa smiled, but her amusement swiftly faded. She and Lars had had two children together, but they hadn't welcomed news of either pregnancy with joy. Such beautiful, beloved daughters had deserved a happier welcome to the world than they had received. Rosa's only consolation was that they didn't know, and that she had done all she could to make it up to them every day thereafter.

Even with Dante gone and friends suffering hardship, the work of the vineyard went on. The grapevines had flourished green and lush beneath the torrid skies of June in Santa Rosa, and the time had come to position the shoots so that the vines would concentrate their flavors in a select few, perfect bunches. Rosa, Lars, and the eldest Cacchione children walked the trellis rows, arranging the vines by hand so that the leaves would receive full sun exposure and not shade the growing clusters of small, green fruit and slow their ripening. The Cacchiones were satisfied only when a grapevine was in balance, which Rosa quickly learned meant that the vine supported a sufficient but not excessive canopy of leaves, enough to support the growing clusters and bring the fruit to perfect ripeness.

Positioning the shoots was a time-consuming, laborious process, and they completed only a third of the vines before it was time to prepare supper. The men continued to work in the vineyard while the women went to the kitchen and prepared a tasty meal of gnocchi, sausage, tomato and mozzarella salad, and crusty bread. Guiditta returned home just as they were setting the table and pouring the wine. She looked pensive, but she assured them that Sal was on the mend and Bea was bearing up well, although she remained terribly worried about her husband. Before they could press her for more details, Guiditta went back outside to call the men in for supper.

Guiditta waited until the children had finished eating and had run off to play before she shared the rest of the news from the Vanelli ranch. According to the doctor, Sal had suffered a mild heart attack brought on by stress, and it was essential for him to reduce his workload and rest until he had fully recovered. "The doctor didn't seem to understand that if Sal spends less time in the vineyard, the work won't get done, and his stress will only increase."

"Mr. Vanelli should visit Dr. Reynolds and

get a second opinion," said Dominic.

"He absolutely should," declared Rosa, although she had never met Sal's doctor and had no reason to question his diagnosis. "Dr. Reynolds is a miracle worker."

"The Vanellis could use a miracle or two right about now," said Guiditta ruefully. "They've decided to sell their vineyard."

"But they've farmed that land for almost forty years," cried Francesca. "And his father before him. Mr. Vanelli swore he'd never give it up. Jack London offered him a fortune for it, and Mr. Vanelli turned him down again and again, remember? That's one of his favorite stories, how he bested the famous writer and daring adventurer Jack London."

"I know, dear, but their circumstances have changed," said Guiditta. "Now the Vanellis are asking far less than Mr. London ever offered. They're getting on in years, and they have no children to take over the vineyard after them. If the uncertainty of farming is taking its toll on their health, it's quite sensible for them to retire."

"*Nonno* and *Nonna* didn't leave their land when they stopped working," Francesca said.

"They had your father and me," Guiditta reminded her, and then she smiled fondly, wistfully. "And they never really stopped working, did they?"

"The Vanellis have Daniel Kuo."

Guiditta laughed. "Yes, and he's a wonderful foreman. No one grows a grape to perfection quite the way he can. But he's not their son, and they don't expect him to care for them in their old age."

"I bet he would, if they asked," said Vince. "He's a real stand-up guy."

"They have too much pride to ask," said Dominic.

Guiditta sighed. "I admit I'm torn. For their sakes I hope they'll find a buyer who can match their asking price, but I'll miss them so much that I'm tempted to steal their 'for sale' sign before anyone else sees it."

Rosa and Lars exchanged a look. Was this their cue, Rosa wondered, or was this the worst possible time to announce that they too intended to move away soon? Lars shook his head slightly, and she gave him the barest of nods in return to show she understood. It would be unnecessarily hurtful to mention their own impending departure at such a time, especially since they still had not settled on a plan.

"I'd like to visit the Vanellis tomorrow," said Francesca.

461

Mabel's eyebrows rose. "Your mother was only joking about pulling up the sign. It wasn't a hint."

"I know that."

"Nor should you try to talk them out of it," said Guiditta.

Francesca looked deflated. "Oh."

"But it would be lovely if you'd stop by for a chat and to help around the house a bit," said Guiditta. "The Vanellis have always doted on you children, and I think a visit would cheer them up."

"I'd like to go too," said Rosa, on an impulse. "If I can be spared for a few hours, and if Francesca doesn't mind the company."

Francesca and Guiditta both assured her she was welcome to go along, so the next morning, Rosa and Francesca set out in the car with another basketful of bread, prunes, preserves, and wine, and a packet of handmade get well cards from the younger children. Rosa drove and Francesca directed her south, in the opposite direction of Santa Rosa, past vineyards and farms to Glen Ellen, a small village in a forested valley just north of the town of Sonoma. They took a side road that wound uphill through a leafy wood, and just as they rounded a steep bend, Francesca pointed out a modest, hand-painted sign that marked the turnoff to Vanelli Vineyards and Orchard. If they had continued on a few miles past the turnoff, Francesca added, they would have come to Jack London's famed Beauty Ranch, where his widow, Charmian, resided in a home called the House of Happy Walls, built a few years after Jack's death. Elsewhere on their vast acreage stood the renovated mid-nineteenth-century winery where Charmian and Jack had lived together and where he had written several of his renowned books as well as papers on his innovative farming methods. Also remaining were the ruins of Wolf House, Jack's magnificent dream home, which had taken three years to build and had mysteriously burned to the ground in 1913, just before the Londons intended to move in.

"Arson?" asked Rosa, intrigued.

"Who knows?" Francesca said. "Could be. Before you ask, I'm sure Mr. Vanelli had absolutely nothing to do with it, despite their ongoing feud."

Rosa laughed. "It didn't occur to me that he might have, until you suggested it."

About an eighth of a mile farther along, the car emerged from the hilly woods into the vineyard proper, rows upon rows of trellises covered in lush grapevines. In contrast to the Cacchiones' land, vast acres of relatively flat, level land framed by gently rolling hills, the secluded Vanelli ranch resembled a stream-cut valley surrounded by thickly forested slopes. A high, towering peak disappeared into a bank of low clouds to the northwest. "That's Sonoma Mountain," Francesca said, just as the road abruptly ended in a broad circle of gravel. "Park here. We have to walk the rest of the way, but it's not far."

Rosa carried the basket as Francesca led the way down a cobblestone footpath that wound through the trees to a stone bridge spanning a wide, rushing creek. From the opposite bank Rosa spied a white Victorian farmhouse with gingerbread molding in a clearing up ahead, but as they drew closer, she saw that it was not one structure but two, one smaller and cozy, the other L-shaped and twice the size of the first. Together the two buildings formed a horseshoe with a garden courtyard between the wings. Partially hidden amid the surrounding trees were various outbuildings, and through the foliage Rosa glimpsed more even, horizontal rows of trellises climbing the steep hillsides. The stunning views of the sun-dappled hills with Sonoma Mountain rising just beyond them took her breath away. Birdsong and the burbling of the creek filled the air with the music of nature, and the breeze carried the scent of grass and fresh berries. It was as lovely and thriving as any farm Rosa had ever seen, and she could not imagine how the Vanellis could bear to leave it.

They found Sal reclining on a daybed on the deep front porch, a green-and-gold Sunflower quilt draped over him despite the warmth of the day. A stack of *Life* and *National Geographic* magazines and a glass of iced tea, dewy with condensation, sat on a white wicker end table to his right, but he paid no attention to them, his gaze fixed instead on a yellow birdhouse on a post in the front yard. At the sight of Francesca and Rosa approaching, he smiled, pushed the quilt aside, and began to rise, but they quickened their pace and called out that he shouldn't get up on their account. He nodded and waved, seeming relieved as he adjusted his pillow and settled back against it. His face was drawn and haggard, and although his silver-gray hair was neatly combed, he evidently had not shaved for at least two days. He seemed to Rosa to have aged a decade in the few weeks since she had last seen him, and the naked worry on Francesca's face told her the young woman shared her shock and concern.

"Now, girls, don't look at me like that," he said gruffly as they climbed the porch stairs. "You'll make me feel like a sick old man."

"We know you're not that." Francesca patted him on the shoulder and pulled a rocking chair up to his side. "How are you feeling, though, really?"

"Bored. Tired." Sal frowned unhappily. "I want to be out in my vineyards, not dozing the day away on the porch. This might be my last summer on the vineyard and I'm missing my favorite season."

"Mr. Vanelli," exclaimed Francesca.

Sal's brown eyes twinkled with amusement. "I called it my last summer here because we're selling the place, sweetheart, not because I plan to be pushing up daisies this time next year."

"Well, that's a relief."

"Listen, girls." Sal lowered his voice, glanced toward the front door, and motioned for them to draw closer. "Bea's been waiting on me hand and foot for days. She needs to get out of this house for a breath of fresh air before she makes herself sick, hovering over me and waiting for me to collapse again. Would you persuade her to take a walk or sit in the garden for a little while?

Anything to give her a little break."

"We can certainly try," said Francesca. "She could take Rosa on a tour of the vineyard."

"I'd enjoy that very much," said Rosa. "How long should I keep her occupied?"

"Until she smiles at least twice and laughs at least once," said Sal decisively. "Then I'll know my old girl's back."

"Consider it done."

"She's going to miss this place," said Sal wistfully as he took in the view from the daybed. "I hope the new owners won't mind if I bring her around to visit from time to time. She'd probably tend the flower garden for free if they'd let her. It's too bad she can't take her roses and daisies with her. She and Luther Burbank go way back."

"He's a famous horticulturist," Francesca added for Rosa's benefit. "He developed the Shasta daisy and lots of other flowers and plants."

"Some of the flowers in the courtyard grew from seeds and cuttings from Luther's own garden in Santa Rosa," Sal said proudly. "Bea can show you which ones."

Rosa set the basket of food on the porch floor and leaned back against the railing. "You've made up your minds to leave, then?"

467

"We have." Sal frowned and shook his head. "That raid on your folks' place, Frannie, was the last straw. Bea's been after me to retire for years now, and the day I left the hospital, she told me she was terrified that this vineyard might make her a widow. Well, the vineyard isn't the problem. Prohibition is, the law and the crime and all that goes with it. For six years, I convinced myself that I could outlast it and someday get back to doing what I love — making excellent wines." He patted his chest ruefully. "Then my ticker told me I probably couldn't."

"Oh, Sal," said Rosa, shaking her head. She had liked Sal and Bea since they first met at the Cacchiones' harvest dance, and it saddened her to see them so worn out from strife and worry. "I'm sorry it's come to this."

"So am I." He gazed off toward Sonoma Mountain. "I'll miss watching the sun set behind that peak, but the view I'll miss most is sunrise over the Mayacamas — that's the mountain range to the east, Rose. Walking the vineyard early in the morning while the fog still clings to the ground, watching the eastern sky brighten with the coming of dawn, all rose and pink and gold —" He paused and cleared his throat. "Well. I've seen it thousands of times. I wouldn't need to see it again to remember it forever, wherever I go."

"Where will you go?" asked Rosa, thinking of her own ill-formed plans. "Have you decided?"

"Yes, we have, and I'm glad to say it's not far."

"Not at all, only a little more than thirty miles away," Bea chimed in as she pushed open the screen door and joined them on the porch. "My brother and his wife own a resort near Cloverdale in the Alexander Valley — twenty-four of the coziest little redwood bungalows you'll ever see, right on the Russian River. We're going to help them run it."

"You can't count on the weather or the wine," said Sal, "but you can always count on tourists from San Francisco."

Francesca brightened. "Cloverdale — you'll be close enough to come back to visit."

"Now and then," agreed Bea, smiling. "And you can visit us. We'll show you the most beautiful places in the Russian River Valley — just as soon as we learn what they are."

Everyone laughed, and Rosa seized her opportunity. "In the meantime, would you show me the most beautiful places on your vineyard?"

Bea hesitated, glancing to her bedridden husband.

"Oh, go on, I'm fine," said Sal. "Show her around. Who knows when you might get another chance?"

Bea agreed, so while Sal settled back to enjoy the children's get well cards and Francesca carried the basket inside to the kitchen and put away the gifts of food and wine, Bea and Rosa strolled arm in arm along the cobblestone footpaths and gravel roads that wound through the Vanelli estate. Sal's father had built the smaller farmhouse in 1862, Bea told her, and the larger detached wing was added in 1915 and included a spacious kitchen, a laundry room, and offices, with sleeping quarters for their workers on the second floor. Bea proudly showed off her lovely flower gardens in the courtyard and the shade garden lush with wild ginger, strawberries, and Dutchman's-pipe she had planted amid groves of cypress, oak, and coast redwood trees. From the gardens they strolled past the barn and the stable, where Bea introduced her to Sal's pride and joy, a team of four magnificent English shire horses, majestic and gentle. Farther away from the house and adjacent to the vineyard stood the winery, a long, low building built of the same sturdy red-wood as the barn, with a gabled roof covered in curved terra-cotta roof tiles.

"It looks humble from the outside," said Bea, sizing up the building fondly, "but the cellar is where the real work of the winery takes place, and its cellar is magnificent."

"Dante says that the quality of a wine depends upon what happens on the grapevine," said Rosa, following Bea inside.

"He's quite right, up to a point," said Bea, smiling. The first floor of the winery appeared to be a single large room supported by redwood columns, and all around them were stored the tools and accoutrements of winemaking — cast-iron grape crushers, redwood fermenters, oak presses, empty casks, and oak barrels stacked on their sides, plugs firmly in place. "An excellent wine begins with an excellent grape, but in the wrong hands, perfect fruit can become absolutely undrinkable wine."

Suddenly they heard footsteps behind them, and they turned to find a man climbing the cellar stairs. He looked to be in his late twenties, of Chinese heritage and handsome. He was a few inches taller than Rosa, with broad shoulders and a slim waist, and his rolled-up shirtsleeves exposed strong, well-developed arms. He grinned at Bea and gave Rosa a quick, curious smile and a nod of welcome. "Undrinkable wine?" he echoed. "Not from this winery, I promise you that."

Smiling, Bea took the younger man's arm and gave him a motherly pat on the shoulder. "And you're a significant part of the reason why. Rose, this fine young fellow is our foreman, lead vintner, and all-around right-hand man, Daniel Kuo. His family has been growing grapes and making wine on this land longer than Sal's has. Daniel, allow me to introduce you to Rose Ottesen, a neighbor and a friend. She and her husband work for the Cacchiones."

They shook hands, and Daniel's dark brows drew together in sympathy. "I'm sorry to hear about the hard times over at your place," he said. "How's Dante holding up?"

"As well as can be expected, from what I hear," said Rosa. Although Lars had gone to see Dante several times, she had not. She thought she could better help the family by staying behind to take care of the household chores and mind the children so that Guiditta, Francesca, and Mabel would be free to visit him. Guiditta probably wouldn't have passed on Dante's complaints even in the unlikely event that the stoic rancher had made any. "It's been difficult, and I don't see it getting any easier anytime soon, but I think they'll get through it all right."

"Please let me know if there's anything I can do for them."

"Of course."

"Daniel," said Bea, "I was going to show Rose around the wine cellar. Would you do the honors instead?"

"I'd be glad to." Daniel led the way down the stairs into the cool darkness of the wine cellar. It was much like the Cacchiones', albeit smaller, and the wine barrels rested on shelves unencumbered by chicken wire and padlocks. Daniel pointed out the barrels that contained the family's legally permissible two hundred gallons, and shook his head in frustration as he indicated the many more that were filled with water to keep the wood from drying out. Someday, he said, he hoped to fill them with new wine — someday, after Prohibition was repealed.

"You always say 'when' rather than 'if,' " remarked Bea.

"I don't believe Prohibition will last," Daniel replied. "It can't. It's unreasonable, the wartime grain emergency is over, and it didn't help the economy the way its proponents insisted it would."

"If Sal and I had your faith, we wouldn't

be looking to sell the vineyard."

"Time will prove me right." Daniel's voice took on a note of gentle urging. "Wait it out. You'll see."

Bea patted his arm and shook her head. "We've been struggling under Prohibition for more than six years, and we can't wait it out any longer. I'm sorry, Daniel, but it's time for Sal and me to move on."

Daniel managed a rueful smile and nodded, and Rosa guessed they'd had the same discussion several times before.

When Daniel finished the tour of the cave, as he called it, he escorted the two women out into the vineyard, where he spoke passionately and in great detail about the varietals of grapes that grew on the rugged slopes. With a sweeping gesture toward the Mayacamas, he lauded the Zinfandel vines that grew along the highest rows on the eastern slopes of the vineyard, some with stocks wider than the span of his hands, with roots so deep they drew rich flavors from minerals lingering far beneath the arid ground. The table grapes that grew on the opposite slopes absorbed their sweetness from the rainwater that soaked into the ground in winter and the sunshine that bathed them in spring, and when plucked and eaten at the peak of their ripeness, they were juicy and delicious and refreshing, better than candy. The particular geology of the V-shaped vineyard introduced intriguing characteristics unique to Vanelli wines, Daniel explained. The Cabernet Sauvignon grapes that grew on the eastern slopes received more sunlight than those that grew on the western ridges, which fell into the shadow of Sonoma Mountain by mid-afternoon. More sunshine encouraged the grapes to grow thicker skins with more tannins, which influenced the flavor of the wine. Sal and Daniel had spent years developing the perfect blend of grapes grown on the sunnier slopes and those cooled in the shade to create a magnificent wine they were proud to call their own. "Of course, Sal's name is on the bottle, not mine," Daniel concluded modestly. "And that's how it should be."

Rosa was so captivated by his tour — and so startled by Daniel's unwitting use of her and Lars's fond old phrase to describe the sweet grapes eaten fresh from the vine — that it took her a moment to detect a strange incongruity in his narration. "Aren't Zinfandel and Cabernet Sauvignon wine grapes?" she asked, looking from Daniel to Bea and back. "I thought you grew only table grapes and prunes here."

Bea and Daniel exchanged a look. "It's true that we still grow wine grapes, and we still make wine," admitted Bea, "but only four hundred gallons a year."

"Two hundred for the Vanellis' household and two hundred for mine," added Daniel. "That's within the bounds of the law."

Rosa was afraid to ask if they too were bootleggers, but Bea answered her unspoken question. "We don't sell our wine. We store it, and we've given some away, but we don't sell it. If we did, we would've quit after what happened to Dante and Guiditta."

Rosa was greatly relieved to hear it.

Daniel finished his tour, with Bea chiming in from time to time with amusing stories about their years on the vineyard. Then he bade the women good-bye so he could return to his work. Rosa thanked him and promised to carry his best wishes home to the Cacchiones. Daniel seemed remarkably knowledgeable about the cultivation of grapes and winemaking, and Rosa was touched to see how much he cared for the Vanellis and regretted their imminent departure. She hoped the new owners would recognize how valuable his knowledge and experience were and would allow him to keep his job, if he wanted it.

With Daniel Kuo staying on as foreman,

she suddenly realized, the new owners could surely be as successful as the Vanellis had been — even if they were novice vintners who had never grown a grape.

"Bea," she asked after Daniel left, "you said that Daniel's family has grown grapes and made wine on this land even longer than the Vanellis have. Did his family work for the previous owners?"

"Indeed they did," said Bea. "Daniel's great-grandfather came to California for the Gold Rush and stayed on to help build the railroad. He had no family back in China depending upon him to send money home, so he saved every penny in hopes of buying land, since he had been a farmer back in China." She sighed and shook her head. "No one would sell to him, and this was years before the Alien Land Law would have made it illegal for him to own property hereabouts anyway. Eventually he took a job as a picker for Sal's grandfather and worked his way up to foreman. Over the decades, most of his descendants left the Sonoma Valley to find work in San Francisco, but a few have always remained, including Daniel."

As she spoke, Bea led Rosa up the western slopes to the prune orchard, where the blossoms of spring had given way to hard, green fruits slowly growing and ripening in the warm sunshine. Harvest would begin in August, and the Vanellis were counting on a bountiful crop to help them pay their debts and moving expenses. From Bea's description, Rosa gathered that the cultivation of prunes wasn't significantly different from that of apricots. A rancher who had grown one of the fruits successfully could certainly master the other.

As they reached the northern boundary of the ranch and turned around to head back to the house, the women fell into a contemplative silence. The Vanellis' love for the land was evident, and Rosa considered it unfair and unfortunate that they felt compelled to leave. She could not imagine how new owners could possibly appreciate and cherish their vineyards and orchard as much as the Vanellis did — although she knew she herself would.

As they walked on, Rosa glimpsed another outbuilding through the prune trees, its weathered, sun-faded walls blending almost invisibly into the leafy wood that bordered the orchard. "What's that over there?"

Bea glanced over her shoulder but didn't pause. "Oh, that's just the old prune barn. We don't use it anymore. I've been after Sal to tear it down before it collapses, but we never got around to it. It's a nuisance and an eyesore."

"Fortunately, you can't see it from the house or the road." Rosa supposed that made it easier to put off the chore of tearing it down — out of sight, out of mind. "When Guiditta told me how close your land is to Sonoma, I never guessed it would seem so remote, so secluded."

"It is rather isolated, isn't it?" Bea replied thoughtfully. "We're far enough off the main road that we don't get many tourists passing by. It's quiet and peaceful, and we like it that way, but I suppose it would be too isolated for some folks."

"Bea," Rosa began, and then hesitated, reluctant to hasten the Vanellis' departure from the land they cherished or to prosper from their misfortune. "Are you and Sal sure, I mean, are you absolutely certain that you want to sell?"

"Oh, Rose, if you only knew how many months we anguished over this decision, you wouldn't need to ask." Bea slowed her pace as they reached the edge of the vineyard and the charming farmhouse came into view. "Our minds are made up, and we know it's for the best. We hope to move out as soon as the harvest is done."

"I suppose that means you'd be glad to

find a buyer soon."

"Yes, indeed, although who in their right mind would want to buy a vineyard during Prohibition?" Bea laughed, and Rosa joined in weakly. "Fortunately, we've already received an offer, and even though it's less than half of what we hoped for, we're inclined to take it. Sal's heart can't take another season, and I'm not sure mine could either."

Rosa stopped short. "Bea, you can't take that offer."

Bea halted too, regarding Rosa in puzzlement. "Well, I admit it's not ideal, but I'm not sure we'd get a better offer if we stayed through the winter, not in these uncertain times." She resumed walking. "Sometimes you have to take what you can get."

Rosa quickly fell in step beside her. "Bea, don't do anything until I can bring Nils to see your land. I think he'll love it as much as I do, and I know we can beat that other offer."

Now it was Bea's turn to stop short in astonishment. "You and Nils want to buy a vineyard?"

"And the orchard, and the house, and those magnificent horses, and whatever furniture you want to leave behind — everything." Rosa read the uncertainty in the older woman's eyes and knew she wondered how two hired hands could possibly have the means to buy a thriving forty-five-acre ranch and all that went along with it. "We both come from generations of farmers and ranchers so we know what we're doing, and we can meet your asking price. Please tell me you won't sell to anyone else until Nils has the chance to see the property."

"Well, I can certainly promise you that. We weren't planning to accept the other offer unless nothing else came along before the end of the harvest season." Bea reached out and clasped Rosa's hand in both of hers, beaming. "Bring Nils by as soon as you like, and bring your children too. I know the Cacchiones hold your family in the highest esteem. I can't tell you how it would comfort us to know we're entrusting our land to worthy stewards."

They settled on Sunday afternoon for the next visit, and after agreeing to keep the matter between themselves and their husbands for the time being, they walked back to the house, their footsteps quickened by hope and anticipation.

For the rest of the day Rosa felt as if she might burst from keeping her secret, and as soon as the children were tucked into bed, she took Lars by the hand and led him outside to the creek, where already the ocean fogs were rolling in. There she told him all about Vanelli Vineyards and Orchard and the unexpected outcome of her visit. The property was secluded and yet still accessible to schools, markets, church, new friends, and the train to San Francisco. There was a vineyard and winery for her and an orchard for him. The farmhouse seemed cozy and charming — from the outside, anyway — and the new kitchen and laundry room in the adjacent building sounded ideal. It was far enough away to throw any pursuers off their trail, but close enough that the move would not be too disruptive for the children. Most important, it offered them what they most wanted and needed — a home and land of their own — and they could afford it.

Lars mulled over her words, tempering her enthusiasm with cautious questions about the wisdom of buying a vineyard in the midst of Prohibition — or whether someone with his history should have anything to do with a winery in the first place.

His unexpected reluctance caught Rosa entirely off guard. "I'm not worried that you'll fall back into your old ways."

"Maybe I am."

"I know you won't. I know you have more willpower than that."

"Rosa —" He ran a hand over his chin. "It's not a matter of willpower. It — it's more than that. The temptation to drink, the craving — it's always there. I just . . . do my best to ignore it."

"But I've seen the Cacchiones offer you wine several times a week since we came here, and you've never once taken a sip."

He smiled crookedly. "Well, I was always more of a gin man."

She seized his hands. "Then we won't make gin. Lars, I know you can stay sober. I know you can, for me and the children. I know you won't let us down."

"I don't know how you can be sure of that. I've let you down before."

"That was years ago," she said vehemently, her hands tightening around his, hard and callused from a lifetime of ranching. "You've changed."

"Maybe I haven't changed enough."

He looked so stricken, so full of self-doubt, that her heart ached for him. "I'll never offer you wine with your meals the way Dante and Guiditta always do." They not only offered, they urged, barely stopping short of putting the glass in his hand. "You can tend the orchards and the grapes, and never set foot in the winery. I'll never make more than two hundred gallons. I won't even make that much, just enough to learn how."

"It would be better if we made no wine at all. Rosa —" He hesitated and pulled away from her, emotion contorting his face. "My drinking cost me a lifetime of happiness with you. Lately I've felt as if we've been given a second chance. I don't want to risk losing you and the children again."

She took a deep breath. "Very well. If that's the way it has to be, we won't make any wine. We'll sell the wine grapes instead."

He eyed her, uncertain. "Are you sure?" When she nodded, he said, "Don't forget, the money's yours, not mine. You don't need me to buy this vineyard and winery and do whatever you like with them."

"What I'd like to do with them is make a home for us and our children. Whether we make wine or grow table grapes and prunes, or . . . or pumpkins and onions is inconsequential." She grasped his arm and turned him to face her. "It's not my money. It's our money. I don't want to do this without you."

He grimaced. "It's John's money. It's the mob's money."

"It's ours now, and that's only right. We'll

do better things with it than they would have."

Lars surprised her with a laugh. "I'm not so sure they'd look at it that way." He sighed as if setting down a heavy burden and held out his arms to her. "Let's take a look at the place on Sunday. If it's all that you say it is, let's make the Vanellis an offer."

On Sunday they borrowed the Cacchiones' car and took the Sonoma Highway south to the Vanellis' ranch. Sal was determined to show Lars his prized vineyards and orchard himself, so he brushed off Bea's admonitions that he should rest and led Lars away. While the children romped in the yard with the Vanellis' two frisky collies, Bea showed Rosa the house and the adjacent building. The farmhouse was small, but more spacious than any home Rosa had ever lived in, and the newer building had all the modern conveniences she could possibly want. After Rosa had seen all she needed to see of the building and grounds, she delicately, almost apologetically, asked to review the books, and when Bea graciously granted her request, Rosa found no irregularities. When Lars and Sal returned from their tour of the grounds and outbuildings, Rosa knew at once that Lars was pleased and impressed. He made a quick, perfunctory survey of the farmhouse and work building, trusting Rosa's opinion that it suited her and the children. Then Rosa and Lars excused themselves and went off alone to stroll through the gardens, where they could speak privately.

They quickly confirmed that the estate was indeed all that Rosa had described and more, and so they returned to the farmhouse and made the Vanellis an offer. They offered all that remained of their savings, knowing the property was worth much more.

Rosa could scarcely believe their good fortune when the older couple accepted.

In the weeks that followed, Rosa and Lars were swept up in a whirl of activity. First they informed the astonished Cacchiones of their intentions, and within a day they opened an account at the Bank of Sonoma so they would be able to pay for their new home with a cashier's check instead of two satchels full of cash, which would surely raise eyebrows and provoke rumors. They arranged to keep the Vanellis' workers on, especially the invaluable Daniel Kuo, who seemed to Rosa to be disappointed that the Vanellis had sold the vineyard so quickly, which she hoped said more about his affection for the Vanellis than his impression of the Ottesens. They took care of the various legal documents and planned for the move from the cabin into the farmhouse, a task made far easier by their small number of possessions and the Vanellis' willingness to leave most of their furniture behind. All this they took on in the midst of their usual responsibilities, working for the Cacchiones, caring for their children, and in Lars's case, assisting with the Vanellis' prune harvest to prepare him for the following year, and all the years that would follow, when it would be his harvest, their harvest.

The Vanellis departed for Cloverdale the week after the prune harvest ended and their fruit was shipped off to the dryer and then to market. Soon thereafter, only a few days before grape harvest was expected to begin on both the Cacchiones' vineyard and the Ottesens', Rosa, Lars, and the children moved into their new home.

The Cacchiones treated Rosa, Lars, and the children to a farewell feast the night before they moved away, and the following morning, Guiditta came down to the cabin to see them off. After packing their few belongings, Rosa had swept and scrubbed the cabin from cellar to attic, a small gesture of thanks to the Cacchiones for offering them a safe haven.

When it was time to go, Rosa and Guiditta exchanged tearful good-byes, laughing at their own foolishness because they knew they would see each other again soon. Rosa couldn't help feeling that they were abandoning the Cacchiones when they were most needed, even though Guiditta assured her that wasn't so. Guiditta was delighted that they had found a place of their own where their family could thrive and prosper, and she was also relieved that the Vanellis' beautiful, fertile acres would be in the care of good, capable, trustworthy ranchers. Guiditta promised to offer whatever advice and assistance the Ottesens needed, and Lars in turn offered to help the Cacchiones with the young apricot orchard he had planted for them. They would be so close and in touch so frequently, Guiditta declared, it was hardly as if the Ottesens were moving away at all.

Rosa hung back while Lars helped the children into the ten-year-old Chevrolet Series 490 the Vanellis had included in the purchase. "We've kept your secrets," she told Guiditta, "and now I need you to keep one of ours."

From her pocket she took the newspaper clipping John had sent, unfolded it, and handed it to Guiditta, who inhaled deeply as she read the penciled curse. When she looked up from it, she said nothing, but her expression was wary and questioning.

"If anyone comes around here looking for us," said Rosa, "please tell them we passed through on our way to Canada and you have no idea where we are now. Invent new names for us. Tell them we didn't stay long and you never really got to know us."

"All right." Guiditta folded the paper and returned it. "I knew you were in some trouble. I didn't think you'd leave your home and come so far just to see Dr. Reynolds, but I didn't want to pry."

Rosa smiled apologetically, wishing she could confide in Guiditta completely. "The less you know, the better. I'm sorry."

"I'm sure you have good reason to be cautious." Guiditta hesitated before adding, "You should know that Lupita has been insisting to the other children that Nils isn't her father."

"Is that so?" Rosa had to laugh. "Well, whether Lupita likes it or not, he's definitely her father."

Guiditta smiled, but the concern didn't leave her eyes. "Even so, if she's spreading tales, it might attract unwanted attention your way."

Rosa thanked her for the warning and

gave her one last quick embrace before joining her family in the car. As they drove away, Rosa glanced over her shoulder and watched Guiditta closing up the cabin. She wondered how long it would stand empty before another family in need benefited from the Cacchiones' kindness and generosity.

The children chattered excitedly in the backseat as they drove south along the Sonoma Highway. Rosa took off her hat, closed her eyes, and let the sun and wind caress her face, tousling her dark bob. She could not remember when she had last felt so relieved and hopeful, so content. She thought of the ripe, late-summer produce awaiting her in Bea's kitchen garden and wondered what to prepare for the family's first meal in their new home. The day called for a celebration. If she had more time, she would make her *abuelo*'s tamales. Perhaps tomorrow —

"What's going on?" Lars suddenly said under his breath, and Rosa felt the car slow down. She opened her eyes and threw him a questioning glance before noticing the dark sedan approaching from the opposite direction. First it straddled the lanes, and then it turned to block their way.

Rosa felt a jolt of alarm. "Drive around it."

"Can't. Shoulder's too steep." Frowning, Lars pulled over and brought the car to a halt just as the other driver climbed out of his car. As the man strode toward them, Rosa's eyes locked with his, and she gasped in recognition. Dwight Crowell hesitated, confusion clouding his expression for the barest of moments before he continued forward. He knew the car, Rosa realized, and he thought he had pulled over the Vanellis.

"That's the bad man," said Lupita, wide eyed. "The one who took Mrs. Cacchione and dumped out all their wine."

"Yes, it is. Don't say another word," Rosa warned, instinctively holding Miguel tighter on her lap. The children fell instantly into a tense silence.

"Is there something I can do for you?" asked Lars through the open window, curtly civil, when Crowell reached them.

The agent's searching gaze came to rest on the family's belongings, packed into the backseat with the girls. "Leaving town right before the harvest?"

Lars shrugged. "It's time to move on."

"In Salvatore Vanelli's car?"

"He sold it to us," Rosa said, dislike and

491

mistrust putting a cutting edge to her voice.

Crowell nodded, thoughtful, as he opened his jacket and planted his hands on his hips. "Where you folks headed?"

"South," said Lars. "And we'd like to get going, so we'd be much obliged if you'd move your car out of the way."

"It's just a routine stop. Don't get jittery." Crowell strolled around the car, peering into the wheel wells and beneath the chassis as if he expected to find jugs of moonshine strapped to the axles. "If you've done nothing wrong, you don't have any reason to be nervous."

"We're not nervous," said Rosa, ignoring a warning look from Lars. "We'd just like to be on our way."

"Long drive ahead of you?" Crowell inquired as he completed his circuit of the car and halted by Lars's window. "Driving all the way to Stavanger?"

"Not quite that far," said Lars.

"And you're all going together, just one happy family — the man of the house, his doting wife, and their four great kids."

"That's right."

Crowell grinned sharply. "It's an odd sort of happy family, what with the loving husband sleeping on the sofa every night."

Rosa went cold. The agent had been peering through their windows, or he had broken into the cabin in their absence. What else had he seen? What more did he know?

"What's the matter, Nils Ottesen?" Crowell asked, brow furrowed in feigned sympathy. "What did you do to offend the little woman? Why have you been in the doghouse all these months?"

"I snore."

"Every night?"

Lars held his gaze, unsmiling. "So I'm told. I'm lucky enough to sleep through it."

"Funny thing about Stavanger." Never before had Crowell's resemblance to Lars been more revolting, a cruel distortion of the features Rosa adored. "It's very convenient, isn't it, that you hail from a town whose records were destroyed in a courthouse fire three years ago?"

"It's wasn't at all convenient for the people whose vital records were lost," Rosa retorted, "or for the clerks who had to sift through the ashes salvaging what they could."

"Why don't you just tell us what you want and let us move on," said Lars. "Have I broken any laws?"

"None that I know of, but I'm still looking." Crowell smiled. "And I'm going to keep looking."

"Do as you see fit," said Lars. "It's your time to waste."

Crowell's smile hardened. He nodded to Rosa and waggled his fingers at the children, who shrank back and looked away. He headed back to his sedan, and a few moments later he roared past them, making haste, no doubt, to pester the Cacchiones.

"Lars," murmured Rosa, her voice trembling. "In the new house, perhaps we should, just in case — perhaps the sofa isn't —"

"If we ever share a bed again," Lars broke in harshly, "it won't be to keep up appearances for the likes of him."

Stung, Rosa said nothing more.

Lars started the car and drove on, but the happy mood had been shattered, and no one spoke another word until they turned off the Sonoma Highway onto the winding side road that climbed the forested hills toward their new home. After rounding the steep bend, Lars stopped the car at the turnoff and nodded toward the sign that announced they had arrived at Vanelli Vineyards and Orchard. "We'll have to change that," he remarked, studying the sign before driving on.

"Ottesen Vineyards and Orchard?" said Rosa, dubious. It was the obvious choice, but it felt wrong, since Ottesen was not their true name.

"Ottesen Orchard and Vineyards?" said Marta.

"That's not any better," said Ana.

"How about, Mama's Grapes and Prunes?" suggested Lupita.

Marta shook her head. "That sounds like a roadside fruit stand."

"I like it," piped up Miguel. "Or Mama's Fruits. That's good too."

Everyone laughed, and Lars said that if they didn't come up with anything else before he had time to make a new sign, they'd flip a coin — heads for Mama's Grapes and Prunes, tails for Mama's Fruits. When Rosa protested that they should name their new ranch after the whole family, not her alone, Lars joked that unless she came up with something better herself, and soon, she would be stuck with the results of the coin toss.

Daniel Kuo awaited them on the front porch, a well-read edition of *The Call of the Wild* in one hand and a heavy ring of keys in the other. Rosa accepted the honor of unlocking the front door, and the children raced past her into the house, bounding up the stairs and claiming rooms and beds. Unpacking and settling in took up most of the day, with Rosa in the house and Lars mostly in the barn and stables and nearest outbuildings. Once, in the middle of the afternoon, Rosa and Lars both found themselves in the hallway outside the largest bedroom at the same time. Rosa carried her mother's last quilt, the one Elizabeth Nelson had repaired and named Arboles Valley Star, the one pieced of scraps that carried a lifetime of memories, of hope and regret.

"Help me make the bed?" Rosa asked, suddenly shy. He nodded, and together they smoothed the sheets over the mattress, lay the quilt on top, and plumped the pillows along the headboard.

The task complete, Lars started to leave. "It's not for appearances," Rosa blurted. He hesitated in the doorway, his back to her. "It's not because I'm worried that the sofa will give you an aching back. It's because I love you."

After a moment he turned, but when he merely stood silently looking back at her, she felt tears spring into her eyes and she wished she hadn't spoken. Then he came to her and took her hands. "Rosa, would you marry me if you were free to do so?"

"Of course I would." Did he really need to ask? "I would marry you today if I could."

"Will you marry me when you can?"

"Yes, yes, of course I will."

"Then it's settled. That's good enough for me, for now." He cradled her face in his hands and lifted her chin so that her lips met his.

For weeks they were too busy to worry about a new name for the estate, although Lars and the children often teased Rosa by pretending they had already decided upon Mama's Grapes and Prunes. They settled into their new home, met the few hired hands the Vanellis had kept on after their fortunes tumbled, and set themselves to the work of the harvest.

With Daniel to advise them, they hired additional seasonal workers to pick the grapes — round, ripe, full of color and flavor — the table grapes first, and then the Zinfandel and Cabernet Sauvignon. Every day Rosa woke before dawn and prepared a hearty breakfast for everyone, and then, in the cool hours of the morning, the real work began. In teams of three, the pickers walked the vineyard, snipping the ripe clusters from the vines with sharp and well-oiled blunt-tipped clippers, loading them gently into wooden lugs, and hauling them to the grape house. It was hot, exhausting work, and Rosa was on her feet for fifteen hours a day,

497

cooking, picking, and managing the household. They worked swiftly and against time, determined to harvest the clusters at the height of their perfection, before the first rains of autumn swept into the Sonoma Valley and diluted the sweetness of the berries. She and Lars would have been lost without Daniel, who had welcomed them as his new employers civilly but with less warmth than he had greeted Rosa as Bea's visiting friend. Rosa did not take it personally; she assumed he missed the Vanellis and was preoccupied with the arduous work of the harvest. It was perfectly understandable, but Rosa and Lars would have tolerated it even if it were unreasonable. They needed him. Although Sal had left them detailed records, first-hand experience was far more useful than notes, and precious hours could be lost searching for information that Daniel knew by heart.

The new school year began before harvest concluded, and on the first day, Lupita set off happily with her sisters. Without Marta there to watch Miguel, Rosa could no longer work in the vineyard with the pickers, but she had plenty to do in the house and garden. Daniel proved himself invaluable again when it came time to sell the table grapes, but he admitted his uncertainty with the markets for wine grapes, as the Vanellis had always reserved the crop for winemaking. Hoping for the best, Lars and Daniel consulted with Guiditta and made the most advantageous arrangements they could as newcomers in an already crowded market.

After the last batch of wine grapes was packed for delivery to the train station the next morning, Daniel took Rosa aside and asked her if they shouldn't hold some back in the coldest part of the cellar for their own use. "Bea told me you were interested in winemaking," he said. "I could teach you."

Rosa hesitated. "Nils — my husband — he would rather we didn't."

The look on Daniel's face as he nodded and folded his arms over his chest told Rosa that Daniel had already approached Lars, and had been told to haul every last grape off to market. "Two hundred gallons a year per household is perfectly legal."

"The legality isn't the problem." Suddenly Rosa remembered something Bea had told her on her first visit to the vineyard — throughout Prohibition, the Vanellis' winery had produced four hundred gallons of wine a year, two hundred for the Vanellis and two hundred more for Daniel. If they did not crush that season, Daniel would lose what was probably a significant part of his compensation.

She thought quickly, wishing she had more time to ponder the consequences, but the fruit would not stay perfect long, and they could not afford to lose Daniel to a more practical vintner. "You can make your two hundred gallons," she told him. "I won't make any, at least not this year."

"You'd prefer to watch and learn this time around?"

Rosa nodded, ignoring a pang of guilt. She had not promised Lars she would not learn, only that they would make no wine.

Daniel grinned and thanked her, and as he quickly set off to sort out his allotment of berries, Rosa heaved a sigh and considered herself fortunate. With the work of winemaking to keep him occupied, Daniel was unlikely to quit for at least another few months, giving them more time to win him over.

That evening, as they sat on the front porch watching the children play in the garden with the collie pups the Vanellis had given them, Rosa told Lars about the promise she had made to Daniel, and why. "It's not too late to tell him it's simply not possible. We can return the grapes he held back to the rest of the shipment —" Then, suddenly, she had another thought. "Or we can let him keep them. He could sell them and keep the profits, or crush them and make wine, as long as he doesn't do it here."

Lars mulled it over, resting his elbows on his knees as he watched the children play. "It wouldn't be fair to take something from him that the Vanellis have always granted, especially after you told him he could have it," he said. "Any other vineyard would give him what he wants, and he's too good a worker, too decent a man, to risk losing him all because of my weakness." He settled back against the daybed, putting his arm around her shoulders and lacing his fingers through hers. "All right. Let Daniel make his wine, and learn all you can from him. But I can't help you, Rosa. I won't set foot in that winery. That's not a risk I'm prepared to take, not when I have so much to lose."

"It's not a risk I want you to take," she said. He had returned to her, and she could not bear to lose him again.

At last the long, hard, exhilarating days of their first grape harvest were behind them. Lars, Rosa, and the children joined the Cacchiones for their annual harvest dance, a far more subdued affair than the previous year's, when Dante was a free man inviting

501

friends and neighbors to drink his wine and share in his family's prosperity. There was no wine barrel in the corner of the barn that year, and to everyone's disgust, Crowell and another dark-suited man interrupted the gathering just as they were sitting down to their feast, jotting down the names of the guests and inspecting glasses and mugs to be sure no alcohol was being served. He seemed surprised to see Rosa and Lars among them. "Back in town?" he asked, jotting their names on his pad with a stub of a pencil.

"Only for the party," Lars replied shortly.

"Long way to come for a party," Crowell remarked as he moved on. "I guess that means you didn't go home to Stavanger after all."

Rosa and Lars exchanged a look, and she knew he was as annoyed and dismayed as she was that Crowell knew anything at all about their whereabouts.

As Crowell and his partner circled the room, Alegra Del Bene appeared increasingly unsettled the closer he came to her table until she suddenly went ashen gray and fled the barn. Alarmed, Rosa ran after her and found her in the Cacchiones' kitchen, her head in her arms on the kitchen table, trembling. She quickly sat up and struggled to compose herself, but she would not explain why she was so afraid. When Rosa tried to assure her that Crowell was a hateful bully, but he could not harm her or Paulo if they had committed no crimes, Alegra shook her head bleakly, unconvinced.

Eventually Alegra calmed down enough to return to the party, but only after Rosa made sure Crowell had left. "Don't tell Paulo I was upset," she begged, and reluctantly Rosa agreed. If Paulo knew the truth, he might be able to arrange for someone else to stay with Alegra whenever he needed to leave the vineyard on business. Rosa settled for reminding Alegra that she was welcome to stay with her and Lars whenever she wanted. They had plenty of room, the end of harvest allowed them more time to visit, and Miguel would be delighted to play with his best friend more often. Alegra managed a smile and agreed to take Rosa up on her invitation when she could, and they walked back to the barn together, where the feasting and dancing had gone on merrily in their absence.

Rosa had agreed not to tell Paulo about Alegra's distress but she had made no such promise about Lars. "She's new to this country," Lars said, as if trying to explain her excessive fear to himself as well as to Rosa. "She doesn't understand that ordinary citizens have rights, and that no one, not even a federal officer, is above the law."

How could she, Rosa wondered, when the law no longer made any sense or held sway when it was most necessary, when bribery and intimidation were the order of the day, when a judge could convict a barkeeper of serving alcohol in the morning, levy a fine, and stop by the same man's establishment for a drink on his way home from work? How was Alegra to know which laws would be enforced justly, which would be ignored, and which would be invented on the spot to suit those who would enforce their own will upon others? Rosa was tempted to put the question to Dwight Crowell the next time she saw him, a meeting she hoped wouldn't come anytime soon. With any luck, it would be months before he discovered that the Ottesens and their secrets had only moved away as far as Glen Ellen.

All the more reason not to put their alias on the sign marking the turnoff to their property, or upon any of the fruit crates they sold at market.

Rose had mulled over many possibilities for what to call their new business, and endured ever-sillier suggestions from the children, but nothing seemed to fit. Just when she thought they might have to use one of the children's ideas after all, Lars announced that he had come up with the perfect name. The children tried to tease and wheedle it out of him, but he wouldn't tell them and vowed that he wouldn't until he had made a sign for the post by the road. Rosa thought he shouldn't go to the trouble of making a sign until everyone — especially herself — agreed upon it, but Lars assured her she would love it.

For two days he worked on the sign, out of sight in the barn, shaping a large, round slab from the ancient stump of a coast redwood that had been cut down ages before. From a distance Rosa overheard the sounds of carving and chiseling, and smelled scorched wood, and once, Lars returned from an errand in Sonoma with three cans of paint he quickly hid beneath a tarp behind his workbench. "I can't even see which colors you chose?" she protested, laughing, but Lars insisted on keeping the entire project secret until it was complete.

And then, at last, it was.

One morning Lars called Rosa and the children into the garden, where he had leaned the sign up against a pine tree and covered it with an old cloth. At his signal, the children counted to three and he pulled the cloth away, unveiling an elegant oval with a carved border of grapevines accented with prune blossoms. Painted in the center in graceful script of red and gold were the words, "Sonoma Rose." Underneath, in smaller letters, appeared the phrase, "Vineyards and Orchard."

"That's you, Mamá," said Ana. "You're Sonoma Rose."

"It's perfect," exclaimed Marta, clasping her hands to her heart. "Sonoma Rose Vineyards and Orchard. It's absolutely perfect."

Lars was watching Rosa closely, awaiting her verdict. "Well? What do you think? If you truly hate it, I can make another sign —"

"I love it," Rosa said, smiling. "I do. I wouldn't change a thing."

"Let's hang it up," ordered Lupita, tugging on Lars's sleeve. "Let's do it right now."

Lars laughed and swooped her up in his arms, and for once she didn't scowl and demand to be set down. "Not yet. It's not quite finished."

"What more do you need to do?" asked Rosa. "It's lovely just as it is."

"No, it needs one thing more. I want to

trim the edges with hammered copper. It'll look nice, and it'll protect the edges from the weather so the wood won't split." He set Lupita down and ruffled her hair, grinning. "I thought I'd check that old building on the edge of the orchard for scraps. The other day I glimpsed a flash of sunlight on metal through the window."

"That might have been an old tin can," said Rosa. "Be careful. Bea said that building could collapse at any moment, and the wood is so old and dry it's likely a fire hazard. We should tear it down before lightning strikes it."

"Not before I salvage what I can," said Lars cheerfully, and he set out for the orchard.

Rosa admired the sign a while longer, then kissed the children and left them to their play while she went into the kitchen to start supper. She was peeling potatoes and humming contently to herself when Lars appeared, his expression stunned and disbelieving.

"What is it?" asked Rosa, alarmed.

"I think . . ." Lars hesitated and tried again. "I think I might know why Sal was feeling so much strain. I think I know why he had that heart attack."

"Tell me."

"I think I'd better show you."

Quickly she snatched off her apron and took his hand, and together they hurried off through the vineyard to the orchard, not slowing their pace until Lars brought them to the old prune barn. There, at the edge of the orchard farthest from the house, he halted.

"What's wrong?" demanded Rosa. "Is the roof caving in? Did something fall and strike you? We can have this deathtrap torn down tomorrow if it's too —"

Shaking his head, Lars opened the door and gestured for her to take a look inside.

Within the dilapidated old barn, Rosa discovered a gleaming expanse of copper boilers, rubber tubing, and tin milk jugs; sacks of sugar; charcoal left from burning; and inexplicably, large wooden crates marked on the sides with painted loaves of bread and biscuits and cakes and the words, "Johnson's Bakery." A heavy, sweet, yeasty smell hung in the air.

Rosa had never seen a still except in newspaper photos printed alongside descriptions of intrepid federal agents' raids on hapless moonshiners, but she immediately recognized the contraption for what it was. It was a still, and it was enormous and elaborate and very much illegal, and it was in their

508

prune barn, and there was not a speck of dust upon it.

CHAPTER EIGHT

Rosa stared at the still, incredulous, unwilling to believe that the Vanellis had sold them their estate without mentioning the illegal contraption hidden within their old prune barn. "Do you think it's possible that Sal and Bea didn't know this was here?" Rosa tried to remember Bea's exact words, but all she recalled was that Bea had said — or perhaps she had only implied — that they never entered the crumbling structure.

Lars studied the still, dubious. "I guess it's possible, but I doubt it."

"Maybe someone else built it — one of the hired hands or someone."

"Without the Vanellis or anyone else finding out?"

The only way to know would be to ask. They sought out Daniel first, and when they realized he was in the wine cellar, Lars told Rosa he would wait outside while she went in to question him. He had vowed never to set foot in the winery, and he meant to keep that vow.

"But there isn't any wine there now," said Rosa. "The Vanellis took what was left of last year's two hundred gallons with them, and Daniel's new wine is too young to drink. It's only unfermented grape juice. Wouldn't it be fine, just this once?"

"Rosa," said Lars, pained, "the worst thing an alcoholic can do is start convincing himself that just this once, it would be fine."

Rosa bit her lips shut and nodded, ashamed that she had even suggested it.

She went inside and found Daniel in the cave inspecting the wooden troughs of new wine he had recently crushed. Rosa had worked alongside him all the while, scrubbing the winery clean, sorting the grapes, removing the stems and leaves, and crushing the berries. Later they would press the juice, and Daniel planned to teach her how different oak barrels with different toasts added notes and flavors to the wine, making each vintage unique. He had shared his knowledge generously, openly, and as they worked together, his cool demeanor had thawed. Rosa hoped she was not about to make it ice over again.

"Daniel," she said after he greeted her cheerfully, "did you know there's an enor-

511

mous still in the old prune barn?"

His smile promptly vanished. "I knew about it," he said guardedly. "I've never seen it."

"Did Sal build it, or one of the hired hands?"

Daniel grimaced. "I make it a point to mind my own business."

"Please, Daniel, tell me. If it was the Vanellis', it belongs to me and Nils now, and that makes me very nervous."

"It wasn't the Vanellis', and it doesn't belong to any of the hands, either," Daniel said. "For the past few years, some gangsters out of San Francisco have been renting the prune barn to make grappa. The deal is five hundred dollars a month, no questions asked. Sal couldn't turn down that kind of money, not in these hard times."

"No, I suppose he couldn't." Rosa leaned against a wine barrel and took a deep, shaky breath. "And since the Vanellis switched almost entirely to table grapes years ago, and don't have any old wine in storage, and have never sold wine grapes, Prohibition agents wouldn't suspect them of bootlegging. They probably don't bother coming around often to inspect."

"Strictly speaking . . ." Daniel seemed almost embarrassed to say it. "The Vanellis weren't bootlegging. They were just renting out an unused prune barn."

Rosa could well imagine how Dwight Crowell would regard that fine distinction. "How often do these gentlemen come around to make grappa?"

"About once or twice a month."

"Then they're overdue." Rosa paced the width of the cave, clasping her hands, working the sudden cold out of her fingers. "Maybe the Vanellis told them they had sold the estate and that they shouldn't return."

"Maybe," said Daniel, but he looked doubtful. "Would they have left the still behind? It must be worth something."

The equipment was valuable, even if only for the price of the parts. On the other hand, it was illegal, and if the gangsters didn't have another place to hide such unwieldy incriminating evidence, they might have thought it more prudent to abandon it.

Her head ached, and she clasped a hand to her brow and fought to untangle her snarled thoughts. She felt a sharp, unmistakable surge of anger for Sal and Bea. They had seemed so kind, so generous, so weary and thankful to have the vineyard and orchard taken off their hands. Now she understood why they were so eager to sell the estate and be done with it, so eager that until Rosa and Lars had come along, they had been willing to accept less than half their asking price. And now the burden was Rosa and Lars's to bear, and if Dwight Crowell came snooping around —

"Why didn't they tell us?" she said, thinking aloud. "Why didn't they warn us?"

"Would you have paid as much as you did if you had known what you were taking on?"

With a sudden flash of insight, Rosa said, "You made the other offer, the one they almost accepted."

Daniel nodded.

"Did you offer them so little because you knew their secret?"

"I wasn't trying to lowball them. I offered them every cent to my name," he replied. "I've worked these acres all my life. Can you blame me for wanting to own them?"

"No." Rosa understood all too well what he felt. "I don't blame you at all. I'm sorry."

"It's not your fault. You wanted the land too, and you could afford it."

Silence descended upon them, as cool and deep as the wine cellar itself, but eventually Daniel spoke. "What are you going to do?"

"I don't know," said Rosa. "What would you have done, if the Vanellis had accepted your offer?"

"I'd have collected the monthly rent, looked the other way, and kept my mouth shut."

He answered so promptly that Rosa knew he had decided long before he offered to buy the estate. And if, after he assumed ownership of the estate, the feds had discovered the still on his property, he could have claimed that he had known nothing about it, that he had merely honored a rental contract established by the previous owners. Rosa and Lars could attempt that tactic too, but they were less likely to succeed. Unlike them, Daniel had not made an enemy of Dwight Crowell. He was well known within the community and his people had been in Sonoma County for generations. Not so the Ottesens, for whom no record of their existence before their arrival in San Francisco a year ago could be found.

What if the gangsters were as curious as Crowell about their new landlords? What would they learn from their associates in Southern California?

Shaken, Rosa thanked Daniel for his honesty and went back outside to Lars, who was pacing in the yard. When Rosa told him all she had learned, it seemed as if every word etched new lines of worry on his brow.

"We have to report this to the authorities," Lars said when she finished. "We can claim — with perfect honesty, I might add — that we recently bought the property and only just now discovered the still. It's not ours and they're welcome to haul it away."

"We could do that, but as soon as they've finished destroying the still, they'll drive up to Cloverdale and arrest the Vanellis."

Lars frowned, kicking at the dirt. He didn't want to see Bea and Sal prosecuted any more than she did, even though the couple had deceived them.

"Eventually whoever's been running that still will come around to make another batch of grappa," said Rosa. "How would we explain to them that we got rid of it?"

Lars abruptly stopped pacing. "We can't make enemies of those people."

Rosa laughed, tearfully, helplessly, from the futility of it all. "I know, but what can we do?"

"For now, let's do nothing," said Lars. "Until a few hours ago we didn't know that contraption existed. If I hadn't gone to the prune barn today, we still wouldn't know."

Rosa wished they didn't.

One rainy morning in late October, Rosa and Daniel were in the winery carrying out a task Daniel called "punching down the cap." As the juice fermented, grape skins, stems, and seeds floated to the top of the wooden vats and formed a solid skin, trapping in heat as well as some of the active yeasts needed to transform the sugar into alcohol. Three times a day over the course of several weeks, Daniel and Rosa broke up the caps and pushed them back down into the dark juice with a tool that reminded her of an oversized potato masher. Daniel assured her the procedure was essential in keeping the fermentation process going, that it would prevent the growth of mold and add color, richness, and tannins to the wine. When the cap no longer floated to the surface, he told her, it would be time to press the wine.

They were nearly finished when one of the hands called down the cellar stairs that a man from Johnson's Bakery had arrived and wanted to speak to the new proprietor. When Daniel shot her a quick, wary look, Rosa remembered the wooden crates she had seen in the prune barn and her heart plummeted. The moment she had dreaded had come, and Lars was off at the Cacchione estate advising Guiditta how to prepare the young, struggling apricot orchard for the winter. Rosa was on her own.

"I can finish here," Daniel said, grimacing

in sympathy. "Or I could come with you, if you want."

"I think I'd better see him alone." If she didn't, he might guess how nervous she was, and she didn't want to give him that advantage. Rosa stripped off her gloves, summoned up her courage, and ascended the cellar stairs. Outside, the rain had diminished to a fine mist that clung to her hair and cheeks, and as the sun fought to burn through the clouds, she spotted a delivery van parked in the yard, its doors and sides adorned with the same logo she had seen on the wooden crates in the prune barn. A dark-haired man in a snappy pinstriped suit and hat strolled through the shade gardens with his hands in his pockets, admiring the late-blooming undergrowth, but he looked up at the sound of Rosa's approach. Barely keeping the tremor from her voice, she introduced herself and asked how she could help him.

"I'm Alberto Lucerno from Johnson's Bakery," he said, shaking her hand. He looked to be close to her own age, perhaps a few years older, with short, dark hair oiled and parted down the middle. "Perhaps the previous owners mentioned me?"

"I'm afraid they didn't." If only they had . . . "I — I usually make my own bread.

Perhaps they thought I wouldn't need your services."

"We do much more than bake bread."

"I don't doubt it."

"I hope you're as willing to do business with us as the folks who used to live here were," said Mr. Lucerno earnestly. If she didn't know better, she could almost believe him to be a salesman hoping to win a new client for his bakery — except no one wore a suit that fine to deliver bread and rolls and pastries.

"We'll see," said Rosa, glancing up at the sky as thunder rumbled. "Would you like a cup of coffee and a piece of pie while we talk things over?"

He readily agreed, and as heavy drops began to pelt the ground, he quickly followed her inside to the parlor, where she served him a generous slice of prune pie and poured them each a cup of coffee. He accepted cream and sugar and didn't seem terribly disappointed to learn that the man of the house was not around. "I wasn't aware the vineyard was for sale," he said. "Seems the Vanellis moved out kind of sudden."

"Well, under the circumstances, it seemed best." Rosa took a sip of coffee, wondering if her guest had ever killed anyone. "Perhaps you haven't heard about Mr. Vanelli's heart attack?"

Mr. Lucerno's eyebrows rose. "No, I wasn't aware of that. How's he doing?"

"He's on the mend."

"Good, glad to hear it." Mr. Lucerno nodded thoughtfully. "I guess it's lucky for them they found a buyer so quickly. You and your husband aren't from around here, are you?"

"No, we're originally from Stavanger, but for the past year we've been working for the Cacchione family in Santa Rosa."

Studying her, he finished his last bite of piecrust and set his plate on the coffee table. "Is that so?" He had a sharp, knowing gaze that took in everything, from the way her hand rattled the spoon against her coffee cup to the way her eyes darted repeatedly to the front door as if she couldn't wait for him to leave.

She knew she would be a fool to lie to him.

"I believe I've seen your company crest before," she said, summoning up every ounce of courage she possessed.

"Maybe you've seen our delivery trucks around town."

"No, that's not it." She rested her chin on her palm and tapped her cheek with her forefinger thoughtfully. "I saw it on a bunch of wooden crates out in the old prune barn."

He sat back, rested his right ankle on his left knee, and studied her with admiration. "Well, aren't you a cool customer."

"Let's be frank with each other, Mr. Lucerno," she said lightly, setting her coffee cup aside. "I'm not going to be a customer of any kind, am I?"

He laughed. "Not unless I could interest you in a good glass of grappa."

"It's too strong for me. I prefer a nice red wine." She leaned forward and offered him a small, knowing smile. "Since you're not here to sell bread, and I don't want to buy any grappa, is there anything else for us to discuss?"

"One small matter. The gentlemen I work for want to keep renting your prune barn."

Rosa smiled thoughtfully as if the idea intrigued her, but her heart sank. Until that moment, she had clung to a slender thread of hope that the gangsters' prolonged absence meant that they had found a better place to make their grappa, and that Mr. Lucerno had come to tell them when they intended to dismantle the still and clear out of the crumbling firetrap of a barn. "What are your terms?"

"We'll pay four hundred a month for exclusive use of the prune barn — and for your discretion."

"I understand you paid the Vanellis five hundred a month."

"I thought you said they never mentioned me."

"They didn't." Too late, Rosa realized that might insult him. "I heard it from someone else."

"I wonder how that fella found out." He looked like he meant to say more, but a sudden pounding on the front door interrupted him. Rosa jumped when he instinctively reached for his breast pocket, but she begged his pardon, forced herself to stand, and went on unsteady legs to answer the door.

Dwight Crowell stood on the front porch, rain dripping off the brim of his hat. "So you didn't stop with buying the Vanellis' car, did you?"

"Agent Crowell," she managed to say. "What do you want?"

He stepped forward as if he would walk right through her to enter the house, looming so near she could smell the tobacco and mint on his breath. She drew back as she always did when he came too close, but she kept the doorknob firmly in her grasp in case she had to slam the door shut.

"I want answers," Crowell said. "First off —"

"I can't bother with your questions right now," she said. "I'm busy. I have a guest."

Crowell drew closer and craned his neck, trying to see past her into the parlor. "Yes, I saw the bakery truck parked in the circle. Do you always entertain deliverymen in such high style?"

"That's none of your concern."

"I'll make it my concern, Mrs. Ottesen. Or should I call you Sonoma Rose? I saw the new sign. It led me right to you." He grinned nastily. "That's no name for a rancher's wife. Sounds like the proprietor of a whorehouse." He fingered the collar of her dress. "What would you show me on your winery tour, Sonoma Rose? Can I make a reservation for a private tasting?"

She slapped his hand away, barely resisting the urge to slap his face too. "Don't ever touch me again."

"You heard the lady," said Mr. Lucerno, who had come up behind her unnoticed. He eased the door open wider and eyed Crowell coolly. "I think you'd better leave, mister."

Crowell looked him up and down, and Rosa knew that the incongruity between Mr. Lucerno's fine suit and the vehicle he had arrived in did not escape him. "Says who?"

"Says the guy who can make you go even if you don't want to."

"This is my cousin, Albert," Rosa quickly interjected before the argument could escalate. "He often stops by to visit me when his deliveries bring him to Sonoma. Albert, this is Agent Dwight Crowell from the Prohibition bureau."

"Cousin, you say?" Crowell's steely gaze flicked from Rosa's dark brown hair and eyes and brown skin to Mr. Lucerno's, but whatever family resemblance he might have discerned, it failed to blunt his suspicions. "You two grow up together in Port Hueneme?"

"It was Stavanger, actually," said Mr. Lucerno. "Not that it's any business of yours."

The men stared each other down, the air between them crackling with tension. "Mr. Crowell," Rosa blurted, "if I answer your questions, would you please leave us alone?"

His gaze darted to her face. "For now."

"Then go ahead," she said. "And then go away." Just over her left shoulder, Mr. Lucerno turned a laugh into a cough.

Crowell indicated the downpour with a jerk of his head. "Aren't you going to invite me in?"

"That's not necessary. My answers will be the same whether I give them to you in the parlor or on the porch."

Crowell threw a look of unmasked resentment to Mr. Lucerno — warm, dry, and sipping coffee — and fixed Rosa with a stern glare. "Are you making wine on the premises?"

"Why, yes, of course," she said. "What else would we do with our leftover wine grapes? Waste not, want not, as my mother always says."

"Good old Aunt Mary," said Mr. Lucerno with a chuckle.

"You should go see her more often," Rosa chided him. "You know you have a standing invitation to Sunday dinner."

"You freely admit that you're making wine?" Crowell snapped.

"One hundred and sixty gallons exactly," said Rosa. "Each one perfectly legal. You're welcome to inspect the wine cellar yourself."

"I think I'll do that." Crowell turned on his heel and stormed down the front steps.

Rosa invited Mr. Lucerno to accompany them, but he preferred to wait in the parlor and help himself to another slice of pie. The keys made an angry, impatient jingling in Rosa's pocket as she hurried after Crowell to the winery, but she didn't need them. The door was still unlocked and Daniel still inside punching down the cap. Their sudden appearance startled him, but when Crowell pelted him with questions about the crush and how many gallons of new wine they had made, Daniel answered, unflustered, and his responses matched Rosa's. Scowling, Crowell descended the stairs into the cave and poked around awhile longer, searching for hidden doors or secret stashes until Daniel's silent but unmistakable amusement became intolerable. Crowell stormed from the winery, nearly slamming the door in Rosa's face as she followed swiftly after him, and stalked through the rain across the stone footbridge to his car. Thoroughly drenched, Rosa nonetheless lingered in the gravel circle as he drove away, watching and listening until she was certain he would not double back and drive through the vineyard toward the orchard and the old prune barn. Only then did she dash back across the bridge and into the house, shivering, heart pounding, wet hair plastered to her face and neck.

"He's gone," she told Mr. Lucerno, crossing her arms over her chest, chilled through.

"He'll be back."

She shook water from her dark bob and sighed. "Unfortunately, I'm certain you're right."

Mr. Lucerno looked her up and down as

she dripped on the doormat. His gaze came to rest on her face, and in his eyes she saw a respect and grudging admiration that had nothing to do with the way her rain-soaked dress clung to her curves. "Thanks for not ratting me out to your friend the fed, cousin."

"He's no friend of mine."

"So I figured." He stepped around her to get to the door, but he hesitated, his hand on the latch. "You should get into some dry clothes before you catch a cold. And if that fellow lays a hand on you again, you let me know. I'll take care of it."

"Thanks, but I can take care of myself." As much as Crowell's innuendo disgusted her, she had endured far worse at John's hands. "He's just a bully with a big mouth."

"That's not what I hear. He's new in town, but he's already made a name for himself. Just watch yourself. Don't let him get you alone."

The gangster's concern was as oddly amusing as it was unexpected. "I'll be fine. My husband's usually around, and even when he isn't, there's always someone within shouting distance."

"Glad to hear it." Mr. Lucerno pulled out a thick roll of bills, counted out ten, and handed them to her. "We owe you some

527

back rent. Circumstances . . . made it necessary to lie low for a while, but we're back
on schedule. You know how it is."

Rosa tucked the bills into her dress pocket
without counting them. "Of course," she
said, although she didn't know and hoped
he wouldn't elaborate.

"You can expect regular cash payments of
five hundred dollars the first day of every
month." Mr. Lucerno smiled briefly and
turned to go. "So I'll see you on the first of
November, if not sooner. Usually we work
late at night, so you might not even know
we've been here."

"Just as long as Dwight Crowell doesn't
know."

Mr. Lucerno's eyes narrowed. "Don't
worry about that. We'll take care of him if
he becomes a problem."

"He seems too prideful to accept a bribe."

"Yes, he does," said Mr. Lucerno nonchalantly, and as much as Rosa despised the
agent, she felt a chill. "Thanks for the pie
and coffee." He strode out into the rain, but
when he reached the footbridge, he turned
and called out, "Give my best to Aunt
Mary."

"I will," Rosa called back. She closed the
door firmly, shutting out the rain and the
sound of the bakery truck driving away.

Then she remembered the folded bills Mr. Lucerno had given her, and she took them from her pocket to count them.

She had accepted ten crisp one-hundred-dollar bills.

Lars returned home from Cacchione Vineyards just in time to meet the girls at the bus stop and spare them the long walk up the driveway in the cold drizzle. Rosa and Miguel were on the front porch bouncing a ball back and forth when the old Chevrolet rumbled up to the house and the girls tumbled out, giggling and shrieking as they dashed through the puddles to the house. Lars waved a greeting to Rosa before driving off to park in the old carriage house, but he must have had chores to attend to, because nearly twenty minutes passed before he came hurrying across the yard, pausing on the front porch to brush rain from his coat and hat before coming indoors. Rosa greeted him with a fierce embrace and a long kiss, which he returned gladly. "I'm very happy you're home," she told him.

"Had I known I'd be greeted like that," he remarked, "I would have come home sooner."

She had much to tell him, but it had to

wait until hours later, after supper and baths and bedtime stories for the children. Until then they chatted about the news from the Cacchione family and the sapling apricot orchard Lars had left behind. As soon as the children were tucked into bed, Rosa led Lars into the parlor where only a few hours before an armed gangster had enjoyed prune pie and coffee. Lars stared in disbelief as the story spilled from her, anger darkening his face when she told him what Crowell had said as he fingered the collar of her dress. "If I had been here —"

"You probably would have punched him," she interrupted, "and he would have hauled you off to prison, so it's very good you weren't here. Anyway, I was never alone with him, except while we walked from the house to the winery and back."

"I don't like the thought of a gangster coming to your defense."

Rosa stood and went to the window, glancing apprehensively out into the rainy night. "Better to have him on our side than against us."

"I doubt he's on anyone's side but his own." Lars sighed and leaned forward to rest his elbows upon his knees. "So it sounds like we're keeping the Vanellis' tenants on."

"For now. I don't see that we have much choice." She took the bills from her pocket and handed them to Lars. "I've already accepted their first payment. This is for the past due rent they owe us for September and October."

Lars quickly counted the bills. "A thousand dollars."

"And five hundred more due to us the first of every month."

"That's hardly worth the risk we're taking." Lars shook his head, folded the bills carefully, and passed the bundle from hand to hand as if he wasn't sure what to do with it. "I thought our plan was to convince them that they should find a better place for their still."

"It was, but then Crowell showed up, and —" Rosa sat down heavily on the sofa, her hands clasped together in her lap. "I never had the chance to explain to him how dangerous the prune barn is, for them as well as us, and the next thing I knew —"

"It's all right, Rosa. You did the best you could under the circumstances."

"No, it's not all right. We can't give gangsters the run of the place, especially with Crowell snooping around. It's only a matter of time before he stumbles upon the prune barn, and then what will we do?"

"Crowell never found the Cacchiones' old wine cellar," Lars reminded her. "He doesn't seem to be one for long walks. He might never venture much farther than the winery."

"Maybe not," Rosa replied uncertainly. She hoped Mr. Lucerno and his associates had other, better things to do than make grappa, and that they would visit the prune barn only rarely. As long as the still remained on their property, she would live in fear of its discovery — something that seemed inevitable as long as the suspicious, spiteful Crowell lurked nearby, watching and waiting to catch them in a crime.

More than a year had passed since Rosa, Lars, and the children had fled the Arboles Valley. Sometimes it seemed to Rosa that ages had gone by since she lived in the small adobe on the mesa, watching her children suffer and perish; other times it felt as if they had only just escaped the flooded canyon. Some mornings she woke gradually, her mind and body keeping pace with the sunrise, and in those strange moments between sleep and wakefulness she believed herself to be lying beside John in the bedroom they had once shared. As dread and hopelessness welled up in her, she would close her eyes and wish herself back to sleep, lying perfectly motionless so she would not jostle John awake, annoying him and provoking a sullen temper that would last the rest of the day. When sleep did not return, she would open her eyes, blink confusedly at the unfamiliar patterns of sunlight and fine cracks on the ceiling until she recognized her new bedroom and remembered where she was. Then she would sigh with relief, pull the quilt up to her shoulders, and snuggle closer to Lars, hoping with all her strength that John would never find them.

The children rarely spoke of John anymore. Even Lupita had come to accept Lars as part of their family, although when she was especially angry with her parents she would stomp her foot and yell that someday her real papa would come for her. As infrequent as Lupita's outbursts were, they left Rosa badly shaken. John haunted her nightmares, and the thought of him suddenly appearing on the front porch demanding his children and the now empty valises that had once been stuffed with cash was enough to make her heart pound with fright. More anonymous letters had followed the first John had sent to Rosa Barclay in care of Cacchione Vineyards. When the second arrived, Guiditta kept it for Rosa until the next time they saw each other, hesitating before she held up the envelope so Rosa could see the postmark and the same block printing. Guiditta offered to write, "Return to sender, addressee unknown" across the front and put it with her outgoing mail, unopened. Rosa agreed and asked Guiditta to do the same with any others that might come. Perhaps it would have been better to destroy them, not knowing what incriminating secrets to her past they might contain, but keeping them would prove that she had received them, whereas returning them might convince John that she had moved away. Rosa didn't know how many letters Guiditta had received and returned, but she hoped they were few and far between and that eventually John would give up and stop sending them.

Rosa could not help but think of John and the mobsters he had become entangled with every time she spotted the Johnson's Bakery truck parked out by the edge of the orchard or heard the distant, low hum of the still as she walked through the vineyard. Mr. Lucerno's associates apparently had a lot of work to catch up on in the prune barn after their prolonged absence, for they appeared far more often than Rosa had anticipated.

Although she glimpsed the men only rarely, and only at a distance through the prune trees, signs of their presence were everywhere for those who knew how to interpret them — tire tracks in the gravel, footprints in the dirt outside the crumbling prune barn, a faint sweet and yeasty smell that wafted through the orchard when the wind came from the west, and of course, the delivery truck. By the time Mr. Lucerno returned on the first of November to pay the rent, Rosa's nerves were a tangle of apprehension and worry. Dwight Crowell came by for routine inspections at least once a week, and so far no more of his visits had coincided with those of the men from Johnson's Bakery, but Rosa knew it was only a matter of time until the two factions collided.

Worry kept her from drifting off to sleep at night even within the safe circle of Lars's arms, and nightmares shook her awake before dawn. Dark circles formed beneath her eyes and her stomach rebelled, leaving her ravenous one moment and queasy the next. But despite her distress, when she wasn't brooding over John, Crowell, or the ersatz bakers cooking grappa in the prune barn, she was content and industrious, grateful for her children's good health and affection and for Lars's love. She did not need to pretend to be happy, as she had living in the adobe with John; she *was* happy. But she was also very worried, knowing that their new lives in their beautiful new home on the Sonoma Rose Vineyards and Orchard could be snatched away from them at any moment, and though she tried, she could not hide the physical manifestation of her distress.

One morning in mid-November, she made corn cakes for Ana and Miguel's breakfast and flapjacks for everyone else. She served the rest of the family, placed two steaming flapjacks on her own plate, and was just about to ask Marta to pass the syrup when Ana exclaimed, "Mamá, don't eat those!"

Rosa was so startled she almost spilled her coffee. "Don't eat what? What's the matter?"

"Don't eat flapjacks." Ana's brow was furrowed, her dark eyes troubled and full of fear. "You should have corn cakes instead."

Rosa's stomach was so unsettled that morning that she would prefer not to eat anything. "Why, *mija?*"

"Because —" Ana's eyes darted to Miguel and Lupita, as if they were too young to hear.

Lars set down his fork and studied Ana,

concerned. "Go on, honey. What is it?"

"Because you're like us," Ana blurted. "You can't have flour anymore, Mamá. It makes you sick too, just like me and Miguel."

"Mamá's sick?" asked Lupita, her voice rising with alarm.

"Of course not," Rosa soothed, reaching across the table to clasp Lupita's hand. "I'm fine."

"No, you're not," insisted Ana. "I've seen you throwing up. You've caught what we have."

Rosa muffled a sigh. "No, I didn't, *mija*. I'm just tired, that's all. I've been working too hard."

Marta looked bewildered. "Ana, Mamá can't catch what you and Miguel have. You got it from your father." In recent months she had begun referring to John in that aloof manner, as if she had not considered him her father too for most of her life. "It's not like the measles."

"How do you know?" countered Ana tearfully. "Maybe you haven't been paying attention, but I have. Every morning Mamá nibbles some toast or a flapjack, and then later, in the middle of washing the dishes, she runs away and throws up. I know you do, Mamá. I heard you through the door."

"Rosa," Lars broke in, "is this true? Why didn't you tell me?"

"I —" Was she really ill that often? She was so busy, so preoccupied with the children and the vineyard and the winery and their frequent, unexpected, and unwelcome visitors that she had not given much thought to her upset stomach except to lump it in with the other effects of her ongoing worries.

"Ana," said Marta reasonably, "last night Mama had bread with supper, remember? She didn't throw up then, did she?"

Ana thought for a moment. "I didn't hear her, but that doesn't mean she didn't. She's definitely sick every morning. Maybe she throws up at night after we go to bed."

Lupita set down her fork, looking faintly ill herself. "Can we please not talk so much about throwing up?"

"That's an excellent idea," declared Rosa. "Ana, *mija,* I don't have celiac disease, but if it would make you feel better, this morning I'll have corn cakes instead of flapjacks for my breakfast. Okay?"

Ana nodded, relieved, and soon everyone resumed eating and the children's cheerful patter turned to other things. Rosa replaced her untouched flapjacks on the serving platter and took a corn cake instead, and as she raised her fork to take a bite, her eyes met Lars's across the table. Wide-eyed and startled, he raised his eyebrows in a silent question. She gave him a small, uncertain shrug and smiled weakly.

Lars insisted that she see a doctor that very day. She preferred Dr. Reynolds, but Lars was too agitated to wait for her to make the trip into San Francisco, and he didn't want her to travel alone on the train in her condition. "We don't know that I have a condition," she reminded him, although now that she was paying attention, she was fairly sure she did.

Guiditta and Alegra recommended the same doctor in Santa Rosa, and he confirmed what Ana had unwittingly noticed and Lars and Rosa had suspected. Rosa was pregnant.

Shock soon gave way to joy and worry and concern in equal measure. Rosa had never expected to have another child, and although she had suffered no unusual complications in her previous pregnancies, she was thirty-six and knew there were risks at her age. She worried how the demands of a new baby would disrupt her other children's lives, just as they were settling into a comfortable routine after the series of upheavals they had endured throughout the previous year. Never far from her thoughts was the fear that John or the police or the gangsters they had left behind in Southern California might find them and force them to flee in the night in peril of their lives — but how fast and how far could she run with a child in her womb or a newborn in her arms? And with Dwight Crowell determined to uncover all their secrets and Albert Lucerno directing an intermittent stream of gangsters past their front door, how long could they expect to keep their identities secret?

For Lars, however, Rosa's pregnancy brought only happiness. Although he did not dismiss Rosa's fears, his joy outshone any worries. They were going to have a baby, and this time they would raise the child together from the very first, within the safe circle of a loving family.

"Safe," echoed Rosa. Yes, this baby and all their children must be safe. Every other consideration diminished in comparison.

Before their child arrived in July, Rosa would take every possible precaution to ensure the safety of all their children.

She counted off the worst threats confronting them: John was the first and foremost, but he would remain in prison for at least a few more years. He knew where Rosa, Lars, and the children had been, but not where they were now. If, upon his release, he made his way to Santa Rosa, Guiditta would set him upon a false trail, and they could enlist other trusted friends to confirm whatever story Guiditta told him. Rosa knew, too, that it would not be easy for John to make the journey north, a felon with limited resources and no friends. He could not deplete their bank accounts or sell the ranch to finance a search for the wife and children everyone else believed to be dead, not when Rosa held all the necessary documents within the strongbox she had taken from the adobe. As a precaution, Rosa and Lars passed themselves off as John and Rosa Barclay and met with a banker in San Francisco. They explained that they had recently relocated to the city and wanted to transfer their funds from their old bank in the Arboles Valley to a new account with his bank. The clerk was all too happy to help, not knowing that two weeks later they would, with the assistance of a different clerk, close their new account and deposit the money into Nils and Rose Ottesen's account with the Bank of Sonoma.

Dwight Crowell persisted as a frequent intrusion into their lives. Although Rosa had once dismissed him as a nuisance, as his questions became more probing and his demeanor more malicious, she had come to see him as a menace. Under the law he could show up unannounced to inspect the winery, a right he exploited at whim. Complaining to his superiors would do them no good, as Paulo and Alegra Del Bene had learned. All Rosa and Lars could do to shield themselves from his authority was to tolerate his visits and give him no cause to arrest them — which they could have done quite easily, if not for their aliases and their unwilling association with known criminals.

They could do little more to conceal their true identities from Crowell than what they had already done, but their ties to organized crime had to be severed before it was too late.

They could not simply ask Albert Lucerno to leave, and they could not afford to offend him by demanding that he go. Lars and Rosa talked endlessly about what to do, but for every solution one of them proposed, the other found a fatal flaw. When Mr. Lucerno came by the house to pay the December rent, Rosa warned him, over coffee and a slice of pumpkin pie, that Dwight Crowell had taken to prowling the winery and the vineyard and she worried that it was only a matter of time before he found his way to the prune barn. Unconcerned, Mr. Lucerno assured her that the men he worked for would help pay the Ottesens' legal expenses if they were caught holding the bag. Rosa smiled tightly and thanked him.

Christmas offered them a merry diversion from their troubles, but as Rosa prepared the nursery and felt the first stirrings of the child within her womb, the strain of harboring bootleggers and dodging the law left her constantly exhausted and apprehensive, as if she were caught in a vise, fighting to hold the jaws open while an unseen adversary mercilessly turned the screw. In early January, Rose reluctantly accepted the rent and told Mr. Lucerno that she lived in deathly fear that the decrepit old barn would collapse upon his men while they worked. Without pausing to reflect, Mr. Lucerno remarked that his men were deceptively light on their feet and would probably escape uninjured at the first sign of trouble, and that he was more concerned about the loss of the grappa and damage to the equipment. His merciless indifference chilled her. She realized then that his apparent concern for her with regard to Dwight Crowell had misled her. She would not find a way to appeal to his better nature or sense of decency because he possessed neither.

Increasingly desperate and afraid, she

despaired of finding a way to free her family from the vise grip that inched ever tighter. Then one night, a sudden and unexpected thunderstorm brought the children running from their own beds into hers and Lars's. As she sang the children gentle lullabies to calm their fears so they could drift back off to sleep, she prayed for the storm to increase its fury, to bring gale-force winds down from Sonoma Mountain, leveling the prune barn and destroying everything within it. How, she wondered angrily, could it withstand storm after storm? Why would it not simply collapse under the weight of old age and rot? She had warned Mr. Lucerno that the neglected building was a deathtrap, but as if it had a perverse will of its own and wanted to prove her a liar, it refused to fall.

Perhaps, she suddenly realized, she and Lars needed to give it a push.

While the rest of her family slept, she lay awake for hours, jittery and eager, until the rain ceased and the winds diminished. Careful not to jostle the children, she shook Lars awake, pressed a finger to her lips as he yawned and blinked up at her, and gestured to the door. Carefully they extricated themselves from the tangle of sheets, blankets, and sleeping children and stole quietly into the hallway. "I know what to do," Rosa whispered. "We have to burn down the prune barn."

"What?"

"We have to do it now," Rose insisted, grasping his arm. "We can blame it on a lightning strike from the storm. If we wait, we'll miss our chance."

Lars inhaled deeply, but thankfully he did not need long to make up his mind. "Get dressed. The grappa will burn but I'll fetch some kerosene too in case we need to speed things along."

Swift and silent, they threw on their clothes and hurried out into the fog-shrouded stillness between the storm and the sunrise. The muddy yard was cratered with puddles and strewn with windfall leaves and broken twigs. Rosa went on ahead through the vineyard while Lars stopped at the garage for kerosene. Would the rain-soaked wood burn? Rosa wondered as she strode through the grapevines, stripped of their summer greenery, stark and angular in the predawn haze. The prune barn had to come down that morning. There would not be many occasions when a thunderstorm coincided with the men's absence. It had to come down now, because Rosa could not endure the strain much longer.

545

When she reached the prune barn, she hesitated before throwing open the doors. Lucerno's men had been working hard since she had last stolen a glance inside. The still gleamed spotlessly as before, but many more tin milk cans were arranged in rows along the opposite wall, and a pile of empty sugar sacks three feet tall sat in the corner. She and Lars had to make it look as if they had tried to put out the fire, as if they had tried to save Mr. Lucerno's stores of grappa. With a wary glance toward the ceiling, Rosa steeled herself and entered the barn, the uneven floorboards creaking underfoot. She took hold of one of the milk cans and wrestled it outside, concealing it in the forest between the thick, spreading roots of a coastal redwood. She had dragged two more cans into the forest before Lars showed up with two jugs of kerosene. He understood immediately what she was doing and joined in, but when only five cans remained inside the barn, he put a hand on her arm as she took hold of one and shook his head. "Leave them," he said. "We can't make it look like it was too easy."

She nodded and let go of the milk can. As they left the barn, Lars paused to grab a few pieces of equipment from the side of the still facing the door and carried them outside. "Stand back," he said, and while she withdrew to the forest, she glimpsed him striding back and forth within the barn, spilling kerosene in his wake, careful not to splash any on his clothes.

Her heart pounded as she watched him kick over two of the milk cans to send streams of grappa cascading down the uneven floor. "Lars," she called. "Get out of there." Nodding, he paused in the doorway long enough to strike a match and throw it behind him, and then he ran to join her among the redwoods.

First the only flickering light came from the fallen match, so close to a stream of grappa that Rosa wondered if the liquid would extinguish it rather than burst into flame. Then, with a soft roar, the kerosene caught fire and a line of searing red and orange and blue raced from one end of the barn to the other. And then suddenly it seemed the entire barn was ablaze, flames leaping up to lick the high beams, sparks popping and snapping and rising into the sky. Lars kept a wary eye on the nearest redwoods, and if an ember went aloft and floated lazily back down to earth too close to the trees, he was immediately upon it, stamping out the flames with his heavy boots. Rosa's heart pounded as she watched some of the branches closest to the roof blacken and smolder, and she swallowed back the bitter, metallic taste of fear. If she had given her plan more thought, she would have abandoned it as too dangerous. Now it was too late, and she knew that if not for the heavy soaking rains the night before, the whole forest might have caught fire.

Lars stood a few yards away watching the blaze, but suddenly he strode toward the barn door. "What are you doing?" she shouted, but her voice was lost in the roaring of the flames. Crouching low, he darted into the barn and emerged a heartbeat later carrying two empty, smoldering crates marked with the Johnson's Bakery insignia. He raced inside again and returned dragging two old wooden chairs that had been stationed on either side of the doors. Then Rosa understood. The milk cans full of grappa and the pieces of the still stashed among the redwoods were in pristine condition. The charred objects were their proof that they had attempted to put out the blaze and save what they could after the barn had become engulfed.

Eventually Lars retreated to the forest, coughing and red-eyed, his clothes and face blackened with soot, ashes in his hair. As he shrugged off his jacket and shook it roughly,

Rosa pulled the sleeves of her coat down to cover her hands and brushed the soot and ashes from his face and hair. "I think that'll do it," Lars said hoarsely as the roof caved in.

Before long they heard the shriek of sirens coming up the road, and Rosa imagined the children being jolted awake and finding themselves alone. She reached for Lars's hand, squeezed it, and hurried back to the house, directing the passing firefighters along the gravel road through the vineyard to the orchard. She found the children on the front porch, barefoot in their pajamas, their faces turned toward the orchard, wide-eyed and openmouthed in astonishment.

"Can we go see?" asked Ana, frightened and eager.

"No," said Rosa firmly, putting her arms around them and steering them back into the house. "But you may watch from Miguel's window." They tore away from her and raced up the stairs.

Later she learned that Charmian London or one of her houseguests had spotted the smoke and called the fire department. Eventually they brought the blaze under control, but not before the prune barn and everything within it was utterly destroyed. Curious lumps of metal and twisted wires littered the smoking heaps of ash and cinder, but if the firemen thought they resembled anything other than farm or orchard equipment, they said nothing. Everyone there was aware of the thunderstorm that had passed through the Sonoma Valley that night, just as they knew how a lightning strike could bring down an old tinderbox of a building within hours. The fire chief remarked that the Ottesens were fortunate that they had lost only one little-used outbuilding and not their house or winery, and everyone for miles around was lucky that the forest had been only slightly singed. The caprice of nature could have devastated them all.

The ruins had not yet completely cooled when Mr. Lucerno showed up two days later to inspect the damage, driving a shiny new roadster instead of the bakery delivery truck. Rosa and Lars showed him the grappa they had managed to save before the flames grew too intense and the few other charred, inconsequential items they had snatched up in their last, frantic moments before the heat and smoke forced them to retreat.

"You warned me this place was a death-trap," said Mr. Lucerno, nudging a smoldering cinder aside with the toe of an Italian leather shoe that probably cost more than Rosa's entire wardrobe.

"Thank heavens no one was inside at the time," Rosa said, with a shudder that was not at all feigned.

"I'm sorry we couldn't save more of your property," said Lars, and offered to help load the milk cans of grappa into his roadster. Mr. Lucerno accepted, and when the task was done, he studied the ruins of the barn, frowning and shaking his head, muttering under his breath about the cost of doing business out in the sticks.

"We don't think it's right to keep your money for the weeks you can't use the barn." Rosa handed Mr. Lucerno three hundred dollars, a little more than half the month's rent. "I hope your Mr. Johnson won't be too upset about this."

Mr. Lucerno peered at her curiously. "Mr. Johnson?"

"Your employer," she said. "Johnson's Bakery? I assumed that was his name."

A faint smile appeared on his lips. "No, that's not his name. He will be upset, but he'll understand that this was an act of God. He won't take it out on me." He brandished the bundle of folded bills and tucked them into his breast pocket. "This'll cheer him up a little, this and the grappa you saved.

How soon could you rebuild?"

"Well, that all depends," said Lars, taken aback. "We'll have to clear the debris, and see how much it will cost —"

"We can help you there."

"Much appreciated," said Lars, "but I'd have to fit the work in between the winter pruning and cleanup of the vineyards and —"

"So you're saying it'll be a while." Mr. Lucerno frowned, thinking. "We'll need to find someplace to use in the meantime. Can you vouch for any of your neighbors? They'd have to be folks who know how to keep their mouths shut."

Lars and Rosa exchanged a look and shook their heads. "We just moved in a few months ago," said Rosa. "We haven't even met Charmian London yet, and she's our nearest neighbor."

"I'll tell you what." From the look on his face, Rosa knew Mr. Lucerno was groping for some good news to take back to his employer. "Can we count on you to renew our lease, so to speak, after you rebuild the barn?"

"Absolutely," said Lars. "The day the prune barn is rebuilt, you can move right in and set up shop."

Mr. Lucerno nodded, satisfied. "Good.

Good. I'll tell my boss." He climbed into his roadster, gave them one parting nod, and drove away. Watching the roadster rumble down the gravel driveway, Rosa reached for Lars's hand, flooded by an immeasurable sense of relief.

She knew Lars would always manage to be far too busy to rebuild that old prune barn.

January and February were the months for pruning and cleaning up the vineyard. Lars and Daniel led the teams of workers, and just as on the Cacchione ranch, every member of the family, young and old, played a role. Miguel was old enough to help Rosa pull weeds around the stocks, and after the girls came home from school, they helped gather up the uprooted weeds and fallen grapevine trimmings. Rosa wasn't sure whether it was dark humor or pragmatism that prompted Lars to have the children pile up the debris on the ruins of the prune barn, but after the last trellis row was finished, he and Daniel lit the bonfire on the ashes that rain showers had not washed away. The smell of smoke drifting up into the night sky filled Rosa with anticipation for the coming of spring. Before long mustard growing among the trellises would dust the vineyard in gold, and soon thereafter the grapevines would leaf out, becoming green and lush once more. With the children healthy and thriving, John misled by his returned mail, and the men from Johnson's Bakery gone for good, for the first time in ages Rosa looked to the future with something close to optimism.

The baby growing within her womb gave her even more reason to be full of joy and hope. Friends and family alike helped her prepare for the little one's arrival. To make ready the nursery, Lars built a crib, refinished a secondhand rocking chair, and painted the walls of the smallest bedroom a warm, creamy yellow. Rosa sewed curtains, a dust ruffle, and a cozy Pinwheel Star crib quilt from cotton feed sacks and scraps. For their part, the children eagerly suggested names and argued over whether they should have a boy or a girl. On one sunny, breezy February day, Alegra Del Bene and her youngest son came over for lunch and playtime, bringing along a large carton full of baby clothes her children had outgrown.

"Are you sure you won't need these again?" asked Rosa, lifting the lid and admiring the neatly folded garments, flannel blankets, and diapers.

Alegra smiled, but her eyes were weary

and her skin seemed drained of its radiance. "If I do, I'll borrow them back."

As the boys ran off to play, Rosa took Alegra upstairs to show her the baby's room. Alegra admired the Pinwheel Star quilt and wished aloud that she knew how to make something so soft and comforting for her children. "I'll teach you," Rosa offered. "It's easy, and quilting lessons will give us a good excuse to get together." Alegra accepted so promptly that Rosa wondered whether she was very eager to learn, or just relieved to have a reason to avoid staying home alone. She didn't need a reason. Rosa had given her a standing invitation to come over when she felt anxious or wanted to avoid an unwelcome visit from Dwight Crowell, but Alegra rarely took her up on the offer. Perhaps she didn't want to admit she didn't like to be home alone.

They took Rosa's sewing basket out to the front porch where they could keep an eye on the boys as they played happily with the collie puppies in the courtyard garden, enclosed on three sides by the farmhouse and the adjacent building. After Rosa showed Alegra a few sample quilt blocks, they settled on a simple Nine-Patch for her first project. They were chatting and sorting scraps from Rosa's basket when they heard the distant sound of wheels on gravel and the rumble of a car's motor. They both instinctively glanced up, but from where they sat, a thick screen of redwoods blocked the view of the gravel circle where visitors parked. Seeing no one, Alegra returned her attention to her work, a piece of royal blue and red tartan fabric in one hand and Rosa's best shears in the other, but Rosa recognized the sound of the motor and fixed her gaze on the footbridge. Within moments, Dwight Crowell appeared, striding purposefully toward the house.

"Rose," began Alegra, holding up a scrap of red wool, "do you think this piece would be too rough, or —" Her words choked off as she caught sight of the agent. Stifling a gasp, she dropped the shears, scrambled to her feet, and raced into the house. The door banged shut behind her.

Rosa stood and waited for their unwelcome visitor at the top of the porch stairs, smoothing her skirt and crossing her arms. "Agent Crowell," she said flatly, "what can I do for you?"

He halted at the bottom of the stairs. "I'd like to speak to your cousin."

"He isn't here."

"Then tell me where I can find him."

"He doesn't check in with me," Rosa

retorted. "I'm his cousin, not his mother."

Crowell jerked his head in the direction of the gravel circle. "Whose car is parked back there?"

Rosa was surprised he didn't know; he had recognized the Chevrolet she and Lars had bought from the Vanellis quickly enough. "It's not my cousin's," she said, exasperated. "What'll it be this time, Mr. Crowell? Do you want to see the winery, count the barrels again, knock on the walls in search of a secret room?"

His lips thinned. "I think I have time for all of that."

"Miguel," she called. "Stay in the garden with the dogs, hear me?"

"Okay, Mamá," he shouted back, waving. Alegra's son echoed him, shading his eyes with his hand and searching the porch for his mother. He spotted Crowell instead, and instantly his happy grin crumpled into a scowl of worry and dislike.

Over Rosa's objections that such precautions were unnecessary and demeaning, Lars had heeded Mr. Lucerno's warnings and had asked the hired hands to make sure she was never left alone with Crowell. As soon as Rosa and Crowell headed up the hill to the winery, a hand named Charlie who had been observing them from the doorway of the barn left his post and fell in step behind them. Seething with impatience, Crowell stormed ahead as Rosa and Charlie discussed the improving health of a mare that had fallen a bit lame. As she watched him, it occurred to Rosa that in the year she had known Crowell, his arrogant self-righteousness had become an almost frenzied, malevolent zealotry. She wondered if that was because no matter how many wine-makers he harassed and arrested, he could not dam up the river of alcohol flowing in Sonoma County — wine, grappa, distilled spirits smuggled in by ship from Canada and Mexico, the liquor kept coming. Many officials looked the other way when their neighbors broke the law, justifying their leniency by arguing that they were obliged to focus their attention and limited re-sources on the real villains — members of organized crime, opportunistic hardened criminals — rather than family men, farm-ers and ranchers they had known for years. Not so Crowell, who condemned such police officers and politicians as hypocriti-cal and corrupt. To Crowell, Dante Cac-chione was as much a criminal as a mob boss, Alegra Del Bene as deserving of suspicion as Albert Lucerno. There were no innocent civilians in his war, only lawbreakers and potential lawbreakers.

The wine cellar had not changed since Crowell's last visit except that the new wine was a little bit older, though still undrinkable, but he went through his usual paces anyway, inspecting every nook and corner of the winery. When his search turned up nothing illegal, he left the winery disappointed and more suspicious than before. Rosa was tempted to tell him that perhaps the reason he found nothing incriminating on their property was not because they hid it so well but because there was nothing to find, but she kept the observation to herself. She already did too much to challenge and provoke him. If she were more submissive and meek and showed him the deference he believed he deserved, he might leave them alone, but Rosa could not bring herself to cower and scrape before a man she despised.

Finally he left. Rosa joined the boys in the garden and asked them to help her feed the dogs, glancing to the front door from time to time and waiting for Alegra to reappear. When she didn't, Rosa brought the boys inside for a snack of cookies and prunes while she went to find her friend.

Alegra was in the baby's room, sitting in the corner with her knees drawn up to her chest, staring straight ahead at nothing.

"Alegra," Rosa exclaimed, hurrying to her. "What's the matter?"

"Is he gone?"

"Who? Agent Crowell?" Rosa tucked her skirt beneath her legs and sat down on the floor beside her. "Yes, he's gone, off to torment some other law-abiding citizens. Alegra, please tell me what's wrong. Are you ill?"

"No, I just —" Alegra swallowed hard and took a deep, shuddering breath. "I can't get away from him. He comes into my house, he follows me here —" She wrapped her arms around her shoulders, shivering and bowing her head as if an icy wind buffeted her on all sides. "If I know he's coming, I can prepare myself and it's not as bad, but when I don't expect to see him and suddenly he's there —"

A cold, hard knot formed in the pit of Rosa's stomach, and she had a terrible feeling that something was very, very wrong, something much more than simple dislike. "Alegra," she said steadily, "what has Agent Crowell said to you? Has he threatened you?"

Mutely, Alegra lifted her head and threw Rosa a pleading, tearful look.

"You can tell me," Rosa persisted gently, putting her arm around Alegra's shoulders.

"I've told you, he can't arrest you if you've done nothing wrong. He's not above the law."

"He *is* the law," Alegra cried. "He makes his own law."

"No, Alegra, that's not true."

"It is. It is." Tears streamed down Alegra's face. "Don't tell Paulo. Please. I did it for him, but it would kill him. I know it would. And then I would be all alone, and what would happen to the children?"

Heart pounding, Rosa held Alegra as she wept. "What did you do?" she asked as calmly as she could. "What is it that you don't want Paulo to know?"

The story came tumbling out of her, splintered and broken. How Dwight Crowell had come to their vineyard shortly after his appointment to the northern California bureau more than a year before, demanding to see their sacramental wine permit. How he had invaded their winery to count and tally their barrels and casks. How he had shown up week after week, accusing the Del Benes of selling sacramental wine to speakeasies and hotels up and down the West Coast. How Paulo had threatened him with violence if he ever accused them again. How Crowell began appearing whenever Paulo was away from the vineyard, interrogating

Alegra and demanding that she inform on her husband. Alegra's bewildered, tearful insistence that she had nothing to divulge. Crowell's certainty that she was lying, and his promise that if he could not find evidence against her husband, he would procure it by some other means, and no judge in the county would take the Del Benes' word over his. How he swore he would throw Paulo in prison if she did not testify against him. He would have her deported to Italy and she would never see her husband and children again. When she could not give him evidence of a crime, she desperately offered him money to leave them alone. Crowell seized her by the shoulders and shook her. He did not want her money. He could get money from any nervous bootlegger from Eureka to Santa Barbara. He wanted something else.

"He comes for me when he knows Paulo is away," Alegra finished dully as Rosa listened, dumbfounded by horror. "I put Gino in his room with cookies and milk and toys and I tell him I'm taking a nap. He doesn't take me in my marriage bed — a small mercy. He takes me to the stable, which he says is the most suitable place for a filthy whore like me."

"Dios mío," Rosa breathed, drawing Alegra

into her embrace, holding her, rocking her gently as if she were Ana or Lupita. "Oh, Alegra."

"Don't tell Paulo," Alegra begged in a barely audible whisper.

"We have to tell someone. This can't go on."

"No." Alegra tore herself from Rosa's arms and pressed herself farther into the corner. "Mr. Crowell will tell him it was my idea. He'll claim we were lovers."

"Paulo would never believe that. No one would believe it."

"He'll arrest Paulo and send me back to Italy."

"That's not in his power."

"No? Then why does Dante Cacchione sit in prison even now?"

"Dante was a bootlegger. He broke the law. Paulo hasn't and neither have you."

"Crowell can make anyone look like a bootlegger," Alegra cried. "The trunk of his car is full of bottles and casks and equipment he's kept from raids. He showed it to me. All he has to do is tell a judge he found it on our property and we're finished. Don't you see? No one would believe me. No one would believe Paulo, not even if his friend the bishop defended him. Dwight Crowell is the law." Alegra enunciated the last five words clearly, her accent emphasizing her plight.

"There must be something we can do."

"There is," said Alegra bitterly, "and I'm doing it, God have mercy on me."

Rosa felt searing, helpless rage churning within her. "No. Not anymore. You've got to get away from him. Do you have any family in California who could take you in for a while? Does Paulo?"

"My family is all back in Italy. Paulo —" Alegra hesitated. "Paulo has brothers and sisters in San Francisco and Sacramento, as well as here in Sonoma County."

No place within Sonoma County was far enough away. "Can you take the children and stay with Paulo's relatives in San Francisco or Sacramento for a little while?"

"But —" Alegra shook her head. "I can't. The children have school and — and Paulo needs me —"

Rosa took her by the shoulders. "Paulo and the children need you to be safe. You must get away from this man. Either you take the children and get away, or we have to tell the police what he's done."

Alegra gasped and clutched at her. "We can't. Please, Rose."

"He can't go on raping you at will!"

"But Paulo — it would kill him if he knew.

I couldn't bear it. How would you feel? Would you want Nils to know?"

Rosa inhaled deeply, imagining Lars's anguish and rage. He would want to strangle Crowell with his bare hands. Eventually Paulo would have to know what Crowell had done, what his wife had suffered, but for now, what mattered most was getting Alegra away from him, to keep her safe until they could figure out what to do.

Crowell had to be stopped.

Eventually, gently, Rosa persuaded Alegra to arrange to take Gino for an extended visit to her sister-in-law's family in Sacramento. The older children would be fine at school during the day and at home with Paulo; Crowell always ignored the children. After that was decided, Rosa led Alegra, limp with exhaustion and relief, off to her own bedroom to rest. She slept the afternoon away while Rosa minded the boys. Later, when the girls came home from school, Rosa left the younger children in Marta's care and drove Alegra and Gino home in the Del Benes' car, while Lars, who knew only that Alegra was suffering from some sort of nervous exhaustion, followed in the Chevrolet.

They saw Alegra and Gino safely back to their own home, although Rosa doubted

Alegra felt any sense of security and comfort there. Rosa could hardly meet Paulo's eyes when she and Lars found him in the winery and told him only that his wife was not feeling well. Paulo ought to be told the truth, Rosa thought, with the same stomach-churning anger that had surged up in her before. He could protect his wife better if he knew the dangers she faced. But then an image flashed before her mind's eye — Paulo with his hands clenched around Crowell's throat, Paulo being hauled off to prison, Alegra collapsing in anguish — and she knew she must abide by Alegra's wishes, for now.

Lars drove them home. Staring out the window and blinking back angry tears, Rosa clenched her teeth and balled up her skirt in her fists. She did not know what to do.

"Would you mind telling me what's going on?" Lars asked.

Rosa told him, and as she had expected, his first instinct, like hers, was that they must report Crowell to the police. Rosa reminded him that Alegra had agreed to leave town only on the condition that neither the police nor Paulo be informed, and getting her to safety had to be their first priority. The longer Lars mulled it over, the more he realized that they had to tread carefully. Of course they would have to go to the authorities before long, but who could be trusted, and who would instinctively take Crowell's word over his accusers' simply because of his position, they did not know — and they could not act until they did. Crowell was too powerful. If he struck back, he could ruin them all, picking off Alegra's protectors until none remained.

Rosa hoped an idea would come to her as the burning of the prune barn had, but although she kneaded and pounded the problem in her thoughts, day after day, no inspiration came to her, only anger. So constantly was Crowell in her thoughts that it was a shock when, four days after Alegra's confession, he showed up on her front porch as arrogant and self-righteous as ever, as if his soul were spotless and his conscience clear.

But of course, from his perspective, nothing had changed. He didn't know that Rosa knew the truth.

"What do you want?" she asked, her voice shaking with anger. When he smiled slightly, her anger and disgust surged. She knew he interpreted the tremor as fear. "The usual tour?"

"No time for that today," he said, with something like regret. "I just stopped by to show you something." He reached into his breast pocket and removed a folded newspaper clipping.

There was only one clipping he would taunt and threaten her with, but why he had waited so long, she could only imagine. He held out the report of the raid on Cacchione Vineyards to her, but she didn't take it. "I've seen it," she said. "I was there."

"So many people claim you as a relative," he remarked, reading the caption beneath the photo. "It says here that you're a member of the Cacchione family."

"The reporter made a mistake, that's all."

"It's a curious list of relatives, even if we don't add your cousin Albert Lucerno, who has quite a rap sheet, as it turns out, and looks absolutely nothing like you."

"We're cousins by marriage, not blood."

"Of course you are." Crowell studied the photograph a moment before turning an icy smile upon her. "I wonder who else might claim you as kin if they saw this?"

Rosa felt a cold fist close around her heart. "What do you mean?"

"It should be easy to get the negative from the photographer, and as soon as I do, I'll have copies of this picture sent to every police station, post office, and newspaper in California." He folded the clipping, returned it to his breast pocket, and patted his coat with satisfaction. "Someone will recognize you and your husband, but I doubt any of those folks will be from Stavanger."

"Don't you have anything better to do with your time?" Rosa snapped, fighting off panic.

His lips curved in a slow, thin smile. "The look on your face right now tells me there's no better use of my time than finding out whatever it is you and your husband are hiding." He turned and descended the porch stairs. "See you soon, Sonoma Rose."

Rosa slammed the door and fell back against it, heart pounding, breathless with fear and rage. Within weeks, days perhaps, someone from the Arboles Valley would come forward and identify her as the missing and presumed dead Rosa Barclay, and Lars as her childhood sweetheart who had informed on the mob. The news would eventually find its way to John, even in prison, and he would know precisely where to find them. The Ventura County police would come for Rosa, and mob hit men for Lars.

She paced the length of the parlor, clenching her hands together, taking deep breaths to clear her churning thoughts. They would have to flee. They had no choice but to abandon their new home and run before their enemies caught up with them. But this time they would not be fleeing with two satchels full of cash and the reassurance that they were believed to be dead, drowned in the flash flood that had raced through the Salto Canyon or, in Lars's case, murdered by John's gangster friends. Every penny they owned had gone into purchasing Sonoma Rose Vineyards and Orchard. Crowell's photos proved they were alive. And Rosa was five months pregnant.

An hour passed, two, but the clarity of thought Rosa desperately needed eluded her. She could not bear the thought of fleeing penniless into the night with enemies in hot pursuit. She could not tear the children from the safety and comfort of their vineyard home. She could not give birth in some rundown motel with only Lars's help and no means to pay for a doctor or food or any of the essentials they needed. It was impossible, impossible, and yet what choice did they have?

A sudden knock on the door jolted her into alertness. Crowell, back so soon? Furious and afraid, she raced to the door and flung it open only to find Mr. Lucerno standing on the porch, hands in his pockets, looking out toward the winery.

Her first dizzying, sickening thought was that he had come for Lars, but somewhere in the back of her mind murmured a voice of reason — Crowell had not yet distributed the photos. He had not even had enough time to obtain the negatives. She rested a hand on her rounded abdomen, took a deep breath, and said, "Mr. Lucerno, what brings you out our way?"

Mr. Lucerno turned and offered her a cordial nod in greeting. "I was just passing by and thought I'd check in and see how the new prune barn is coming along."

Rosa felt as if she had been kicked in the stomach, and for a moment she could only look back at him, unable to breathe.

"Mrs. Ottesen, are you all right?"

"I'm fine," she managed to reply. She patted her tummy and forced a smile as if to indicate that only the normal pangs and discomforts of pregnancy troubled her. "I'm afraid we've only cleared away the rubble. This is one of our busiest times of the year on the vineyards and in the orchard. I — we didn't realize the need was so urgent. We assumed you would find another place to work."

He grimaced, clearly disappointed, and gestured to the high hills and the tall, concealing trees all around them. "We haven't found anything as remote and secluded as this, not with such easy access to the pomace we need to make grappa."

"There must be somewhere you could go."

"You might be surprised, but some folks would rather be left alone even if it means passing up an easy five hundred bucks a month." He paused and regarded her with intent curiosity. "You and your husband wouldn't be those kind of people, would you, Mrs. Ottesen?"

It was simply too much. They would never be free of these men who hounded them like jackals, howling and nipping at their heels, waiting to pounce and rip out their throats the moment they sensed weakness. They would never be left alone.

"Yes, Mr. Lucerno," she burst out, "we are exactly those sort of people. Please, please, try to understand. It's too dangerous to have you here any longer. We have young children. I'm going to have a baby. Agent Crowell is constantly breathing down our necks —"

"Hey. Hey." Mr. Lucerno held up his palms. "Take it easy, cousin." With a glance to her abdomen, he frowned and paced the length of the porch, then returned and halted in front of her. "Okay. Listen. You're about to have a kid and that's got you all worked up. I see that. And you're right, that fed comes around so often I'd think he was sweet on you."

Rosa shuddered. "Please don't say that."

"I'm not saying you enjoy it. Okay. Look. I'll tell my boss that this isn't a good place for our operation anymore. But he doesn't like bad news. You've got to give me something to sweeten the taste."

Rosa regarded him mutely, helpless and hopeless. She had no rescued grappa to load into his car this time, no refunded rent payment to make the injury sting a little less. She had nothing to offer him, nothing that he wanted, except —

"I know where you can find Lars Jorgensen," she heard herself say. Her throat constricted in horror at the thought of what she had done, but she could not take the words back. With one sentence she had set foot upon a path she must follow to its end.

Mr. Lucerno shook his head. "Never heard of him."

"I'm sure your employer has." Rosa's voice shook. "Have him ask his associates in Southern California if that name means anything to them and I bet he'll like the answer. They'd probably pay him for the information, or at the very least, they'd owe him a favor."

"Sometimes favors are better than cash." Mr. Lucerno studied her. "All right. Whoever this fella is, how can we get our hands on him?"

Rosa shook her head. "You'll have to figure out that part on your own." It was the only measure of protection she could give him.

"You don't want to implicate yourself. Fair enough. But you've got to give me more to go on than a name."

Rosa plunged ahead, refusing, for the moment, to consider the consequences. "Talk to your boss's friends in Southern California. Get his description and find out what he did to them. Then ask yourself, who showed up around here soon after Lars Jorgensen disappeared? Who looks like him and acts like him, down to his hatred for bootleggers?"

"All right. I can do that. Then what?"

"Your employer can do whatever he wants with this information. All I ask is that you never tell me what that is, and that you and your friends consider our property off limits from now on. Agreed?"

"If the information proves to be as valuable as you think it is," Mr. Lucerno emphasized, "then I'd say you have a deal."

He put out his hand, and they shook on it.

"Thank you," Rosa told him. "Thank you and good-bye."

"I'll miss your prune pie, cousin." He tugged the brim of his hat, nodded, and turned to go. When he reached the bottom of the porch stairs, he suddenly glanced to his right and raised his hand in greeting to someone who stood behind the house out of Rosa's field of vision. As Mr. Lucerno walked on, Lars came around the corner and halted, looking up at her without a word.

He waited until Mr. Lucerno crossed the footbridge and disappeared behind the redwoods.

"Rosa," he said, pained, "what have you done?"

What was necessary, she thought, but could not say aloud. *Only what was necessary. . . .*

Dwight Crowell never returned to Sonoma Rose Vineyards and Orchard. Neither did Albert Lucerno, just as he had promised.

A few days after Crowell's last visit, his car was found abandoned on a rural back road outside Geyserville, the windshield shattered, the sides pockmarked with bullet holes, the driver's seat splattered with dried blood. The doors were closed, the handles wiped clean. The agent himself was nowhere to be found.

A month passed. The detectives investigating his disappearance were stymied, and anonymous sources from within the department admitted that only a handful of tips had come in, all of them useless, and that the trail was stone cold. It didn't look good for the missing agent, they said, a man with few ties to the area, no family back in Los Angeles to speak of, a man whose job was his life. Officials from the Prohibition bureau acknowledged that a man like Dwight Crowell made a lot of enemies in the course of performing his duties. The people of Sonoma County, especially, owed him a debt of gratitude for his diligence and steadfastness on their behalf.

A year after his disappearance, a memorial service was held in his honor in Santa Rosa. No one Rosa knew attended.

EPILOGUE

A month after Dwight Crowell's mysterious disappearance, Alegra Del Bene and Gino came home to Santa Rosa. Rosa sat beside her and held her hand as Alegra tearfully told Paulo how the corrupt agent had intimidated and coerced her. Paulo wept and embraced his wife, declaring that whoever had killed Crowell had done a great service to the community and had spared Paulo the trouble and sin of killing him with his own hands.

Later, Rosa repeated his words to Lars. "I don't disagree," said Lars, gently and with an undercurrent of sorrow, "but I still wish you hadn't struck the match that lit that fire." Then he held her and kissed her to show he understood why she had done it, and that he had forgiven her.

It took much longer for her to forgive herself.

In July, Alegra was there to hold Rosa's hand when she gave birth to a beautiful baby boy.

In the months leading up to the baby's arrival, Lars had asked Rosa if she preferred a Spanish name, like those she had given her other children. Dredging up a painful memory from the first year of her marriage, Rosa told Lars that throughout her first pregnancy, John had insisted upon the name John Junior if they had a boy, and Mildred, after his grandmother, if they had a girl. When Rosa gave birth two months earlier than John had expected and he realized the child was not his, he had immediately changed his mind. "Call her anything else," he had said, handing the baby back to Rosa. "Call her whatever you like."

On her own, Rosa had chosen the name Marta after her father's mother.

When their first son was born, John, certain the child was his, named him after himself. But John Junior died, and after that, John no longer cared what the children were named. They were more Rosa's children than his, he seemed to think, and so they might as well bear Spanish names, like hers. They would die young anyway. It would be a waste to bestow an important Barclay family name upon any one of them.

In suggesting they choose a Spanish name for their child, Lars had only meant to honor Rosa's heritage. He didn't know, and it pained him to recall how Rosa had suffered throughout her marriage to John, a marriage she never would have made except for his own failure to be the man she needed all those years ago. After Rosa finished her story, Lars understood that the best way to honor her and their child was to give the baby a name from his side of the family. And so they named their son Mathias, after Lars's father.

Shortly after Mathias's first birthday, Dante Cacchione was released from prison. He returned home haggard and thin, but with a fierce gleam in his eye that hinted at a newly kindled fire. Throughout his imprisonment, rather than give in to despair and loneliness and boredom, he had devoted his time to the study of the law, poring over an incomplete collection of dated, worn law books kept in the small prison library until he had committed it to memory. He wrote eloquent, compelling letters to the editor of every newspaper in Sonoma County and throughout the Bay Area, shedding light on the lives of his fellow prisoners, how they were treated, how poverty and lack of opportunity had led more men to prison than greed or cruelty or any other oft-cited cause.

When Dante was finally permitted to return home to his family, he became known as a socialist firebrand, and whenever the downtrodden needed an advocate, he could be counted on to speak up for them. He also passionately argued the case for the repeal of Prohibition to any public official who would listen to him — and many more who wished he would give up and go away. But he wouldn't go away, nor would he be silenced. He wove together statistics and anecdotes to prove how the so-called Great Experiment had achieved none of its lofty goals and had created more crime and economic hardship than its framers could have possibly imagined. The more he spoke out, the more other people agreed with him.

But in spite of Dante's withering condemnation of Prohibition, the Cacchione family abandoned bootlegging after selling off the vintages stored in the old wine cellar. If not for their prunes and walnuts, they wouldn't have been able to afford to pay their property taxes, but there was little money left over for other necessities. After a few years of poor grape harvests and dismal wine grape sales, the Cacchiones were forced to sell off acres of their beloved vineyard.

Through it all, they firmly held on to Dante's beloved old Zinfandel vines, refusing to give up all hope that one day they would be allowed to resume the honored traditions of winemaking that their family had followed for generations.

Young Mathias Ottesen was two years old when Rosa and Lars were blessed with another son, whom they named Oscar, after Lars's brother. Baby Oscar was only six weeks old when Rosa learned of John's early release from prison from a newspaper clipping Mrs. Phillips sent her from San Francisco.

The same article also provided a terse account of John's death.

John had served two years of his five-year sentence on federal racketeering charges and had been granted parole on account of good behavior. Three weeks after his release, a hiker had discovered his broken body at the bottom of Salto Canyon, and after a thorough investigation, the coroner had concluded that he had jumped to his death.

What the newspaper did not record, and what Rosa never learned, was that in the aftermath of John's suicide, rumors swept through the Arboles Valley like summer fire through chaparral. Some people thought he had killed himself out of prolonged grief for his drowned wife and children. Others, more cynical, noted that with his postmaster job gone and his ties to organized crime severed, John had realized he would actually have to work for a living again, and he had preferred to die. A few people whispered that he had not intended to take his own life but that he had fallen to his death after fleeing in terror from the ghost of Isabel Rodriguez Diaz, whose spirit was known to haunt the mesa.

Rosa found no satisfaction in the news of John's death. Someday, when the children were old enough to understand, it would fall to her to tell them that he had taken his own life. She didn't know how she would explain to them something she could not understand.

When he was three months old, Oscar Ottesen made his first trip to San Francisco to attend the wedding of his parents, Nils Ottesen and Rosa Diaz. When they applied for the marriage license, Rosa was able to produce her birth certificate, but Nils Ottesen, a native of Stavanger, California, had nothing to show except his driver's license and voter registration card. But the five older children confirmed his identity — he was Nils Ottesen, their pa — so the city clerk shrugged, accepted their fee in cash, and signed the necessary documents.

The newlyweds and their six children spent the weekend enjoying the sights of the city and the hospitality of Mrs. Phillips's boardinghouse. Each morning they breakfasted upon waffles with strawberries and whipped cream — except for Ana and Miguel, who had corn cakes with their strawberries and whipped cream instead. Although they still had to follow Dr. Haas's banana diet, they were so healthy and vigorous that Mrs. Phillips declared she hardly recognized them as the poor dears who had crossed her threshold four years before.

Rosa hardly recognized herself as the same haunted, despondent mother who had brought them there.

In October 1929, the stock market crashed and the nation reeled.

The following February, the House Judiciary Committee surprised the nation by announcing that it would open debate on measures that could possibly lead to the modification or even repeal of Prohibition.

The news did little to lift the spirits of weary grape growers and winemakers in Sonoma County, who knew that congressional hearings and debates could drone on endlessly but lead nowhere, and that bills could stall in committee. In the meantime, fear and force bound Prohibition enforcement agents, gangsters, vintners, and ordinary citizens together in a barbed-wire net of violence.

Federal inquiries discovered that the Prohibition bureau was rife with corruption — something Rosa could have told them years before, sparing them the trouble and expense of a lengthy investigation. In the aftermath of the report's release, hundreds of enforcement officers around the country were fired for falsification of official records, extortion, bribery, theft, forgery, perjury, conspiracy, and a host of other crimes, but the bureaucratic housecleaning seemed to make no difference. Crime syndicates remained as firmly entrenched as ever, and the newly hired replacement Prohibition agents enforced the laws no better than those who had been dismissed.

The harvest of 1930 was expected to be one of the most bountiful in years, but the combined blows of an enormous surplus of grapes and devastatingly low prices brought on by the Great Depression threatened the California grape industry with total collapse. More grape growers uprooted their vines and planted other crops. More wineries closed.

Rosa and Lars hung on. With every change of season they told themselves that Prohibition was inching toward its inevitable demise. If they endured and economized, they could keep Sonoma Rose Vineyards and Orchard afloat until Rosa and Daniel could sell their young wines and make more than two hundred gallons apiece. In the meantime, Rosa would learn and perfect her craft. So many gifted winemakers had been forced from the profession. Much knowledge and skill had been lost, but Daniel was an excellent teacher, and he knew many retirees who were more than willing to nostalgically reminisce about the golden age of California winemaking with Rosa, who served them lunch, strolled with them through her grapevines, and remembered the details and nuances of every story they told.

Rosa and Lars knew they were much better off than most other families those days. They had the farm, so even in that time of widespread poverty and hunger, their children had plenty to eat. They would tighten their belts and count their blessings and hang on.

■ ■ ■ ■

In 1931, Sonoma County suffered through blistering heat waves, drought, and terrible insect infestations. But even though grape growers sent the smallest crop of grapes to market in ten years, the ongoing economic crisis meant abysmal sales and negligible profits. The usual rules of supply and demand didn't apply when no one had money to spend.

The poor and the desperate from across the country flooded California seeking work — not looking for a handout, but a job, a place to sleep, and the means to feed their families. Rosa and Lars hired as many men as they could, sheltered as many as the dormitory and the barn hayloft would hold. It was never enough. Sometimes Rosa went off alone and wept when she had to turn away men in threadbare clothes and shoes held together with twine because Lars had no more work for them and they could not afford to take on anyone else. But Rosa never turned away women with children. Somehow they all managed to make do with a little less to help one more mother and child.

In 1932, Herbert Hoover asked the American people to elect him to a second term. "Why not?" asked Lars sardonically. "He did so well with the first one."

Rosa had never been happier that women had won the right to vote as she was on Election Day that November. She was among the first in line at her polling place, and after she pulled the lever for Franklin Delano Roosevelt, she murmured a prayer that the New Deal he proposed would bring a new era of pulling together for the common good to a nation in dire need of change. Throughout his campaign, Roosevelt had promised to correct the great national mistake that was Prohibition, and Rosa fervently hoped he would prevail. Change was in the air, and soon, she hoped, a refreshing wind would blow justice and common sense their way.

Roosevelt was elected in a landslide. On the same day, nine states, including California, held referenda on Prohibition, and the voters overwhelmingly called for repeal. Prohibition had been dealt a fatal blow, but it was not dead yet. It remained the law of the land.

Sonoma Rose Vineyards and Orchard flourished. In any other era the family would have prospered, but the Depression meant that they barely managed to get by. Even as Rosa struggled to make ends meet, she never forgot to thank God for her children's health and to count her blessings, nor did she forget the loyal friend who had spurred her to flee the adobe after John beat her and went off to murder Lars. If Elizabeth Nelson had not been with her that day, Rosa would have picked herself up off the floor, calmed the children, washed her face, and paced through the house while she waited for John to return with blood on his hands and news of Lars's death on his lips. If she had not fled that night, she would still be living in the adobe, a widow struggling to raise her two remaining children. Rosa knew this as irrefutable fact because everything that had happened to her from that day forward turned on the pivot of her decision to heed Elizabeth's warnings.

If Rosa and the children had not taken flight that day and sought refuge in the canyon, Lars would not have found them there, rescued them from the flood, and driven them to the safe obscurity of Oxnard. While it was true that Lars had come to the adobe looking for her after he returned to the Jorgensen ranch and discovered what John had done, by then the police searching the Barclay farm had found the contraband in the hayloft. They would not have let Rosa leave with Lars. She wouldn't have gone to Oxnard or taken Ana and Miguel to see Dr. Russell at the hospital, so he would have been unable to refer her to Dr. Reynolds. Without Dr. Reynolds, she never would have learned the cause of her children's mysterious illness. Ana and Miguel would be dead; Mathias and Oscar never would have been born.

Every good thing in Rosa's life since leaving the Arboles Valley depended upon Elizabeth Nelson, the catalyst of her escape.

Despite the crushing restrictions of Prohibition and the hardships of the Great Depression, Rosa and Lars were getting by in Sonoma County. They did not need a rye farm in Southern California that they could never visit. And Rosa owed Elizabeth a debt of gratitude she could never fully repay.

Even so, Rosa and Lars resolved to try.

They hired a San Francisco lawyer and arranged for him to travel to the Arboles Valley to offer the Barclay farm to Elizabeth and Henry for five dollars an acre. Mindful that the Nelsons might not be able to afford even that nominal amount, they authorized the lawyer to offer them other terms: In exchange for farming the land, maintaining the property, and paying the property taxes, the Ottesens would pay the Nelsons a modest salary and let them keep any profits they earned from whatever crops they decided to raise. The Nelsons would pay the Ottesens quarterly payments of fifty dollars, which would be put toward the five-hundred-dollar purchase price. In five years, the title would be transferred to the Nelsons and the farm would be theirs, free and clear. The lawyer informed the astonished couple that the Ottesens hoped the Nelsons would rename the farm Triumph Ranch. "Mrs. Nelson, especially, loved the name you suggested," Mr. Tomilson reported to Rosa and Lars after he returned from the Arboles Valley with all the necessary papers signed and notarized. He shook his head and smiled sheepishly. He had thought the name an odd request and had expected the Nelsons to decline, even though Rosa had assured him they wouldn't.

Eight years before, Henry and Elizabeth had come to the Arboles Valley full of hope and ambition, believing they held the deed to a thriving ranch, confident that they would prosper on fertile acres beneath sunny California skies. The swindler who had cheated them out of their life savings had shattered their dreams, but they had endured the blow with grace and had resolved to rebuild their lives, undaunted. In the midst of her disappointment, Elizabeth had looked beyond her own heartache and had reached out to a grieving woman and a lonely man. Rosa and Lars owed her everything. And now the Nelsons' dream of Triumph Ranch could finally come true.

In anticipation of President-elect Roosevelt's inauguration on March 4, 1933, Congress passed a resolution to end Prohibition if a majority vote of state conventions from thirty-six of the forty-eight states ratified a Twenty-first Amendment to the Constitution nullifying the Eighteenth.

In the months that followed, one state after another voted for repeal — including, on July 24, 1933, California. Although the magic number of thirty-six had not yet been reached, the outcome already seemed inevitable, so the federal government closed down the Prohibition bureau. Six days after California voted for repeal, all Prohibition agents in Sonoma County were to be relieved of duty. They did not go quietly. A few hours before midnight, by which time they were expected to have closed out their files and turned in their weapons, agents raided a popular Sonoma watering hole, confiscated a small amount of alcohol, and, since the proprietor wasn't in at the time, arrested the chef. The unfortunate man was hauled off to the county jail in Santa Rosa, where he was photographed, fingerprinted, and arraigned on charges of liquor possession. Whether he paid his $750 bail before or after the agents who arrested him became obsolete was the subject of some debate among the disgusted citizens who read about the arrest in the paper the next morning. To Rosa the eleventh-hour raid seemed spiteful, pointless, and all too reminiscent of something Dwight Crowell would have organized and taken part in with malicious glee.

All that summer, states held conventions to vote on the Twenty-first Amendment, Sonoma County grape growers predicted a modest harvest, and vintners prepared to make wine. Everyone kept busy, watching and waiting.

It wasn't until November 9 that Kentucky, Ohio, Pennsylvania, and Utah voted to repeal the Eighteenth Amendment, bringing the total to thirty-six states. The Twenty-first Amendment to the Constitution had passed.

Prohibition was finished. . . .

For months, like grape growers and winemakers throughout California wine country, the vintners at Sonoma Rose Vineyards and Orchard had been working almost without rest in anticipation of the day in early December when the repeal of Prohibition would officially go into effect.

On December 5, 1933, winemakers and brewers, bottlers and coopers, grape growers and hops ranchers across the nation welcomed the end of Prohibition with joyful celebrations — or, for many others, with sober contemplation of their sacrifices and the long road they had yet to travel before they could rebuild all they had lost. Rosa, Lars, their children, and their friends quietly rejoiced, thankful and relieved and mindful of the work that lay ahead. But their mood was jubilant. After many long, hard years, promise was in the air and prosperity seemed within their grasp.

Daniel had taught Rosa everything he knew about winemaking, and although she still had much to learn, she was confident that someday she would create a truly magnificent wine. Dante Cacchione and Paulo Del Bene promised her that she would never forget the day she tasted the first vintage that would bear her name. "But which name?" Lars asked her ruefully when no one else could hear.

There could be no question of that. She had no doubts. She knew who she was. Rosa Diaz Barclay had perished in the flash flood that had swept through the Salto Canyon more than eight years before. That despondent, broken woman was no more. In the years to come, tourists who made their way up the steep, winding road through the lush forests of Glen Ellen to sample her vintages would know her as Sonoma Rose, and she would be content if they never knew her by any other name. She was Rose Ottesen — grape grower, winemaker, wife, and mother — and her heart, at long last, was at peace.

ACKNOWLEDGMENTS

I am deeply grateful to Denise Roy, Maria Massie, Ava Kavyani, Liza Cassity, Christine Ball, Brian Tart, Nadia Kashper, Melanie Marder Parks, and everyone at Dutton and Plume for their contributions to *Sonoma Rose* and the Elm Creek Quilts series.

Numerous people graciously assisted me during the research and writing of this novel. Geraldine Neidenbach, Heather Neidenbach, Marty Chiaverini, and Brian Grover were kind enough to read yet another manuscript on a tight deadline and provide the timely, insightful comments I have come to rely upon. I sincerely thank Gaye LeBaron, Sonoma County historian and author, for examining the manuscript with a careful eye and helping me rid it of inaccuracies and anachronisms. Friend and problem-solver extraordinaire Fran Threewit earned my gratitude by making my research trip to Sonoma County smoother, easier, and much more fun than if I had gone it alone. Others who offered their expertise include Greg Berruto and Jack Gilbert, Benziger Family Winery; David Coscia, Southern Pacific Historical & Technical Society; Kevin Grant, Sebastiani Vineyards & Winery; Jennifer Hanson, Sonoma State Historic Park; Cara Randall, California State Railroad Museum; Gery Rosemurgy, Broadway Quilts in Sonoma; and Ruth Straessler, Santa Rosa Railroad Square. My sincere thanks to you all.

I am indebted to the Wisconsin Historical Society and their librarians and staff for maintaining the excellent archives from which I drew research resources for this book. The following works were especially instructive: Louis J. Foppiano, et al., *A Century of Winegrowing in Sonoma County, 1896–1996* (Berkeley: The Bancroft Library, University of California, 1996); Stefano Guandalini, M.D., "A Brief History of Celiac Disease." *Impact: A Publication of the University of Chicago Celiac Disease Center* Vol 7 No 3 (Summer 2007): 1–2; Sidney V. Haas, M.D., "The Value of the Banana in the Treatment of Celiac Disease." *American Journal of Diseases of Children* Vol 28 No 4 (October 1924): 421–37; Gaye LeBaron and Joann Mitchell, *Santa Rosa: A Twentieth Century Town* (Santa Rosa, CA: Historia, 1993); Robert M. Lynch, *The Sonoma Valley Story: Pages through the Ages* (Sonoma, CA: The Sonoma Index–Tribune, Inc., 1997); Vivienne Sosnowski, *When the Rivers Ran Red: An Amazing Story of Courage and Triumph in America's Wine Country* (New York: Palgrave Macmillan, 2009); Lee Torliatt, *Golden Memories of the Redwood Empire.* (Chicago: Arcadia Publishing, 2001); Honoria Tuomey, *History of Sonoma County, California, Vol I.* (Chicago: S. J. Clarke Publishing Co, 1926); Ventura County Star, *Ventura County Looking Back: A Photographic History of Ventura County: The Early Years.* (Battle Ground, WA: Pediment Publishing, 2006); and Simone Wilson, *Sonoma County: The River of Time* (Chatsworth, CA: Windsor Publications, 1990).

Most of all, I thank my husband, Marty, and my sons, Nicholas and Michael, for their continuous love, support, and encouragement. You have enriched my life beyond measure with laughter, hope, love, and joy, and I am forever thankful.

ABOUT THE AUTHOR

Jennifer Chiaverini is the author of the *New York Times* bestselling Elm Creek Quilts series, as well as five collections of quilt projects inspired by the novels. A graduate of the University of Notre Dame and the University of Chicago, she lives with her husband and sons in Madison, Wisconsin.

CPSIA information can be obtained
at www.ICGtesting.com
Printed in the USA
FFOW051126150313
992FF

JUN 0 6 2013